Age of the Fallen

AGE OF THE FALLEN

Mark Olmos

VMI PUBLISHERS • SISTERS, OREGON

Published by
VMI Publishers
Sisters, Oregon
www.vmipublishers.com

ISBN: 978-1-933204-90-1
ISBN: 1-933204-90-7

Library of Congress: 2009930777

Printed in the USA

Cover design by Juanita Dix, j.d. Design, www.designjd.net

Dedicated to my children
and to their generation of spiritual warriors.
May they succeed where we failed.

Table of Contents

Prologue

EVERYDAY, EVERYWHERE, THERE IS AN UNSEEN BATTLE THAT RAGES BETWEEN GOOD AND evil that impacts the destinies of men and nations.

We feel it all around us. We see it in the news. We sense it when we take the time to be still. It's not in the pages of religious books, but right outside our window, in our neighborhoods, and even in the safety of our own home. We hear the voices; we are repulsed by random thoughts; we feel the presence of unseen forces.

Evil is not mindless or random. It is embodied in the form of fallen angels that hate both the Creator and His creation, and struggle against the angels of heaven to destroy God's greatest love: mankind. In this task they are patient and relentless and carry the skill of tens of thousands of years to the spiritual battlefield.

But God created a powerful way to counter them. Despite popular belief, it wasn't through grand religious institutions that fall into corruption so easily. Instead He raised up small bands of spiritual warriors and gifted them with the ability to see into the spiritual realm and engage the enemy with His truth. Throughout history they have existed all over the world, from every walk of life. They are chosen to walk in the shadows, to fight in the background, and are always present somewhere during key turning points in history. They prowl dark alleys and the places where dark deeds are done, receiving their orders from heaven and then giving their very lives to stop evil's advance in their generation. Unfortunately, not all of them succeed.

One such a group of warriors lives in Japan, a land long lost spiritually amidst its technological wonders and world-renowned efficiency. Aiko and her group of teenage friends combine dangerous faith, sacrificial loyalty, and youthful passion to do what very few in history have ever done.

They live by a simple rule. Choose sides, and make a difference.

Chapter One

The Ultimate Lie

THE NEWSPAPERS WOULD SAY THAT SHINJI MATSUOKA, A SIXTEEN-YEAR-OLD STUDENT experiencing trouble adjusting at school, had a mental breakdown and hanged himself in his own room. But there was more to it, much more.

◆ ◆ ◆

On a night like any other, while he drifted on the edge of sleep, a jagged sword slashed violently into Shinji's brain. His eyes opened suddenly. There was no blood, no ripped flesh, and no scream…it was a spiritual wound. The demon who stood over him leered as fear penetrated the sixteen-year-old's mind and started to grow. Shinji didn't see the evil angel, but the demon relished the look of dread spreading over his young face, as the wound took effect.

Shinji looked anxiously across his darkened room and swallowed hard trying to get rid of the tacky sour taste in his mouth. He glanced at the open door of his closet, which had grown more foreboding each and every night. A chill went down his back. He thought he saw something move in the shadows. He could feel a presence there, like somebody watching him. He was sure of it. His body started to tighten into a small, protective fetal position and he pulled his covers up to his eyes, trying to look away. He heard a rustling sound as the curtains of his bedroom window came to life, gently blowing, as if some unseen creature had just invaded his room. Shinji stopped breathing for a moment and strained his eyes to focus in the darkness. Did he see a face in the shadows, eyes staring at him with hatred? Was that an evil growl he heard, or the wind shaking the rafters? As he took a deep breath he smelled that elusive strange odor that had settled in above the smell of unwashed clothes weeks ago. It had the stench of something old–no, something ancient.

They were now in position to finish their foul work. The demons laughed, knowing he couldn't see or hear them unless they wanted him to. Fear was taking over slowly but surely.

Finally, the logical part of Shinji's brain resisted. *Th-there–there is nothing there. You're just being...stupid.*

The hate-filled, invisible presence left the closet and moved quickly to join the attack, driving a ghastly black spear into Shinji's heart. Gripped by terror, the teenager sat up and hyperventilated. What was wrong? Why couldn't he breathe?

The creature that had entered by the window cruelly slashed him with a horrible-looking axe. Each slash added fear upon fear, thrusting him toward panic, and Shinji fought it as rationally as he could.

They were too strong. Too experienced. Their silent laughter rippled over their victim, and he twitched and shuddered. Nothing could oppose them or their lies.

The fallen ones had studied him for months. They knew what images to draw from the things that Shinji had put into his brain, and had allowed into his life. They knew the names of all of his friends and enemies, his favorite TV shows, and what scared him the most. They had observed his motives and listened to his hopes and dreams, as well as his fears and uncertainties. They struck with spiritual weapons at key moments in his life, discouraging him, confusing him, and causing him to doubt everything that he knew. They tempted him to think immoral thoughts, and do immoral things, so they could heap a mountain of guilt, regret, and shame on him, and create a wall of lies between him and his only hope. Then they watched, and waited, and plotted to drown him in anguish. It was easy, because he was fallen too, after all. Now, at last it was the perfect time; now they had him.

The demons looked at each other, smiling, and began speaking lies into Shinji's terrorized and bewildered mind. "Everyone hates you...you worthless, useless, insignificant loser! Your parents are ashamed of you; your siblings laugh at you; you have no real friends!" The demons circled him as the wounds festered, nudging him toward despair.

"You are one huge mistake, a disgusting embarrassment, a horrendous joke! Everyone laughs at your hideous ears and stupid fat face! Look how attractive other guys are; you are just repulsive and ugly!" The demon could see him starting to lose it.

"Face it, you're a failure, you stupid little retard! You fail in school; you fail at home; you fail in life! You fail at everything you ever try because that's what losers do!"

Shinji clamped his hands over his ears. This was their cue to get louder and more abusive. They mocked him until he started whimpering and then scratched himself so deeply that he ripped open his pajama top. There were already scars from weeks of scratching. New welts appeared on his arms and chest, and dark blood oozed from his wounds. The demons smiled at the self-mutilation. "Almost there," their looks said to each other.

"Rope; get the rope! It will be all over in a moment. No more pain, just peace and vengeance. You'll show them. They'll be sorry. You'll get the last laugh; get your ultimate revenge. They'll feel so bad. You'll ruin their lives like they ruined *yours*!" they chanted relentlessly into his brain.

Shinji, still whimpering in despair, scrambled from the bed and made his way to his closet where he had hidden a thick rope, already tied with a special strangulation knot that he learned about on a suicide Web site. He tugged it from under a pile of clothes and fastened it to a hook he had installed on his closet wall, hidden behind his hanging clothes. He then walked to the center of his room, looked up at the cross beam, and threw the noose up with one quick motion. It hit the edge of the beam and got snagged on a small nail sticking out of the wood. At first he was confused, and grateful that he had missed, but then, as if pulled by invisible hands the rope slid over and the noose fell into place and swung gently beckoning to him. He had measured it weeks ago, so it hung at the perfect height. His despair returned and he took the chair from his desk and placed it directly under the rope.

The demons backed off, wanting him to feel a sense of relief and empowerment as he took *their* solution into his hands. When he had finished preparing he paused a moment and sat on the edge of the bed, staring into the darkness, hoping for one reason to stay alive.

None came.

The demons coordinated their attack this time and ran horrible spiritual weapons through Shinji's heart from the front, back, and sides. They chanted evil incantations and shoved him to the last step before death–absolute and complete hopelessness.

He was there now, in that suffocating moment, feeling only hatred, failure, pressure, disappointment, and shame. Shinji stood up and stepped onto the chair and looped the rope around his neck. It felt stiff and rough against his skin as he pulled on the noose to make it snug. He hesitated. A demon whispered, "Life is so worthless! Death! That's the final great adventure! Go on, kick the chair away!" Shinji blinked, said a brief good-bye, and took a deep breath. He looked down and bent his knees, took a short hop, and kicked the chair in midair, just like he had practiced.

The house shook as the rope went taut and the chair clattered to the floor. The loud creaking continued while Shinji swung from side to side, life seeping from his body. The sound was enough to wake his parents.

The night was filled with the screams of a young family that found their eldest son hanging lifeless in the middle of his own room. The mother, wretched over her loss, the father put his fist through a wall in anguish, and his younger siblings cried in horror and confusion.

Later, others would wonder if there was something they could have said to Shinji. Teachers would wonder if there was something they should have seen in him. The world would shake its head at the loss of one more promising young life. All the while, the creatures of hell and death would respond as they always did when evil prevailed–with celebration. They would gloat over the lifeless body of a desperate teen, enjoying the horrible death, the torrent of grief, the rage toward God, and the confusion that suicide left behind. Then, they would eagerly move on to their next target.

♦ ♦ ♦

Across town, another teenager soberly watched an on-the-spot reporter on television as he talked about the continued rise of suicide in the city and the sad death of Shinji Matsuoka. As they showed the grieving family, following the body of their son, covered by a white sheet and wheeled into an ambulance, her hands slowly clenched. Then she felt a whisper in her heart and pulled out her phone.

It was God's turn to move.

Chapter Two

Teens Interrupted

KOH AND KAI WERE CLEANING UP IN THE BACK AFTER ANOTHER BUSY DAY AT THEIR parent's café. Koh huffed and put another set of dirty plates down by the steaming sink to be washed when he saw them; uneaten, untouched french fries. He paused and looked back to see if his brother was watching, wiped his hands on his apron, and stuffed three into his mouth at one time.

"You're not eating food off the plates again, are you?" yelled his brother from the other room.

"Hmmph. Do you think I'm some kind of sicko?" he said, trying to swallow fast.

"Uh, yeah." Kai emphasized the *yeah* by snapping him in the butt with a dish towel as he walked into the kitchen. "And no one would argue with me on that," he added matter-of-factly.

"Hey, I'm normal, everyone else is messed up." Koh chuckled to himself, taking more soggy fries and dipping them in ketchup. He could hear his brother's phone ringer go off. It played the old *Batman* theme song.

"Yo!" he said into the phone while he pulled the plate away and dumped the fries into the trash. Koh frowned in despair. His brother always did this to him, always imposed order on the unstructured way he approached life. Kai listened intently for a few seconds. "Right. We'll be there." He flipped the phone closed and squared his shoulders, his gaze dipping to Koh's belly before it met his eyes. "Looks like you get a chance to work off those fries." Koh smiled. "*Batman and Robin* baby."

♦ ♦ ♦

"All right, be patient, everybody—one step at a time. We are going to take down the boss tonight. If we rush, we will all surely die." Takumi flipped his headset mic out of the way and took a sip of Coke. Nine animated adventurers in addition to his own hefted medieval weapons across the war-torn landscape on his monitor. He pushed up his glasses and adjusted his mic.

"Remember, without our shadow priest we have only a sixty-seven percent chance of success. So, that means, Warriors, you must charge in together and time your war stomp to stun-lock the guards for exactly forty seconds. Then our shadow priest will cast the weaken-mind spell followed by another war stomp. The rest of us just attack with the highest d.p.s. weapon that we carry." He listened to a question on his headset.

Fujimoto, the sixty-fifth level elven warrior, complained for the third time tonight that he needed to loot first so he could complete his armor set.

"No, Fuj, you got to loot last time. Yasu needs the enchanted bracers of the Owl too."

His phone rang, playing the *Mission Impossible* theme. He muted his headset and answered. "Hey Aik. Uh-huh, you sure? Right. See you there in exactly thirty-one minutes." He hung up and looked at his computer screen. "Whew, okay." He thought a moment and then unmuted his headset.

"Okay, Mathemaniacs, an emergency popped up. I need to go." He cringed at their heated protests. "Yes, more important than killing the Lich King." He thought again and then added, "Uh, I can't tell you everything, but it has to do with a beautiful girl." He smiled big at their responses. "Yeah, I knew you guys would understand. Tomorrow night, then? Okay. Out."

Takumi looked at his watch, grabbed his backpack, and left his room.

♦ ♦ ♦

Both girls were screaming, because they had never gotten to the seventh song together and were trying hard not to be the one to make a mistake. They stood side-by-side on large game pads that registered each step as they tried to keep up with the Dance Dance Revolution video game. Mai was graceful and flawless while Ishi was tireless and determined. Both were perspiring.

"Give up, little one. I can do this all night," Ishi challenged without breaking her concentration on the scrolling screen of arrows.

"I've finished this game three times." Mai glanced sideways at her friend.

"No way! That's not fair, you've danced all your life."

"Aren't you tired, Ish? You can quit if you want to," Mai grinned.

"Never!" Then Ishi changed tactics to something guaranteed to throw her much younger friend off balance. "Hey, I saw this really cute boy checking you out on the train today." Mai's eyes opened wide in shock and her jaw dropped. She squealed and broke rhythm, turning on Ishi and playfully trying to tackle her to the ground. "Ah, I win. I win," Ishi claimed as Mai continued to pull at her.

Ishi's phone rang, playing a popular hard rock song. "Stop, stop, I need to get the phone." Mai went limp and let her get to her bag to fish out her phone. "Hey, girl. Uh-huh. I'm with Mai." As she listened, she closed her eyes briefly. Two vertical lines formed between her eyebrows. "We'll be there." She closed her phone and sighed.

"No sleepover?" Mai asked, knowing the answer.

"Time for a different kind of dancing, Mai-chan." Both girls took a few moments to pack their bags and left together.

♦ ♦ ♦

"Boom! Yeah baby!" Michio hollered as he blasted another baseball into the net. Five other players were watching him hit with admiration, glad that he was on their team. He was not only the largest player, but also their best hitter. The mechanical pitching machine whirred and issued another pitch. "Boom! Yeah!"

"Mich, you don't have to say, 'Boom,' just hit the ball," his shortstop pleaded, breaking up the group in laughter.

"Hey, it works for me," he said adjusting his batting gloves and smiling, then added with his pinky extended, "Uh, Kaz, what do you say, 'Tink'?" he teased. The group let out a loud, extended "oooooh" and waited to see if Kaz would fire back. He just laughed along with them, taking the ribbing like a teammate should. He knew it was only jock-talk.

"All right, then…boom!" Kaz said when Michio hit his next ball. That started a chorus of "booms" from the whole group each time Michio hit the ball. Finally, after three "booms," there was a *whiff* as he missed one on purpose while they boomed again and he pointed over laughing. "Gotcha!"

His phone rang in his sports bag playing a Japanese video game song, "Neraiuchi."

"Hey, Mich, it's your girlfriend," someone teased.

"No, no, it's his mommy."

He wiped the sweat from his face, opened it, and answered, ignoring his mockers. "Hey, what's up? Uh-huh. Okay, then, let's do it. I'll be there." He hung up and started packing up.

"See, it *is* his mommy."

"Sorry, guys. Gotta split. See you all tomorrow!"

"Tell your girlfriend I enjoyed my date with her last night."

"Tell mommy to tuck you in."

Michio smiled and looked back one last time. "I'll go boom on you if don't be quiet." He pointed in feigned anger and then laughed and headed out.

They all headed for the station, leaving the concerns and joys of their teenage lives behind, preparing to step into another world altogether.

Chapter Three

AIKO

AIKO HAD BEAUTIFUL BUT INTENSE EYES. EVEN THOUGH THEY WERE CLOSED, THEY expressed both confidence and concern. She was a picture of concentration: her regal, slender figure on one knee, her lips speaking silent words into the heavens, her heart and ears tuned and listening for an answer, one hand raised toward the stars and the other on the hilt of her sheathed sword.

The night was warm and industrial smells filled the air. She had arrived early to survey the site they had been summoned to. First to arrive, last to leave, that's how she liked it. On the outskirts of town, on a hill overlooking an abandoned warehouse, she was seeking confirmation from God when she felt a sudden prick in her spirit.

Trouble.

She immediately opened her eyes and caught the slight movement of two shadows moving toward her from the trees on her right. Without the slightest hint of hurry she lowered her hand, glanced down, and veiled her spiritual sword. Now she looked like any other seventeen-year-old girl, sad and alone, staring into the night because of boy problems or stress at school.

Two approaching demons smiled wickedly at each other, relishing their good fortune, and moved in for what they thought would be some unexpected fun.

They were wrong.

◆ ◆ ◆

Kenji woke up suddenly, gasping for breath. He was sweating. He was experiencing yet another terrifying nightmare, shivering from fear as his eyes darted nervously from one shadowy corner to another. He felt cold…so cold. His mouth was dry.

Darkness crept all around him, but a dim light revealed a large empty warehouse of some kind. And at his feet…the faint gleam of gunmetal. He felt a sudden shudder in his heart. Fear pushed the breath out of him; so he lay alone in the unknown darkness, gulping for air and hoping that he wouldn't fall asleep again. Then he heard the horrible voices again.

The demon leaned over his trembling victim and continued to drive his axe into his defenseless heart. "Listen, why go on? Face it; you are a failure and an embarrassment. Why live another worthless day? Tomorrow will be the same old thing. Come on," came the sickly sweet voice. It was relentless and enticing, "think of the peace of just sleeping forever…think of the release…end it…now!"

Kenji cried out in anguish and clamped his hands tightly against his ears to stop the persuasive voices that attacked him from within. He looked again at the gun that lay at his feet. Relief. He reached out, feeling the hard cold metal and picked up his deadly savior.

♦ ♦ ♦

"Roboto!" the guys chorused as the train doors whisked open and Takumi strode in. He found Koh, Kai, and Michio in the first car, their usual meeting place. Koh and Kai gave him a high five as the train pulled out.

"Hey, partner. Ready for butt kicking?" Michio raised his loosely curled hands. Takumi bumped fists with him, nodding.

"Hey, guys." Then he looked around the car. "The girls?"

"Next stop." Kai said, glancing at his watch.

"So, Tak," Koh said, "did she tell *you* anything? What's up tonight?"

"You probably know as much as I do. He calls. We go out."

No new information. Koh slouched back.

"But…" Takumi continued, causing everyone to lean in, "her voice sounded different…more urgent." He pushed up his glasses and shook his head. "I'm not sure what that means." The train started to slow. "Could mean something big," he finished as the train stopped and the doors slid open.

"Hey, guys." Ishi greeted them with Mai following close behind. Then she looked closely at Koh. "Koh! Wipe the ketchup from your mouth." Koh frowned and reached up to feel the corners of his mouth.

"Ha! I told you to stop eating food off the plates again!" Kai accused.

"Hey, they were untouched…and I…" Koh tried to explain but Ishi cut in.

"Okay, that's disgusting." Ishi scolded. But before Koh could defend himself she continued. "Let's get focused. Somebody's watching, right?" Her voice filled the car. The guys exchanged quick guilty looks and nodded unconvincingly.

"Of course."

"Yeah."

Takumi just smiled at the guys' attempt to avoid another scolding. "Don't worry, Ish, I'm keeping watch. Nothing so far." Ishi nodded at Takumi and then looked at the other guys with knowing eyes and one hand on her hip.

"Uh, yeah. Nothing so far," Koh confirmed, squinting his eyes and looking around.

"Good, because tonight could get rough, stay alert." Ishi warned, causing questioning looks on all their faces.

◆ ◆ ◆

"I say we scare her, horrify her. Make her cry, make her run." The first demon scowled as he looked Aiko over closely.

"No, idiot." His black tongue licked his lips and yellow drool dripped past his fangs, down the corner of is mouth. "You need to learn to take your time and enjoy tormenting these humans, especially the females. If you scare her, she runs off screaming. But if you play with her…" He took a long, lustful look at his prize and put his crooked nose next to her neck and whiffed deeply. "They are as worthless as the dirt they are made from. Sooo easy to manipulate and discourage. Check her belongings and get her name," he commanded.

"But the Overlord is waiting for our scouting report."

"He can wait. This won't take long. Now, get her name."

Aiko sat looking randomly into the night, waiting for them to make their move. One of the demons now hovered in front of her while the other examined her bag looking for a name. As their dank smell engulfed her, she fought the need to hold her breath and felt her stomach churning, but willed herself to stay focused. She continued to look straight ahead past the demon, seeming completely oblivious to their presence.

"Ha! Aiko. That's the name of this little piece of filth." The demon chuckled and rubbed his scaled palms together. Aiko crossed her arms closely as if she had gotten a chill. The demons threw back their hideous heads and laughed wickedly. They loved when a human spirit could sense something evil nearby.

"Aiiiko," the demon began sweetly. "Poor little Aiko…" Aiko looked around as if she had heard a whisper. She started to look confused. The demons leered at each other. "Ah, this one *is* sensitive, good." Then the one not speaking to her remembered something.

"Wait…didn't the captain say…"

"Shut up!" He turned to Aiko again and brushed up against her, speaking right into her ear. "Is it a boyfriend? Or maybe a two-faced friend at school…"

"I'm telling you, that name–" The demon on Aiko held up his hand to shush his partner and then eagerly reached to his side, pulling out a jagged sword. He licked its edge with anticipation.

"How about a little despair to go with your evening…maybe some murderous and hateful thoughts aimed at your family…" The demon raised his sword and continued to taunt as Aiko slowly turned to look at him. His smile disappeared when Aiko's eyes cleared and focused directly into his. He faltered.

"Never talk about my family that way," she said evenly without a hint of fear. Both demons stepped back quickly. The one who had been speaking awkwardly lunged and drove his sword toward her heart, but as it reached her chest it struck against the sudden appearance of blue translucent breastplate, glancing away harmlessly. Aiko stood. The moment she was erect she was fully armored. She wielded a glowing sword at her attackers. Her lips curled in a fierce challenge.

"We must report this," One demon whimpered.

"To the Overlord. Thanks for the information." Aiko smirked. Both demons looked at each other accusingly. She gripped the sword in both hands. "Anything else I need to know?"

"Think twice, Warrior, before you get involved. You will be making the biggest mistake of your life if you choose to get involved."

Aiko lowered her sword and cocked her head, looking at the demon thoughtfully. "Okay." She nodded slightly. Then in a sudden movement her sword flashed and decapitated the demon in front of her. Without a pause, she spun, driving her sword into the heart of the other, who now stood helpless as truth worked its effect on one who lived by lies.

"I've chosen."

Both demons burst into clouds of sulfurous dust.

♦ ♦ ♦

Kenji cried out again in despair. He had heard the relentless, tormenting voices pushing him for months now. He had tried alcohol at first to drown them out, then drugs to mute them, but they only served to numb his will and grant them greater control over his life. And now the voices were louder and more convincing than ever. They always had one message that they cast from shadows of darkness in penetrating voices, tainted, magnetic and so compelling. "Meaningless. Everything is so meaningless! You'll always be a loser!"

Unable to silence these tormenting voices, tonight he sought the only option left. Trembling, he put the gun to his head. The hard, cold metal ground into his scalp. His finger slid up against the trigger and started to pull.

Then there was a shift. Somewhere, somehow...something changed.

The voices in his mind fell silent. He heard a surprised, angry cry. Then the new voice spoke clearly and calmly. "Help is coming." He stared at the gun in bewilderment.

Chapter Four

SENT ONES

THEY ALL CONVERGED, ACCORDING TO INSTRUCTIONS, AND FOUND AIKO WAITING, focused as always.

"Okay, tonight's going to be different. Armor up!" She then explained the unique mission to her team, who exchanged nervous glances.

"A retrieval? So we are going to bring somebody out with us?" Takumi asked. Aiko nodded as the Warriors gazed over the crest of the hill, wondering what awaited them. From a distance they could already see demon squads slithering in and out of the shadows.

"That's a first for us." Ishi said, stretching her arms above her head and then touching her toes. "Are we ready for this?"

"She's right. Helping someone is one thing, but taking one away from the other side while they guard him? That's new." Kai added.

Up to now they had guarded the approaches to schools, cleaned out stations, or stopped attacks on the train in order to relieve others from spiritual harassment. The idea of handling the responsibility for someone's life, in a rescue-type mission where demons gathered in larger numbers, weighed on them. They could all feel the stakes getting higher.

"And, I think we can expect much more resistance. I ran into a patrol that mentioned an Overlord."

"Wait now…uh, what's an Overlord?" Koh asked while he fussed with the wrapper on a candy bar.

Kai shrugged his shoulders. "Probably something big and ugly. But, a patrol? Like, they're expecting someone?"

Aiko paused. "We've met their captains, and they handle eight to ten Grunts. So an Overlord probably handles four to six captains. Say maybe up to sixty."

Koh stopped for moment, stunned, and then slowly pushed the candy bar into his mouth. Aiko had trained them for large group battle tactics, but they had all hoped that they would never have to use them. Thus far, the most they had faced was ten demons and, even then, Aiko had handled four single-handedly. All of them had sustained vicious wounds in that fight.

One by one, they shifted their gazes away from the amassing enemy. Ishi spoke up, trying to get everyone focused. "Okay, remember, shoulder to shoulder takes away their numeric superiority. Back to back in emergencies, and never ever leave your partner," she reminded everyone, exchanging nods with Aiko. They all took a deep breath, looked up into their leader's eyes, and nodded.

Then Michio announced, "I counted at least twenty-three just on the outside; seven at a barricade and over fifteen or so past that. Then, there's a gate, which they will probably lock. Who knows what's in the building after that?"

"There are *exactly* twenty-eight in plain sight," Takumi corrected as he gazed past Michio's large frame.

Michio looked at him dismissively and turned back to Aiko, who was finalizing a plan as they spoke. "Are you sure about this? They really do seem to be waiting for us." Michio shook his head, moderate concern in his deep voice.

She blew out a short breath and glanced into the heavens one more time. "Yes," she said, looking at him. "It's tonight. Everyone check your gear," Aiko ordered, already checking her own.

The six Warriors that she led partnered up. It took them ten seconds, each one turning around slowly to be checked. They tapped on each other's armor to be sure it was secure. They made certain that all of their weapons were present and would release in an instant. One quick glance into each other's eyes gave an unspoken commitment. They always fought in twos.

When the check was complete, they huddled together.

Aiko instructed them firmly, "Okay, I'll go over the top and take the captain. Ish and Mai, watch my back, okay?" The two girls nodded, promptly reaching for bows that were slung on their backs. "The rest will follow. As soon as he falls, take out the six guards."

"How long will that take?" asked Kai.

"Yeah, we don't want you to be trapped," added Koh, who was licking chocolate off his fingers. "If you're not careful…"

"Less than one second," Aiko interrupted matter-of-factly. Koh stopped licking. Koh raised his eyebrows and whispered to Kai, "That's why she doesn't have a boyfriend." They grinned, holding back their laughter. Ishi rolled her eyes.

Aiko continued, businesslike. "We fight our way up the road toward the gate and hope it's not locked. If it is, we may need to fly you over, Mai-girl, to unlock it for us. We have to make this a quick retrieval. There's no telling how many they will gather if we take too long. Remember, tonight we're on turf they control."

She placed both hands on Mai's shoulders. "Now be careful, little one. If something goes wrong, Michio will have to break the door down. Stay defensive and protect yourself."

"I'll be okay," Mai murmured, looking at her feet as always, as she calmly brandished a gleaming sword in each hand.

"Okay. Ish, you rejoin her on the other side. Once the gate is open, we fight our way to the stronghold. I can't beat the Overlord alone, but I'll keep him busy till you take out all the guards. Be sure you banish them or make sure they leave the battle, because if they come up from behind..."

"Oh yeah. Attack from behind in the alley–ouch!" Michio remembered.

Some of them nodded and smiled painfully, while others rubbed their behinds. Demons preferred to attack from the rear or the flanks when they could. Getting hit with a full barrage of flaming arrows from behind in an alley near the high school had cemented the lesson in their minds.

"They missed me," Koh declared nonchalantly. Everyone turned.

"I...uh...didn't get hit," he added apologetically but with a hint of personal triumph.

"Uh-huh. That's because you used me as a shield." Kai pointed to his backside. "Couldn't sit for a month because of you," he exaggerated while slapping his brother on the back of the head. There was a pause, then the group let out a light laugh that broke the increasing tension of the imminent attack.

Aiko's face broke into a smile for the first time. "Okay, okay, that's why we plan, right? After you finish the guards, we take down the Overlord together and find whoever it is we are supposed to help. Any questions?"

Takumi spoke up from deep thought. "If there are twenty-eight outside..."

"Or so," Michio interjected.

Takumi ignored him. "That means we will definitely be facing up to fifty or sixty tonight, and an Overlord. I want to emphasize that we kill fast and move quickly." He earned his nickname, "Mr. Roboto," by being methodical and efficient. It also made him a great captain for the math team at school.

"Yes," Aiko agreed. "No lingering. This is our first Overlord."

Koh had to ask one last question. "Uh, how will we know which one is the Overlord?"

"I agree with Kai. Big, ugly, and very hard to kill," Takumi answered.

"Let's stay focused to the end. Watch out for each other. Remember," Aiko said, pausing, "someone once fought for us." They all nodded soberly in agreement. She looked at each of them in turn. "The Master will be with us." She raised her gleaming sword into the air. "For His Honor!" In unison, the Warriors raised their weapons and repeated, "For His Honor!"

Aiko looked at the group, took a deep breath, nodded once, and charged over the rise. Sprinting the short distance to the barricade, she flipped up and over six guards, landing in front of the surprised captain. Before he could make a sound or pull out a weapon, she deftly sliced him in half crosswise. He imploded with a *whooosh* and disappeared, leaving a cloud of sulfurous dust. Banished in less than a second. The remaining six guards growled and drew their weapons. Aiko turned to face them, standing in the residue of their defeated captain, taking a defensive stance.

"Face me and die!" she challenged. Their eyes glared with hatred as they pulled jagged weapons and moved in to attack. Just then, the six Warriors leaped over the barricade in unison and let out a shrill battle cry. In midair, the two girls loosed arrows that flew past Aiko's head. She spun to attack a large guard. He raised a wicked ax, and his drooling grin promised he'd bury it in her. The air around her buzzed with a rank stench. Pulse thrumming, she leveled her sword at his heart. Two arrow tips sprouted from his chest; he burst, sulfurous particles blasting her face as he disappeared. When she spit the foul taste from her mouth and turned back, her Warriors had finished with the guards and stood waiting for her command. "Let's go!" Aiko shouted, thrusting her arm in the air.

Filled with adrenaline, they rushed up the road toward the gate, expecting a fight, but the whole area was deserted and deathly quiet. They came to a stop with puzzled looks.

"Where are they?" Ishi asked.

"I'm sure I counted twenty or more," Michio said, searching every shadow around them.

"I can smell them," Koh said with a sour look on his face.

"Careful…they're here," Aiko said. A grim realization shone in her eyes. "They're cloaked." The Warriors strengthened the grip on their weapons and kept straining their senses in all directions for any sign or smell of a demon.

"I hate it when they do that." Koh shook his head and took bigger whiffs of the air.

"Yes, they're all around us…can't tell how many," Takumi said, eyes closed, concentrating, listening.

They could feel an invisible force gathering all around them. They looked quickly from side to side, pointing their swords wildly toward any movement or sound that broke the silence of the night.

"We're surrounded." Ishi looked toward their rear, wondering if their escape had been cut off. She glanced at her leader, waiting for orders.

Aiko called out, "Circle!"

As they began to move, there was a rushing wind like a giant veil being suddenly pulled across the sky. A harsh guttural voice pierced the night, ordering an attack. All around them, demon warriors appeared wielding cruel, twisted weapons. Their eyes glowed with loathing and their evil snarls filled the air.

The Warriors let out a collective gasp as they stumbled into a circle formation and formed up shoulder to shoulder. Well over thirty demons began moving in, eager for a kill.

Michio swung his sword from side to side. "Maybe this wasn't such a good idea."

"We are *so* dead." Koh looked defeated.

"They've got the advantage," Takumi said, counting their opponents and calculating their chances.

"Not for long. Everyone hold!" Aiko commanded as she dropped to one knee. She extended her hands, head bowed and eyes closed. The demons gasped and cried out when they saw her go down. They rushed into the Warriors to try to stop Aiko.

"Go defensive!" Ishi called out. Aiko, in deep concentration, whispered to heaven.

There was a deafening crash as the demons slammed into the waiting Warriors, forcing them back one step. Sparks lit up the night as deadly scythes, spears, and axes sought out the small, encircled group. The Warriors cringed at first impact and all found themselves eye to eye with a vicious fallen angel. Its foul hot breath bore down on them. Their weapons locked. A harsh, grating sound like fingernails on a chalkboard pierced their ears as lies collided with truth. They slowly regained their footing, sought out the shoulder next to them, and held. After a few moments two and three demons joined the attack on each Warrior. Demon blades started to slip through and find their targets.

"Aaah! Watch my right!"

"Ouch! There are too many!"

"Ugh! Spear, Look out!"

"I'm hit, I'm hit!"

Each terrifying demonic attack that hit a human spirit caused a burning, hissing sound in the spiritual dimension. Lies embedding in heart and mind sent up a sulfurous stench. Each lie implanted a doubt, a discouragement, a weakness, a paralyzing fear. The growing spiritual pain caused each Warrior to waver. They struggled to maintain their focus, and with hardened determination continued to stand and fend off the attack. But just barely.

"Hold! Everyone *hold*!" Ishi ordered with authority. "Aiko? *Hurry*." Ishi yelled, without taking her eyes off her opponent.

Suddenly Aiko stood and yelled, "For His Honor!" A loud boom shattered the night. The ground shuddered as a blue shockwave of heavenly power thundered outward like a massive sledgehammer from the Warriors' circle. The demons were thrown back shrieking. They fell to the ground stunned. The Warriors stood unscathed, breathing heavily.

"Now! Take them!" Aiko ordered as she charged, sword flashing.

In unison they cried out and rushed into the dazed group of demons who were trying to recover.

Takumi moved like he was performing a kata, going from one opponent to the next with deadly efficiency. He banished each demon with a single strike earning his name, "Mr. Roboto."

Michio stood at his side swinging an over-sized sword that only someone with his brute strength could wield. He rushed in attacking two or three demons at a time, hacking, punching, headbutting, and filling the air with his war cry when he banished an enemy.

Ishi's sprinted into the fray in a blur. She slashed one demon into oblivion, roundhouse kicked another, and then expertly dueled a captain, locking swords with him and then using her black belt skills to pound him senseless before she decapitated him, causing him to burst with a *whoosh*.

Mai danced gracefully across the battlefield like a poised and deadly artist banishing demons in her wake. With two short swords flashing, she spun, flipped, fought from a kneeling position, and while leaping high into the air. A look of fierce concentration radiated from her eyes.

Koh and Kai attacked like a synchronized fighting machine. They stood back to back and went spinning into their enemies like a wheel of death. Their hearts beat as one as they banished one demon after another with perfect teamwork. While Kai called out pre-choreographed attack moves, Koh whooped and bantered with the enemy.

Aiko charged fearlessly into the thick of the battle. She moved with the poise and confidence of a veteran. He sword was fast and her footwork was flawless, but most of all she was wholly committed to what she was doing and banished each demon with ferocity.

Cries filled the night and the stench of banished demons hung in the air as the few remaining fallen angels fled. The Warriors turned to each other, trying to catch their breath. Ishi called out, "Everyone okay?" They had mostly arm wounds, burns, and scratches. Only Koh had taken a spear thrust that slipped through his armor and penetrated his right shoulder. He held it gingerly.

"God, I *knew* I would get hit tonight! It's payback for that alley thing." He grimaced. "Uh...I think I can go on. I'm left-handed anyway."

"No you're not!" his brother corrected. Koh looked absently at both hands.

Michio was rubbing a bump on his forehead from too many headbutts.

They were all hurting from minor wounds. Aiko evaluated the situation and looked toward the gate ahead of them. It stood ten feet high and twenty feet across and was covered with rust and grime. It guarded the only entrance to their destination and was closed tight.

"If they were waiting for us here, what will we find when we open that gate?" Ishi asked, bent over with hands on hips.

"It's like we're storming their home field or something. What's going on, Aik? Are we supposed to be here?" Michio asked for everyone.

Aiko replied confidently, "I'm sure this is the night and this is the place. We go on." She motioned them to stay back and ran up the gate and found it locked. She struggled with it for a moment to be sure and then gave up. Aiko rejoined the group and motioned for Mai.

Mai stepped forward, looking down. "Still want me to go over?"

Aiko paused, knowing her young friend could land in the middle of another large group of guards. Once in the air, there was no turning back.

Aiko looked at her. "I couldn't hear anything on the other side, but I know they are there, so you'll have to be quick and protect yourself until we get in." Then Aiko looked up at Michio. "Mich, get something heavy and pound on that door hard just before she goes over. Make them think we're forcing it open. That will buy her a few seconds."

Michio looked around and picked up a large piece of lumber that was a former part of the barricade. He liked bashing things. As he held it, he whispered a prayer, and the wood started to glow with a faint blue outline. He turned to the gate as the other Warriors stood back. He looked to Aiko for the order to begin. Mai retreated from the gate to give her time to accelerate, and Ishi waited on one knee with hands clasped together and opened toward Mai's approach.

"Good. Everyone get ready. Koh, you're wounded. Move to the back with Kai. Heal up and guard our rear. Okay, Michio, let them know we're here." Aiko then turned to Mai and signaled.

The mighty Warrior beamed. He liked it when Aiko was intense. He reared back, lifted his front leg, and swung the lumber like a bat. "Boom!" he yelled. In the meantime Mai sprinted toward the gate with her feet barely touching the ground, picking up speed with every step. As the door shuddered and creaked, Mai, at full speed, stepped into Ishi's hands and leaped high into the air, while Ishi popped up and hoisted her hands high over her head. She flew gracefully over the gate, pulled in her knees, flipped, drew two swords in midair, and dropped to the other side. The Warriors listened, bracing themselves. There was a quick series of slices, thrusts, and parries. A demon cried out followed by a *whooosh*. A locking mechanism began to turn and there was a loud *click*. The large door swung open and revealed a force of fifteen demons who whirled in surprise. Michio caught three of them and sent them flying into the night with a mighty swing of his lumber.

"Everyone inside!" Aiko and the other Warriors charged in and quickly cut down the rest.

"I could get used to *this*!" Michio said, looking fondly at his glowing piece of lumber.

Aiko, still all business, ordered, "Okay, let's keep moving." Then she stopped and called out, "Mai. Mai!" Aiko cried out when her eyes found the little one against the wall.

"I…uh…had to turn my back for a second. No one to watch–" Mai spoke painfully with tears filling her eyes.

She sat leaning against the wall beneath the locking mechanism she had opened. There was a fiendish axe buried between her shoulder blades. The Warriors rushed to surround her. Aiko, eyes glistening with tears, knelt next to her, took hold of the axe with both hands, and pulled hard. Mai gasped in pain as it came out. The wound was smoldering deep in her spirit. Aiko placed both hands on the wound, closed her eyes, and began praying as a tear rolled down her cheek. The wound slowly closed, but Mai still cringed in pain. Aiko tightened her lips and wiped her face and stood up. "Something's not right." She peered into the darkness beyond the gate.

"Hey, look at this axe," Takumi said, examining the weapon.

Ishi took it. "This is not a Grunt's axe. It belongs to a…"

"Slayer," Aiko concluded with growing indignation.

"Oh man, not a Slayer." Koh rubbed his sore shoulder. "Can tonight get any worse?" he complained.

"What is a Slayer doing here?" Michio asked, with everyone gathering around now.

"A suicide is in progress. He's here to end a life. We're not just retrieving." Takumi looked at each of them somberly. "We're here to stop someone from killing himself. We have to hurry," he urged.

"Let's find him." Aiko looked into the night coolly. "Ishi, keep healing Mai, but quickly. Kai and Koh, you stay here in support. Takumi and Michio, let's go," she said sharply.

As he watched the three Warriors trot off, Kai shook his head. "Oooh, she's mad now."

"Oh, yeah. Mad *and* in a hurry," Koh agreed, still holding his shoulder. The brothers glanced at each other with raised eyebrows.

Kneeling by Mai, Ishi sighed in relief. "The armor stopped it from penetrating too deep."

"It hurts, Ish..." Mai grimaced. Ishi prayed, but kept glancing after Aiko.

The gate had opened into a small abandoned parking lot with a path leading up to a metal door, which stood ajar. The three Warriors rushed to the door, paused and peered inside, and together entered a large room with a high roof and a musty smell. It was unfurnished other than a collection of rubber tires of assorted sizes, broken pallets, empty barrels, and twisted pieces of metal. Trash littered the floor and the room smelled of rust, spoiled food, sweat, and urine.

"There!" Takumi said, pointing.

In the far corner of the room lay a young man curled up on the ground. His eyes were closed and he was trembling violently and moaning as if in a nightmare. Over him hovered a powerful, beautiful creature with extended pinioned wings. In its gleaming hands it held a golden spear.

"Look Aik, a Watcher. You were right." exclaimed Michio. They glanced at each other and then back to the angelic guardian.

The next moment, the Warriors saw him, the evil Overlord. He was hovering over the boy in the darkness, held at bay only by the Watcher's presence. His red glowing eyes pierced the darkness and communicated only one thing–pure and absolute hatred. He stood eight feet tall and sinuous muscles rippled over his torso and limbs. Glistening black scales covered him from head to claw. In his hands, he carried a spear with a razor-sharp barb and a round shield bearing a bloody pentagram. He was poised to pounce, but kept snarling in frustration at the powerful Watcher.

"Big, ugly, and hard to kill." Michio sighed.

"Why do I always have to be right? And, uh, the kid has a gun. Do you see it?" Takumi pointed.

"What now?" Michio asked Aiko.

Aiko surveyed the scene. "Wait."

Just then the Watcher looked up at Aiko and her two friends. He acknowledged them with a nod. He stepped back, and with one powerful rush of his wings disappeared into the night. The Overlord jumped back in surprise. Looking over his shoulder, he saw the Warriors and scowled.

He spun quickly to face them, raising his weapon.

"This one is *mine*. Go play elsewhere," he growled. "*Children.*" He turned his back to them and advanced toward the boy to attack and take his prize.

Aiko's eyes darted from wall to wall and searched out every corner of the room in an instant. She knew it was another trap.

"Mich, Tak, you see him?" she asked, looking at them sideways.

The two Warriors did a quick search. There was one unaccounted-for Slayer, who had left an axe in Mai's back. They looked back at her with empty expressions.

"There in front, directly between us and the Overlord, partially cloaked. He's using the shadows. See him?"

"Got him," Takumi whispered.

"Wha…" Michio squinted.

"Good! Take him together." Aiko darted toward the Overlord. As she did, the Slayer uncloaked and swung a large axe at her in a deadly arc. Just as she reached him, she curled and rolled narrowly under the blade. It passed within an inch of her. She continued her roll beneath his legs and on past him toward the Overlord as he thrust his spear toward the unconscious boy.

There was a loud *ring* as her sword blocked the Overlord's weapon just before it hit its mark. He turned, seething with anger, and roared at her.

The now fully visible Slayer, in the meantime, had swung so hard that missing Aiko had thrown him off balance and out of position.

"*There* you are!" Michio said in exasperation, and cut a swath across his midsection with his long sword. A split second later, Takumi's blade cut off the Slayer's axe hand. Blood spurted, and his weapon clattered to the ground. The demon roared in agony and turned ferociously on the Warriors, who thought they had already won.

"Uh, shouldn't he go, like, *whoosh*, now?" Michio stuttered.

"Not enough damage," Takumi yelled. "We have to cut deeper to banish this one!"

Just then, a punch came out of nowhere, caught Takumi square in the chest, and sent him flying into the wall with a loud thud.

This menacing Slayer had four arms.

They hadn't seen the other two appendages in the shadows. The other hand grabbed a surprised Michio and lifted him off his feet, causing him to drop his sword.

Meanwhile Aiko was confronting the Overlord. "You've lost. Now disengage," she challenged, buying time till the others could join her. She would need help with this one. *Guys, where are you?*

The Overlord growled at her with hot, putrid breath, then smiled mockingly as he drew himself up in front of the young Warrior, towering over her. She stood to meet him, unflinching and unafraid.

"I've lost? Little one…why would you think you even have a chance?" he jeered.

"Because we are here, and He is with us. It's over," Aiko said without blinking.

The demon roared, shaking the room. He laughed at her.

"The barrens are a long way off. Leave this one or I *will* banish you!" Aiko challenged.

"You pitiful skank! You think you can beat me?" he sneered.

"I didn't say *I* could," Aiko said calmly.

He stopped smiling. He knew what that meant and he hated it. She knew how to harness strength beyond herself. A knowing, evil look crept over his face. He remembered his instructions on this one.

"I know where your brother is," he mocked. "Makoto. That's his name, isn't it? He's one of us now. Very helpful boy."

Aiko gasped as the painful ridicule seared into her heart. Her sword lowered just a bit.

"You're lying!" she cried.

"We have a Slayer picked out for him when he is ready. He'll serve the Dark Lord and die, and you'll be too late," he mocked.

She felt her confidence draining as her heart filled with a mixture of grief and rage. *Makoto, where are you?*

"Aiiiiko!" It was Michio. She looked quickly to the side to see him lifted high over the head of the Slayer. She saw Takumi lying crumpled and unconscious against the wall. Suddenly, she heard the sound of a spear whistling through the air toward her.

She cried out in alarm as she struggled to get her sword up in time.

The weapons collided, sparks seared the air, and the force of the blow knocked her to the ground.

"Aiiiiko!" Michio cried again. The Slayer was winding up to throw him into a pile of sharp scrap metal.

The Overlord pushed his weapon down hard against Aiko's sword, pinning her to the ground.

As the Slayer reared to fling Michio down, two arrows streaked through the air from the direction of the door and buried deep in the demon's chest. He gasped and dropped Michio, who hit the ground with a crash.

Ishi and Kai burst through the door yelling, and sprinted toward the Slayer. As he grabbed for the arrows in his chest, they drove glowing swords deep into his belly. He cried out. There was a large thud behind him. He froze with an anguished look on his face and fell forward with a large axe, his own, buried in his back. He hit the ground hard and burst into dust.

Michio stood angry and panting, "*That* was for Mai!"

Aiko's eyes narrowed. She turned and pushed herself up onto one knee. She looked deep into her enemy's eyes and stood, yelling, "Aaaiiiyaaah!"

She forced herself powerfully up against the weight of the Overlord's weapon and sent a flurry of strikes, driving him backward on the defensive. All her enemy could do was parry and retreat as she pressed her attack. Suddenly, she paused for a second and stood straight up, dropping her guard, looking the demon in the eye, inviting a strike. This prompted him to rear back with his spear to attack. The other Warriors caught their breath as Michio cried out in alarm, "Aiko, noooo!"

Ishi stopped him short. "No, wait…watch."

The demon lord recoiled, ready to strike. In the blink of an eye, Aiko stepped inside, past his shield, under his spear, and leaped up onto his chest. She was eye to eye with him. Her left arm slipped around his thickly muscled neck, and her right arm drove her sword into his chest to its hilt, piercing him all the way through.

Shock filled his face, and his arms went limp. He writhed in pain, unable to break Aiko's hold on him. She felt him shudder and shake as he started to lose material form. "I…hate…you, worthless idiot!" He spit yellow slime at her face and roared.

"I love my brother, and you can go to hell!" she shot back.

She closed her eyes and whispered a quick power prayer. Her sword became a white-hot flame burning within him. Her whole form glowed with burning light. The demon cried out in defeat. She pushed away from him as his body collapsed inward and with a *whoosh*, he left a stinking residue of sulfurous dust. She caught her sword as it fell and stood wiping her face with the back of her hand and coughing. She turned quickly to the others. They were speechless, transfixed on her as the glow around her dimmed.

"What? Everybody okay?" Aiko asked.

They couldn't find words. They had never seen her glow like that before.

"Ish?" Aiko nodded toward the boy who was their mission, and Ishi sheathed her sword and made her way over to him.

"Check Takumi!" Aiko directed. Michio ran over and leaned over his partner.

Takumi was laying flat on his back, blinking his eyes, and trying to sit up. "How…did…I miss that? Should have known…He caught me off…"

"What? You didn't count the arms?" Michio said in fun, helping him up.

"I thought you couldn't take him yourself," Kai observed, walking over to Aiko. "By the way, what was that glow thing you did?"

"He shouldn't have mentioned my brother," she said, still trying to understand what had just happened as she sheathed her sword, now wiped clean.

Ishi was kneeling over the curled-up boy. "I don't know who you are, but you better be worth this." She started to lift him and motioned to Michio.

"Is it just me, or are these getting tougher?" Michio asked, lifting the boy into his arms. "We've gone from street fights to major warfare."

"It wasn't so bad," Koh said, still holding his arm. Everyone stopped to look at him. Kai slapped his shoulder.

"Ooow! Heeey!" Koh whined, grabbing his wound overdramatically.

"He's right. This is unusual. Patrols, guards, ambushes?" Ishi added with a questioning look at Aiko.

"That's an organized defense, not some roaming fallen angels making trouble," Kai concluded.

"Let's get out of here. We'll talk later," Aiko answered. She turned to Michio. "How is he?"

"Well, he has a gun." Michio acknowledged pointing to the gun near where Kenji was lying.

"Had," Ishi said as she took it and tossed it far into the rubble.

They all gathered around Michio and the boy cradled in his arms. Mai and Koh limped up, healed but clearly hurting. Takumi stepped forward, shaking the clouds out of his head. There was a momentary pause as seven teenage Warriors looked at the reason for their battle.

"What's your name?" Ishi asked as gently as she could.

"Uh? Ken…Kenji," he said, shivering and sounding very disoriented. He looked from face to face nervously. "Who…who are you?"

They all looked at Aiko for an answer.

"We were sent to help you," Aiko said.

"Who sent you?" Kenji whispered as he started to lose consciousness.

"Answers later. For now, trust us; we're friends." She turned to the others. "Okay. Coffee Shop everyone, let's go!" The Warriors trotted off into the night.

Chapter Five

Journey Home

Kenji felt himself floating...

Moving...

Voices...

"Don't bang his head on anything," a girl's voice ordered.

"He ain't heavy. Besides, a knock might be a good thing...you know, wake him up," a deep, husky voice responded.

"Mich, not everyone likes banging his heads against hard things," said another guy, teasing. Several voices laughed.

"Did you see me catch those four guards with one swing?"

"For the tenth time, *yes*, and it was three."

"Did you see me save your butt with that arrow?"

"Dude, I love the way Mai-chan flies..."

"How are you, Mai-chan?"

"Better."

"Someone watch Tak, he keeps wandering away. I think he hit that wall too hard."

"Hey, Tak, how many fingers?"

"Give me a break! I just need some ice."

Several voices chuckled.

"Ish, take point with me, they may have one more surprise for us," a strong female voice suggested.

"No, they won't! An Overlord got banished tonight and they're scared."

"Wow, he was big."

"And ugly!"

"I would have charged him too, but my shoulder..."

"Sure you would," an unbelieving voice answered.

"Hey...no...really...I would...I would have."

"Oh, Aiko, that was so cool. 'Go to hell!'" said a voice imitating her.

"And then whooosh! Man, you stuck him good," a playful male voice added.

"She's not a man," shot back a girl's voice.

"You *know* what I mean."

"Okay, guys, quiet down, there might be trouble in the station."

There was a pause, then the sound of an approaching train.

Kenji's eyes started to open. He slowly focused on a tall, attractive girl with short hair who was looking around, alert. Her eyes met his for a moment and a smile formed on her lips. "Almost there," she said, as Kenji's eyes drifted closed again.

A train stopped and the sound of the intercom announced the destination.

"Let's go, everyone. Someone pull Takumi on!"

There was the sound of doors closing. "Okay, everyone can relax." There was a collective sigh. "Ish, keep your sight on to watch out for surprises. I'm sure word is out already."

"Anyone have anything to eat?"

"Are you *always* eating?"

"No. Well, most of the time…oh…here."

The sound of a package opening could be heard, followed by a crunching noise.

"I could use some food right now too."

"I just want coffee."

"A Coke would be good."

"Who's taking the new guy? What's his name again?"

"How about Mister Near-Impossible-to-Save?"

"Mister Meat-Grinder."

"Mister Ambush-Man!"

"Mister…"

"Okay you two, stop it, he might hear."

"His name is Kenji!" said a girl's irritated voice.

"Okay…okay…don't get huffy."

"Who's taking Kenji?"

"We'll decide at the Shop."

"It's just that…well…we've had tough fights before, but this…you gotta ask…who is this guy?"

"I know…" Everyone went silent.

A voice announced the next train stop.

"This is it. You got him, Michio?"

"Light as a feather."

"Show-off."

"Hey, I'll take a show-off like him in a battle any day."

There was laughter.

"Did you guys see me hit those five guards?"

Groans.

Moving…floating again…

"Oh, grab Tak quick, he's still on the train!"

"Whooaa, that Slayer did a number on him."

"Takumiii, gonna tour the city, are you?"

"Okay, let's move. Ishi what do you see?"

"Mostly harassers and a few Grunts. They see us and they're backing off. No more fights tonight, I think."

"You lead and I'll cover the rear."

"Right."

"Stay close, everyone. Let's go heal up."

Then, there was silence.

Chapter Six

Coffee Shop

It was a pleasant coffee shop. It had six round tables, each with two chairs, along with a counter, lined by six stools, and a well-maintained toilet in the back. The whole place had a home-style feel and smelled of freshly baked pastry and coffee. On a television set hanging in the left corner over the door, a baseball game was in its final inning. There were no customers, but the Friday late-night crowd would be in soon. In the back, connected to the main customer area, was a long room with a large, low table that filled most of the space. It was surrounded by eight comfortable chairs. In the far corner of the room, a wraparound couch lined the back wall. In front of the couch was a small coffee table.

Michio gently placed Kenji on the couch while the others dropped their backpacks on the floor and plopped down wherever they could. Everyone got busy cleaning up and took turns healing one another with quick prayers. After a few minutes, they relaxed.

Kenji felt himself waking up. He could smell food cooking and heard voices all around him.

"Hey, hey, guy?" said deep voice.

"His name is Kenji," a girl's voice said sharply from across the room.

Kenji's eyes opened to see a large teenage boy bending over him. Despite his intimidating size, he seemed very good-natured.

"Keeennnjiiii," the big boy huffed, looking across the room, still smiling. "Oh hey, you're awake. Here, drink this. It's tea. It'll help clear your head."

"Wh…where am I?" Kenji managed to say as he took the cup with shaky hands, and took a sip. He took a deep breath as the warm liquid went down smoothly.

"It's Coffee Shop."

"Which…coffee shop?"

"Just Coffee Shop," he said, smiling. He looked back and called out. "Hey guys, he's awake." They all looked up from what they were doing.

"What happened?" Kenji asked as he sat up and blinked his eyes open wide. He took another sip of the tea.

"You almost didn't make it," the tall girl with short hair spoke.

Kenji looked down, trying to remember any part of the night's events. There were the nightmares and the mocking voices, the drugs, wandering the streets terrified, and the–it came to him and he looked down at the ground with sudden realization.

"Uh…where's the…uh…?" Kenji checked his pockets.

"Gun? It's gone for good," another girl said with a sense of finality. She had a ponytail and an athletic build. She looked like she was waiting for him to complain.

Kenji instinctively tried to react but it just wasn't there.

Come on…don't let them push you around. Intimidate, threaten, be cool.

He knew that a gang leader needed to stay in control at all costs, fearless and intimidating. But for some reason he couldn't call it up. He simply *wasn't* angry and he couldn't fake it. He felt as though he wasn't himself, or maybe for the first time, he was. What was going on?

"I'm Aiko. This is Ishi and Mai," said the tall, short-haired girl, pointing.

Kenji nodded to the ponytailed girl and to a younger-looking one with short, light brown hair almost hiding behind her.

"I'm Michio," the big guy said and slapped him on the back. Kenji cringed and mouthed a muffled "ooowww."

"He's the one who carried you a pretty long way." Aiko patted Michio's shoulder.

"Thanks, I guess…but wh–"

"The one with the ice pack on his head is Takumi," Aiko interrupted. "The two eating back there are Koh and Kai." They both waved without looking up from their furious eating.

"Oh, no, they're racing again. How disgusting." Ishi shook her head.

Kenji looked them over and, with a bewildered look on his face asked, "Who *are* you? Do I know you?"

"Yes, and he does it again!" Koh yelled with hands raised, dancing, and food still hanging out of his mouth. Kai started knocking his head on the table. "You must have cheated!"

Kenji's expression became even more incredulous.

Aiko noticed Kenji watching Koh and Kai. He pushed his long hair back with his hands revealing a strong, handsome, but wearied face, with circles under his eyes.

"I'm sorry," Aiko said. "You don't need this right now." She turned to the brothers and spoke sharply, "Guys, this is important."

"Okay, sorry." The boys sat like scolded puppies.

"Now," Aiko said, "what we are asking is *who* are *you*?"

"We've never had to fight so hard for someone," Ishi said in a serious tone.

"Yeah, like they didn't want to let you go." Michio crossed his arms.

"Or like they're afraid of you turning," Takumi said, still lying back, looking sideways from under his ice pack.

Kenji looked at each of them like they were speaking a foreign language. "What *in the world* are you talking about?"

"It's more like *which* world are we talking about." Michio glanced at everyone.

"Hey, you guys remember your first night?" Aiko stated more than asked. Everyone grunted in agreement, nodded, or said, "Oh yeah…" Aiko sat next to Kenji and looked him in the eyes.

"Hear me out, okay?" She sighed and continued. "You were going to end your life tonight."

Kenji looked at her in disbelief. "Oh…uh…"

After a pause, Aiko continued. "But it wasn't just you. Someone or something was pushing you; voices in the night or in your dreams?"

"More like nightmares," Takumi added.

Kenji looked up and met her gaze. "But how…"

"Think about it." She paused. "There is more to the world than just what we see or what we can measure. There is more to us than just bodies that go back to dust when we die. We all have a sense of eternity, a soul that will go on forever; a spiritual side."

"Wait! Is this some kind of cult?" Kenji asked suspiciously.

"Hey, I said *that* too!" Koh said, standing.

Aiko's quick look told Koh to be quiet and so he put two hands up and closed his mouth and sat down. She turned back to Kenji. "No, this is not a cult, not a religion, but a reality, a very real, true, hard-and-fast reality."

Kenji settled down a little. "Okay, so we might be spiritual. And?"

"Do you believe in God, Kenji?" she asked.

He paused, weighing his answer. "Yes, and no. I mean I've always thought He was real, but trust me, He must have given up on me by now."

"No, He hasn't. Tonight He knew you were in trouble and that they were trying to end your life, so He sent us. Whether you believe it or not, you really do matter to Him."

"*Who* was trying to end my life? Who are 'they'?" he asked, starting to get exasperated.

"The fallen ones, demons," she said simply. Everyone took a deep breath. This was always the hard part.

Kenji stood up and waved his hands. "Wait a minute! Who exactly are you?"

Aiko looked at the others, then at Kenji, and said in measured tones, "We...we're on the other side; spiritual Warriors. We're committed to the God who made everything that there is, and to His Son, who is the greatest spiritual Warrior of all time–and our Master. When He calls, we go in and remove demonic influences that are trying to destroy people. It gives them clarity, restores spiritual sight temporarily, and offers a chance to change sides," she said very deliberately.

"Temporarily?" he asked.

"If you don't choose sides, they move in again to fill your mind with deception and blind you to the truth. So, *not* deciding *is* deciding," Aiko explained, knowing he wouldn't get it.

"So, this fight you had tonight, was for me against some kind of monsters?

"Not monsters. They're fallen angels; demons who work for the Dark Lord and whose only purpose is to destroy you," Aiko answered.

Kenji sat down. "I'm sorry, you all seem like really nice people, not my usual crowd, but I just don't believe a word you're saying."

"Tonight was different," Aiko continued. "What they were saying"–she glanced at the other Warriors–" is that there was an unusual amount of resistance surrounding you. As you can see, some of us got knocked around. Usually, it's two or three, maybe five at the most, but for you..."

"Fifty-one Grunts, one Slayer, and one Overlord, so a total..." Takumi calculated.

Aiko interrupted, "Uh, Tak..."

"Oh, right." He smiled apologetically.

She paused, and then spoke with added sincerity, "Kenji, who are you?"

Kenji hesitated and looked up, deciding whether or not to say anything. "Trust me, you don't want to know." He got up to leave.

"Please," she insisted gently.

He stopped and looked at them hesitantly. "Okay, look, it's not who I am, but maybe who my father is. Have you ever heard of the Red Dragon Group?"

"City's worst and most powerful organized gang," Takumi replied, as though giving an answer in history class. "Drugs, prostitution, extortion, gambling, and other unseemly ways to make a profit." He looked at Kenji for confirmation.

"Yeah, my father..."

Suddenly, there was the loud *crash* of tables being kicked over. The door burst open and a hulk of a man dressed in an ill-fitting suit, with a permanent scowl on his face, stepped into the room, looking at each teenager, searching.

His gaze rested on Kenji, and he grinned.

"He's here!" he called back to some unseen boss.

Aiko glanced at Ishi. A signal. Ishi put on her Truesight just as another man walked into the room. He was very well dressed and had a manner that was arrogant, thoughtless, and evil. The pungent odor of cigar smoke entered with him and something else, something ancient. At first glance, Ishi gasped and went white stepping back, almost stumbling. Aiko went to help her and turned toward the man who ignored all else but one.

"Kenji!" a raspy voice spoke. His piercing eyes bored into him.

"So, you're okay? I had word you were kidnapped," he lied, "but I'm glad to see you are in *good* hands." He cast a look over to Aiko and spit on the ground.

Kenji was frozen with fear.

"Uh, Fath–"

"Shut up and get to the stupid car!" he screamed, grabbing Kenji by the throat with one hand and pointing violently toward the front door. His eyes bulged and filled with rage like they were going to explode. He shoved Kenji to the floor, releasing him, and then stood calmly fixing his cuffs and adjusting his suit. Then in an eerily gentle voice he added, "You and I will talk in private like a father and son should." Kenji got up and scrambled toward the door, where the henchman grabbed him by the collar and held him roughly. Kenji's father turned to Aiko and the others. He took out a cigar and lit it. Koh started to weakly point at a No Smoking sign, and got a face full of smoke for the effort.

"Do you know who I am?" Kenji's father asked as he blew another puff of smoke.

"You're Ryudan. I've seen you on TV. You're head of the Red Dragon Group," Takumi answered from under his ice pack.

"Very good, smart boy. Then you know who you are dealing with. Or do you?" He moved close to Aiko, right up in her face. There was something behind his eyes, something deep, something evil. She went rigid and he moved even closer, suffocating her with smoke as he whispered in her ear.

"I know what you did tonight, tch, tch, tch. You should mind your own business," he threatened. He leaned in and smelled her hair, running his hand up her arm.

Michio took a quick step toward him clenching his fists. Aiko shot a look at him, shaking her head slightly, stopping him in his tracks. Ryudan chuckled. She tried to contain herself but her skin crawled in revulsion. She could feel the evil pulsing in his touch. Kenji was watching from the door, struggling against the grip of the henchman.

"You found me! Okay? Let's go," he called out.

Ignoring him, Ryudan whispered, "I knew your sister. Nice little girl. So sad to lose a sister, such a tragedy."

Aiko's lips started to quiver and tears filled her eyes.

"Your brother will also be lost soon, and then *you*. Nothing or no one in this godforsaken *universe* can stop it!" He spit in her face. Aiko looked down, and wiped the warm ooze from her cheek as though defeated. He laughed wickedly and backed to the door, watching the pain he had just dispensed, with deep satisfaction.

Just as he turned, Aiko replied in a trembling voice, "No." He stopped and looked up, still smiling triumphantly, but mildly disappointed that she wasn't in a heap of despair.

She continued in a more measured tone, glaring at him through tear-filled eyes. "There was a shift tonight in the heavens. You felt it and you are trembling in your silk pants. That's why your boss sent you here. You're just a slave."

Ryudan stopped smiling and paused, trying to stay composed. Before he could form words, she continued, "It's *your* turn soon. You know that the One who made the universe will send us, and there is absolutely nothing *you* can do to stop *us*."

"You wanna die *that* bad, you little piece of trash?" he growled, throwing his cigar to the ground and shaking his finger at her.

"I'm already dead, Ryudan. Your threats mean nothing to me. When the Master gives the word, I'm coming after you myself." She spoke with a strong, penetrating gaze.

Ryudan shot a glance to his henchman, who released Kenji and lunged toward Aiko, raising a hand to strike her. As his hand came down, Ishi blocked it. He grunted and swung the other hand, which she stopped easily as well. The henchman stepped back and reached for the gun under his coat.

"Wait! Not here, you idiot," Ryudan ordered. "We'll be seeing them again soon. Playtime is over," he added with hate. "Let's go. Kenji, move!" The henchman spit on the ground in front of Ishi, who looked at him unmoved, and then stormed out.

As Kenji was pushed out he looked back at the Warriors and Aiko standing there defiantly. Her eyes met his, and she softened, remembering her mission. She hurried after them as they left the shop, and watched as Kenji was shoved into a black limousine.

"Kenji?" she called to the open window. "The voices…you won't hear them tonight." His eyes met hers again as the window started closing. The limo screeched off into the night, leaving Aiko standing alone in a cloud of exhaust fumes.

The Warriors were visibly shaken as they caught up and gathered around her. They all let out a collective sigh before finding their tongues.

"Okay, that *never* happened." Kai said.

"Whoa, so all that fighting tonight was for nothing," Koh complained.

"Ishi! What did you see?" Aiko asked eagerly.

Ishi looked up ominously. "He's a carrier. I saw at least five demons *in* him, maybe more. I've never seen anything like that. Scary!"

"That much evil in one person, and he came here on our turf?" Michio asked.

Aiko was considering what had just happened. "Well, Takumi, I guess we got our answer about Kenji?" she said, looking at him.

Takumi was quiet, processing everything that had just happened. His forehead was red from the cold pack, his hair was damp and out of place, but his eyes were intense. Suddenly, with uncharacteristic drama, he spoke.

"Just take the darkest place in the city, I mean pitch black darkness–enemy territory–filled with slaves who are blinded by that darkness, and you light only one match, or one small candle, and that light, that one small light, will be seen by a whole lot of people."

"Kenji." Mai stated what they were all thinking. "Maybe he'll help turn the tide," she hoped, quietly, still staring in the direction of the limo.

Aiko put her arm around Mai. "If they don't kill him first. Remember a light in a dark place can be seen by *both* sides."

"Hello, but Kenji's gone, with the demon dad," Koh said, pointing down the street. "So we lost him. It's over."

"I hate to say it, but he wasn't getting it, Aiko. Koh may be right. They won this round," Michio admitted.

Aiko stood thinking. After a slow deep sigh she said, "Let's get home. We did what we were called to do. We answered the call and we took care of each other. We need to trust His plan even though we can't see it now."

"I'd rather know *now*." Koh crossed his arms.

"Actually, I'd rather it were more predictable too." Takumi pushed up his glasses.

"Then we wouldn't need faith or trust, would we? And without trust..." she paused.

"There *is* no power," they finished in staggered unison.

"Pray for Kenji tonight. There's still time before his window closes," Aiko said, looking in the direction of the limo again.

"Come on, Takumi. I'll make sure you get home," Michio offered.

"Thanks. My head still hurts, especially when I think," Takumi answered.

"Just don't do no counting, that always hurts my brain." The two partners got their backpacks, waved, and walked down the street.

"We've got some cleaning up to do," Kai said, excusing himself and walking back in. He motioned Koh to follow. "Sorry, Aiko, but I don't think we'll ever see him again." Koh shrugged his shoulders and followed his brother.

Aiko looked over at the girls. "Ishi, you got Mai?"

"Yeah, come on, little sister." She playfully wrapped her arms around the twig of an eighth grader, who smiled widely.

"Ish?" Aiko put a hand on her shoulder. The two girls' eyes met. "Thanks for watching my back tonight."

"Forever and always, sister. Oh, and I heard what he said to you. I'm so sorry."

Aiko's eyes narrowed. "No Ish, *he's* the one that will be sorry." Her fists clenched and she cast one last look down the street. Then she softened and looked tired. "That's enough for one day. Come on, I'll walk to the station with you." The three teenage girls shouldered their backpacks, Mai put on earphones, and they walked arm in arm into the night.

♦ ♦ ♦

Kenji lay down in his room and stared at the stars through his window. It was the clearest night he had seen in a while. It was quiet and peaceful. He took a deep breath, sighed, and slipped into a peaceful sleep.

Unseen, a powerful Watcher gripped his spear and settled over him for the night's duty.

Chapter Seven

THEOLOGY

"MAKOTO! THERE'S A MONSTER IN MY CLOSET! MAKOTO!" AIKO CRIED AS SHE PULLED HER sheets *up to her terror-filled eyes.*

Makoto came running into the room. "Where, Aik?"

The frightened ten-year-old pointed to the foreboding darkness of her closet. Her thirteen-year-old brother turned and then walked slowly toward the darkness. "It's okay, Aik-chan, I'll get rid of it for you." As Aiko watched, just for the flash of moment, she saw her brother standing, covered with translucent armor, wielding a sword. Two glowing, hate-filled eyes bore down on him. The vision horrified her and she screamed, "Makoto!"

He came trotting back to her bed. "They're gone, scaredy-cat."

"Why won't they leave me alone?"

He put his arm around his little sister to comfort her. "They're afraid of you, Aik-chan."

She looked at him for a moment. "Will you teach me to fight them too?"

Makoto chuckled. "Someday we'll fight them side by side! Okay?"

She hugged him tight.

The sun peeked through the window, sending a beam of light directly onto Aiko's closed eyes, and she twitched. She was on her knees at the side of her bed. She had drifted off while talking with God. She groaned as she pushed through the temptation to slip into bed. It wasn't the first night she'd slept on her knees.

"Okay, I'm up, I'm up." Raising her hands, she focused and prayed, "Master, fill me with Your power and lead me through this day to honor You." She got up and stumbled into the bathroom for her quick morning routine, and twenty minutes later she was walking briskly out her front door with her backpack.

Coffee Shop was always her first stop, where she would sit and study her sword manual. This contained her Master's teachings and techniques in spiritual swordsmanship. Often, the others showed up there as well, but after last night some of them would be waking up too sore to drag themselves to Coffee Shop at seven o'clock on a Saturday morning. As she turned the corner, she could already taste the hot tea. She reached for the front door.

A male voice called out from across the street. "You were right!"

"Huh?" She turned and looked in his direction.

"The voices *are* gone, and I want to know why." Kenji hunched his shoulders against the cold and shoved his hands in his pockets.

"Does your father know you're here?" she asked, glancing up and down the street, knowing the danger he was risking.

"You don't think I care what my father thinks, do you? I am, uh, more of a momma's boy." He spoke in a half-joking tone. Then he muttered, "I hate my father."

She looked at the black-clad, gangster-looking, tattooed hoodlum standing on the curb. Despite the mafia garb, his eyes didn't match the look. They were sincere and curious. She grinned and shook her head. "Uh, you are no momma's boy." *Master, what is going on?*

She put on her sight for just a moment and looked up and down the street again. Nothing. Satisfied it wasn't a trap, she managed an inviting smile, and he trotted across the street to join her.

"No one else thought you'd come back," she said as he stepped up onto the curb.

"What did you think?" he asked.

"I just do what I'm told and trust God," she replied simply.

"Okay, that's where you lose me. You talk about Him like you actually *know* and can *hear* Him. I've known some religious people, but it was more like rituals and stuff. Can anyone actually hear God?"

She thought for a moment. "I need tea." She opened the door and looked back at him, leaving the door open.

Koh and Kai's parents owned Coffee Shop. The brothers worked shifts there but must not have been up yet, because their mom served Aiko and Kenji tea and cookies. Aiko took a sip of her steaming tea and let it go down to warm her, and looked up at her unexpected guest.

"No beer, huh?" Kenji joked, looking at his tea. "Um, right," he said as he took a sip.

"Why did you come back, Kenji? Was it just the voices?"

He thought a moment. "No, not just…" He broke into a sudden laugh. "I've never heard anyone talk to my father like you did last night. I thought you were dead on the spot. I've seen my father do such cruel things to people who serve him a cup of coffee that's too cold, or show up thirty seconds late for an appointment. I mean, my father is a cold-blooded murderer. Well, he's more of a monster, ever since..." He shook his head and looked into the distance for a moment. "After he trashed you and threatened you, you just held your ground and spit it back in his face, and the thing is, you were right! You scared him real bad. I mean, scared the sh–um, I mean the life out of him. So I thought, what is it that this girl believes so strongly, that you would risk your life like that? No one believes like that." He paused. "When I woke up this morning from my first peaceful sleep in years, I just thought...I gotta know."

Aiko smiled and wiped a tear that was forming in the corner of her eye. She straightened, took a deep breath, and silently thanked God. "You see, God created everything, but He made us different. He made it possible for us to know Him."

"What does that mean?" Kenji asked.

"Um...like you know and trust a friend."

"With God? But..."

"Let me tell you more, maybe it will get clearer. A beautiful and powerful leader among the angels grew proud and self-deceived until at last he tried to take over God's throne."

"Can anyone do that?" Kenji asked, interested.

"No, God is all powerful, but pride can distort how you see reality. There was a battle in heaven, and the angel was cast to the earth with one-third of the heavenly creatures that had chosen to follow him. He was consumed with hatred and became utterly evil. He has many names, but we know him as the Dark Lord.

"So those are your monsters...uh...fallen angels, or demons?" he asked.

"Yes."

"So, there are good angels too, then," Kenji observed.

"Yes, and they help us." She started to warm up. "Since the Dark Lord couldn't defeat God, he went after God's greatest creation, mankind. Using every bit of cunning and evil he could, he deceived man and got him to rebel against God. This made all of mankind a slave to evil. Our world became fallen."

"Oh, I know all about that," Kenji said, staring at his hands and running a finger over a 666 tattooed on his right wrist.

"We all do, Kenji, in some way," Aiko reassured him. "You see, the Dark Lord knew that because of God's sense of justice, He would now have to punish His most precious creation. So, God banished man from His presence and appointed a day of judgment where man would pay the penalty for his bad choice. The Dark

Lord thought he had won, and he gloated in the victory." She paused to see how Kenji was taking all this.

He rubbed his chin. "Last night, you said we have to choose sides, but I've never had a chance to choose before."

"That's because we're all born into darkness. The first person kind of set it in motion for all of us. We're all fallen."

"So, I'm on the wrong side already?"

"Yes. We all are. To be fair, God had to punish us with the same standard." She paused. "Yet, He didn't give up on us," Aiko added, with the hint of a smile. "He loved us so much that He sent a Spiritual Warrior who would come to undo all that the Dark Lord had done. First He had to beat him in combat showing Himself worthy to stand for us."

"So He won?"

"Oh yes! First time ever the Dark Lord was beaten by a man."

"Why did He win? I mean, what did He do different?"

Aiko spoke with wonder, "He was God's Son."

Kenji turned his head slightly in disbelief. "So, why didn't He end it? You know, just wipe out all of the bad guys?"

Aiko nodded. "At the time, that would have included *us*. He had to find a way to defeat evil without losing us."

"So how…"

"He died in our place. He voluntarily laid down His life by allowing Himself to be struck down and punished instead of us. He died so we wouldn't have to," she said with her eyes glowing with gratitude.

Kenji sat up straight and ran his hand through his hair. "Wow."

"He proved that He was God's Son by coming back to life and returning to heaven, having accomplished His mission. Before He left, He raised up an army, empowered them to fight, and sent them out to win the world back for His Father."

"So, that's what you are, part of that army?"

She looked at him reflectively. "All around us, every day, the battle rages. In some lives, it's a subtle current slowly distracting people from God. In others, it's a vicious frontal attack designed to destroy them. When He calls we go out to try to make a difference."

They sipped their tea and Kenji thought deeply. It wasn't an uncomfortable silence. He looked across the table at this remarkable girl as she ate peacefully and allowed him to process these new thoughts. He couldn't believe how clear his mind was, and how the things she shared resonated with his whole being. He felt as though he had heard it before somewhere, or at least part of it.

They paid their bill and left Coffee Shop to walk in the brightening morning.

"So, how does it work? How do you, like, start off?"

"You already have a spiritual side to you, so you just turn your heart and thoughts to God and talk to Him about it." Aiko looked intently at his face to see how he would respond. *Will he turn?* she wondered.

"So, I just tell Him I want to change sides?"

"You tell Him that you want the forgiveness that His Son provides, and pledge your life to follow Him with all your heart," she explained.

He was silent for a long while, then said tentatively, "But what if you are unusually bad? There must be some who can never cross over? I mean, some things can't be forgiven." Images of broken children and grieving families scrolled through his head, and in the background looped the terrified screams of countless innocent victims."I'd love to think that God is forgiving as you say, but all I've seen is random evil, chance success or failure, and a world that seems to favor the strong and powerful. Take what you want. Destroy anyone who gets in your way."

Aiko got in his face and spoke firmly. "That what the Dark Lord wants you to think. Kenji, God meant for life to be better than that. He was so determined to get you back that He sacrificed His own Son for you! He wouldn't have done that for nothing. He can forgive anything and everything you've ever done."

Kenji met her eyes for a moment and then looked down. "Ummm, I overheard what my father said to you. What happened to your sister?"

The question caught Aiko off guard and her throat began to tighten. She looked away as they walked, trying to gather herself.

"Her name was Shiho, my little sister. We were very close. She depended on me. I always protected her," she said, remembering. They walked on in silence.

"So, what happened to her?"

"My sister met a boy. I warned her from the beginning. He was into drugs and he slowly dragged her in too. She was trying to help him but instead she became an addict. Anything for love, you know?" She paused to take another deep breath.

"What did your parents–"

"They weren't around by then. I spent nights holding her when she woke up screaming from nightmares. She would lay in my arms weeping for hours, so frightened." They stopped walking and stood facing each other. She looked up at Kenji. "She couldn't get the voices out of her head. Then, one day she left for school and didn't come home. I searched the whole city for her, but I was too late. I got a call. She was only fourteen. They said it was suicide."

"What did you do?" Kenji asked.

Her lips tightened and she took a breath to compose herself. "I chose sides." Kenji was visibly moved. His eyes were moist, but there was something else. Anger was rising in him. She sensed it wasn't rage, but self-loathing.

"But how did my father know–"

"About my sister?" she finished for him. "Demons use drugs to destroy people. Drugs weaken the will. The fallen ones that empower and use your father's organization, the ones who tormented my sister, they told him."

Kenji raised an eyebrow. "He talks to demons?"

"They can talk to us the same way I'm talking to you right now when they need to. Not only that, he's provided fertile ground for their work, so they seem to work overtime with your family." She reached down, lifting his wrist and looking closely at the 666.

It was too much. She could see him struggling and getting more frustrated. He pulled away from her.

"I can't do this. I'm just fooling myself," he said sharply.

"What is it?" she asked.

"Don't you see, I'm a part of my father's world," he replied with disgust. "I probably sold drugs to your sister or her boyfriend. My job is to get the young ones addicted." He ran his hand through his hair roughly and started talking louder and louder. "I've beaten, tortured, deceived…"

Aiko couldn't keep from crying anymore. Tears were streaming down her cheeks and she was biting her lip so she wouldn't start sobbing. *Shiho. I'm so sorry I wasn't there.*

"I've made the rounds outside the schools giving free hits so we could hook kids, and taught them how to get the money to pay for their addiction. I've watched so many of them slowly destroy themselves and I couldn't care less." He kicked the ground hard.

"Stop! Stop it!" Aiko turned her back to him. She was trying so hard to befriend Kenji, confused now as to why God had asked her to do this. When she turned back, Kenji was walking away.

"Wait!" she called out.

He turned, still walking. "There's no place on your side for me. I belong in hell. I'm evil, like my father. Stay away from me, I just destroy people," he yelled back at her, desperate self-loathing staining his voice. He broke into a run and headed up the street.

Aiko felt utterly deflated. "I'm sorry, Master, I wasn't strong enough." The next moment, a thought hit her and she put on her sight. A quick look around revealed nothing until she focused upon the area where Kenji had run. Two demon harassers, about to turn the corner, looked back. When they saw that she'd spotted them, they smiled wickedly. One of them made a rude gesture while the other spit out, "You just lost one!" Then he drove his claws into Kenji's skull, looked back, and winked at her.

She cried in anguish as she fell to her knees. Kenji's window was closing. "I messed up. I lost," she conceded, filled with defeat, and sat, shaking her head, weeping on the ground. Her eyes slowly closed, and her trembling hands rose toward the heavens.

Chapter Eight

Ishi's Run

"So what do we do?" Ishi asked, looking with concern at Aiko.

"His chance to change sides is gone," Koh said, stuffing the last piece of a hamburger in his mouth.

"Don't you see? They're fighting 24/7 for this one, and he ran after hearing the truth? Doesn't look good," Takumi said.

"Still, he *did* come back, that's something," Michio replied, walking to Aiko's side and glaring at Takumi and Koh. He was trying to cheer up Aiko, who hadn't said a word after spilling the whole episode to the group.

They spent Sunday afternoons at Coffee Shop to share what they were learning and sharpen their warrior skills and teamwork, but today, when Aiko walked in, the atmosphere had gone straight to crisis mode.

Aiko spoke in a quiet voice, "We need to find him. I know he's starting to get it. I could see it in his eyes. We need to find him before the chance is gone."

"Uh...doesn't running away from you qualify as *gone*?" Koh remarked skeptically. Kai hit him on the back of the head.

"They're attacking him hard. I'm so stupid! I should have looked for them." She stood up, disgusted, then wilted back into the chair. She took a deep breath and continued. "There may be more fighting before we get him clear to change sides."

Ishi stood decisively. "Then we find him. We do know the part of the city his father works in. And we could divide up and watch the clubs and surrounding streets." She looked at the group for approval but got only blank looks. Takumi just shook his head.

"I see him pass my school in the morning," Mai interrupted, peeking from under her long bangs.

Everyone riveted on her. Ishi knelt in front of her.

"Mai, is he there every day, at the same time?"

She nodded. "Just about...I recognized him that night."

The whole group began to process this new lead.

"Whoa, someone really is keeping us in the game," Michio exclaimed, clapping his hands together. The momentum was shifting back.

Everyone looked at Aiko, waiting for orders. Her face hardened a little. "Okay, everybody, listen...this won't be easy. They'll be expecting us again."

♦ ♦ ♦

Across town Kenji slouched in a chair, deep in thought. Unseen to him, in the spiritual dimension, a powerful Watcher protected his mind. He was oblivious to the clamor that surrounded him and the spiritual struggle going on with demons pressing in to get past his guardian. Loud music pounded the walls and the air smelled of tobacco, crack pipes, and burnt chemicals. It was a small mansion that may have been beautiful at one time, long ago, but its beauty had been replaced by something filled with decadence and depravity. This mansion had now become a drug house. Looming voices reverberated everywhere, some angry, some laughing, some paranoid, some woozy, but all high. Young prostitutes, both male and female, were preparing for the night's work. Also, spread throughout the house were enforcers. These trained killers appeared to drink and flirt with the girls, but they had clear orders, packed handguns, and had the black hearts to use them. It was one of Ryudan's candy houses. Kenji was in charge here, but his father had sent some extra henchmen because of his disappearance the other night and discovery in the safe house of the enemy.

Kenji was ignoring everyone today. Anyone brave enough to get in his face would find a blank stare. His mind was a battlefield. He couldn't get events of the last two days out of his mind...or Aiko's words.

"You have to choose sides..." her voice echoed.

"I'm a killer...no forgiveness for killers."

"God is a forgiving God...He proved it..."

"Come on...how many have you destroyed?...and you're so good at it...so many people fear you!"

"Just have a sincere talk with Him...tell Him that you want His forgiveness and pledge your life to Him..."

There was a cold splash over Kenji's lap and he angrily jerked himself up. He heard laughing from a couple stumbling past him. "Sorry, man, I think I dropped my beer on you. I'm sooo sorry. Ha-ha-ha-ha!" Kenji stood and shoved the drunk to the ground and raised his fist. His heart filled with rage. He breathed heavily and looked hard at the trembling man on the ground and then the anger turned into disgust and he stormed out of the room through the front door entrance, wiping his pants.

There was a large porch with a long bench that the lookouts used to lounge on. He walked up to three of them who were drunk, and was about to say something lewd and threatening to them, but instead reconsidered his words. "Give me some space, would you?"

They hurriedly stood up and walked away. Kenji watched the waning light of the day and tensed as he felt a great conflict raging within him.

Demons desperately sought to retake lost ground and engulf him in deception, but a heavenly Watcher sent by the Warriors' prayers was buying him time.

"Kenji," said a sweet, alluring voice. "So what's a girl got to do to get some candy around here?" It was Junko, a fairly new customer. She was sixteen years old and came from a broken family. She struggled to fit in at school, and was insecure, but pretty–the profile they looked for. She looked like just another young woman in her twenties with makeup and sultry clothes, selling her body for money to buy drugs.

"Hello? Anyone there? Come on, most guys can't take their eyes off me," she teased, trying to charm him.

Finally, he looked at her, and his heart sank. *How many have I destroyed without even thinking?* For a moment he saw Shiho, Aiko's sister, in Junko's innocent face. Kenji couldn't form any words. Clamping his jaw shut, he turned away and ignored her.

"Well, uh, Kenji," she said in a sweet but irritated voice. "Am I at the wrong address?"

"Don't worry, baby, I'll take care of you." The deep voice of an enforcer came from behind Kenji. He turned and watched the enforcer reach into his pocket for a packet of powder. "You got the money, right?"

"Uh, no..." She replied haltingly, then, gaining her composure, she smiled sweetly. "But, I can pay in other ways."

"Can you now? This is a big hit." The henchman leered at Junko, licking his lips and swallowing.

Kenji felt sick. "Stop." He shoved the packet back into the enforcer's pocket and glared at him. "Beat it!"

"Just doing what I'm paid for," he said, backing off.

Kenji looked at him with hardened eyes until he had disappeared from sight.

"Hey, what the..." Junko sounded desperate.

"Shut up. Listen to me. Get out now. Go back home, go back to school, do whatever you were doing before. I never want to see you here again."

She looked at him in total confusion. "But..."

"No, don't you see. If you stay here, you're going to die. That's what we do here; we destroy. You're worth more than that."

"Huh?" Her eyes got moist and she blushed. She looked down and shook her head like she didn't believe him.

Kenji spoke even louder. "Look, just turn around and never come back. Get out of here!" he screamed, pushing her away.

He watched as she stumbled down the path, tripping in her high heels, looking like an awkward little girl playing dress-up. As she was about to turn the corner she glanced back, still confused.

What Kenji didn't see was the newly dispatched Watcher hovering over her.

Kenji turned to the heavens. "God, what am I going to do? I've never been a big believer." He paused. "Okay, I've never been a believer, period, but..." He paused again, thinking. "Aiko makes You seem so real. Okay, here's the deal. If you show up tomorrow, we'll talk."

Kenji made his way home, not realizing the terrible battle he had just unleashed in the spiritual dimension for his soul.

♦ ♦ ♦

The plan was simple. On Monday morning they would approach the school from different directions, covering every route Kenji could take. They would stay in contact with their cell phones, and converge ready for a spiritual fight wherever they found him.

They had been outmaneuvered before the day started.

Aiko was suspicious the moment she woke up. Her spirit was prompted to be careful. She slid straight to her knees and infused God's power into the day's activities with her hands raised to the heavens. As she left her home, she immediately put on her sight. A harasser demon waited at the end of her street. "All right, here we go," she said to herself. She walked quickly toward him, switching to the spiritual dimension and pulling her sword. She wasn't playing around today.

"It's the holy orphan who thinks she's gonna change the world," he said, mocking, and then pulled a long blade from its sheath.

"I don't have time for this," she said curtly, and leaped into an attack. He blocked her first swing, but couldn't react when she spun and cut him in two. She kept walking right past him without breaking her stride.

Twenty feet ahead another one waited. "Come on, little girl..." *Whooosh.* He disappeared as she sliced him in half from head to crotch. She turned the corner and saw another one standing at the end of the street where she had to pass; she sighed and quickened her pace.

Suddenly, she saw *him* walk past, just in front of the harasser...it was Makoto, her big brother who'd gone missing. She froze in her steps. "Makoto?" She broke into a run, ignoring the harasser, who cackled wickedly. When she got closer, she caught a glimpse of him rounding the next corner. "Makoto!" She kept running toward him, but he turned again into an alley. Her heart pulsated as she followed blindly and finally saw him standing at the very end where a fence blocked the way. He was surrounded by demons; one she hadn't seen before. Instead of being large and brutish, he was a tall, thin, robed demon with no face. She hesitated for a moment as Makoto looked toward her, blinking his eyes...*it was him*!

She leaped forward and at the same time five demons moved to the attack. The alley allowed them to face her two abreast; the fight was on. She cut and chopped her way toward her brother, glancing at him between opponents. A sword grazed her neck, sending a hissing burn, but she kept on pushing toward him. When she finished the last one, she heard a ghastly demon voice.

"You don't think getting him back will be *that* easy, do you?"

She looked up and saw the strange demon standing in her path. Makoto was pulled through a hole in a fence to a waiting car.

"Makoto! Stop!" Her voiced reverberated in the alley as she reached both hands out toward her brother.

The demon laughed. "This one is reserved for a special death, and you will witness it!" He glared at her as Makoto was shoved into a door. He turned to leave.

Aiko couldn't do anything, unless...She whispered a quick prayer and her sword glowed. She tossed it up and grabbed the hilt in a throwing position. "While I'm alive, you can't have *him*!" She let the sword fly. The demon whirled only to see the glowing weapon hurtling toward his face. He didn't even try to react as it buried itself to the hilt between his eyes. Aiko waited for him to disappear, but instead of an angry cry, she heard a laugh. The demon calmly reached up and pulled out the sword, which abruptly stopped glowing.

He tossed it to the ground and hissed, "Next time it will be my turn!" Aiko froze, and gaped at him with confusion.

The next instant, the car took off with the demon flying over it. Aiko sprinted to the fence and watched the vehicle speed down the road, turn the corner, and disappear.

"Aaaaah!" She shook her hands and paced from side to side. She looked down the road one more time and then bent down to fetch her sword. Her phone rang. She looked at it and she gasped when she saw that she had missed five calls.

♦ ♦ ♦

"Come on. Hurry up, man!" Kai shouted, pounding on the bathroom door.

"Some things you can't hurry, dude," Koh said calmly.

"Hey, it's not like you're making a work of art in there. Hurry up! We have to make the seven-oh-five, or we'll be late."

"I'm on it. Keep your shirt on. It's a waste of time going after Kenji anyway—he won't turn."

Kai was losing it. "That's not your call. Now hurry!"

There was a flush, and the sound of water running in the sink. The bathroom door opened and Koh stepped out with a backpack slung on his shoulders and a big smile on his face. He let out a long, satisfied sigh.

"Come on, Kai, we'll be late." He snickered.

Kai's eyes narrowed and he grabbed Koh's shirt threateningly, but then decided it was the wrong time to start an extended fight. He let go and grunted in frustration. "OK. Let's go. Aiko and the others will be waiting. Be sharp, there's gonna be a fight today."

They walked through the kitchen of Coffee Shop to say good-bye to their parents, but they weren't there. They entered the dining area just in time to hear the crash of ceramic mugs exploding on the floor. Hot drinks splattered everywhere. Their mother gasped and cried out their father's name. When they rushed in, she was cradling him in her arms while a concerned customer dialed Emergency on her cell phone.

Their two backpacks dropped simultaneously as they rushed to their father's aid. He was awake and grabbing his heart, looking confused. Mother stared up at them, wide eyed. "I need you to stay here while I go to the hospital with Father."

Kai pulled out his phone while Koh helped their mother. He slammed his fist on the nearest table as he dialed. He got Aiko's voice mail. "Okay, this isn't good."

The brothers exchanged worried glances. Whatever had happened just now was worse than it looked.

♦ ♦ ♦

Michio and Takumi met early at Takumi's request so they could get to the station on time. The platform was filling up fast with morning commuters.

In addition to his backpack, Michio was carrying his favorite bat, which he was gripping, looking up and down the polished black wood.

"Hey, you coming to the game later? Central High has this pitcher that no one can hit. I mean *no one*. But today he meets the mighty Michio!"

"Is he a lefty or righty?" Takumi asked mechanically, not taking his eyes off a small portable chess set he carried.

"Lefty, I think...yeah, southpaw."

"You're toast," Takumi concluded.

"How can you say that? You gotta believe, Roboto-san!"

"Your batting average is one hundred points lower against lefties, and if this guy is as good as you say, you're toast," he said, making a move and looking up at the discouraged cleanup batter.

"Okay, that's it." Michio squeezed the bat so hard his knuckles turned white. "You come to the game, and when I get to home plate I'm gonna point my bat at you wherever you are sitting just to say, "I'm gonna prove you wrong."

Takumi smiled. He had inspired his friend again without his knowing it. "I hope you do. But I wouldn't bet on it." He turned back to his game with a grin.

"Hey, baseball isn't all about numbers, you know?" Michio said sitting down next to his skeptical friend.

"Actually it..." Takumi stopped mid-sentence. He glanced at his watch and stood up. The others on the platform were getting restless, and the crowd was too big; something was not normal.

"It's begun," he said quietly.

Michio picked up on it immediately. "Late."

They looked at each other and thought the same word. *Kenji.*

"Could it be...?" Michio said, scratching his head.

"No. There is no such thing as a coincidence. Everything is spiritual. You know that."

A voice came over the loudspeaker apologizing for the delay, which would be for at least twenty-five minutes. Takumi pulled out his cell phone while Michio walked through the crowd of people, many of whom were picking up cells to call in late, when he heard the whispers. "Suicide." A broken and bereaved businessman had jumped in front of a train. It happened all the time, but rarely on this track.

Michio walked back to tell Takumi what he knew, and found him frantic.

"Aiko, pick up. Pick up!" He flipped his phone closed. "Koh and Kai are out. Their father collapsed this morning." He was talking fast. "I can't get in touch with Aiko. Now, we won't make it this morning either."

"Ishi and Mai?" Michio asked.

"They're were my next call." He speed-dialed them.

♦ ♦ ♦

Ishi loved Mai like a sister. She was the most remarkable eighth grader; very shy around others, but hardworking and confident, and a completely different person when she danced…or fought. She had a simple, naive, and fearless faith.

And Mai loved Ishi. She wasn't stuck up for a junior in high school. Although she came off as a tomboy and dressed like one, she couldn't hide the fact that she was pretty. The fact that she didn't flaunt it made her more attractive. Mai loved her intensity too. Ishi had a deep reservoir of passion for God, for life, for friends. She did everything at a sprint.

The girls were holding both hands on the porch of Mai's house, sending up prayers for the day's battle and empowering each other. They finished, looked up smiling, picked up their backpacks, and bounded off the porch in the direction of the station. They were the last to leave for the school because they were the closest.

"So, you coming to Michio's game today?" Ishi asked as they walked, adjusting their backpacks.

"I'd rather see you play soccer," Mai said sheepishly.

"Come on, girl, there's a cute bat boy in the ninth grade that you will be meeting next year." Mai turned red, giggled, and bumped Ishi playfully as they walked. A mischievous look crept over Mai's face.

"I saw you looking at Kenji."

"What? We were all looking at him…all of us girls," she said, starting to blush.

"No, we were looking, but you *looooked*."

Ishi thought, *Was it that obvious?* "No. Don't you start, girl. He's a drug dealer!"

"But if he turns…"

"He's got a lot of changing to do."

"We've all come a long way, Ish," she said wisely.

"Yeah, we have, little sister!" Ishi grabbed her in a brief headlock and rubbed her hair. Mai screamed in fun. "Well, he does have kind of a noble look when he's unconscious, so if he promises to sleep the whole time, I could date him." Both girls laughed.

Suddenly, the phone rang and interrupted their horseplay. Ishi fished it out from her pocket and answered.

"Hello," she said, still smiling at Mai. A moment passed and then her smile faded. She stopped walking. "What? No way! Okay, I'll get there. You guys find Aiko. See if you can help Koh and Kai's family. Mai and I've got it from here."

She hung up, grabbed Mai's hand, and started dragging her to the nearest street corner. "Let's go!"

"What's wrong?"

"How much money do you have?"

"Five hundred yen for lunch."

"Get it out now. The others are delayed, fighting started earlier than we thought. Traps everywhere. Truesight, girl." Ishi ordered.

"But the train, we'll miss it." Mai pointed back in the direction of the station.

"It won't come on time." She looked up and down the street and saw what she was looking for. She called out, "Taxi!"

The driver saw her and in an instant pulled up, with the door opening automatically. The girls dived into the cab and barked out the name of the school.

"We're in a hurry!" Ishi added.

The cab lurched forward and began weaving in and out of traffic. Ahead, Ishi could see that the traffic had stopped.

"Is there another way we can get there fast?"

"Don't worry," the cab driver replied, smiling, "I've done this for a long time." The cab swerved into a side street and after several turns was back on a main road, closing in on the school. Then they hit a gridlock again and the two passengers leaned over the seat, looking forward anxiously. Traffic was at a dead stop.

"No! Not now. Not now. Aah!" Ishi drummed hard on the seat. Mai sat next her gripping the seat and biting her lip. "What do we do? What? What?"

"Get out here!" he ordered. The girls took the cue, wondering why he was so insistent. He looked out of the window at them both, smiling.

"You'll have to run from here. Give your bag to the little one so you can make it on time. Mai, you'll have to catch up fast, she'll need you. You'll find him in the station closest to the school." He pointed ahead.

The girls turned toward the subway station, but when they looked back, the driver and the cab had vanished. They locked eyes and shouted simultaneously, "Watcher!"

Ishi shed her bag and threw it to Mai. A look of determination was etched on her face. She recoiled and glanced at Mai. "Hurry Mai-chan!" She bolted off like a sprinter on a fast break in a championship game. Mai followed walking as fast as she could under the weight of two bags.

♦ ♦ ♦

Kenji had had a restless sleep filled with the ongoing conflict in his mind. He had refused drugs or any of the other mind-numbing substances he was used to. He was starting to feel the excruciating pain of withdrawal, but he welcomed the pain. It took the focus away from the battle raging in his soul. He vaguely remembered asking God to show up, but he superstitiously didn't want to think about it. If it happened, it happened.

He wasn't sure where he was going this morning–he was seeing everything with different eyes. He instinctively headed toward his usual route to the trains and school; maybe he would see Aiko. He was giving God His window.

As he headed toward the entrance to a station, a kid came up to him. "Can you help me out?" It was the usual opening for a drug deal. Kenji stopped, pulled out of deep thought. "What?"

"Come on, Kenji, I'm a regular, got something for me? I got money." He was a sophomore who had been strung out on meth for a year. He was unusually skinny and unkempt. His vacant eyes had dark circles around them. He jittered and picked at the scabs on his arms.

Kenji's face twisted with revulsion and, instinctively, he turned the other direction. He'd forgotten about the stream of steady customers he would see on the way to school. He had been out of it for a few days so the need would be desperate. A foul knot of words spewed from his lips. He shut his mouth fast. *Okay, I shouldn't have said that today. Guess that seals it for me. But why do I need to be assaulted by my sins* today? He heard a car coming to an abrupt stop nearby.

"Just heard about an accident on the trains, can I get you somewhere, sir?" It was an enterprising taxi cab driver. *He must have seen me leave the station*, Kenji thought. *At least I can avoid the crowd.*

"Ummm...yeah, sure." The man scurried out and opened the door, allowing Kenji to step in.

"Take me to the station by the intermediate school." The man nodded and took off.

"What kind of accident?" Kenji asked.

"Suicide jumper." Kenji thought he saw some emotion welling up in the driver, but he turned away, busy with his driving and looking guarded as he turned down backstreets to avoid traffic.

The car came to a stop. Kenji handed him the fare and jumped out. The cab driver took off again and in a moment had disappeared from sight.

A barricade blocked the station entrance, and policemen were busy explaining the situation to the commuters. As Kenji walked past the scene, he heard a girl calling out. He stopped and inclined his ear in the direction from where it came.

"Someone help!" It was coming from down in the station. He looked around and wondered why no one else was reacting. He went up to the nearest police officer, who was talking to five people at once, and tried to get his attention.

"Excuse me." Kenji pulled at the policeman's sleeve.

"Not now kid, can't you see I'm busy," he said while he continued to wave his arms to calm frustrated commuters.

"Someone, please, help!" The voice sounded more desperate.

Kenji yelled this time. "Hey. Didn't you hear that?" The officer didn't even look at him this time. "You must be deaf."

Kenji gave up trying to get his attention and ducked the barricade, unseen in all the confusion, speeding down the steps toward the voice. It was completely dark. *Must be a power problem*. He heard the voice again at the end of the platform, in the pitch-black darkness.

"Hey there? You okay? I'm here to help. Don't be afraid." He squinted, hoping his eyes would adjust to the dark as he carefully stepped toward the voice, feeling the way in front of him with his hands.

"I can't see you. Please help me. I'm over here."

Kenji wandered toward the voice, trying to call up a picture of the platform from memory.

"Okay! It's gonna be fine, just keep talking."

Silence. He listened hard and kept walking.

"You still there? Hello?"

Out of the darkness came an animal-like hissing sound. Kenji stopped in his tracks. He heard another sound that was very familiar to him. It was the sound of a butterfly knife being swung open. He could feel himself breathing hard.

"Kenjiiiii, beeee afraaaaid," a guttural voice hissed. Kenji tried to run, but couldn't move. He stood numb and frozen, waiting to be stabbed to death.

♦ ♦ ♦

Up and down the street, heads turned at the white blur that ran by them toward the station. As she dodged, ducked, and hurdled, Ishi saw the world passing by her fast. She strove to maintain her speed while avoiding people, pets, strollers, cars, and street vendors of every size, shape, and height. She almost fell once, but miraculously recovered her balance without breaking her stride. Her Truesight revealed demons and Watchers clutched in deadly combat. The Watchers were giving her a clear path. With one block to go, she hit a higher gear and bolted toward a barricade, surrounded by a crowd and guarded by policemen.

A few blocks back, Mai rounded the corner, running as fast as she could with her double load of books.

In the station, Ishi thought. *Can't waste time with crowd or the guards*, she decided.

As she approached, she slowed and carefully timed a cartwheel that built her momentum as she flipped over the crowd, somersaulting and landing at full stride, and down the steps in an instant. The guard was too busy stopping the surging crowd to follow her down.

♦ ♦ ♦

Kenji trembled. The voice struck fear down to the marrow of his bones. He felt a coldness creeping over his soul. Next, he heard the sound of running steps.

As Ishi plunged into the cool darkness, she felt their presence. Cloaked demons. When she reached the bottom of the stairs, the emergency lights flashed on, bathing the platform in red. She searched quickly for Kenji and saw him near the end of the platform, standing in front of a teenage girl.

The lost girl blinked in the light, but she smiled sweetly and thankfully, moving her hand behind her back.

"Thank you. I was so scared! Can you help me?" she pleaded, as she reached out to him.

Kenji panted shallow breaths, full of fear that he couldn't shake off. His eyes darted around, looking for the source of the evil voice. All he saw was the girl.

"Oh, there you are. D-did you hear that voice?"

"What voice?" she said, stepping closer to him, looking vulnerable and confused.

Ishi took a closer look at her as she approached. *God, what is this?* This was a first for her. A demon, a Slayer, had manifested into the physical world, an ability that all angels had, both faithful and fallen. But it was extremely rare. *How do I fight this one? Master, lead me.*

"Kenji! Get away from her," Ishi yelled.

Kenji was taken aback by the urgency in her voice. He turned and looked at her, stepping reluctantly backward. The demon pulled the knife out and lunged toward Kenji's chest. Hate filled its face.

"Kenji, watch out!" Her scream echoed off the walls.

He turned in time to see a small teenage girl trying to knife him. A veteran of many knife fights, he instinctively caught her hand.

"Hey! What are you doing?" he exclaimed, totally confused. Her face went instantly from angry to harmless and confused.

"You scared me…the voice…I thought it was you." Before he could respond, she was launched backward by a powerful kick.

"No," Ishi cried, sending the demon girl flying back. She immediately charged after her.

"Hey! Wait! What are you…" Kenji raced after them.

Ishi ignored him and landed three solid punches to the girl's face, sending spit and blood everywhere. Next, she spun a roundhouse, sending the girl into the wall with blood pouring from her nose.

"Ishi?" Kenji cried, rushing up and grabbing her by the sleeve. She looked at him with a desperate intensity and pushed him away.

"Let go of me!"

"You're going to kill her," he warned her.

Because of Kenji's diversion the demon girl had a chance to recover. She pulled out the knife and waited for Ishi's attack. Ishi came in punching, but this time found a knife waiting and jerked back her hand, bleeding. Now, the tables were turned and the demon attacked, swinging at her face and stabbing at her heart. Ishi was on the defensive, backing away, ducking, blocking the knife-hand with her arms. She didn't see a piece of loose tile as she backed away, and stumbled backward. She reached back to break her fall, but exposed her chest by doing so.

The demon lunged with the knife high over her head. Ishi hit the ground then tried to get her hands up, but it was too late, the demon was plunging the knife down.

Kenji caught her knife-hand in midair. He grabbed the girl, immobilizing her with a bear hug and staring at her in disbelief.

"Stop! What's going on here?" he yelled.

The girl looked at him, and to his horror, she changed. Her soft brown eyes turned to glowing, yellowish orbs filled with hatred. Her sweet smile turned to a ghastly growl, exposing a mouthful of fangs lined by blood red slime.

"You're going to die today, you little filth," she said with a deep, guttural, evil voice.

Terror gripped Kenji and he fell back, paralyzed by fear. The demon girl stood over him, scowling. She glanced around and spoke in a hellish tongue, giving orders to unseen allies. Suddenly, Kenji felt invisible hands close around his throat and lift him in the air. He flew across the platform and was pinned to the wall. The demon wiped the blood from its face, closed its eyes, and transformed back into its spiritual form. When it turned to finish off Ishi, she wasn't on the ground anymore. She stood fully clad in armor of light, and wielding a sword glowing with heavenly power.

"You sure you want to do this, skank?" the demon spit out. Ishi stood unmoved, on guard.

"I'm leaving with Kenji." Ishi's voice echoed in the station.

The Slayer pulled out a terrible axe and stepped toward Ishi, towering over her.

"You little idiots make me sick! You think you are so powerful, so where are your friends now? Your God couldn't stop us from keeping them all away, even your weak leader was taken down! Maybe this is your day to die."

Ishi didn't blink. "Kenji! Turn to God, can't you see that this is all real now?" she called past her opponent.

Kenji gasped for air and strained to see what was happening. He heard voices, and as he looked, he was filled with amazement. Ishi stood clad in some kind of glowing armor. She held a long sword and stood before a hulking monster.

"Too late, his life is almost gone and you have to face me alone."

Ishi moved toward the demon, watching the huge ax and adjusting her attack.

"I'm here alone because the Master allowed it. I trust Him. I exist this very moment for one reason alone; to send you to hell! If I must die to do so, *then let it be!*"

"Then you will die alone, skank." He swung powerfully downward, aiming to split her in two.

Kenji's lungs screamed for air. He felt an iron grip around his neck, powerful fingers squeezing the life out of him. He felt dizzy. "This is what it feels like to die," he thought. It was getting dark. *God, if You're there . . .*

Then he saw a light.

Two lights.

They streaked toward him like shooting stars. The grip around his neck suddenly released and he felt the ground crash into him from below. Air rushed into his lungs. For just a moment, he saw two ghastly beasts trying to wrestle gleaming white arrows out of their hearts, then *whoosh*. They were gone. He blinked his eyes wildly, trying to figure out if he was dreaming.

Just then, a train horn blared in the tunnel, and a faint rumble began.

Mai banished a third demon with her bow before they realized another Warrior had joined the fight. Kenji had crashed to the ground nearly unconscious. Three more demons uncloaked and rushed her, while one stayed back to finish Kenji. In a flash, her bow was slung and two swords were unsheathed. She stood on one foot like an eagle, both hands extended high. She glanced at Ishi in front of the Slayer, blocking thunderous blows, and then at Kenji being lifted by the last demon toward his death. Her young face hardened.

The train was closer.

Her yell echoed in the station as she began her dance. She attacked in a full sprint, leaping high just before them and landing rolling in the middle of the three fallen ones. She gracefully spun on her knees, slicing both demons on the sides of her in two. *Whooosh! Whooosh*! Immediately afterward, she rolled toward the last surprised demon, shoving both swords simultaneously into his heart. *Whooosh*!

Meanwhile, the demon was dragging a semiconscious Kenji toward the track.

The train's horn reverberated as it approached yet closer.

Mai stood and quickly spun, flinging two swords with all her strength.

The first hit the demon carrying Kenji. He cried out and then vanished, dropping Kenji on the edge of the platform. The second hit the Slayer engaging Ishi just beneath his arm as he was coming down with his ax. He roared in pain.

Kenji felt himself starting to fall and grabbed for the edge, but he was too weak. He went crashing down on the track.

Ishi sidestepped the ax from the demon who was now distracted by the pain of Mai's sword. His errant blow hit the ground hard, shaking the platform. Ishi stepped on the great axe handle and then swung with all her might at the wrist of the Slayer. Its black claw dropped to the ground, accompanied by a shriek of anguish and loathing.

The platform rumbled with the impending arrival of the train.

"You're coming to hell with me," the demon cried above the din of the approaching train. He morphed back to human form and brandished the switchblade with his remaining hand. Ishi shifted back to the physical focus as well and charged the demon.

Mai had leaped down on the track and watched the train rushing toward her as she prayed for strength to lift Kenji's dead weight back onto the platform.

"Come on, come on, come on. Up! Why are guys so heavy?" she groaned anxiously. She could see the eyes of a surprised conductor cringing for impact. She grunted and strained with all her strength, crying out as she inched Kenji upward.

The demon stabbed hard at Ishi, who turned instantly, allowing the knife to glance past her chest. She jerked its wrist backward, dropped back, and placed her feet square on the demon's waist, kicking hard and sending it flying over the platform.

At the same time Kenji rolled back onto the platform and a nimble flyer leaped onto the platform, crossing the demon's trajectory.

The next instant, the train caught the demon in midair, speeding down the track with it, away from the station. Mai landed gracefully on the platform.

Ishi rushed over and hugged her.

"Mai. Oh girl! Are you okay, little sister?" she cried out in relief, looking her up and down.

"That was too close," was all Mai could say, her voice trembling.

"Okay, no time, the train won't banish the demon–he'll be back with help," Ishi said quickly.

"What do we do?" Mai asked, her eyes wide and her face pale.

"We have to end the battle," she said with finality. "Help me, Mai." They dragged Kenji to the wall and sat him up. "Keep watch now, girl."

Mai put on Truesight and scanned the area.

"Kenji, can you hear me?" Ishi shook his shoulder. "I need you to listen to me!"

"Uh…am I awake?" Kenji said weakly, trying to regain his senses.

"Yes, what did you see?"

"Hmmm?" He focused his eyes on Ishi. "I must be sleeping."

"Kenji, you're not dreaming."

He suddenly sat erect and looked around wildly.

She gripped his chin and made him look at her. "*What* did you see, Kenji?"

He thought for a moment, pushing his hair back and moving his eyes to and fro and then back to Ishi before it hit him–hard. She lowered her hand from his face, and he stared at the ground, realizing something deep. "There was a creature and you had this glowing sword and…whoa, it really is real…just like Aiko said."

She gave a sharp sigh. "Listen, Kenji, you must matter to God big-time, because you were supposed to die twice and we were sent to stop it. I've never heard of anyone being able to see a spiritual fight before."

"But that girl..."

"Was a demon."

"But..."

"Angels can do it even though it's rare. They can manifest as humans."

"But why?"

"They don't want to lose you, they hate you, and they want your soul. Kenji, you can stop this battle right now."

As he stared at her she spoke simply, but with authority–and urgency. "Choose sides." Mai looked back to see how he would respond. Ishi paused, watching him think for a few seconds. Then she risked the question. "Would you..."

"Yes... *Yes!* I believe...that God loves me...I need Him!"

"Ask Him to forgive you, and commit yourself to following the Master from now on," Ishi guided, trying not to sound too rushed.

Kenji looked up and formed the words awkwardly. "Uh...God? You kept Your end of the deal, so I'm keeping mine. Forgive me of anything that keeps me from You. And Master? Be my leader from now on."

♦ ♦ ♦

As Aiko pushed through the crowd to the entrance of the station, she felt a sudden shift in the heavens and a feeling of overwhelming relief and joy. "He turned," she said to no one in particular. She smiled, and then laughed. As she looked up again, Michio and Takumi pushed through the crowd, elation written all over their faces.

"Did you feel it?" Michio said excitedly.

"Of course she felt it," Takumi said, without taking his eyes off her.

She smiled. "All of heaven felt that. Let's go help our friends."

Like a rush of light flooding a dark musty room for the first time, Kenji's soul was cleansed with forgiveness, filled with the joy of being loved, and renewed with the feeling of ultimate value and meaning that the God of all things cared about him. He felt a warmth rush through his body from head to toe. He looked up to see Ishi and Mai with tears streaming down their cheeks. They both threw their arms around him and gave him a long hug.

"Come on, let's get going, I know some people who aren't too happy right now," Ishi said, regaining her composure.

"Uh-oh," Mai said with foreboding. "Ish...look."

Kenji didn't see anything, but both Warriors saw at least a dozen demons heading toward them with the one-handed Slayer in the lead. Ishi sighed, closing and opening her bleeding hand, checking the damage for the first time. She looked back at the approaching enemy. *Maybe this is my day to die.*

Both girls stood up and braced themselves to meet the onslaught, but when the demons were twenty feet away, they stopped abruptly with fear etched on their faces. The Slayer tried to get them to move forward but they wouldn't. Ishi turned toward the stairs and saw three figures marching down.

"Aiko!"

Aiko didn't even draw her sword.

"Thank God!" Ishi said, relieved.

"Yes!" Mai said, glad.

The demons shrank away from the Warrior leader, flanked by her armed friends. She turned to them. "It's over. Unless you want a long trip back from the barrens I suggest you go and try to figure out how you're going to explain this failure to the Dark One," Aiko said steadily.

At her reference to the Dark Lord, the demons shuddered, and turned in retreat. They had failed their mission and were beaten.

Aiko turned to the girls, who stood there sweating and bleeding, with torn and dirty clothes from their demon brawl. They both had tear-streaked faces and looked extremely relieved.

Aiko walked up and hugged Ishi and Mai together. Michio and Takumi joined the hug.

"I'm so sorry we left you to fight alone, Ish, Mai-chan."

"Us too," Michio added.

"Hey, if Roboto hadn't been quick on his phone we wouldn't have gotten here either. Besides, He was with us," Ishi said, glancing up.

"Uh..." It was Kenji, who was just standing by.

Michio pushed through the crowd and grabbed him in a great bear hug.

"Oowww...thanks...but...okay...thank you!" he said, cringing from bumps and bruises. His face was smashed against the strong shoulders.

"Mich, let him down, man, he's fresh out of battle," Takumi instructed. He came up and gave a warm handshake to Kenji. He simply said, "Brother."

Kenji then looked up into Aiko's moist eyes as she gazed knowingly at him.

Yet another victory, she thought. *Thank You, Master.*

"Thank you, for not quitting on me," Kenji managed, not fully sure what changing sides really meant.

Takumi snapped his phone closed again. "Good news, everyone, school is canceled. Apparently, because of their attacks everything went crazy today."

"You're telling me," Ishi replied. Mai came up and looked at Ishi's bleeding hand and started a healing prayer.

"By the way, Kenji *saw* the fight." Ishi watched Aiko, Michio, and Takumi. Their heads whipped up, and they stared at Kenji with their mouths open.

"Really?" Aiko studied Kenji for a few seconds. "Well, welcome to a whole new world. Let's regroup and get Kenji started." The Warriors trotted off into the morning together with Kenji.

As they left the station Aiko saw Takumi frowning as if he was solving a complicated math problem. Their eyes met and he shook his head slightly and spoke so only Aiko could hear him. "Do you realize what we just got ourselves into?"

Aiko nodded. "Ryudan."

Chapter Nine

Past Tense

"So what's first?" Kenji asked.

They were all settled in at Coffee Shop and still trying to grasp what they had gotten themselves involved in. They had spent all day debriefing, making sure that Koh and Kai's dad was okay, and getting to know Kenji, their new, dark-looking friend. Here stood the son of a gangster, who from top to bottom looked criminal, except for the humility and thankfulness that shone from his face–the look that shone from everyone who had just met the Master; that change was what Kenji himself was trying to understand.

What now?

"Well, there are some things you need to leave behind," Takumi began.

"Do you carry like cool knives and stuff?" Koh held out his hands with an expectant look on his face. "Can I see them?"

"Koh!" several voices scolded.

He raised his hands innocently. "What? Just trying to help him turn over a new leaf. Jeez!"

"Yeah? Sure it isn't a fascination with evil?" Kai challenged. "No offense, Kenji." Koh looked hard at his brother, started to wag a finger, and opened his mouth to respond.

"Guys." Aiko's firm voice caused Koh to stop, cross him arms, and glare once more at Kai.

"No, no, it's okay. I figured this would have to go," Kenji confessed as he pulled out a switchblade and placed it on the table. There was a muffled gasp in the room as the weapon clattered on their table that was only used for drinks and snacks before. "And uh, well..." He pulled out a small pistol from the back of his pants and placed it next to the knife. "I uh, *have* to carry that, in my world, that is." Only Mai let out a surprised squeal and stared with eyes like saucers. She looked up at Ishi, who seemed disappointed. The others just bit their lips and raised eyebrows.

"You mean *had* to…but not anymore," Ishi added, breaking the uncomfortable silence.

"Right. Had. But I didn't load it today, if that means anything. Wished I had in that subway." He tapped the gun on the handle lightly and then pulled back his hand.

"It wouldn't have made a difference. It was a spiritual creature you faced today," Aiko explained, and Kenji just nodded.

Koh reached for the gun. "So have you like killed–"

"Uh, hands off!" Aiko ordered and then added, "and no questions for things already forgiven. Kenji will share what he wants to in time." Koh shrank back like a scolded child, with a disappointed look on his face.

"Well, to be honest, I'm no killer." Kenji said, pulling out a pair of brass knuckles and dropping them by the other weapons. "Well, not directly anyway. No killer instinct is what my father used to say. No taste for blood." He took a deep breath and frowned. "He, on the other hand, gets pleasure from hurting others. But with a few drinks and some drugs, I had enough anger to beat the sh–"

"Oh!" Takumi jumped in his seat. "Um, yeah, that's another little change, uh, language."

Kenji looked confused. "Language? You're kidding, right? You have rules about language? Oh…you mean *sh*–"

"Whoah, yeah, that's one of them." Takumi raised his eyebrows.

Every head turned to Aiko. She looked at Kenji thoughtfully. Then she glanced up and around the air like she was looking into the unseen world. "*They* talk that way. Demons. They belittle and trash every thing precious and pure that God made. So, we choose not to. But it's not about rules. It's *never* about rules. We just want our language to reflect our hearts."

"See, what comes out of our mouths comes from our heart…new heart, new words," Takumi said like he was completing a logical equation.

Kenji was nodding. *New heart, huh?* "Okay, wow, I can do that, I think. But give me some time on it?"

Everyone nodded in support.

"But when you slip just say, 'Heat of battle,'" Koh advised with a serious look on his face. "That's what I do."

It was Ishi's turn to glare at him.

Michio put an encouraging hand on Kenji's shoulder. "If I can do it, you can do it. I used to be an awesome trash talker. The change just comes naturally."

Ishi had recovered from her disappointment over the gun. "Don't worry. We always help each other out. We're not perfect, we just try to keep moving forward." She grinned.

Mai glanced at Ishi curiously as she spoke.

"God's part of the change too. He'll help you," Aiko added.

After a short pause, Kenji nodded his head in agreement. "Whew, okay. Hope He's patient." He patted his pockets to confirm that he had no more weapons.

Aiko then got busy rummaging through her backpack. "Um, let's see. I have a new weapon for you." She pulled out a worn, small black manual and held it out toward Kenji. "This will have to do for now. It's used, but nothing's missing."

Kenji glanced down at the table in front of him surveying the tools of his trade for the last four years. He had been around them all his life, and been allowed to use them from the age of thirteen. In the briefest of moments he remembered shoving the gun up against terrified enemies or flashing his knives at anyone bold enough to try to stare him down. He remembered the sick feeling of a jaw or ribs breaking from the force of the brass knuckles. *That's over now.* He glanced around the room and saw a group of the sincerest and most extraordinary people he had ever met. He then looked at Aiko who was holding up a book, no, not just a book, a new life altogether, in front of him. Her eyes had a gentle love about them, but burned with fierceness and strength deep within. She could see him thinking and just waited patiently. Kenji glanced up for a moment. *God is real. I saw what I saw. I've seen evil all my life. Now I've seen good defeat it. I'm choosing sides.*

I choose God.

Kenji took the manual, turned it over, and flipped the pages. "So does everybody…?" He began but stopped as seven manuals were pulled from back pockets or backpacks and held up instantly. "Okay, I'll start from the beginning, I guess." He pushed his hair back and concentrated on the first lines of the first page.

"Ishi why don't you help him get started?" Aiko said, putting her hand on her shoulder.

Ishi looked surprised and a little embarrassed. "But Takumi could–"

"No, you got to him first. I think it's in the plan."

"Right. You're right. Okay. Here tomorrow, seven A.M.?" she said, trying to sound as natural as possible. Mai looked at her sideways and couldn't hide a grin.

"I'll be here. Thanks," Kenji agreed, for the first time really *looking* at her. Ishi just nodded and then looked at Aiko, who gave her a short nod.

Kenji shifted in his seat and took a deep breath. "But, uh, that will only work if I'm still alive." Everyone looked surprised, except Aiko and Takumi, who glanced at each other.

"Let me go with him?" Takumi asked Aiko. They had discussed this earlier and knew what had to be done. They also knew it would be dangerous. She looked over at Kenji, waiting for him to answer.

"No, no way. This is something that I have to face alone," Kenji said shaking his head.

"Whooaa. Wait. Go where, with who, and do what?" Koh asked, looking from face to face and half-squinting his eyes. The others just looked at Kenji and then at Aiko and then back again, waiting for someone to explain.

"I need to get out. I, uh, need to leave the business officially." Kenji paused while the others looked on with sober and concerned looks. "The only problem is, there is only one way to do that with Ryudan. It's complete loyalty or nothing. No one leaves and lives. No one."

"I think you will be the first." Takumi said. "Because first of all you are Ryudan's son, and second of all–"

"God is with you now," Ishi finished. Takumi nodded.

He continued, "Exactly. Kenji, He wants you alive. So nothing on this earth can kill you." Kenji thought a moment and tilted his head, understanding soaking in. Takumi pushed up his glasses. "The offer is still open. I'll go with you."

Kenji looked at him with admiration. *Why would you do that? You must be one killer math team captain. Guess they're not all wimps.*

"Come on, guys. I say we all go," Michio thundered, throwing a fist into the air. Everyone started to nod, except Koh, who looked around in disbelief. "Aiko?" Michio asked, wanting her go ahead.

She looked hard at Kenji, praying silently.

Then Kenji spoke up. "No! I can't let you do that. It's a different world. I know I'm changing, but I still know how that world works. I'll walk out of that room miraculously or get a bullet in the back of my head as I walk out." The others protested, but Aiko ended the discussion.

"I agree. You have to do this one alone. I think we're destined to cross paths with Ryudan again, sometime soon. For now, he goes in alone," she concluded for everyone. "But Kenji?" She looked at him hard. "This is the last time we will ever let you go in alone, and if you are held against your will, we're coming after you. I promise you that."

Everyone nodded or grunted in agreement to one of their greatest values; they loved each other with reckless abandon and now Kenji was part of them.

Kenji looked around blinking in amazement. Then after a deep sigh he looked at his watch and stood up.

"I know where he is right now. I, uh, I'll see you tomorrow." He turned to go and glanced down at the weapons on the table. Paused. He looked at the book in his hand intently and then at the group. "Only one way to find out, right?" Then he walked out of Coffee Shop with everyone watching until the door closed behind him.

Aiko turned to everyone.

"Anyone interested in covering his exit?" Aiko asked. The room exploded with responses.

"Yes! Thank you!"

"I thought you'd never ask!"

"Oh yeah!"

"Let's do it!"

"As long as we don't get too close," Koh said running his finger along the barrel of the gun on the table.

Aiko motioned them to gather around her. "Okay, Takumi, figure out where we can meet him as he leaves his father's place. Ish, it's across town, figure out the train schedule and make sure everyone has enough money for the trip there and back. Everyone, we're talking defensive escape, a moving rear guard." After fifteen minutes they bounded out of the safety of their sanctuary into the fallen world to provide spiritual escort for Kenji so he could make it back *if* he made it out of his talk with Ryudan alive.

The ambiguity of the happenings in the spiritual world the past few days was about to be cleared up with absolute certainty. Someone very important had changed sides and when word got out, hell would have to respond.

Chapter Ten

RUN

KENJI'S FATHER SCOWLED AT HIM WITH LOATHING. "WHY AREN'T YOU DEAD?"

He leaned forward over his desk with a cigar pushed into the corner of his mouth, puffing smoke like an angry chimney. Two henchmen stood in the shadows of his plush office. One was by the wet bar that was always fully stocked and the other was standing beside a worn, comfortable reading chair by a large bookshelf that covered an entire wall, filled with books on the occult and strange genealogies that Kenji had never bothered with.

Kenji glanced at the armed bodyguards and then returned his father's glare. "I want out."

His words hung in the air for a moment. He heard one of the guards chuckle and noticed the other one shaking his head. His father waved his cigar at Kenji and said sarcastically, "Oh, I see. You want out. Just like that?"

Ryudan looked at him up and down, shook his head, and sat down. He took a puff from his cigar and tapped it over a black ashtray in front of him. "That's impossible. Now get out of my office." He put the cigar back in his mouth and turned to some papers on his desk.

"I'm not asking."

Ryudan cocked his head to the side, looking directly at Kenji, who continued, knowing that the next statement was likely to set off an explosion. "I'm gone. I've uh, I've...changed sides."

Ryudan froze. The color drained from his face and then a moment later came rushing back a deep red. His breathing became heavy, then he started to tremble with rage. Between clenched teeth he hissed, "What did you say?"

"I'm done here. I'm done destroying lives and destroying myself. I've chosen a new way."

"You...have...no...idea..." Ryudan growled, standing up from his chair now and throwing his cigar to the ground. "Boy, you messed up bad this time." He now stood and started to pace behind his desk. His henchmen reached into their coats and took a step toward Kenji waiting for their orders. "I should have killed you earlier, I should have killed *her*," he roared.

"Leave her out of this! She has nothing to do with you."

Ryudan let out a breath of disgust. "You really are an imbecile. I'm not talking about your new holy skank." He gripped his desk with one hand and ran the other roughly through his hair. "You have no idea…"

For a moment Kenji thought his father would pull out a gun and just start shooting. Then something very eerie happened. Ryudan's eyes slowly glazed over, his head jerked from side to side, and then he looked at Kenji perfectly calm. "I've known for a long time that you weren't worthy to carry on the family business. You are a complete failure and total embarrassment to me. There's too much of your mother in you," he said with disgust.

Mother? Kenji gasped. His father had *never* mentioned his mother. From his earliest memories he was told that she was missing or dead. It was as if she never existed until this moment.

Ryudan continued talking to himself. "At least there is another. Someone much more suited to our family legacy. Yes, yes, this one is no longer needed, but he should be turned back first for the sake of the family name." He then turned to Kenji again. "Why aren't you dead? You need to be dead."

Kenji took a step back. He was riveted by the mention of his mother, wanting to ask a million questions, but he knew he had to get out of there. His father's bizarre behavior scared him.

"Like I said, I'm done here. I'm leaving. I'm out." He turned to leave and felt the hair on the back of his head stand up in anticipation of a bullet entering his brain from behind.

In a deep, guttural tone, Ryudan spoke as Kenji crossed the room to let himself out. "Losers belong on the losing side. You'll be of no consequence in the end, but we'll still get to you. We can't let you live. We'll get to them too. Your new friends have no idea what they've stepped into, loser."

♦ ♦ ♦

Nearby, Aiko reviewed the plan one more time. "Okay, remember, once he leaves I'll slip in behind and cover his back and follow him to the station where we will all meet up. Mich and Tak, you guys hold anything that comes up from his left.

"Got it!"

"Affirmative."

"Ish and Mai, you watch the right side." Both girls nodded, looking up the street. "Kai and Koh, you lead him out. Clear the way in front of him and take anything that gets by us."

Koh was about to protest shaking a half-eaten beef stick. "Wai…"

"Don't you worry none, Koh, nothing's getting by me." Michio declared confidently.

"Um, *us*," Takumi corrected.

Koh then looked worriedly over to the girls' side. Ishi looked at him hard. "You have something to say?"

Kai put his hand on Koh's shoulder. "Come on. You and me, Batman and Robin…let's show 'em what we can do." Koh sighed and nodded slightly.

Aiko stood ready to move. "Nobody armor up till you're about to attack, and keep moving toward the station. Okay, positions," she ordered. The Warriors trotted up the street.

They had to cover Kenji for five city blocks before he got to the station. They expected an attack from the rear and then for a call out to any demons in the area to converge on them once they knew the Warriors were there. Evil had lost Kenji's soul, but now they had to stop him from ruining their plans.

♦ ♦ ♦

Okay, God, if You're real, this is where You show up. Kenji walked out of his father's office and down the long hallway lined with lounging henchmen. They glanced up and watched him as he walked with purpose toward the stairway that led down almost directly to the rear exit of the building. Ryudan appeared at the door of his office as Kenji continued to walk.

"You're worm food! I'm going to rip your soul to pieces, and your friends' too! You're a complete failure and a disgrace to this family line. I'm going to erase you permanently!"

As he continued to move, Kenji reached into his pocket and gripped the sword manual and turned to face his father one last time. The henchmen instinctively pulled out their guns. Ryudan raised a hand. "Don't bother, he doesn't have the guts." They all froze, weapons at the ready.

Oops. Kenji abruptly stopped, realizing what they were thinking, and decided to pull out a small manual from his pocket. When they saw it they all relaxed a bit.

Ryudan sneered at the sight of his son holding the enemies' book. "So, you want to fight?" Ryudan's eyes glazed over for a moment and he extended a hand toward Kenji. It was trembling with dark power.

Kenji felt a chill run over him from head to toe and his vision changed. Like the flickering of a television with poor reception, the hallway changed. At one moment he saw the henchmen standing facing him with their guns and his father glaring at him with hatred. In the next moment there was a flash and he would see dark creatures coming out of the walls with their evil glowing eyes staring at him. *God, what's happening to me?* He stumbled backward, still facing his father. His vision changed back, the henchmen were chuckling, and Ryudan let out a long, deep, evil laugh. "Still want to play?"

Kenji's eyes darted back and forth. "What the…" He started to get up and the scene flickered again. The demons were moving toward him now, and from behind Ryudan another robed demon appeared and came directly at him. This one had no face but wielded a horrible-looking sword. His nose was filled with an ancient, evil smell. Kenji looked around wildly, wondering what to do. He remembered the manual in his hand.

A new weapon, she called it.

With no other option available, he held up the manual in front of him as if would ward off his attackers. The demons slowed at first and then started to sneer and laugh. As the scene continued to flicker, Kenji thought he saw a ripple forming around him. He looked closely at himself and saw an outline of something. *What?* It was faint, and shimmering on and off so he couldn't make it out. In his hand a flickering blue outline seemed to be attempting to coalesce into a gleaming blade.

A sword!

He struggled to his feet again as the scene flickered back to real life. He heard his father's mocking voice. "Good-bye, maggot."

When the scene changed back, the faceless demon was only a meter away from him. He saw a glint of metal as a sword started a downward arc to slash Kenji across his heart. The developed instinct of street fighting kicked in and he dodged. He heard a crash of metal hitting the floor. *God, was that real?* Then the scene went back to normal. Kenji looked around wildly while backing up. *Where…No, he's there. He's going to attack and I can't see him.* Kenji started to stumble backward and pray desperately. Then he got his answer. It was one word whispered directly into his mind.

Run.

He was only a few meters now from the stairway and bolted down as fast as his legs could carry him, skipping three or four steps at a time, with both hands on the rails. The scene flickered and he could hear the growls coming up behind him. Then it changed back to just his heavy terrified breathing and the loud pounding of his shoes on the metal stairs. He finally reached the double doors and pushed so hard that he lost his balance and fell on the ground, scraping his hands on the rough pavement. Ahead of him was a long alley that extended thirty meters to an opening that led to the road and five blocks later to the train station. *I'll never make it.* He pushed up off the ground and turned around just as the scene flickered again. *I'm dead.* He was surrounded by demons and the faceless one was there in front of him like a hunter ready to collect his quarry. Then it spoke.

"No escape. Nowhere to hide. Nothing but despair...death," it hissed. Kenji was petrified.

God, if You're there . . .

Instantly there was another light. The demons looked up in surprise at something or someone behind Kenji. Kenji turned and craned his neck back for a look. *What the...*Advancing up the alley was a Warrior in armor made entirely out of light, carrying a sword that glowed. Then he heard her voice. "Kenji!"

"Aiko?" The scene flickered back and Kenji saw Aiko running up to him in an empty alley. She helped him up and repeated heaven's answer to his prayer.

"Run."

Kenji looked at her wildly and then up the empty alley and took off willing his legs to run as fast as they could. He was out of breath and looking fearfully from side to side. *What's happening to me?* He turned back and saw Aiko standing in a cloud of dust with her sword held low and several demons backing up.

Run. I'm going crazy. Just run. He looked back one last time before he reached the end of the alley and saw Aiko start up the alley toward him, looking over her back toward where the demons were. Without warning, he collided with someone as he left the alley.

"Whoooaa, dude, calm down." It was Kai. He grabbed Kenji by the sleeve and hurried him along. Koh was there looking back.

"Calm down! I'm not even calm. You expect him to be calm?" Koh whined.

"Gotta keep our heads," Kai said while he led them toward the station as Aiko had ordered.

♦ ♦ ♦

Aiko glanced forward and saw that Kenji had turned the corner. She had surprised the demons but they were regrouping. Now sure that Kenji was with Koh and Kai, she took a deep breath and turned to face the demons again.

"No more running." She held her sword out, glanced at her arm, and a glowing shield materialized. *Hold as long as you can.* She noticed the demons were conferring with the faceless one.

They're going to try to cut him off. They'll cut through the buildings. Aiko charged. *Have to get them all…now.*

♦ ♦ ♦

"Okay, that's one block," Koh counted desperately.

"So far so good," Kai answered.

Kenji was dazed. "What's happening? I…back in the alley there were–"

Kai grabbed his arm and pulled suddenly. "Whoa. What did you see?"

"I'm not sure. It's stopped now." Kenji said blinking and rubbing his eyes.

"Two blocks." Koh's voice cracked as he looked behind them.

"Stay sharp." Kai stopped and threw his arms out, stopping the others. "Twelve o' clock. Coming up out of the…ground." He paused a moment and then snapped his fingers. "They're using the sewers. They're trying to cut us off. Koh, flank attack on my order."

Kenji looked around wildly. "What? How do you know that?"

"In spiritual form they can pass through material objects but they can't see through them. They need a clear line of sight like we do. They're using the sewers to get ahead of us without us knowing." Kai spoke fast as he and Koh armored up and pulled out their swords.

As the demon hit street level it pulled out its weapon and snarled. Koh and Kai charged, then crisscrossed paths and moved in from the flanks. The demon paused, unsure what to do, as Koh attacked. The moment the demon turned to meet his attack Kai struck him from the blind side and burst him into a stinking cloud of yellowish dust.

"I hate sewers. Hey, if they get to the station before us in force–" Koh pointed ahead.

Kai frowned and looked up and down the street. "Okay, I'm thinking we need to get ahead of them. Kenji, forget what I said about calming down. Run!" The three set off down the street.

♦ ♦ ♦

Aiko could see the robed demon waiting and watching while she dispatched the last of five demons that tried to get past her.

"I told you it would be my turn the next time, Called One." The robed demon brandished his evil weapon and started circling Aiko.

Oh great. Him. Okay, God...I need some help.

She glanced back at the alley again.

The demon followed her gaze after Kenji and looked back at her. "Oh, *he* can wait. I'll get to him, like I got to your brother." He smiled wickedly. "Like I'll get to you." He raised his sword and attacked, coming down hard on Aiko's waiting shield.

She cried out, absorbed the blow, and went to one knee. She then quickly rolled toward him, driving her sword deep into his stomach. She waited to hear a cry of pain but none came. Instead a powerful hand slapped her across the face and sent her flying into a pile of trash cans. The demon laughed. "You can't hurt me, weakling. You see your God's power is limited. Or didn't you know that?"

She hurried to her feet and got ready for his attack. "Okay then, I'm here. If you think you can take me, try." Aiko took a defensive stance and raised her sword.

"Ha. You are a bold one. You're in enemy territory and fighting a superior opponent. You're going to lose." The demon attacked viciously, slashing from every direction. Aiko backed up and blocked every attack. "It's only a matter of time before you fall," he spit at her. She wiped the sweat from her forehead with the back of her sword hand, reset her defensive stance, and circled her opponent.

What is this creature? What do I do? My sword doesn't hurt him. Then it came to her. *Only one chance; Run.*

"You look worried, Called One. Doubting your God, are we?" He lunged at her again.

Aiko blocked the attack, spun, and brought her shield full force into the chest of the demon. It sent him flying backward into an alley wall where he disappeared momentarily. When he came rushing back out of the wall Aiko was on one knee with her hands upraised looking the demon in the eye and speaking under her breath to God.

The demon didn't have time to react. A wave of power erupted outward from Aiko and the demon was thrown back with great force into the building again.

A few moments later when the demon charged out of the building, he was accompanied by eight more demons. But Aiko was gone.

♦ ♦ ♦

"This is strange." Takumi looked up and down the street. "Nothing." He looked across the street to see Ishi and Mai waiting too. Ishi looked at him and shrugged with a question on her face.

Michio frowned. "You think Aiko's in trouble?"

"I…I'm not sure." Takumi looked up the street, thinking deeply. But his thoughts were interrupted by the sudden appearance of three guys sprinting up the street toward them, pumping their arms furiously.

"Hey," Ishi yelled, waving her arms trying to get their attention as they flew past. When they went by without a pause Ishi looked over at Takumi with more questions in her face. Then they heard Koh's long cry.

"Sewers!"

"Shoot, that's why we haven't been attacked. They've been passing underneath us the whole time, gathering at the station in force. Mich, we gotta go."

"What about Aiko?" Michio boomed.

"We'll get Aiko. You guys go on." Ishi yelled, immediately grasping the situation.

"No, Ish, we need your speed again. If Koh and Kai run into an ambush, they'll need help fast," Takumi explained excitedly.

Ishi nodded and spoke quickly. "Okay, Mich and Mai, wait for Aiko. Tak and I will get to the station. Okay, Roboto, I hope you do wind sprints for the math team. Armor up, everybody!" She and Takumi took off down the street after the boys.

Michio and Mai looked at each other. They had never been partnered in a fight. They looked like a great bear and tiny ballerina standing next to each other.

"Okay, Mai girl, let's find our leader."

She nodded and waited for him to lead. They took off down the street toward Aiko.

♦ ♦ ♦

It was a small obscure station that had a paved turnaround area in front for taxis. There was a manhole in the center of the street right where they had to pass by. It wasn't a busy time so it was deserted.

"Wait. Slow down." Kai puffed while he looked around carefully with Truesight on. The boys were breathing hard and their gazes darted from side to side. Kenji still looked like he was in shock from his glances into the spiritual realm. Then Kai sighed thankfully and turned to Kenji and Koh, who had their hands on their knees. "Guess we got here first."

Koh looked past him and stood straight up. "Oh sh–" Before Kai could stop him the expletive came out. He was about to scold him but caught his meaning and spun quickly.

"What? What's going on?" Kenji asked, seeing nothing but an empty street.

Demons began to rise from the ground all around them, growling and pulling out ghastly weapons.

"I vote run," Koh said. He and Kai stood instinctively back-to-back and began slowly turning to count their adversaries. Kenji stood by helpless. "Okay, too late. We're surrounded. Nice work, Brother." Kai ignored him.

"Kenji, they're after you, just kneel down here between us. We won't leave you," Kai promised. Kenji did as he was told, wishing there was more he could do. But street fighting was no good against unseen enemies.

"Speak for yourself," Koh complained, still looking for a way out.

"Okay, try to kill in a three count and we'll use a rotating switch. When I hear a whoosh I'll call it out, okay? That should keep them off balance."

"Yeah, for the first ten seconds. Then what? Run?"

"We hold till the others arrive. Koh, rotating switch, are you ready?" Kai confirmed. Koh just shook his head in doubt.

♦ ♦ ♦

Michio and Mai didn't have to go far until they saw Aiko running up the street toward them with a determined look on her face. They glanced at each other, not sure what to do since Aiko never ran from a fight. Then they saw it, unlike any other demon they had faced so far. It was just turning the corner far behind Aiko, accompanied by a group of Grunts. When she saw Michio and Mai, she raised her sword to point straight ahead as she approached them.

"Come on, guys. Let's get to the others." Michio turned and ran with surprising quickness for a guy his size. Years of baseball wind sprints were serving him well today. Mai glided, her feet barely touching the ground. The three of them made for the station at full speed.

"You okay?" Michio asked as he ran.

Aiko wondered if she should tell them, but decided against it. "Delayed them as long as I could but I think a lot slipped by."

"Yeah, they're using the sewers."

Aiko shook her head. *I should have thought of that. Come on, girl.* "Then we have to hurry to help our friends." She glanced over her shoulder. They still had time.

♦ ♦ ♦

The demons lurched forward to attack, and the Warrior duo lost all brotherly hostility and banter and became a perfectly synchronized unit.

Kenji knelt between them, looking from side to side and listening to their quick chatter.

"Ready. And switch!"

"Oh yeah, they don't like that."

"Nice work. And switch. And watch Kenji!"

"Give the boy a sword."

"Switch."

Like a machine, the two Warriors coordinated their actions so they were continually attacking and moving, causing the gathering mob to have to adjust its angle of attack constantly. After a few fruitless attempts to take the Warriors, the demons changed tactics and went after Kenji to split the Warriors' attention. Their numbers were still growing.

"Whoa. Kenji, get down! Shoot! An arrow got by me!"

Suddenly Kenji clutched his heart as a feeling of dread just exploded inside. Then a chill ran down his spine and fear clutched his mind. It was spreading. His eyes closed shut and he grimaced in pain. He grabbed his thigh and then reached out toward Kai.

"Okay, go defensive. Ouch. Back-to-back right over Kenji," Kai called out. "Kenji, stay with us."

"Won't last long this way. Ah, got my shoulder again. For crying out loud. Running would be nice right now," Koh whined.

Suddenly a rapid series of whooshes came from the back of the demon mob, causing confusion. The boys looked over and saw Ishi cutting her way through to them. A few moments later Takumi joined her.

Ishi barked orders. "Tak, take Koh's place. Koh, heal Kenji now. Then get back in the line. Stay defensive, everyone."

"All right, but Kai let the arrow through, not me."

Kai threw a quick stab over with his eyes while Koh knelt next to Kenji, whose eyes were cringed shut.

"Where are all these coming from?" Takumi wondered.

"Stay focused, the others will be here soon," Ishi encouraged.

After a few moments Koh rejoined the line with a worried look. "I hope so, because we're talking seconds before we go down, not minutes."

Then, like an angel from heaven, Mai dropped out of the sky with swords flashing and they became a circle of five. The others blinked in surprise as she took a place next to Ishi. Everyone exclaimed, "Mai! How? What?"

She turned to the others. "Aiko said get ready to move."

Koh turned. "Huh, when?"

"Now." As she spoke another disturbance started at the back of the mob and rumbled toward them. With all the demons facing toward the center, Michio was able to lower his shoulder and plow his way through, swinging his sword wildly with Aiko following in his wake. She called out to the others.

"Get Kenji and fall in behind." She glanced at her watch and nodded.

There was a pause as the demons turned toward all the confusion. Ishi pulled Kenji up and supported him. "Time to run, Kenji. Are you with me?"

He stood up, shaking his head and blinking his eyes to clear his mind. "Yeah, I'm okay now I think. Let's get out of here."

The Warriors parted slightly as Michio rumbled through and fell in behind with Aiko covering the back. "Let's move to the platform." They instinctively formed into a formation like a rugby scrum and pushed their way forward, carried along with Michio's momentum. When they reached the gates they quickly fished tickets from their pockets and rushed through to the platform while Aiko stopped and held the surging mob at bay. Just then the train pulled in for its ten-second stop. They all rushed into the first open door. Ishi and Takumi stopped and looked back for Aiko.

"Aik, we're all here," Ishi called out. Aiko disengaged and leaped over the gate and rushed, with flaming arrows following her all the way. The bell rang for the closing of the door. Aiko was almost there when she arched her back and cried out and stumbled. Both Ishi and Takumi reached out and caught her before she could fall, and pulled her into the closing doors. Everyone plopped hard into a seat except Ishi, Takumi, and Aiko, who fell to the floor together. The train started to move.

Aiko pulled herself up to her knees. Everyone was gulping for breath and glistening with sweat. "Everyone okay? Anyone need healing? Is Kenji okay?" A few moments of silence went by. She looked up and everyone was staring at her as she tried to catch her breath.

Ishi broke the silence, kneeling next to her. "Sister, why do you fight alone?" Aiko was smoking from all the wounds she had received. There were three arrows in her back. Her arms were covered with burns and there was a slash on the back of her neck.

She squeezed her eyes shut and her lips pressed together hard. "Uh, I'm okay. Just heal me up. Heal up, everyone," Aiko said, unable to hide the tear rolling down her cheek. Ishi started to pull the arrows and pray her leader's wounds closed. She glanced at Aiko's face as she prayed. Her hardened courage couldn't hide the fact that she was in horrible pain. She wiped a tear that was forming as Ishi prayed the last wound away. "Thanks, Ish," was all she said as she started to push herself to her feet.

Kenji was watching intently as everyone partnered up and prayed for each other. After a while Ishi moved over to where he was and examined his spiritual wounds. "Let me see here how well Koh healed you. Hmm, not bad, I'm surprised."

"I heard that." Koh acted like he was offended, but he was more relieved. "I'd say I more than pulled my weight today, holding the line practically alone."

Kai cleared his throat. "Uh, right. I seem to remember a certain s-h word coming out of your mouth."

"Not."

"Oh, yeah, bro…you said it."

"I said shoot. Right, Kenji?"

Ishi warned Kenji, "Better *not* to remember than to get involved." But Kenji had started to answer already.

"Sorry, man, you said *the* s-h word," Kenji admitted.

Koh looked liked a cornered animal. "Well…"

Everyone said in a chorus, "Heat of battle?"

"*That* is exactly right." He clapped his hands together. "Okay, change of subject. Mai, are you taking flying lessons? How'd you do that?"

She looked up from under her bangs. "Mich threw me from a running start." Her eyebrows went up. "He's super strong."

"Yeah, I was scared at first. I thought I threw too hard, adrenaline and all. I was sure you'd end up on the roof of the station." Everyone chuckled, breaking the tension. Relief started to settle in as everyone relaxed.

Koh continued, "Oh man, it was like an angel from heaven." All the guys grunted in agreement. "So totally cool, I gotta say."

Mai blushed and looked down and then over to Ishi, who was sm
partner. Michio came over and gave her a high five.

"So Kenji, did you say what you needed to say?" Aiko asked. Everyo
bered why they had come again, and listened for Kenji's answer.

"Uh, yeah. He, uh, didn't take it too well."

"Ya think not?" Koh said, crossing his arms.

"He did something to me. And I uh, well, I…saw things again." Ke
confused and troubled. "It was like in the station, but I felt so helpless."

"Don't worry. Now that you're clear of your past, we'll get you up to s
geared up," Aiko promised. Takumi and Ishi looked directly at her with
ing eyes and she just nodded, causing them to smile. Kenji looked do
book that he had clutched in his hand the whole time, wondering what
ing.

"Anybody else hungry? All that running, you know." Koh said, rub
stomach.

Aiko smiled. "Yeah, actually. I am. Good job, everyone. Let's eat."
nodded in agreement.

Before Aiko turned to look out the window of the train she caught Ke
ing at her intently. She met his gaze. *Okay, God, where is this going? Where wi*

Chapter Eleven

Retreat

KENJI WAS HYPNOTIZED BY THE ROLLING COUNTRYSIDE AS IT SCROLLED BY HOUR AFTER hour accompanied by the rhythmic clackety-clack of the tracks. He was lost in thought. The past three weeks had changed everything in his world. One moment he was on the brink of suicide, the next he was rescued by strangers who showed up and fought for him. He looked across the aisle again at Aiko, who was either resting or praying, he couldn't tell which. She was leaning against Ishi, who also slept with earphones on. As he often did, he replayed his mental tape of the battle in the train station and then his escape from Ryudan. Ishi and Mai had saved him. Koh and Kai had stood over him.

Ishi. Her face was now so peaceful; that day it was filled with intensity and fury, but not hate. Her eyes opened and he quickly averted his gaze. Her eyes closed again. *What a day that was*, he thought, shaking his head. *What a week.*

It had been quickly decided that during school break it would be best to get Kenji out of town. They would all have come, but Michio had a baseball tournament, Mai had a family trip, and Koh and Kai had to help watch the shop so their father could take it easy for a while.

"Kenji, you play chess?" Takumi asked. "I'm tired of playing myself."

"Ummmm…" Kenji shrugged.

"Come on, just a friendly game." Takumi prompted as innocently as he could.

"No thanks, Tak, I wouldn't give you much of a game," Kenji responded flatly.

"Here, you move first." Takumi pushed the small travel board between them while adjusting his glasses.

Kenji sighed. "All right, now let's see…these guys move one." Kenji carefully moved a pawn out.

"Or two spaces on their first move," Takumi responded, moving almost without looking.

"So who is this guy we're going to see again?" Kenji asked as he moved another piece.

"Akira. He's an old spiritual Warrior who helped train us all." Takumi moved again with a glance at the board.

"How did you meet him?" Kenji hesitated with a piece in his hand, moving here, there, and then down.

"Actually, he's the Warrior that came after Aiko. He freed her. She freed us," he said, again moving quickly and looking around the train as though this game wasn't enough to fully engage his mind. "That kind of makes him our spiritual grandfather."

"So Aiko is your spiritual mother?"

"Don't go there," Aiko said without opening her eyes, apparently listening while fully awake. Ishi sat up and looked around, getting her bearings.

Takumi smiled, "Hey, I didn't say it, he did. I just laid it out for him and he followed the logic."

Meanwhile, Kenji was struggling with his next move. He felt someone watching, and looked up to see Ishi across the aisle studying the board and making faces. When he attempted a move, she gave him a severe look that said, "How can you miss it?" Kenji then grabbed the queen. She nodded and he slid it out, as she smiled approvingly. He dropped it, sat back and sighed. "Your move, Tak. So how old is Akira?"

Takumi again just glanced at the board and moved quickly so he could talk. "I believe he is fifty-eight. Right, Aiko?" Aiko nodded, without opening her eyes. "He's been with the Master for forty-two years, so he's a dangerous spiritual Warrior," he continued.

Ishi and Kenji were moving again while he was talking. "Okay, Tak...I moved. By the way, what's with the Roboto thing?"

Takumi made a face. "Oh, that's my nickname. I just like being efficient," he said, smiling and moving quickly.

Ishi gasped out loud and jerked in her seat. Takumi and Kenji looked at her. "You okay?" Kenji asked.

"What?" Takumi said at the interruption.

She sat calmly, with a grin on her face. "I'm fine, Mr. Roboto! My leg's falling asleep," she lied. When Takumi glanced away, she bore a hole in Kenji with her eyes, looking down at the board and at him alternately.

What am I missing?

"Did you move?" Takumi said, looking out of the window.

"Gimme a sec." Kenji glanced up at Ishi, who was climbing the walls because he didn't see it. *Another look . . .*

Ah, there it is. Wow...no way, he thought, and smiled, deciding to have fun. Finally, he moved a piece. "Takumi, you like riddles?" Takumi turned from the window to Kenji as though he were ready for a fresh challenge. "Try me."

"How do you ask for the bill at an Australian restaurant?" Kenji posed. Takumi suddenly appeared interested, and then repeated, "How do you ask for a bill at an Australian restaurant? Hmmmm..." It only took a second. He caught his breath and shot a look at the chessboard. "Check mate? Wait..." He kept looking at the board in disbelief, turning it around. Aiko let out an amused chuckle and opened her eyes. "Takumi lost? Ha, Australian restaurant, that's good." Ishi couldn't hold it any longer; she burst out laughing, stepped across the aisle, and high-fived Kenji, who was chuckling to himself.

"Oh, Roboto, you...you...should have seen"–she curled up, laughing–" the look on your face." She was crying now and Aiko was laughing too. Kenji was grinning from ear to ear with pride, and mimicked in an overdone Australian accent, "Check mate. And g'day!" after which he leaned back and laughed for the first time in a very long time.

"Man, this is so embarrassing," Takumi stammered, glowing red and peering at the board in confusion, but still smiling.

"Don't worry, Roboto, it took two of us to beat you," Ishi confessed. He looked at her with narrow eyes.

"You have to admit you weren't paying attention." She pointed out the window and around the train cabin.

"Yeah, Tak, don't feel too bad, I was toast without her help." Kenji looked at Ishi again and gave her another high-five.

"If you want revenge, you can play her alone. I'm never gonna play you again, so I can keep bragging rights."

Takumi sat back, weathering the fun. "No, you can't play Ishi in anything."

"What do you mean?" she replied, feigning annoyance, with hands on hips.

"She beats you up if you win," he said, mocking her.

She started to make a threatening face and formed fists with her hands, when the door of their car opened and the conductor stepped in for a routine walk-through. Or perhaps someone had complained at all the noise? Ishi sat down next to Aiko, and the others quickly composed themselves, with amused looks etched on their faces. Takumi straightened his glasses and started packing up his board as the conductor stepped to the next car.

Kenji sat back, thinking warmly, *God, these are cool friends*, looking at each of them in turn. When he got to Aiko, she was studying him with her head slightly cocked to the side.

"Long way from last month, huh?" she said.

"You have no idea," he replied with meaning and gratitude in his voice.

"Okay, I guess you should know more about Akira and what we'll be doing this week." She paused, and took a deep breath. Everyone sat up to listen.

"Akira is a master swordsman. He's been fighting the spiritual war since he was a teenager like us. As Takumi mentioned, he was the Warrior that came for me and introduced me to the Master. He took me under his wing and trained me with a group of teenagers that God used him to free. He's spent his life fighting. He's a teacher in a local high school, but his life mission is pushing back the darkness by training spiritual Warriors. We're going to spend a week with him just resting and learning."

"Thank God for that," Ishi said.

"I second that," Takumi added.

"Yeah, it's been pretty tough lately. The enemy seems to be going after us more personally than before," Aiko explained.

"*And* they are showing up in greater numbers," Takumi added, shaking his head.

"But," Ishi started, "we seem to be getting stronger too. I mean, there are demons we banish in single combat, that used to take all of us."

"It still hurts though," Takumi noted with a pained expression upon his face. The girls nodded.

"He's leading us into the thick of the battle," Aiko announced prophetically.

"How do you do it?" Kenji asked. "I just saw a small part of it and it horrified me. My knees were wobbly and I could barely breathe. I mean, I'm surprised I didn't lose it and go crazy."

"Maybe you did. I call it crazy, stupid, committed." Takumi smiled. The Warriors looked at each other, wondering how to explain it.

Aiko leaned forward with her elbows on her knees. "They are created beings just like us, but we know the Creator Himself and He places His Presence within us. We walk *with* Him and He *with* us. We are still just creatures, weak and full of imperfections, but when we walk onto the battlefield in His name, all the power of the universe is behind us. So, we don't fear. The moment you think *you* can handle something alone, you are in trouble. Our greatest strength lies in the fact that *we can't*, but *He can*. When you walk with that faith, you're unstoppable." She looked at him wondering if he was getting it.

"It kinda makes sense. I guess I have a lot to learn," he reflected rubbing his chin.

"Don't worry, Akira will explain it better than me," Aiko said.

"But no one lives it better than you, sister!" Ishi said, throwing her arm around Aiko. Aiko smiled at her next in command.

"No, I'm just a learner too with a long way to go." Aiko redirected the attention, but Takumi wouldn't let it go.

"Kenji, the night you were saved, Aiko had to face an Overlord alone."

"Overlord?"

"The one in the station who Mai and I took down; big, ugly, deadly. That's a Slayer," Ishi said grimly, giving him a starting place.

Takumi continued, "They're present at suicides. They exist to kill and they're hard to take down, but they are given orders by Overlords who are even more powerful. They command up to a hundred Harassers, Grunts, and Slayers. Anyways, Aiko faced one alone, the one that was going after you. She took him alone."

"We all fought, and what did I just say? We're never alone." Aiko continued to refuse the attention. Her mind went to the one she hadn't been able to handle. *If only they knew.*

"All I'm saying is that if you were to get the call to go to hell itself, there is no one better to have at your side," Takumi finished, with love and pride in his leader.

"She helped save me," Ishi said.

"And me," Takumi added. Aiko looked down, her eyes moist from the deep expression of loyalty. They paused for the moment.

"And me," Kenji said.

Aiko smiled and replied, "God did the saving, we were just along for the ride, but this is the Warrior you can thank, Kenji," she said, pulling Ishi to her side. "Have you seen this girl run? I think the enemy underestimated how fast she could get to the station that day, and how tough she is."

Kenji looked at Ishi, who looked down embarrassed. "Ummm…it's what we do," she spoke almost without thinking, "no matter who it is, you know?" she said awkwardly.

"Well, thanks for getting there," Kenji said sincerely.

"And Mai was there too, so, I mean…"

"Uh, 'You're welcome' would be fine, Ish," Takumi said, amused.

"I gotta go to the bathroom," she blurted out and left abruptly.

Takumi and Aiko exchanged quizzical looks. Kenji watched her leave and then just sat back again, with a sense of thankfulness filling his heart. Aiko finished, "Now it's your turn to fight, Kenji. This week you'll be trained in spiritual warfare by one of the best there is. I hope you're ready. It's the next stop."

He looked outside again as the train sped further into the country where Akira waited.

Chapter Twelve

Akira

Kenji saw the old Warrior waiting on the platform when they arrived. They stumbled off the train with their bags and there he was, standing with a quiet presence about him that seemed to radiate. He looked younger than the fifty-something years he had lived, and was endowed with an energy and strength that many a person several years his junior would have envied. His short hair showed signs of graying on the sides but his face looked young, yet wise at the same time. He beamed with contentment and genuine love for his students. They gathered around him and dropped their bags.

Aiko was first.

"Aiko," he said, looking at her intently. "My, look at you. So good to see you in one piece; I've heard that you've been busy. Time to rest, huh?" He gave her a big fatherly hug. She just managed a "Sensei."

Then He turned to Ishi. "Ishi."

"Sensei," she said, and threw her arms around him.

He lifted her up, laughing. "Still a fireball I see, and you're getting very strong, my girl." He set her down and rested his hands on her shoulders.

He next turned to Takumi, who bowed deeply. "Sensei."

Akira grabbed him and pulled him into a hug. "Come here, Warrior. No need to be so formal. We're at war."

"So we are," Takumi said, smiling widely.

"Still a chess champion I trust?" The girls shot a look at Takumi, smiling but pressing their lips together to stifle a laugh.

"Ummm…I still play," he replied, glancing at Ishi and flaring his eyes slightly.

Akira finally turned to the newcomer. Kenji stepped forward.

"Sensei…I'm…"

"I know you. You're Kenji. I'm Akira. I know your father," he said, looking directly at him. Kenji was speechless. There was a brief pause as Akira looked him over.

"This is truly amazing," he declared, with a voice that was filled with wonder. "I am overjoyed to meet you…again."

"But how…?"

"Answers later," he said as he picked up Aiko's and Ishi's bags. "Come, men, don't let the ladies carry anything. I have a friend waiting to take us up the mountain."

♦ ♦ ♦

The night passed like a dream. First, they were taken up to Akira's mountain retreat and settled into their rooms. Next, they joined him for a prolonged dinner and catch-up session. Aiko shared everything that had been happening in the city and recounted the battle for Kenji. Akira listened very carefully, asking questions to fill in the details. This was the first time Kenji had heard the whole amazing story. He could almost see the hand of God directing the events that led him to change sides. Akira laughed when he found out that Kenji had seen spiritual combat, but became grave when he heard that a demon had manifested as a human. He seemed unusually quiet and reflective when they spoke of Ryudan's possession by five demons.

The theme of the night was demonic escalation. Aiko and her friends had started with hallway scuffles or banishing two or three in an alley. Now they were facing small armies. At the same time, their own powers were growing. The whispers in Aiko's heart were taking them deeper into the teeth of evil in the city.

They now sat in silence around a stone fireplace, staring at the dancing fire. The aroma of burning wood filled the room and its warmth chased away the cool mountain air. They sipped their hot tea as they waited for Akira to speak.

"What's going on?" Takumi said, putting down his tea.

"Something big is coming, isn't it?" Ishi said without turning her gaze away from the fire.

Aiko was silent and intense as if she already knew the answer.

Kenji looked around the group. "Uh, has anything like this ever happened before?"

"Oh, yes," Akira answered. He paused a moment. "Every generation, in key places around the world, the Dark Lord tries to set up a stronghold that will serve the purposes of evil for that period; but God will send His own to oppose them."

"Spiritual Warriors?" Kenji asked.

Akira looked back at the fire. "Yes."

"So, it's not just fighting random daily battles, it's actually strategic, like chess or war," Takumi said, raising his voice.

Akira nodded and continued, "Key figures are destroyed, key cities are taken, and the younger generation is targeted to pervert the future." He paused again. "But unlike war, there are no rules for the Dark Lord. He hates with all of his being, and he'll go after you and the ones you love," Akira said grimly.

Aiko's look hardened. She was still silent.

"But we win, right? I mean, we're the good guys and God is…well, God, so we have to win," Kenji said sitting up straight.

"Yes…and no." Akira took a stick and stirred the fire. "A spiritual Warrior has the potential to win every time, but the enemy is cunning and relentless and sometimes entire generations are impacted."

"But, once we win it's over, right? I mean, the world becomes a better place and all that." Kenji was frowning now and looking around waiting for an answer.

Akira chuckled at Kenji. "The tide has almost been turned for good in many settings, only to fall in the next generation and become even worse than it was before."

Kenji opened his mouth and raised his hand to speak, but Akira answered before he could get out his question.

"I know, I know, how is that possible? The truth is, the spiritual war in this era never stops. After a great victory, people become complacent. They feel safe and stop carrying their swords. Or, if they do carry them, they are just for show. They have large gatherings of warriors, but they never go to war, and they become weaker and weaker. So, when the enemy reappears, he sweeps the warriors aside or causes the leadership to fall, leaving the rest to scatter."

Akira struck the burning log and embers and sparks flew in every direction. A full minute of silence passed as they processed this truth.

"What happened to your generation?" Ishi said gently. There was a long pause before Akira answered.

He looked at them. "We lost…twice." He paused again, looking into the fire. His eyes were filled with memories. After a few moments he sat up and slapped his knee. "Okay, bedtime, everyone. Training starts early."

Aiko broke her silence. "Wait, there's one more thing." She sighed. "I faced a demon last week that I couldn't beat." Everyone but Akira froze.

"You never mentioned…" Takumi touched her arm.

"I was afraid. I hit him square in the face and nothing happened. Another time

I drove my sword deep into him and he just mocked me and then came after me." Aiko looked to Akira for an explanation.

Akira paused again and took a deep breath.

"Sensei?" Ishi leaned forward.

"They're called the Resistant Ones. We call them Goons. You can't harm them, not without much spiritual preparation or a special spiritual gift." He paused again. "They show up when the enemy is about to make a big move."

"You mean a big fight?" Kenji asked.

"In a manner of speaking. So then, get some rest. The training is just in time. I'll have to teach you some things I didn't plan on." Akira stood.

"So, we'll be able to beat the Goons?" Aiko asked.

"Umm…no, I can't teach you that."

"But!" came from everyone.

"Good night, Warriors. See you early." Akira ended the discussion.

As the Warriors made their way to their rooms, Akira went to his garden, knelt, and began to pray with raised hands.

He wouldn't sleep at all this night.

Chapter Thirteen

SPIRITUAL WORKINGS

"WHO ARE YOU?" AKIRA ASKED.

"Uh...what do you...uh?" Kenji stammered.

"Who are you?" he repeated.

"Um...Kenji? Is that what you are looking for?"

"Who is Kenji?" he challenged.

"Uh..." Long pause. Akira stared deep into his eyes.

"That's enough for now." Akira turned to leave.

"Wait, just one question? That's it?" Kenji called after him.

Akira stopped without turning. "Yes, but that is the most important question of all." He paused and then walked away.

Kenji took a deep breath. "Okay, who am I...I'm...I'm Kenji." He sighed. What was he missing? He had no clue. He gazed at the rising sun as it cleared in the horizon. He had been asked to meet Akira at dawn. He had come expecting some kind of...well, he really didn't know what to expect, and now he was stumped. *What was that all about?*

"I can't help you."

Kenji turned to see Ishi walking toward him from under a tree from where she had obviously been watching "However, I will tell you that it has to do with your fear and something that Aiko tried to explain to you."

Kenji felt his forehead wrinkle as he strained to remember. "But what..."

"Gotta go. I'm next. Talk to you later," she said and trotted off in the direction Akira had gone.

"Hey, Kenji." Takumi arrived beside him. "Let me guess, who are you?" he teased.

"Yeah, can you...?"

"Sorry, Akira's waiting for me too. Later."

Kenji was left hanging with a question on his face.

"Hey!" he heard an encouraging voice greeting him.

He turned to her. "Aiko, can you give me a hint?"

She stopped, and looked at him with a grin. "Why in the world would you ask me anything at all, when you can now personally ask God yourself? He's waiting to answer you." She started off. "Have a nice day."

Kenji watched her walk off with her confident stride, and glanced up to the heavens tentatively.

"Hmmm...okay...here goes...uh, God...can You help with this? When I think of who I am, all I can think of is my past...my father...my life. I'm a drug lord's son and a gang...well, ex-gang leader. I guess I've never really tried to figure this out; I was whatever I needed to be at the time. Okay, God, I'm feeling really stupid now and I don't know what to say. Who am I?" Kenji grew quiet, and after a few moments realized that he was actually listening for God's voice. That's when he thought he heard it.

"*You're My child.*" It wasn't an audible voice and yet in his heart he knew he had just heard someone speaking to him. Somehow between the confusion and the revelation, he knew that he had just received his answer. "I'm Your child. That's who I am."

An hour later he was with the whole group and Akira was speaking. "A Warrior's identity is his strength, and is what his enemy fears most. Mere humans are child's play, just cannon fodder for demons. But a Warrior of the King, someone who partners with God in life, can't be stopped. Kenji, the enemy will do everything they can to make you forget who you are, but you mustn't forget...it's your strength!"

"Now," he said, standing up, "it's time to see the whole world in a different way."

"Truesight," Takumi said, looking at Kenji.

"The ability to see into the spiritual world and to interact with it," Akira explained before Kenji could form the question.

"Let's go to town." The Warriors leaped to their feet and followed as Akira led them out, talking while they made their way down the mountain.

"Why don't you explain to Kenji how it works?" Akira instructed.

"Spiritual beings occupy the same space that we do, but in a different dimension," Takumi started.

"So, they have to travel distances as we do, avoid obstacles when they can, because they can't see through them, and they exist in time like we do," Aiko added.

"The problem is that it's a *spiritual* dimension that coexists side by side with our reality, so you can't see them unless you have Truesight. You can feel them sometimes, like a chill or a sudden feeling of dread, or evil," Ishi chimed in.

"But be ready. Once it goes on, you may wish you never had it," Takumi said soberly.

"It's pretty bad at first…scary." Ishi shivered.

"But then you realize that they are the ones who should be scared." Aiko's eyes narrowed a bit.

"They sure look a lot scarier than we do," Kenji observed.

There was a collective nod in agreement.

"Once you can see them, you can then resist them in that dimension," Akira affirmed.

Kenji was still trying to grasp it. "But, what do I look like in the real world while I'm fighting in the spiritual world?" he asked.

"Kenji, remember, the spiritual world *is* real. What you mean is the physical world." Akira gently corrected.

Kenji nodded, beginning to understand.

"Spiritual warfare happens at the speed of thought." Akira made a fast motion with his hand. "Demons will attack with lies, twisted ideas, or perverted thoughts that are intended to change your beliefs."

"Wait! That's it? Isn't that like sticks and stones?" Kenji asked.

"No, much worse. Their attacks aren't meant to offend you. They hate you with a passion and want to destroy you. So, they try to get you to believe in lies. Kenji, what we believe becomes our reality." Akira paused for emphasis and looked him straight in the face. "Remember this, a single idea can change the world. So if that idea is a lie…"

"Yes." Kenji ran his hand through his hair as his mind wandered back to his season of torment. "They make you feel like a loser. Like everyone is watching you and laughing at you. They make death seem like an escape. But if you don't know that evil is coming after you…"

"You believe the lie that you have no value, and act on it."

Kenji sighed hard and looked at Akira. "So, how do we fight back?"

"They will try to stir your fears and jab at your insecurities. You need to counter them with truth, very quickly. You must have that truth firmly set in your heart and have the presence of mind to resist them. If not, they will bash at your beliefs until they become doubts, and then plant their lies, ones that diminish your value, your worth, your purpose…your life," Akira finished soberly.

"So while I'm countering these lies, do I look like a crazy man to others?"

"Not really. As you walk across a street, or sit calmly in a room, or walk in to take your seat in a classroom, they can come at you, but you can step into that world and oppose them. To others, it will seem as though you are concentrating on something else or daydreaming for a moment. In reality, you're banishing Fallen Ones." Akira paused a moment to let Kenji process these new ideas. "To you, it will seem like the real world moves in slow motion, because a battle in the mind can take place in the blink of an eye. Occasionally, a demon will choose to blow his cover and attack you physically. They punch, kick, bite, push, stab; anything to kill you."

"Uh, yeah, I remember…scary…like…" Kenji began.

"Fighting a monster. Others will see you thrown to the floor or pushed up against a wall by some invisible force." Akira finished for him.

"What can I do when that happens?"

"It's very complicated, because we have only one brain. So, to see in both worlds and react in both at the same time is very difficult, but sometimes necessary. Demons usually choose to stay unseen, so they will try to keep major battles in secluded areas so they can use all their force against you."

"But why?" Kenji started.

"Kenji, the whys are a mystery to us all." Akira had finished the lesson.

"Oh yeah. Sensei, *why* is it that Kenji was able to see before receiving the gift?" Takumi asked.

Akira looked carefully at Kenji. "I'm not sure. Family trait, perhaps? All we need to know is that God allowed it," he said simply.

"Uh, so how do you get this special power to see?" Kenji asked.

"You already have the gift, Kenji. It comes when you trust the Master. You just have to activate it." They had reached the outskirts of town, and he stopped in front of an empty lot. "Close your eyes briefly and say in your heart, 'Through His eyes.' The world will fade slightly and the spiritual realm will sharpen. Ready to try it?"

Kenji hesitated. "Do I really want to do this?"

"Good question," Takumi said. Aiko and Ishi stood to the side, already looking at the lot with their sight switched on and wondering how Kenji would respond.

Akira asked, "Have you chosen sides?"

Kenji paused, and nodded slowly. "Yes, I have."

"Then, it's time to see the battlefield, 'through His eyes.'"

Kenji closed his eyes nervously. What if nothing happened? What if he couldn't see what they could see? There was only one way to find out. "Okay, here goes." In his heart, he stretched out his faith to God and prayed, "*Through His eyes.*"

The moment he opened his eyes, nothing had changed. He took a breath to speak, when suddenly it was like looking through a lens that was going from fuzzy to focused, only it wasn't the lens that was changing, it was the world itself.

The world didn't really fade, but another world that coexisted side by side, a spiritual world, started to sharpen. Impressions became visible, intuitions had voices, feelings had colors, and spiritual beings had form and substance. The next moment, he saw them.

"The Fallen Ones," Kenji breathed in fear. "Uh...can they..." Just then, a group of three wiry and evil-looking demons locked eyes with Kenji and examined the group from across the lot. They conferred with each other without breaking their gaze and started reaching for weapons that were slung over their scaly backs.

"Oh yes, they can see you. They might even know you," Akira answered in a measured tone.

"This is so weird," Kenji replied, stepping back to be sure he was nestled safely with the group. The others stood unconcerned, but ready to help Kenji understand what he was experiencing.

"Uh, should we do anything?" he asked Akira.

"You mean fight them? No. There's a basic set of rules when you fight." He motioned for Aiko to explain.

She took her cue. "We fight when the Master sends us, and engage anyone who stops us from our mission, or when we are challenged directly. Otherwise, we just pass by."

Akira stood in front of Kenji and explained with emphasis, "You see, Kenji, the battle is strategic, not just a bunch of random scuffles or back-alley fights. There is a Divine purpose every single time you pull your sword, either to advance His cause or put a stop to theirs."

When they looked toward the demons again, there were eight of them snarling, planning, becoming agitated. Kenji stumbled back into Takumi. They all looked toward the gathering attack.

Akira smiled. "Good! They responded faster than I thought. They are challenging you. Okay, armor, everyone. Time to teach Kenji how to fight."

Suddenly, glowing translucent armor appeared on each Warrior except Kenji. He instinctively examined himself and the others, with a question on his face.

Again, Akira took the lead. "Kenji listen to me, we need to move quick." The demons advanced toward them.

"Who are you?" Akira shot the question.

"Uh…oh…I'm a child of God." Kenji suddenly felt a warm, glowing feeling in his heart.

"Will you live right for the Master?"

"I will live right." He felt a pulse from his heart and a faintly blue glowing breastplate appeared on his chest.

"Will you let truth be your guide?"

"I will let truth be my guide." His heart pulsed again. An armored belt appeared around his waist.

"Can anything take you from the Master's hand?"

"Nothing can take me from the Master's hand." A helmet appeared around his head and then faded from view. He felt it still there. "Uh…is it…?"

"Yes, don't worry. We have to hurry." The demons were halfway to them.

"Will you go where He sends you?"

"I will go wherever the Master sends me." There was a pulse and armor covered his legs and feet.

"Uh, could we hurry this along?" Ishi asked drawing her sword.

"Almost there, don't worry. Now Kenji, only two things left."

The Warriors were deployed with drawn weapons around Kenji and Akira as the demons closed, snarling and challenging them with filthy words.

"Trust and truth," Akira said simply. "Do you trust God with all your heart?"

"I do, I trust God!" Nothing happened. Kenji closed his eyes. "God, help me with this one! I really do trust You, I'm just a little new…" Suddenly, a shield appeared on his left arm, translucent and glowing.

The demons attacked. Akira quickly stepped to the side, out of the battle. He called back, "Trust your armor!"

Two demons attacked each Warrior. Kenji backed away from the demons who came at him. He heard an odd bursting sound and felt a wave of heat wash over him from Aiko's direction. When he glanced over, he saw Aiko standing in the midst of a cloud of yellowish dust and the second demon was backing away. Her sword was glowing.

"Sword? What about my sword?" Kenji ducked and a demon sword glanced off his helmet. He quickly raised his shield to block an ax coming at him. "Akira?"

"Good Kenji, move your feet, use your armor."

Kenji ducked again and smashed his shield into a demon, who fell backward. "Uh, about that sword!" Kenji said, looking pleadingly at Akira. He heard two whooshing sounds as Ishi and Takumi each cut down a demon.

"I told you what you needed. You have to figure it out from there," Akira said, watching calmly.

"Uh, you said, trust"–he ducked–" and truth!" He blocked.

"Uh, I believe the truth!" Nothing happened.

"I live the truth." Nothing.

"I speak the truth." He fell back.

"Ouch…I love the truth!" He rolled, avoiding an ax. "Uh…help?"

"Truth has so many meanings in a fallen world like ours. Some people feel like they can make their own truth. Others don't believe it exists at all," Akira called out as Kenji got hit square in the chest, the sword glancing off. "The Dark Lord has blinded the minds of the world to truth and flooded the world with his lies. What's the answer, Kenji?"

"I don't know what it is!" Kenji tripped and fell to his knees. His shield was down as he tried to push to his feet. He looked up and saw the demon swinging his ax for a head shot.

There was a loud *ring* as a glowing sword stopped the blow, and quickly sliced the demon's head off. The head hung in space over the body. Kenji watched as the eyes blinked at him and then *whooosh*. There was a bursting sound, a heat wave, and the demon disappeared with Ishi standing there in the cloud. She looked right at him before moving to finish off her own attacker.

"Not what, but *Who*, Kenji!" Takumi called out, not able to remain silent any longer.

Kenji got it. *Of course, not what, but Who!* He shouted out in a loud, piercing voice: "The Master is my truth." There was a powerful pulse from his heart as a long sword appeared in his hand. When Kenji looked up, there were no more demons. The fight was over. He thought the others had dealt with his last one, so he turned around.

There was a faint whisping sound. "Kenji! Look out!" His second adversary reappeared just behind him, winding up to cut into him. Before he could do anything, he saw a quick movement from Aiko's direction and a sword come hurtling at him. He was certain it would hit him in the head, but instead, it whistled by and he felt the rush of heat as a demon dematerialized.

Kenji fell to the ground emotionally exhausted.

"Take a deep breath and disengage. Pull your heart back," Akira instructed.

Kenji did as he was told and found himself lying in an empty lot on the outskirts of town with Akira and his friends standing over him.

"You okay?" Takumi asked. "I'll always remember my first time." He chuckled and shook his head at the memory.

Kenji stared up, overwhelmed.

"You did good," Aiko said, with a small encouraging nod.

"You call that good?" Kenji said, getting his breath back. "I almost died!"

"Not while I'm alive," Ishi declared, and then looked surprised that she had spoken aloud.

Takumi, Aiko, and Akira exchanged quick glances and Takumi's eyebrows rose a bit.

"I mean we fight as a team…you know?" she added, recovering.

"Uh, right."

"Yes, we do."

After a brief, awkward silence Akira pulled Kenji to his feet.

"I have some questions," Kenji began.

"It's called cloaking. Even in the spiritual world they can fade from view because they are spiritual beings," Akira intercepted.

"About training. Have you ever considered teaching the armor and sword thing *before* a group of demons shows up?"

Now Kenji's emotions were catching up to his fear, and he felt vulnerable and exasperated. The Warriors responded with a smile and held in muffled laughter. Akira also smiled.

"Well, Kenji, do you think you will ever forget how to armor up or how important it is?"

Kenji looked at him and took a deep breath. "Please, say that's all for now?" They couldn't hold it any longer; the Warriors had a good laugh and Akira joined them.

"Let's eat and debrief; you'll get all your questions answered," Akira gently encouraged Kenji, placing his hand on his shoulder.

The warmth of Akira's hand caused Kenji to pause. Without parents to guide him he'd been left to be raised by an evil world. It was different now. He was learning to trust again.

They walked back to Akira's place and talked all afternoon.

Kenji learned that demons couldn't be destroyed, just banished. They were sent to far-off places away from human contact and had to make their way back in real time to civilization. They called it the "Barren Places."

He learned about Watchers and how they were able to encourage, strengthen, and protect, but that the larger tasks were left to Warriors. Both demons and angels could influence humans but not make choices for them. However, at times they could intervene and even, on rare occasions, attack physically.

It was evening now, and Kenji found himself alone on the porch looking at the stars. Someone spoke from behind him.

"Can't stop looking into that other world, huh?" It was Ishi. She was wearing a jogging suit and carrying her shoes. She had a ponytail holder around her wrist, but her hair was down. She walked over and sat down next to Kenji.

He turned to her and smiled. "Wow, I didn't recognize you at first. No ponytail. You look..." Kenji watched Ishi watching him. "Different."

She didn't smile, but proceeded to put her glossy hair up.

Wow.

"Yeah, I can't stop looking...I mean...into the other world." He peered into the sky again using his Truesight. "I'm just wondering what's going on there, and yes, still a little afraid." He turned back to her. "Oh, you're still wearing your armor! Hey, how come I have to *put* mine on and you don't?"

"That will change. At first you have to deliberately choose each commitment, but soon you become what you are choosing. At least that's how Akira explained it. Now I have to intentionally remove it." She paused for a second. "Before each battle, it's important to check it. Sometimes, we might be sagging in one area and be vulnerable to attack. Here, I'll show you. Stand up."

Kenji stood facing Ishi; they both put on Truesight.

"Okay, first I'll turn slowly and you just give me a little tap or punch on my shoulders, knees, back, and then head." Ishi instructed. She turned slowly as Kenji tapped on her armor. Her cheeks blushed red and she avoided his gaze.

"Like this?" Kenji asked, following her directions.

"Yeah. A little *harder*, Kenji." He tried again. "Come on, hit me."

She faced him to demonstrate, but a voice called out from just inside the house. "Are you two lovebirds fighting out there?" Takumi asked in a teasing voice.

Ishi looked in his direction and was flushed with embarrassment. "Takumi, I'm going to hurt you!" She heard Takumi laughing, followed by Aiko's voice.

"Tak, leave them alone."

Ishi looked at Kenji and there was fire in her eyes. "Like this." She punched Kenji hard, forgetting that his armor wasn't on yet. He went down, the breath knocked out of him. She gasped, with eyes opened wide in shock.

"*Oh!* I'm so sorry, Kenji." she stammered, picking him up and checking to see that he wasn't injured.

Kenji coughed, sputtered, and caught his breath. He was half laughing, trying not to look like a wimp. He had been hit many times, but not by a black belt. "No, I'm okay...okay, girl. I get it...tap harder...okay."

"Sorry, sorry," Ishi kept repeating, dusting him off.

"No, okay, turn around." Kenji continued the inspection, tapping harder this time.

With each tap of Kenji's hands, Ishi visibly controlled herself. From time to time she would glance up into his eyes. When she finished her turn she seemed a little out of breath. "Uh…okay…now look for my sword and pull it out just a bit to be sure it's ready to release." Kenji moved closer and reached to her side, pulled and released. She was inches from his face. She held her breath for a moment. Their eyes met.

"Like that?" he said as he finished with her sword.

"Good," she said, her voice cracking. She reached up, tightened her ponytail, and composed herself.

"Okay, your turn, now put on your armor," Ishi said, facing him.

"Okay, I've been waiting to show someone this. I've been practicing. Watch!" Kenji stood back and slowly closed his eyes. In an instant, his armor appeared. He looked at Ishi for approval.

"Nice. Speed of thought, you're getting it, and let's see…" She tapped his head and the outline of an invisible helmet met her hand. "Good. Now turn around…" They repeated the drill with Ishi tapping Kenji's shoulders, knees, back, and head.

"Uh, tell me again why we can't see the helmet?"

"Oh, the helmet guards our thoughts, which is very important, but thoughts are unseen, so the helmet is too. The other pieces guard our lives and actions, which are visible; we see them in the spiritual world. Is that more confusing?" Ishi asked.

"No, I think I get it," he replied, wrinkling his forehead.

They sat down again.

"Well, never, ever forget your helmet. Head shot, that's a killer blow," Ishi said, giving him a playful punch on the side of the head.

"What, really?" Kenji looked over, surprised. Ishi went quiet and just looked at the sky.

"Yeah, it is." They both remained silent for a moment. "Serious stuff, huh?"

Kenji turned to her. "Hey, Ish, thanks again for today. You are always saving my butt." She returned his gaze. They were so close, he could smell her shampoo.

"Gotta look out for the new guy, you know? Aiko helped too, remember?" She reached down to put on her shoes.

Kenji smiled. "Ish?" She looked up, and sat up.

"Yes?" She looked at him expectantly.

"I, uh…" He looked down, and then back up right into her eyes, gathering courage.

"Uh huh?"

"I, uh…I mean…" He let out a breath. "I think we make a good team," he finally blurted out. She looked deflated.

"Right." She finished her shoes, jerking her laces tight, and stood up abruptly. "I'm going for a run. See you, teammate," she said with the hint of an edge. She ran off and left Kenji feeling cold. He watched as she ran down the road.

"I thought the math team was bad with girls!" Takumi chuckled lightly as he sat down beside Kenji.

"Did it look as bad as it feels?" Kenji asked.

"Oh yeah. I'd say you just registered an all-time low on the awkward scale." Takumi paused. "So, you like her as much as she likes you?"

Kenji watched her running into the distance.

"There's just something so pure and strong about her, you know? Something, well, something that I feel I don't deserve."

Takumi picked up a small stone and threw it into the night. "She's definitely focused, Kenji, and right now, she likes you, so you may want to figure out things before you get too far along and hurt her. Does that make sense?"

"I guess you're right." Kenji watched her turn the corner and disappear into the darkness.

♦ ♦ ♦

Akira stood in battle stance across from Aiko, who looked confused. Both Warriors were in full armor.

"Are you ready? I'm going to attack you like a Warrior of light would, not a demon. It will seem odd at first, but think of it like fighting a mirror image. Same moves, same techniques, same defense, and same truth."

"But…same truth?" This advanced lesson was changing the way she saw things. Why would she need to learn this? "I'm not sure I understand," Aiko admitted.

"Truth is dangerous in the wrong hands."

She waited, trusting him.

"Okay, let's fight. It will come to you."

Two hours later, Aiko was dripping with sweat and breathing heavily.

"Good!" Akira noted, looking as fresh as ever. "Let's sit awhile." They both sat cross-legged on the floor facing each other.

"Sensei, I have to know why. Is someone in our group going to turn?"

Akira looked at her thoughtfully. She had already suffered so much for a young Warrior. She had lost a sister to suicide; her brother had disappeared and most likely had turned. Makoto had been a promising Warrior; and then there were her parents. Gone.

"It's about Makoto, isn't it? I'm being sent to…" She stopped and looked at Akira, needing answers. Akira nodded slowly.

"As you know, Warriors are secure. The Master never loses one and the Dark Lord knows this. Our souls are safe when we die, but while here on earth, we can be neutralized. He can make sure we take no one with us. To do that he will look for weaknesses and spin a silky, almost invisible, web in that area. It's hardly noticeable at all, but each day he will return and add a layer to that web…and attack several areas at once. After thousands of layers, the silky web is like a steel cage and becomes a launching point the dark forces use to pull down the Warrior at will. Soon, defeat is not only expected daily, but accepted as reality. They are serving the Dark Lord and don't even know it."

"Can they turn back?" Aiko asked with concern etched across her face.

"Yes, they can, but it's very, very painful. Someone has to get close and cut deeply to clear out the webs, which at times have penetrated every part of a person."

"How will I know?"

"You can't miss it. It's like a growth in his soul; a spiritual cancer. You'll know it when you see it. That's the only way you can get your brother back. You'll have to hurt him, he may hate you for it, and he could even die. If the pain is too great, the demons will offer an easy escape."

"Suicide? I could drive him to…" Tears formed in Aiko's eyes. She took a couple of deep breaths to maintain control, set her chin and wiped her gathering tears. "When will…?"

"You know the answer to that."

"God's time," she whispered, looking down at her sword and gripping it tightly. She looked directly at Akira. "I'll do anything for him. I'd go to hell for him." Her eyes flared with fierceness and passion.

"I believe you would, my dear. I'm glad you feel that way," Akira replied grimly. He took a deep breath. "Now, I have two more things to show you that you can teach the others, that will be essential," Akira spoke more lightly, standing up in an attempt to shift the mood.

"I want to know everything." Aiko stood and wiped her face.

Akira nodded and began his lesson. *Good girl, Aiko. You'll need this intensity to make it to the end.*

Chapter Fourteen

Sad Story

During the rest of the week, Aiko spent most of her time with Akira. Ishi, Takumi, and Kenji were sent out to problem areas in the town to invite attacks so that Kenji could learn more about combat. Sure enough, the demons attacked.

"Stay at my back! They like to come up from behind, cloaked."

"There. There! Don't hesitate, take them."

"Does this ever stop getting scary?"

"Not for them." They laughed.

"I'm hit!" Owwww…my hand. It's smoking."

"Don't worry, there's a prayer for that. Here, let me take your hand."

"You never hold my hand when you heal me!"

"Takumi, I'm gonna kick you someplace. Hmph. Okay, let me pray…"

"Ouch…huh? It heals that fast?"

"Yes, except the really deep ones, those take longer. Still hurts a bit though, huh?"

"Kenji watch it, behind you!"

"Whoa. How'd you do that? Was that your shield?"

"Yup, Aiko taught me last night. Just extend your faith toward the person and materialize your shield in front of him. It's really cool. So, we can protect each other from a distance in a big fight."

"I want to do that too."

"Me too."

"Okay…First…"

♦ ♦ ♦

It was their last night with Akira. In the morning they would be heading home. They sat around the stone fireplace, resting from the day's training and letting their stomachs settle after another great meal. They were all quiet and reflective.

"Please, Akira, can you start to connect the dots for us?" Takumi asked.

Akira looked at Takumi carefully and then said simply, "Kenji." They all nodded and Kenji sat up and leaned forward.

"Yes, and about my father…"

"Ah, I knew this day would come." Akira took a drink from his cup and sat back. "His name is Kentaro." He spoke gravely, as though revealing a lifelong secret. "He wasn't always Ryudan." Again he paused, remembering. "Kenji, what do you know about your mother?"

"Oh, my stepmother is"–he searched for words–" a really bad person. I never really knew my real mother. She was…uh…a prostitute." He looked down at his hands. "My dad didn't even know for sure that I was his child. I don't know what happened to her. I think she's dead."

"That's because your father has worked hard to keep it from you. And he *is* your father. Your mother is alive and the reason you are here at all. She has prayed for you every single day of your life." Akira stopped to let that sink in. All eyes looked at Kenji, who didn't know what to feel, except shock. Not a sound could be heard but the crackling and occasional pop of the fire.

Then Akira continued. "How can I say this? Do you know what a generational curse is?" he asked. Everyone looked puzzled. "It's one of the most powerful strategies in the spiritual war. You see, the key to victory on either side is to perpetuate and multiply their influence in the world with each new generation. Sometimes the Dark Lord and his forces will establish strong control over a very influential person or family. To perpetuate their work, they will work to control the whole family from one generation to the next. So, they will especially go after the children and work on them while they are young. They prepare them to wield the power of evil and carry out the Dark Lord's will."

"Don't they have a choice, the children?" Kenji asked.

"Oh yes, that's why we fight, and why I was sent." He took another drink from his cup and put it down. "Even if it's a generational curse, each person in the new generation must choose. There are a lot of things working against them, and often they choose to continue the evil. Kentaro's family was especially evil. They had even gone so far as to open themselves to demonic possession because such great power came with it. So, Warriors for generations have fought, yet failed to make a difference with them. No one succeeded in breaking the curse, but then something happened that even the Dark Lord didn't anticipate. Kentaro fell in love with a woman named Mayumi. She was a beautiful woman with a good heart; your mother, Kenji."

Kenji mouthed her name. "Mayumi." The other Warriors were all watching him with concern. Ishi's eyes were filled with compassion for him.

Akira continued. "Kentaro got married early, again a surprise, and they had you soon after. The demons were worried and moved up their plans to possess your father, and I was sent with my team to stop them. It was felt that perhaps Kentaro, with his wife and new son, would renounce his heritage of evil and follow the Master."

"Was there a fight?" Ishi asked.

"Not at first, and that puzzled us. I had many good talks with Kentaro, even began to build what I thought was a friendship. I shared with him on many occasions, but he just wouldn't turn. The world was swallowing him up, and the Dark Lord kept promising more and more power to him. You mother tried to flee with you when she saw what he was becoming. Then one day you were stolen from your home. Kentaro put a death warrant on your mother's head. That cleared the way for him to receive the blessing from the Dark Lord."

He paused, and said in a most serious tone, "For the passing on of the curse, hell came to town, and there was a big fight. I went in with seven Warriors..." Akira looked deep into the fire. "...and came out alone."

All the Warriors caught their breath.

"You see, we didn't think *he* would be there...but he came to seal the deal himself...the Dark Lord." There was another gasp in the room. Only Aiko remained unmoved and her eyes narrowed. Akira said, "I saw his bodyguard cut down my friend, and our leader."

"My father," Aiko said evenly, "and my mother fell there too." She looked at Akira for confirmation.

"Yes, there was a fire, a trap, and your mother refused to leave his side," he said sadly. "No one expected...well." The atmosphere in the room was thick with shock and wonder. Akira continued. "So, Kentaro made his choice and became Ryudan. He was infused with power to take over the underworld and promote the spread of evil."

"What about my mother?" The words sounded strange in Kenji's mouth.

"She chose too. She became a follower of the Master. You see, she had listened in to every talk I had had with your father. It was unexpected," he said with a smile. "Of course, your father kept searching for her, because he knew that as long as she was alive she would protect you with her prayers. But they could never find her, thanks to the Watchers and the few remaining Warriors. So, you have been protected from the curse all your life by the prayers of your mother."

"That's why they wanted Kenji dead," Aiko concluded.

"He was prepared by his mother to break the curse." Takumi connected the dots.

"It would have been devastating for that family to turn. It could signal a turning of the tide. It would echo across the land," Akira added.

"What would they do without Kenji?" Ishi asked. "Don't they need someone for their curse?"

"Kenji, are you ready for another surprise? You have a half brother. He lives in another city. He's from your father and stepmother, who knew your father before he met Mayumi. They needed you out of the way so he could take your place. He was named after your father."

"So that's why it was so tough that night!" Takumi said.

"That's why they kept fighting so hard afterward," Ishi said.

"They will keep fighting until the generation is safe–that is, safely evil," Akira said, "but they have a problem. You see, there is an opposite of the generational curse: a generational call. These are families who follow hard after the Master and produce Warriors that carry the faith and experience of a thousand years into battle.

"When the Dark Lord finds them, he unleashes all his deadly power to eliminate them. Sometimes, only once in hundreds of years, both sides try to break the generational power of the other at the same time, and two champions meet and fight till one generational line is broken, the curse or the call."

"Aiko," Takumi exclaimed. "Her family..."

"Yes, so when you saw Aiko confront Ryudan, you were looking at two epic champions that represent thousands of years of preparation, but Aiko surprised them–you all did. The Master had you attack first."

" Kenji turned," Ishi said, looking at him with admiration.

"Yes, before they could get Kenji out of the way, you got to him. So, an heir to a curse has turned, which upsets the balance; they fear what he might do to upset their plans," Akira said with a note of finality.

They all silently reflected upon the enormity of what Akira had just spoken.

"Heaven and hell have placed champions on the table," Akira murmured.

"Someone's going to lose their queen," Takumi contemplated, thinking of chess again.

The room fell quiet and all eyes focused on Aiko. There was deep concentration etched on her face while she looked into the distance toward some far-off battlefield. At that moment she felt so alone.

After a few uneasy moments Ishi stood and placed a hand on her shoulder. Takumi then stood and rested his hand on the other side, followed by Kenji, who flanked him. Aiko looked at her friends with misty eyes. She stood.

"What do we have to do, Akira?"

Akira looked closely at them standing there, and his serious face changed and softened into a smile.

"Love each other. It's something that they will never understand, something that they can't plan for. Stay unified and loyal to each other."

"They're going to try to get him back, aren't they?" Takumi asked.

"I don't know, but from what I can tell, and from what I've experienced, I'd say they'll come for him," Akira admitted.

Ishi asked, "Will it be bad?"

Akira paused, then nodded sadly. "It will be like a battle at the gates of hell. Hell is coming to town, again."

Chapter Fifteen

SHADOWS

KENJI WAS QUIET FOR MOST OF THE RIDE BACK, AS WAS AIKO. THEY BOTH SEEMED resigned to their destinies. Neither could guess what was really coming. Only Ishi and Takumi talked about the possibilities.

"I'm worried about Aik," Takumi said, to break the silence.

"Me too, Tak." Ishi looked over at her friend again. "I still can't believe it. I mean, Akira is her mentor and when he went with a team of people into a disaster no one, I mean no one, came out with him."

"It's not her life that she's worried about," Takumi said pointedly.

"I know, she never thinks of herself." Ishi shook her head. "She'll give her life to save any one of us."

"Then there's Kenji. What will he have to do?" Takumi wondered.

"I saw his father that night. Takumi, he had at least five demons in him…five! That's potentially ten weapons to face at once, operated by five different warped minds. Will he have to face his father?" They both glanced over at Kenji with worried looks.

Takumi thought a moment. "I can't see it any other way. Kenji is the one who has to choose, and somehow he may wonder if there's any Kentaro Senior left to love."

Ishi nodded. "I didn't think of that." She paused for a moment and then let out a sigh. "Tak?"

"Yes?" He looked at Ishi.

"Let's never leave them alone. And I mean *ever*. Okay?"

"Good, yes! I'll stick by Aiko and you stay by Kenji. Always watch their backs."

"Maybe Kenji and I can handle Ryudan if the whole team is there?" she added hopefully.

"I don't know what or who Aiko will have to face, but I'll do anything to protect her."

They looked at each other and considered their predicament. Would they end up like the last generation, two players in a sad story?

Kenji was staring out of the window as the train came to a routine stop at a small station. Another train had just arrived parallel to theirs but was facing the opposite direction. Kenji did what he'd been doing all day, and switched on his spiritual sight. But this time something he saw made him gasp.

"Uh, guys–Truesight…look at that train," he said, pointing. The others were pulled out of deep thought or conversation and looked over to see what had Kenji so excited.

"Oh would you look at that!" Takumi said immediately.

"Aiko, what's up?" Ishi threw up her hands.

On the train beside them stood a group of five teenagers, foreigners with backpacks and headphones, and they were all wearing spiritual armor. They too were turning to a tall blond young man and asking questions. Two more ran from across the aisle and joined them, making a total of seven in all.

Aiko was quiet but intense. She looked over, and after a moment placed her hand on the glass and smiled. She glanced to the others quickly. "Smile guys, they're family." Just then, the trains starting moving apart, and the blond young man put his hand on the glass as the others started animated waves. Then he mouthed silent words, "For…His…"

"Honor!" Aiko and the others finished aloud with him as the trains pulled apart. Their eyes were fixed on each other as they pulled away; the reaction was the same. The groups gathered around their leader for an explanation.

Aiko sat down with a knowing look of realization.

"Okay, now it makes sense," she said, looking at them. "Akira said there would be others; help from unexpected places."

"So, there are others? That's good news. Did you guys know that before?" Kenji asked.

"I've seen others," Aiko said, looking away. Kenji looked over at Ishi and Takumi.

"First time." Ishi shrugged.

"Me too," Takumi said with his face still pressed to the window.

"Wait, didn't Warriors fight in larger groups before? Isn't that what Akira was talking about in his generation?" Kenji asked.

Aiko turned back and looked at him. "They tried to get unified and stay unified. As they gathered in larger groups, fewer and fewer of them actually engaged in the fight. Somehow, the enemy planted his people among them to distract them and to cause disunity and complacency. So, when the battle came, they were beaten back. There were too few trained to stand in front of a demon and send it to hell."

"It's different with us." Takumi rubbed his chin. "A definite shift in strategy. I can see what Akira is doing, what you are doing, Aiko. You want us to be dangerous, always effective."

"Yes, and to fight as one," she said, nodding.

"Now, if the Master sees fit to pull these teams together in one fight..." Takumi crossed him arms and slowly shook his head in awe.

"Wow." Kenji wondered again where this would take him.

Ishi sat up and turned to Aiko. "When did you ever see another Warrior, Aiko?"

Aiko quickly looked away again. "Makoto...my brother," she said, deep emotion welling up within her. She sat back and took a deep breath. "I guess it's time to tell you. He followed after my parents' faith, and I thought I did too. After my parents died in the fire when I was a child, my heart hardened toward God. I was always told that our family was different, special, because of a call. Yet, when I saw what that call did to them, I started to doubt God. I promised I wouldn't let anything happen to the rest of my family and became very protective of them. Makoto tried to rebuild my faith, but I started to resent him because he represented the God who killed my parents. It was then that I started to hear voices in the night...dark ones. I welcomed them because they put a voice to the anger that was consuming my life. I wanted anything that would keep me away from God. Later, my sister got involved with the wrong guy and disappeared and even Makoto started to change and get angry."

She paused, starting to tear up.

"When Shiho disappeared, it was the only time Makoto and I were really close again, because we spent weeks going down every street and dark alley looking for her together. After she committed suicide, I confronted him and told him that his God was cruel. I saw him begin to sink deeper and deeper into depression, and one night he went out and didn't come back for three days. I found his training manual on the kitchen table. He never went anywhere without it, but there it was." She stopped for a moment and pulled a small book from her backpack. On the cover, in faded embossed letters, was the name "Makoto."

"One night, with him still gone, I stood on the roof in a storm, soaked, ready to jump off our building. I'd had enough pain." She paused, shaking her head. "Akira saved me. He had come to help us make arrangements to move into yet another uncle's place and found me just in time. Little did I know that Akira was fighting an amazing spiritual battle for my soul. He may feel like he lost his generation, but he never stopped serving the Master. That night, I chose sides once and for all and vowed to stop evil from destroying more families...like it did mine." Her voiced trailed off.

"Wasn't Makoto encouraged?" Ishi asked.

"Yeah, didn't that help?" Kenji added.

"I'm not sure he even knew. I was so excited to tell him when he returned, but one day he burst in and starting yelling something about knowing who hurt Shiho. Akira touched me while they argued and it activated my Truesight, and I saw Makoto, ready for battle, but now I know that his armor was weak. He was filled with rage. Well, he burst out of the door and even Akira couldn't stop him."

She stopped, tears now rolling down her cheeks.

"What happened?" Ishi asked.

"Ambush," Takumi said. "Right?"

"Akira bolted out the door, and then right back telling me to pray hard. I found out later that Akira fought the whole night for me, but he had to let Makoto go. You see, they had chosen that night to finish the job and to wipe out the generational call on my family, but Akira stopped them."

"And Makoto?" Kenji asked.

"I stopped hearing from him. It's been almost two years now." She looked up at them. "Instead of killing him right away, they decided to use him, for what I don't know...but"–she took a deep breath–" I'm going to stop them and get him back."

Takumi and Ishi exchanged doubtful looks.

They all sat back, looking tired from the new revelation.

Kenji looked outside the window. "Maybe the others will help?" he said, trying to be positive.

"That would be nice." Aiko spoke simply but unconvincingly.

"You two need to know that Ishi and I have decided to be your shadows," Takumi said. "We're not going to leave you alone till this is all over. The team will help too. Don't even try to disagree or Ishi will punch you," he said with a smirk.

"*Ouch!*" Takumi yelped as Ishi punched his arm.

When Aiko and Kenji turned away again to their thoughts, Takumi and Ishi exchanged a determined nod.

Neither imagined the cost they were about to pay to be shadows.

Chapter Sixteen

Catching Up

It was late Sunday night before they could all get together again at Coffee Shop. Aiko had spent the last half hour trying to explain what they had learned from Akira.

"Okay, wait," Koh cut in, wrinkling his forehead. "Go back to the part about the generational thingy."

"That's the beginning, numbskull!" Kai scolded.

"Okay, I didn't miss this." Ishi rolled her eyes. Michio stood up as if to make an announcement, interrupting their banter.

"Right, I'm hearing you guys. It sounds bad," he declared seriously. "But, quick subject change–we *won*!" He pumped his arm in the air. "And you missed a great tournament. I batted five hundred with two home runs, and I saw Mai in the crowd," he added, pointing to the little dancer sipping a hot chocolate.

"My parents *made* me go," she said, looking amused, "but it was good because I knew someone who was playing."

"Did you see the bat boy I told you about?" Ishi tilted her head playfully. Mai looked at her, smiling as though she had been caught doing something wrong, and blushed while the rest of the group teased, "Whoooaaa!" This stopped abruptly when Ishi shook a fist at everyone in defense of Mai. "Hey!" she said standing in front of Mai with crossed arms.

Aiko was glad for the distraction. She loved it when the whole team was together. They were, after all, just teenagers. She knew they trusted her and felt secure while she was around. "Congrats on your game, Michio." She started clapping, and everyone joined in the applause.

"Thank you, thank you, and if we are not kicking some serious demonic butt in two weeks, we're going to the finals!" Michio completed his celebration by pumping his fist in the air again. Everyone shared Michio's victory and offered congratulations.

"Okay, I'm going to say it because I don't think she will," Takumi began, making things serious again. "I think Aiko and Kenji are in danger. Here's why."

"Wait, is this the thingy that I missed?" Koh interrupted with his mouth full of popcorn.

"Yes, so listen this time," Ishi scolded.

The Warriors were briefed on all they had missed. Takumi spoke of Akira's failed battle, the generational curse colliding with the generational call, Kenji's background, and Aiko's family. Aiko and Kenji sat, watching their reactions. Finally, after an hour Takumi finished and everyone was somber.

"Okay, uh, let's go over the dying part again," Koh said, looking worried.

"Uh, yeah, just how does that happen when we're fighting spiritually?" Kai finished his question.

Pushing through her emotions, Aiko took a deep breath. "They can influence evil people to do evil things against us, like when Ryudan's henchman tried to hit me and Ishi stopped him. That was a physical attack caused by what was happening in the spiritual world."

"You mean he could have killed you?" Koh interjected.

Aiko nodded. Michio stood up. "Not while I'm here!"

The rest of the group all agreed.

"That's right."

"Never."

"Over my dead body."

"I'd die first."

Koh's eyebrows went up and he took a deep breath. "Wow, that's really heavy. Honestly, I think I'd probably be under the table."

"I'm *sure* you would," Kai confirmed. Before Koh and Kai started bickering again, Takumi returned to the main subject.

"It might appear in the paper as a random fire, burglary gone wrong, or drive-by shooting, but evil often does have a role," he explained.

Aiko, continued, determined to get them focused. "We always knew the stakes were really high, but up to this point, we've only been saving lives. Now, we have to lay *our* lives on the line, like my parents did." They were all quiet for a few moments.

"Could it change things, in a big way?" Michio asked.

"Yes, it might even begin to turn the tide of the battle here." She stood up and faced her friends. "You guys know what's been going on." She paused. "We hear about it every day. The suicides, the hopelessness, the spiritual poverty." Her voice grew more intense as she spoke. She looked into the air around them. "They've been in control for centuries and now there's a chance we can push back the darkness." They all let that sink in as they calculated the cost versus the possible victory.

"What about Kenji's part in all this?" Kai asked.

"We don't really know, except that what we did that night was a complete surprise to them and really upset their plans. They'll be coming hard again for him before this is over," Aiko answered.

"I think I might have to face my father," Kenji looked at his hand and turned it so he could see the 666 tattoo. He curled it to a fist. "to break the curse in my family line once and for all."

"What about you, Aiko?" Michio asked with concern in his voice.

She paused and looked up briefly. "I'm going after my brother, and anyone or anything that gets in my way will feel my sword. That's my battle, I don't expect any of you–"

Ishi shot up. "I'm going too. We're all going. Don't even think anything else, sister!" They all stood and took a small step toward Aiko and Kenji, except for Koh, who sat sulking.

"Guess the vacation is like, way over," Koh looked despondent.

Everyone looked hard at each other. They stood silently in a circle for several minutes. Aiko knew they were all praying.

It had been a long night and they all had to get ready for school the next day. Aiko decided to close things. "Okay, let's get home. Thank your parents again, Kai and Koh. Let's all get some rest, and stay close to Him, and to each other. God will let us know what comes next."

They didn't have to wait long.

Chapter Seventeen

Ambush

Everyone went home in small groups; Ishi and Takumi kept their promise to stay close to Kenji and Aiko.

"Thanks for walking with me. I feel like a little kid," Kenji said to Ishi and Mai, who stood looking up at the tall apartment building where Kenji stayed.

"You sure this is safe?" Ishi glanced up and down the street.

"Yeah, should be, it was cleaned out by the police recently," he said, remembering his old life. He had access to several apartments in town that were used for meetings, drug deals, prostitution, or a hideout, but this one had been vacant for a while because of a recent police raid. It was safe for now and it wasn't too far from Coffee Shop. After looking around, Ishi turned to Kenji.

She had a serious look on her face. "Okay, remember: Be careful! Use your sight everywhere you go and if you have to leave, just call and we'll come and go with you."

"Okay, Mom," Kenji said with a big smile on his face. Mai giggled. Ishi glared at him, but after a moment also broke into a smile and punched him. "*Ugh.* Guys are such dorks."

"All right, all right, I'll be careful." Kenji raised his hands, surrendering. He looked into her eyes sincerely. "I promise."

Her eyes softened a bit. She blushed and looked down for a moment and then back into Kenji's eyes. "Good." Mai watched, unable to stop smiling.

"Okay, let's go, Mai-chan." She hooked arms with her friend and turned to leave.

"Bye, Kenji. Remember, just call," Ishi said, waving with her free hand.

"Uh, thanks. See you, girls." He watched them go down the street arm in arm. He saw Mai teasing Ishi about something and Ishi taking her into a playful headlock. They looked back from a distance and then turned the corner toward the station.

Kenji fished some keys out of his pocket and went to his fifth-floor studio apartment. It had a large couch in the middle of the room, a coffee table, a television set in the corner, a small kitchen and tiny bathroom and shower. It had been cleaned but still had the aroma of a place that had seen many parties filled with smoke, alcohol, and drugs.

Kenji dropped his swordsman book on the coffee table and went to the refrigerator. *Something to drink?* It was empty.

He grunted in disappointment. The drink machines in the station had all been vandalized and weren't working. He looked out his window at the street below where there was a convenience store across the way. He started to move for the door and then stopped, catching himself. *Okay, think, Kenji.* He walked over to the window again and this time turned on his sight. *Okay, nothing. They must have meetings too, I guess.* Finally, he decided. *Okay, just a quick run.* He walked out of his door but suddenly remembered something and walked back in. He went over to the coffee table and picked up his sword manual. He recalled what Aiko had said during training. "Take it everywhere you go…learn it, think it, live it."

He stuffed it in his back pocket and walked out the door.

After paying for a drink and some snacks, he walked outside the store, immediately opened one of the drinks, and took a long gulp.

Suddenly, from around the corner, he heard a cry.

It sounded familiar. *Ishi! Mai!* He ran to the corner of the store and looked down the dark alley.

Kenji saw four men pawing a young girl. She was pushed up against the wall, screaming as she tried her best to escape.

"Calm down, gorgeous! You're a whore…this won't take long."

Kenji froze. He couldn't see who the girl was. *I could use a gun right now. Wait, no.* He looked around quickly but the streets were deserted. He ran back to the double doors of the convenience store, cracked it open, and yelled, "Call the police! A girl is being raped!" The store owner's eyes opened wide and he turned to pick up the phone. *Ishi, Mai…hold on,* he thought desperately. Kenji then switched on his sight and turned the corner in full armor with his sword out.

What Kenji saw horrified him. There was a Watcher in a violent struggle with three demons who were blocking his way to protect the girl. A small sense of relief filled him as he saw that it wasn't Ishi or Mai, but, she was familiar. Three other demons were chanting, "Rape, power, lust, rape, power, lust…" into the minds of the four hoodlums. As Kenji raced toward them at a full sprint, one young man turned and signaled the others. One of them punched the girl's face, and she crumpled to the ground. The demons charged him.

Okay, God...what I am doing? Kenji prayed silently. He skidded to a stop with his sword at the ready in battle stance. The demons surrounded him and unsheathed their weapons. Kenji noticed that the four men just stood and watched. *Why?*

"Hello, Kenji," growled a demon. "Long time no see."

"He thinks he's one of them," another one mocked.

"Do you thirst for new meat, Kenji, is that why you're following the new girl? Nice fresh..."

"*Silence*!" Kenji commanded in the Spirit. The demons' mouths locked closed and they were muzzled. Rage welled up in Kenji at their filth and evil.

A demon swung a sword at Kenji from the side. He blocked it with his shield and attacked. It took three swings before Kenji wounded him. He caught him off balance and drove his sword into his heart. The demon burst and disappeared.

The two remaining demons attacked with muffled growls of rage. Kenji blocked two swords simultaneously with his shield on one side and his sword on the other, then quickly spun, slashed a demon across the belly, and blocked a second attack from the other. As his second victim vanished in a stinking cloud of smoke, the third one backed up.

"Not bad for a beginner," sneered a mocking human voice, "but then you were always meant to be special."

As Kenji turned to follow his last opponent, who had moved in the direction of the voice, he saw that five more demons had joined the fight. They moved in to surround him.

Oh no...I can't.

"Kenji, we came to take you home," said the same voice, from the young man who Kenji could now see was more evil-looking than the others. Kenji gripped his sword. What had he gotten himself into?

"You know I'm gone. I've chosen! I just want the girl. The police are coming soon, and..."

The sinister young man started laughing. "Police...oh no!" he mimicked in mock despair. "Guess we should hurry." Then he hardened his tone. "Besides, our father is waiting."

Kenji froze and looked closely at him.

"Oh, and by the way, I have something for you." The hoodlum leader reached into his pocket and pulled out a thick lock of hair. It was a ponytail, and he threw it at Kenji's feet. "And, check out Masa's new headset," he said with scorn. Kenji looked over and saw a rugged-looking muscle-bound hoodlum in a tank top undershirt nodding his head to the beat of some unheard song being played into earphones; *Mai's earphones.*

It happened before Kenji could get control. *No. Ishi. Mai.*

"If you've done anything to hurt them," he screamed, "you're dead!" The five demons closed in and the rest was like a nightmare. Kenji was turning, blocking, slashing, feeling searing swords penetrate armor that seemed to be weakening. After a terrible struggle, he felt himself grabbed by human hands, and he saw the face of the man who had done all the talking. He felt the point of a needle penetrating into his arm and a searing liquid fill his veins.

"Time to go home, Brother."

The words echoed in his mind as he felt himself slipping deeper into the horrible, familiar nightmare, accompanied by demons. As he lost consciousness, he heard one final order.

"Makoto, get the whore. Let's go, Ryudan is not a patient man."

Through the blood covering her eyes, the battered young girl saw something lying on the ground next to her. She heard a scuffle and angry voices; her mind was numb from pain and her heart ragged from fear. She didn't know why, but her trembling hand took it. It felt like a small book and she hid it in her clothes. Rough hands lifted her up and a voice gruffly commanded her, "Okay, whore, let's go, you did your job."

No one noticed the item she had picked up, except the Watcher who now hovered over her.

Chapter Eighteen

Kentaro

It had happened so fast. Ishi and Mai were still talking about Kenji as they stood with the evening dinner and bar crowd, waiting for a train. They didn't notice the four men that slowly converged on them. When a packed express train stopped in front of them, they were lifted off their feet and forcibly shoved into the already crowded car.

"Hello, skanks. Just so you know, Kenji's dead tonight," a disdainful voice sneered at them from behind.

Ishi tried to react but there were so many people around, she couldn't risk an unaimed kick or punch. She struggled to see her attackers, but they held her in a vise-like grip.

"Let go of me!" she cried. A blunt instrument struck each girl, snapping their heads forward, ending their struggle as their knees buckled.

They were pushed in and they could feel their belongings being pulled from them. As the doors closed, Ishi's ponytail was pulled so that the sliding train doors closed on it. It was yanked hard and her head hit the doors. The horrified people in the car saw four hoodlums laughing and mocking through the window as the train started to pick up speed. The men ran alongside the train. People inside the train stepped back, unsure what to do.

Ishi's eyes closed with pain and she cried out. Mai was on her knees, barely conscious, looking up helplessly as her best friend screamed out in anguish, kicking her feet and grabbing the back of her head.

Suddenly, Ishi's head came loose from the door and she dropped to the floor with a thud. The other passengers gasped. Mai crawled over and tenderly placed her shaking hand on Ishi's shoulder.

"Ish...Are you all...oh...no," she said sadly.

Ishi looked at her and slowly reached back to touch where her ponytail should have been. Her hair had been chopped off unevenly and it was a frayed, bloody mess.

She was breathing hard in shock and terror. She closed her eyes and tried to get control. *Kenji's in trouble. Need to . . .*

Mai was terrified and whimpered, looking at Ishi's sliced hair.

Ishi was on all fours and closed her eyes again, fighting the searing pain in her head. She moaned in agony, trying to shake the disorientation. She grabbed for her phone but it was gone along with her backpack. She looked at the floor again and whispered, "Master, please..." Mai tried to stand up and wilted again. Ishi glanced up, grabbed a handrail and pulled hard. As she stood, the pain exploded again in her head.

"Mai..." She reached down and helped her get to her feet. Mai almost fell backward, but Ishi caught her, cradling her head with one hand and grabbing her arm with the other. She felt something wet and warm on her hand and pulled it away to see fresh blood. She glanced at the stunned crowd and pleaded with them. "Please...I need some help here! I really need a ph...a ph..." The world went black, as both girls slumped to the floor. The concerned crowd slowly converged to help them.

Thirty minutes later, on the station platform, Aiko was kneeling over Ishi, while Takumi looked on and Michio paced back and forth with clenched fists.

"Ish? Can you hear me?" she asked gently. "Ish?"

"I swear if they're hurt, I'm gonna..." Michio growled.

"Michio, please." Takumi held up a hand to calm his friend.

Mai started blinking her eyes. "Uh...uh...is Ish okay?" she said weakly as she tried to sit up. Michio stopped pacing and rushed over.

"Mai! Don't try to move. You'll be okay," Aiko comforted. Takumi knelt by her.

Ishi sat up like a bullet. "Kenji!" Pain shot from her head to her toes and she lay slowly back down with Aiko assisting her. "They're going to kill him...probably too late...What time is...?"

"Ish, just rest, it's only been thirty minutes."

"But how did you find...so fast?"

"They called us from your phone. They claimed you were dead."

Their thoughts were interrupted as a voice called from across the platform. "Okay, my parents are here, their car is waiting." It was Kai. Koh came running over.

"Those evil cowards!" he grumbled when he saw the girls.

Picking up on the intensity of the moment, Michio chimed in again. "I swear," he said in tears of rage, " Those guys are gonna pay for what they've done!"

Fighting back the tears in her own eyes, Aiko stood up decisively. "No, everyone stop. Now is not the time to react. Let's take care of our friends and hope that God will lead us to Kenji in time. Let's not ever be *like* our enemies. Turn your rage into prayer. We'll have our chance."

Koh and Kai picked up Ishi, placed an arm each around their necks, and walked her to their family car. Michio tenderly gathered up the little dancer, cradling her in his arms as he followed them. The police were talking with the parents, making arrangements to meet them at the hospital.

"Michio, go with them and watch out for them," Aiko said firmly, putting him on spiritual duty. She knew that would help channel his frustration.

"What about you two?" Michio asked. Takumi wanted to know that too and looked over at Aiko for the answer. She looked over the city, trying to make a decision.

"We need to find him." Aiko spoke in measured tones.

"But..." Michio started to say.

"The girls need you, stay close," she responded. He still looked at her as though he disapproved.

Aiko sighed and looked at Michio. "Don't worry, we'll just find him and then call you." She turned to the look at the city again. "If we can."

"I won't let her out of my sight," Takumi assured everyone evenly. Michio nodded to his partner and got into the car.

Aiko and Takumi watched as it sped off toward the hospital.

"What are we going to do?" Takumi asked her when they were alone. She looked over the city again and then at her friend.

"We're going to get Kenji back." Then she paused and shook her head. "I think I'm going to die soon, Tak, or sometime really soon," she said matter-of-factly.

She had never ever spoken like that before. Takumi fixed his glasses and swallowed hard. He touched her arm. Then he formed two simple words.

"Not alone."

Aiko looked over and their eyes met. She saw the intense loyalty in him. *You really would, wouldn't you, Tak?* she thought, with a sense of deep gratitude in her heart. *But I won't let you do that if I can help it.*

"So, where do we start?" Takumi said, looking toward the center of town.

"I think you know where they would take someone as important as Kenji," Aiko replied, inviting a guess.

"Ryudan." Takumi answered. "He has several clubs and drug houses we could check out."

"Kenji told us where most of them are." Aiko put her hands on his shoulders and faced him. "Are you sure you want…"

He nodded quickly. "Even if it's to hell itself. I'm not letting you out of my sight."

She took a deep breath and ran down the station steps with Takumi following close behind.

Chapter Nineteen

INSIDER

NOTHING. IT HAD BEEN TWO HOURS AND AIKO AND TAKUMI WERE FRUSTRATED. THEY walked into the emergency room waiting area and were eagerly greeted by the others. It was midnight now.

"Well?" Michio stood quickly and ran to meet them.

"First, how are they?" Aiko said, looking toward the emergency room patient area.

Kai answered. "So far so good. Just a nasty bump on the head and some stitches. They're doing some tests to make sure there are no fractures."

"It's taking forever." Koh slouched even deeper in an armchair.

"So, what about Kenji?" Michio said, looking alternately at Aiko and Takumi.

"Nothing. We looked everywhere that was logical, now we need a miracle." Takumi looked down and shook his head in defeat.

Aiko also shook her head in frustration. "Master, we need something. Anything."

At that moment, Takumi's phone rang. He looked at the number.

"It's Ishi's phone!" He shot an alarmed look at Aiko.

"Go ahead, Tak." She stepped close to him. Everyone gathered around him, trying to hear the conversation.

Takumi flipped the phone open and held it to his ear. "Hello?"

"Uh…mmm…is this Kenji's friend?" a young girl's voice asked nervously.

"Yes it is. who is this?"

"He…he…needs your help. I…"

"Okay, okay. can you tell me where he is?"

"I can't talk…wait," she whispered, her voice shaking. Takumi placed his hand over the phone quickly and looked at Aiko.

"Someone, a girl, is trying to help Kenji from the inside."

He put the phone to his ear again and everyone leaned in, straining to hear.

Takumi closed his eyes and pressed the phone tighter to his ear. He heard voices, music, and garbled sounds as though the phone was being pushed deep into a pocket.

He waited until he was sure she must have forgotten she was on the phone. "Hello? Hello? Are you there?"

"I can show you…wait." She stopped abruptly again.

He turned to the others. "She's going to show us–" He caught his breath. The others leaned forward in anticipation.

Takumi's eyes opened wide as he listened. There were angry voices and a series of slaps. He could hear a terrified girl pleading for her life as the beating continued and the voices grew angrier. "Oh no," he gasped and looked up sadly. "They caught her." The others gasped and looked down. Aiko slowly shook her head.

The phone went dead. "Hello?" Takumi looked at the phone and hung up.

"So much for the miracle." Koh threw his hands up.

"Poor girl. She took a huge risk to call us. Who is she?" Aiko asked.

Takumi, still stunned, replied, "She, uh, she didn't say."

"Maybe, she'll try again." Michio pointed to the phone in Takumi's hand.

"If she's alive. Isn't anyone else worried about how serious this is getting?" Koh looked from face to face. Everyone ignored him.

Aiko reached up and ran her hand through her hair in frustration. "Okay. Master, we need a target…come on!" She hit her fist against her thigh.

"Coffee shop," Takumi declared. "They know that's our hangout. That's where she'd go if she could get to us."

"That's a long shot." Michio crossed his arms and nodded. "But better than nothing."

"Or how about an ambush? Isn't that what tonight is all about?" Koh pointed toward the hallway where Ishi and Mai were being treated. Everyone sighed in silent agreement.

Aiko looked at everybody, seeing the concern in their faces. She took a deep breath of resignation. "Then you'd better pray for us."

Aiko looked at Takumi and nodded.

"Takumi and I will go and wait. Please keep us up-to-date on things here."

"I'll go open up," Kai volunteered. "You'll need coffee anyway, and if there's trouble, you could use another sword."

Chapter Twenty

WHORE

TIME HAD SLOWED DOWN. TAKUMI'S ADRENALINE HAD LONG SINCE SUBSIDED AND HIS energy level had dropped like a rock. His head was on a table, his glasses were tilted on his face, and he was drifting in and out of sleep. His eyelids felt so heavy that they kept drooping closed. He forced his eyes open again, but didn't have the energy to lift his head from the table. It was 1:30 A.M. Kai was sleeping on the couch in the back.

He saw Aiko standing at the window like a beautiful statue, watching and praying. Her eyes were still burning with intensity, her long slender form stood ready, ever vigilant. Her eyes scanned the darkness and responded to each movement. He blinked and put on his sight for a moment. He loved seeing Aiko in armor. She looked like a warrior princess, but one that was battle tested and fearless. What appeared as a cross work design on her breastplate were actually dents and scratches from the many fights that she had been in. Her razor-sharp sword was glowing in her hand. When a group of demons saw her coming after them, they knew they were in for a fight and would probably lose. Takumi managed a tired smile at the thought.

Aiko felt him watching her and looked over. He blinked a question to her.

You need me up right now?

In her eyes, he saw the concern of a big sister, the love of a friend, and the care of a leader. She gave a short wave and shook her head. *No, you're fine. Rest, Takumi…take your rest.* Takumi slept…for two minutes.

"Takumi!" Aiko said sharply.

He bolted upright, knocking over the table. "What is it?" he gasped, fixing his glasses.

"I'm not sure…a taxi just stopped outside." She motioned him to look. He watched closely. The taxi light was on and the driver was waiting for a young woman's fare as she opened her purse.

Junko furiously searched through her bag, crying. She was still wondering at how incredible her escape had been. They had left her lightly guarded, assuming she was near death from her beating. She had opened her swollen eyes just in time to see her guard pass out, probably from bad drugs. That had allowed her to stagger out of a side door and stumble to the main street. Miraculously, a taxi had appeared. She wiped her face again with an already blood-soaked handkerchief and tried to clean some more blood off the plastic-covered car seat. "Sorry…I'm sorry…I don't know where…" She turned her handkerchief over again and again, looking for a spot that wasn't already red.

"Here try this," a caring, intelligent voice said. A hand reached in and gave her a fresh, clean handkerchief. She hesitated for a moment and then reached out and took the cloth and glanced up to see a young man with glasses paying the cab driver.

"Is this enough?" he asked.

"That's fine, son. Better watch out for this one, she's been roughed up a bit," the cab driver offered. The young man opened her door and gently helped her out. She was confused. She hadn't felt gentle loving hands like this…ever.

Of course that will change soon, she thought. *When they find out who…and what I am.* Then she heard the voices.

"*Whore…filthy little sex toy…you're trash…how many men–*"

The young man got a distant look in his eyes for a second.

Junko blinked, uncertain what was happening. The voices had stopped suddenly. A whiff of something rotten blew past on the breeze.

Footsteps approached, and two kind-looking strangers peered at her. The young man took a step toward her, and she instinctively stepped back. She pulled her clothes around her and only then realized how bad she looked. Her clothes were torn and were stained with blood. Glancing down, she could see that her arms and legs were bruised and she had no shoes. She attempted to fix her hair and found it matted with dried blood. She felt large swollen bumps around her eyes and could taste fresh blood seeping from the corner of her mouth. She looked back down, shame crawling through her heart.

"I'm Takumi," the man said, "and this is Aiko. I believe you called me tonight." He slowly extended a hand toward her. Junko blinked the tears out of her eyes and wiped her face again. She tried again to adjust her clothes and short skirt, pulling it down a bit. She felt like dirt and trash in front of these two. *What am I doing here? I don't belong here!*

"Please come in, and let us help you. You can tell us what you wanted to say when you called." Aiko also extended an open hand toward her.

Junko forced a wry smile and without looking at them directly, stammered, "I can't go in there, unless you serve whores." She suddenly felt two hands grab her shoulders. They were firm, but at the same time gentle. They turned her to face Takumi, who moved close and looked into her eyes. "Please, never say that again…ever." It didn't sound as though he meant it to be a scolding, and it didn't feel like one. She sensed he meant to correct and dispel a lie that she had accepted. She glanced nervously into the eyes behind the glasses and she saw sincerity, and something else, but she couldn't find the words to describe it.

"Uh…" She reached in her purse, pulled out a book, and without looking up, held it out toward Takumi. "He needs you. I wrote directions." She had thought that she might just leave the book, expecting to find revulsion and condemnation from these "good" people that she had heard so much about from her old associations. Takumi took the book. She tried to turn and go.

"Wait! What's your name?" he asked, putting his hand on her shoulder to stop her.

She waved her hand and looked away. "Believe me, you don't want–"

"Please," he said in a gentle tone, still resting his hand on her.

"I'm…I'm…Junko," she replied, almost ashamed to have a name after the way she had lived. She still couldn't look up.

"Come on, Junko, let's get you cleaned up." She paused and felt the warmth of Takumi's hand on her shoulder. She glanced at Aiko's face and saw kindness. *Where else would I go?* She slowly turned in resignation. Aiko came and took her from Takumi's grasp and walked her into Coffee Shop.

Thirty minutes later, she was sitting at a table in an oversized bathrobe with Aiko kneeling in front of her, tending her wounds. She held an ice pack to her head and face that a surprised Kai had produced when Aiko woke him up to make introductions. Takumi came over with a tray. For the first time, Junko lifted her eyes to get a good look at her helpers.

"Okay, this is special tea," Takumi said, smiling at her as he set the tray on the table. "It will help you heal, and it's rather good." He then sat and took her hand, examining some cuts. She pulled back tentatively, but something about how he looked at her made her trust him. She slowly extended her hand.

Takumi turned her hands over in his.

"Let's see what we have here." Trying to put her at ease, he smiled at her again. "Don't worry, I got an A in First Aid class," he said, pushing his glasses up. "Actually, an A in every class, but, uh, you don't need to know that, do you?"

She managed a grin. "Thank you."

Takumi and Aiko tenderly bound her wounds. They both tried hard not to react to the savagery that she had been through. They held back their emotions calmly as they worked with her. There were mostly cuts and scrapes from being thrown to the ground, some welts from a belt or something similar, and contusions from punches around her face. One ear was bleeding, the lobe torn where an earring had been ripped from her flesh. Her arms and legs were covered with bruises, and there were strangulation marks around her neck.

Takumi felt his stomach churning and caught his breath. Aiko put her hand on his shoulder and squeezed a "*Please, hold it in*" to him. The rage and anger threatened to fill his eyes with tears, but he saw Junko glance at him and he forced a smile. He was sure she didn't know just how bad she looked. "Let me know if I'm hurting you," he said tenderly. *I'll never let anyone treat you like this again!*

For Junko it was just too much. She was being loved and tended to in a way that made no sense at all. Her body was being treated with respect and care…by two strangers who seemed more like family. She actually felt safe. It couldn't last. Tears started rolling down her cheeks and soon she was crying uncontrollably; the night, the beating, the rape all caved in on her. She felt arms surrounding her and something else, something was happening on the inside that she couldn't explain. An invisible shield was blocking fear, revulsion, and anger.

Aiko was on her knees, eyes closed, and one hand extended. Kai, behind the counter, paused from cooking breakfast and joined her, bowing his head.

"Master, please, the healing for this precious girl needs to go deep. Tonight, they took everything they could from her, yet You preserved her to do Your will. Won't You please do a miracle in her heart tonight? Protect her from evil and what evil has done to her. Let her know that nothing can steal the preciousness that You made her with." She petitioned silently for half an hour on Junko's behalf while Kai finished a good breakfast for them all.

When Aiko opened her eyes, she saw a surprised look on Takumi's face. Junko had fallen asleep in his arms, like a little child hiding in her father's embrace. Takumi looked over at Aiko, wondering what to do.

"Just hold her, Tak. Let her know she's not trash," Aiko said gently.

"But Kenji?" he whispered.

"Yeah, aren't we in a hurry?" Kai asked, placing plates in front of everyone.

"He'll let us know. For now, let's take care of her. She'll help us in good time." There was the noise of a car outside. They all looked up as car doors opened and closed. The front door burst open and everyone walked in.

"We thought you'd like to see for yourself…huh?" Michio stopped abruptly when he saw Takumi cradling a young woman.

Ishi and Mai came in the door and Aiko ran up and hugged them both. "Wow, I'm glad you're okay, I'm so sorry."

"Uh, Aiko?" Ishi peeked over her shoulder. Both she and Mai opened their eyes wide at that sight of a young bandaged girl in a bathrobe–fast asleep and gently cradled in the arms of the math team's captain.

Koh arrived immediately afterward and ceremoniously greeted everyone. "Hey, everybody…whoooaaa, is there a half-naked girl on Roboto's lap, uh, wearing my bathrobe?" At that moment, Junko stirred and lifted her head from Takumi's chest and opened her eyes. She instinctively pushed closer to Takumi. Everyone stared, waiting for an explanation. Aiko nodded at Takumi.

"Uh, right. Everybody, this is Junko," he said nodding toward her as naturally as he could. The bathrobe slipped off a shoulder as she straightened up and Takumi awkwardly started, stopped, and then adjusted it for her, glancing at the others and clearing his throat. She pulled it around herself and looked at them. There was an awkward silence.

"She's the incredibly brave girl who risked her life to help Kenji," Aiko added with admiration. Everyone nodded and acknowledged her with smiles.

"Naked…lap…" Koh said.

"She's not naked!" Ishi said, scolding him.

"She's about your size, Ish," Aiko suggested, ignoring Koh.

"I have some spare clothes in my soccer bag, if she doesn't mind sweats. Ummm…Kenji?" Everyone looked at Aiko for the answer. Aiko turned to Junko.

"I…I can show you where he is," Junko said, looking a little scared. Aiko smiled. *Brave girl*, she thought.

"First we rest, but we can't wait too long. This is going to be costly," Aiko said grimly, feeling the weight of leadership.

Ishi stepped up, her head swathed in bandages. "But, we have some time now. That's why we rushed here. Did you hear the news?"

Aiko and Takumi looked at each other and then at her closely.

Michio laughed. "We tried to get her home, I promise. But she said this was important."

Koh trotted over to the counter, grabbed a remote, and switched on the TV. A late-breaking story was being replayed again and again. They all watched for a few minutes. A well-dressed man was shown being arrested by the police in front of a five-star hotel.

"That's Ryudan!" Takumi exclaimed. "What happened?"

"Got picked up tonight in connection with a murder," Michio said, nodding his head.

"What time?" Aiko and Takumi asked simultaneously.

"That's the good part," Ishi said. "After they hit us, we assume they went right for Kenji. That had to be about ten thirty. Well, according to that story, Ryudan was arrested at ten thirty five!"

"So, when they called him to report that they had Kenji..." Takumi tilted his head.

"He was already on his way to jail with no phone or ability to give orders," added Michio triumphantly.

Aiko and Takumi breathed a sigh of relief. They had some time. *Heaven and hell colliding*, thought Aiko.

"Now that's what I like to hear," Koh declared, clapping his hands, uncharacteristically positive. Then he paused and changed his tone. "But you know his lawyers will get him out in a few days, a week at the most."

"They won't do anything with Kenji till Ryudan is there. They can't, he's too important," Ishi countered.

"So, we have time to find him, and we also have a chance to recover a bit," Aiko said, still watching the TV report. Everyone nodded.

Junko had watched the whole thing curiously, thinking, *There's something*...right *here, but what?* She'd never seen or felt anything like it.

Aiko looked over at Takumi and Junko. "Thanks, Junko. You have no idea what you mean to us," she said with heartfelt earnestness. Everyone gazed at the lost sheep who had been spit out of the evil world.

Kai walked in with more plates of food, and the energy level in the room went up. Freed from the urgency of the night, Junko's new family gathered around her.

"Michio! Don't even think of hugging her, you'll break her," someone yelled.

"Uh, right." He took her scratched and bruised hand in his large strong one and shook hers gently. He looked over with playful eyes at Takumi, whose arm was still around her.

"Hey, don't mess with Tak's girl." Koh called from the side.

"*Koh!*" four voices shouted simultaneously.

"Okay, okay...That's my robe..."

Ishi came next. "Okay, Tak, Mai and I will take over. Come on, Junko, let's get you out of that awful robe!"

Mai managed a weak smile but couldn't hide her reaction as she started taking a visual inventory of Junko's wounds. Ishi was focused on handling Junko gently and missed the look that passed over Mai's face. Her hands were shaking as she reached to take Junko's arm. She had been forcibly robbed and then had watched her best friend and hero tortured and humiliated; now it was this poor creature. Ishi cued her to help Junko up.

"Oh, sorry, okay," Mai said, and tried to look away then realized she would have to settle some issues later. She would never be the same again.

Takumi moved over and both girls came alongside Junko and helped her to her feet. She couldn't fail to see the fresh bandages and Band-Aids on both girls. She looked at them with some surprise and silent questions.

Ishi noticed her observation and answered, "Yeah, rough night, huh?"

Ishi and Mai walked Junko to the bathroom, and Takumi was relieved of his new friend for the time being. He took a deep breath and stood up, fixing his glasses while stretching his legs, having sat immobilized for a while now. The room was strangely quiet. He could feel the sidelong glances he was getting.

"What?" Takumi said.

Michio put his hands in the air innocently. Koh started laughing and Kai and Michio just had to join him. "Roboto, you had to see the look on your face," Koh started. The boys had a good laugh. Aiko held an amused expression, and then had a thought.

"Tak, you talk to her okay?" she said, inviting him to share the truth with Junko. "I think she'll listen to you."

"Right, but are you sure she'll want a guy?" Just then Ishi and Mai walked in with Junko. Everyone nodded approval at the new clothes, but Junko, like an insecure puppy looking for her master, searched the room to find Takumi and then made her way to his side, almost hiding behind him. She glanced up at him to make sure it was okay, and then down at the ground again.

Aiko didn't have to say anything else to him. She just grinned, raised her eyebrows and quickly spoke before anyone else could react to Junko's innocent loyalty. "Let's eat!"

They all sat down, and Junko the "whore" had the best breakfast she had ever had, surrounded by new friends. By noon that day, thanks to Takumi, not only were her wounds healing nicely, but her heart and soul were completely and miraculously healed when she chose sides and invited the Master into her life.

Demons for generations would pay dearly for that day.

Chapter Twenty-one

TRAITORS

"PLEASE DON'T COME, AIKO.

Ishi, what's happened to you?

Little Mai, what did they do?"

Kenji's tortured mind was filled with thoughts of fear for Aiko and the others. For all he knew, Ishi and Mai had been killed; he felt sick to his stomach with worry. The drugs forced into his body had turned his thoughts into nightmares. In his drugged semi-coma he could switch on his sight from time to time and look at his spiritual surroundings. From the first moment he wasn't sure whether this was all a horrible hallucination, reality, or some convoluted combination of both.

The moment his sight went on he saw wall-to-wall demons, like a pit filled with writhing snakes slithering over and under each other, never quite sure where one began and one ended. The room was jam-packed with the presence of evil. He also heard their voices.

"No power here... your kind has no power here!"

"Hate... hate... hate... hate you, Kenji!"

"Welcome home, Kenji, you little maggot!"

"You can't win... never win... you're too weak!"

"We're waiting for them... let your friends come and die... but first we'll have some fun!"

Demon laughter reverberated through his ears, mocking him, and evil voices spewing lies and torment tortured him relentlessly; in this environment evil was not even thinly veiled; it thrived.

He pulled back his sight and tried to clear his head. He lay slouched on a deep couch in a crowded room. It seemed to him that he was in a drug house or club. There was loud thumping music and the sound of voices talking, men's laughter, and glasses clinking. Cigar and cigarette smoke filled the air, but couldn't hide the evil ancient smell he had come to know. Its stench was overpowering. He felt dizzy as though he was floating. He saw a blurry figure sitting next to him, and strained to focus his eyes as the profile began to sharpen.

Huh? No, it can't be! Is that Aiko? Did they…? His thoughts became conflicted and confused.

"G-go…g-get away…we have no power here…run!" he mumbled, waving his arms. He heard mocking laughter from somewhere close. The Aiko figure next to him turned to face him. It wasn't Aiko at all. It was a young man who just watched him while another voice went on scorning him in a tone that made him shudder.

Kenji heard someone else ask impatiently, "Is it time yet?"

"No," the 'Aiko' man answered tersely. "Another thirty minutes or so. We don't want to kill him before Ryudan gets here." His voice was emotionless and empty.

"Right," came the reply, fading into the distance.

"Uhhhhnn…where…where am I?" Kenji managed to mumble feebly, and then everything went blurry again, a swirling world of evil and hatred. "Ai…Aiko…don't come here…" he moaned, while the relentless, demonic voices continued with their torrent of taunting accusations and whispers.

"See that, Makoto? He's your sister's new man, she is a prostitute after all," a sarcastic human voice scoffed. Several voices laughed in an evil chorus.

"I don't have a sister," an emotionless voice said.

"Whatever!" came a cutting response.

The name caused a moment of clarity and realization for Kenji. *Makoto?* He was here. Aiko's brother was still alive. He struggled to speak.

"Ma…Ma…Makoto…you have to get out." Snickers and more laughter filled the air. "The…they have to kill you…they'll kill you…all of you…" Kenji forced out as he put on his sight again and looked in the direction where Makoto was sitting. What he saw horrified him. Demons were scary to look at because of their monstrous features, but Makoto's ugliness was worse.

You could still see the remains of a Spiritual Warrior…but he was warped and covered with deformities. His head was lopsided by a spiritual growth the size of a softball that glowed beneath his skin. It seemed to be attached to his brain, pulsating, with tendrils extending out like cancerous fingers reaching into almost every area of his body. The effect on his face was horrible. Each orifice had tiny black veins covering and controlling them. His mouth, ears, nose, and eyes were matted with living evil.

Another growth about the same size bulged from his chest. It was attached to his heart. In the same way, it was covered with pulsing veins that extended from his chest to other areas of his body. The tendrils were so thick and taut that his arms were pulled in close to his body and his hands were half clenched with his fingers curled inward.

Yet, behind this horrible creature, Kenji could see a resemblance. Makoto had Aiko's eyes. He could see that they were sad and managed to peer through the prison of evil that surrounded him now. Kenji couldn't take the horror of it any more. He pulled back his sight, looked up at Makoto and whispered again. "They'll kill you…"

Makoto leaned forward and his eyes flared with anger. "My choice!" he hissed.

"But, you already chose sides. After all He did for you…"

"Don't you preach to me, you naive idiot! You have no idea. No idea. No right!" he spit back.

But Kenji caught something in Makoto's eyes that he wasn't supposed to see…regret.

"What did they promise you?" Kenji said, his head now clearing from the drugs. He saw Makoto looking away and then back at him, still very agitated. "I'm out. I get an out, life away from the war. I get to live a life taking care of *me*," he spoke with intensity.

"I know these people and they're lying to you. Makoto," Kenji said sincerely. "They're using you to get to your sister, and when they get her they'll finish off your family."

"No, I get to leave. When this is all done, I get a life. You, on the other hand…"

"You're willing to sacrifice the life of your sister for that?" Kenji challenged.

"Her choice," he hissed. "She can walk away too."

Kenji reached up quickly, grabbing Makoto and pulled him down so that they were eye to eye. "She won't, and you know it. She'll come here, and she'll fight because she loves you–more than you will ever know."

The words hit Makoto like a hard slap in the face and he wavered. It was as if something deep inside, a tiny fragment of a memory, caused him to take a moral pause. He blinked his eyes and they darted from side to side as he struggled. Finally, his face hardened and he tore Kenji's hands away and pushed him back on the couch. "She's dead to me."

Another voice cut in. "Well, well, well, how touching, and how–what's the word?–ironic. It's our two back-stabbing traitors." More laughter erupted in the room.

"Makoto, the great spiritual warrior, now turned smart, and Kenji, son of Ryudan himself, spitting in the face of all that he knows; going over to the other side and turning complete idiot. Tch, tch, tch, you have no idea of how much that hurts us, Kenji."

More evil laughter reverberated, filling the room. Kenji turned to see the young gang leader who had apprehended him. Makoto backed off as he approached.

"Oh my, I've been terribly rude, men. I haven't properly introduced myself. I'm..."

"Kentaro," Kenji said, glaring at him.

Kentaro, Kenji's half brother, jumped on Kenji and grabbed his shirt. He screamed a series of obscenities so foul that even the men around him cringed.

"Don't you ever, ever interrupt me again or I'll rip your lungs out! Do you hear me?" He breathed heavily, inches from Kenji's face. Kenji looked at him spiritually and saw that he was not yet possessed. *The curse hasn't been passed on yet.* Relief flooded him. *Master, I need Your help right now.*

"The girls who were with me–" Before Kenji could finish, Kentaro struck him hard in the Adam's apple. Kenji grabbed his throat, coughing and trying to breath.

Kentaro's phone rang. His tantrum was disarmed and his anger turned to controlled contempt. "Worried, are we?" he smiled and fished out his phone from his pocket. "You'll all die soon anyway." He sneered and backed off to answer his phone while watching Kenji still trying to breath. "How long? Two weeks! How did that happen? Then fire the morons! Yes, the lawyers!" He jabbed his free hand in the air. "Then waste the witness and make him worm food!" He paused, listening a moment. "Yes...I said yes; but I think we're wasting our time. Yeah..." He looked over at Kenji. "It's real. But hey...if Makoto can turn...yeah." He paused, listening closely and frowning." Okay, we'll wait." He hung up and huffed in disappointment.

Kenji whispered under his breath, trying to speak.

"What's that? You have to speak up." Kentaro casually put his phone away. "Or are you too scared to talk?"

Kenji looked down at the floor and spoke softly again. Kentaro grabbed his long hair and jerked his head. "I said speak up!"

Kenji bored a hole in his half brother with his eyes. "I said...you're nothing." The whole room caught its breath. Kentaro's face was filled with rage as he reached back and pulled out a gun and put it on Kenji's temple. "You call a bullet nothing!" he yelled.

"Go ahead, Brother." Kenji looked directly at him. He paused with Kentaro shaking in anger. "You can't because you are nothing," Kenji said calmly. "I know how it works. You exist to serve Ryudan. You're a slave, nothing more."

Kentaro reared back and slapped Kenji hard with the butt of the gun. The force of the blow sent him reeling back on the couch. He could taste blood oozing from the corner of his mouth. He heard the hammer of the gun being cocked and felt the cold metal pressing against the center of his forehead.

"No, Kenji, I'm something that you are not: *loyal.* I'm loyal to a legacy, to our family. You are nothing but a selfish piece of filth and a traitor. But, thanks to you, that legacy falls to me. You might think I'm nothing, but soon, very soon, I'll have more power at my fingertips than you can imagine, and you–you and your girlfriends will be dead." He pushed Kenji's head back hard with the muzzle of the gun and stormed off, shouting.

Terrible pain was shooting through Kenji's head and it blurred the world again momentarily. As he listened to Kentaro ranting, the only thought he kept repeating to himself was, *Thank God, they're alive!* His eyes cleared and found them fixed on Makoto, who was now moving toward him with a needle in his hand. Rough hands immobilized Kenji while he was being drugged again. He looked over to Makoto, who met his gaze impassively waiting for the drugs to take effect.

"She'll come for you…Aiko's coming…don't let them…" Darkness and nightmares slowly enveloped him as he slipped again into a suffocating, restless sleep.

Chapter Twenty-two

Dark Angel

"Okay, now, you don't have to do this if you're not ready," Aiko said with concern, peering from beneath her sunglasses.

"No, I'm fine. Really," Junko said, trying to assure Aiko and the others. They adjusted their clothes one more time and got ready to turn the corner.

They were sure they had at least two weeks to go after Kenji, but had decided that sooner was better than later. Today, they were going to pinpoint the location in the late afternoon and planned to return to get Kenji back in the wee hours, when even drug dealers would be sleeping.

They had gone to a secondhand clothing store to buy clothes that would disguise them to the casual observer. The girls wore baggy pants, T-shirts, jackets, and some form of hat. Ishi had been to a hairdresser to give her a new short-hair look and now sported a beanie. Aiko and Junko went for baseball caps worn backward. Mai looked different, though. She had been unusually attentive to her disguise and had chosen a dark alternative-rock look. Everything was black, including a lacy short skirt she wore over her fitted pants. Instead of a hat she tinted her hair with red and green streaks. She was still the adorable, shy Mai, but there was something bolder about her. Ishi wore stylish black-framed glasses. Aiko and Junko wore sunglasses to cover their eyes, but Mai painted her eyes with a deep dark shadow and dark lines.

Junko looked over her shoulder at the convenience store where Takumi, Michio, Koh, and Kai would be watching from. Kai was on a pay phone just outside the store, faking a phone call, and Koh was next to him with a bag of chips and a soda, eating away. Takumi and Michio were inside the store in front of the magazine rack because the window had a full-length view of the street where the girls would be walking. Takumi was making Michio turn his magazine right side up. He saw Junko looking, and winked. She smiled, and turned back to the girls.

Aiko reviewed the plan one more time. "Okay everyone, remember. We walk up the street talking, Junko talks us through how to get in. We get a good look, count guards, any side doors we see, and lookouts, and we're out, down and back in five minutes. Don't look at anyone directly; they may recognize us since they've hunted some of us already." Ishi looked over at Mai, who just looked down, avoiding her gaze.

"And Junko." Aiko put a hand on her shoulder.

"I know, but don't worry." She looked at herself." I used to show a lot more flesh, they won't recognize me. I doubt if they looked at my face much." All the girls grunted in agreement.

"Okay, then," Aiko said with determination. "For His Honor." The girls replied in unison, "For His Honor." Aiko led them around the corner.

This area of town was dirty. It had small shops that were all controlled by Ryudan. There were liquor stores, pawnshops, an accounting office, a key stall, a launderette, and dubious-looking clubs, all scattered randomly throughout the area. The girls walked at a leisurely pace and talked as naturally as they could until Aiko gave the signal.

"Let's take a look." They were approaching their target. It was one of the most popular men's entertainment clubs in the city. On the surface it offered three stories of exotic dancers, billiards, karaoke, and cheap drinks. But on the inside, behind closed doors, were prostitution, drugs, illegal gambling, and other gang-related business done in Ryudan's personal office.

The moment their Truesight went on, they all gasped and broke their first rule. They stopped in their tracks. Junko took a few more steps, then turned back wondering why they had stopped. She didn't have the sight gift activated yet. Although only two burly guards in business suits sat outside the front doors, the spiritual view was different. There were demons surrounding every square inch of the building. It appeared to be a way station, a hub of demonic activity. Even the roof was covered with demons peering around or talking with one another. A captain would appear, give orders, and four or five demons would take off together. Then, a group of between seven and ten would arrive on black wings and disappear into the building.

"Uh, this must be the place," Ishi said, catching her breath.

"Pssst, let's go." Junko waved her hands at them and glanced at the outside guards. Aiko shook off a sense of foreboding and grabbed Ishi, and they started to move again. Mai followed slowly, staring at the building.

"I think they have everybody inside," Junko commented in a quiet tone. Her voice was shaking a bit. "They usually lounge outside in the afternoon so you could count them." They continued past. "Okay, you see the club has only three public floors, but there are actually five floors. There's an elevator in the corner closest to us right now, just inside the door and then right, but you have to pass a guard who will check you for weapons. It goes to all the floors."

"What's on the fourth floor?" Aiko asked.

"Mostly rooms, some for gambling and some for…for…" she said, struggling.

"Okay, Junko, I understand. That's okay." Aiko stopped her from continuing.

"But there's one party room big enough for forty or fifty people. It's where the rich junkies get their drugs. It's on the far corner of the building, because that's where the fire escape is in case of a raid. They'll pick pretty girls off the dance floor and invite them to be eye candy for the wealthy drug addicts in exchange for a free hit. It's called the Candy Shop. That's where Kenji should be," Junko explained.

Aiko stooped, pretending to tie her shoe, and took a good look. "I wish we could see in that door. How many are there today? I wonder if Kenji is really there." She shook her head. *God forbid we pay a huge cost for nothing,*

"I just wish we could be sure. If Kenji isn't there…" Ishi stared at the front door.

"I'm sorry, I'd go in, but the men who…" Junko's voice cracked.

Aiko stood. "No, I'd never ask you to do that. Is there any other way we can be sure?"

"With all the spiritual activity, this must be the place." Ishi walked next to Aiko.

"Okay, keep moving, we've stopped for too long already," Aiko ordered.

The girls kept moving, but Ishi turned back. She didn't see Mai. "Mai?" she called gently. That caused the other girls to turn around to look for her.

The next moment, they all froze.

They saw the slender, black-clad form of a young girl crossing the street and heading straight for the guards in front of the door. Ishi started to bolt after her.

"Wait!" Aiko pulled them into the cluttered pawnshop they were next to. "Watch her from here, Ish." Aiko went straight down on her knees, raised her hands, and started praying with her eyes fixed on Mai.

Junko, not knowing what to do, waved at the shop owner who'd watched them come in, and tried to stay calm. "Just browsing."

Ishi paced in short steps, eyes riveted on Mai, opening and closing her fists. "What are you doing? What are you doing?"

Takumi and Michio had dropped their magazines and had their faces pressed against the glass, eyes wide open. Kai slowly hung up the phone and scolded Koh, who was fiddling with another snack bag, and pointed past him toward Mai. Koh looked and dropped the bag.

Mai sauntered up to the guards and said something to the obvious leader. He looked her over carefully, broke into lewd grin, and made some remark to her. Then Mai gave him the finger while the other guard broke out laughing and slapped the burly chest of the one who had insulted her. Finally, the head guard nodded agreeably. Mai threw her arms around him, kissed his cheek, and disappeared through the door.

The mouth of every Warrior hung open, except for Junko, who commented, "Wow, nice move. How old is she?"

"Fourteen."

"That's why. They love the young ones," Junko replied, shaking her head.

They all held their breath, interspersed with desperate prayers.

Inside, Mai did everything she could to control her nerves. Even though she maintained a calm pace and glided from room to room, her mind was racing a million miles an hour. *"Breathe…breathe…"*

Okay…God, how do I count these? Master, please help. Okay, at least twelve workers…and spiritually…let's see…looks like maybe fifty on this floor…mostly Grunts…wait…captains over there…Overlord…okay,…second floor…"

"Hey, sweetie, starting early tonight?" a voice called out. Mai flashed a sweet smile and kept walking. She kept her armor off, knowing it would tip off the demons. People were too busy drinking and flirting to notice the dark angel moving through their midst.

♦ ♦ ♦

"Should I go in?" Michio asked impatiently.

"No, wait for Aiko to signal. That's the plan," Takumi said.

"Plan! What plan? It went into the trash the moment Mai walked in that place," Michio complained. They glanced at Kai and Koh, who were watching. Koh looked at them and ran his hand across his neck. Takumi scolded him with a look. Michio rushed out the door.

♦ ♦ ♦

"Please, let me go!" Ishi pleaded, looking to Aiko for permission.

"Just wait a minute, she got in, Ish. Let's give her a chance," Aiko suggested with a slight tremor in her voice. "Just keep praying."

At that point, four men appeared around the corner and burst into the pawnshop. The girls all turned to see Takumi, Kai, and Koh trailing after Michio, who was pounding one fist in a cupped hand. Aiko faced them quickly before they could speak and said very directly, "Calm down and start shopping or we are all dead." She had that insistent look on her face. That stopped Michio for the moment. The others followed orders by awkwardly looking at the shelves for something interesting to focus on.

"Spread out, for crying out loud," Ishi added.

Michio faced the shelves but kept an eye out of the window at the club. Takumi stayed near him to keep him calm and tackle him if he bolted.

"Do they sell food here? Hey, I had a MP3 player like this before…wait, this *is* mine!" Koh said.

Ishi got in his face. "Do you know what inconspicuous means?" she whispered sharply. When she saw the blank look on his face she added, "Blend in or I'll kick you."

Koh forced a smile and raised his eyebrows. "I love shopping," he murmured weakly, and then turned back to the MP3 player he was holding.

Just then Aiko's phone rang. She pulled it out and took a quick look at the number calling. "Oh no…please no."

"What?" Ishi walked over to Aiko who stood now.

"Who is it?" they said in unison, gathering around her.

Aiko took a deep breath. "It's Ishi's phone again."

"Ishi is right here, so why would she call us?" Koh asked seriously.

Kai turned pale and started to shake his head. "They have Ishi's phone and now they have Mai." They all turned to look at the club where Mai had been captured.

"It's a text," Aiko said, slowly opening her phone.

"I'm out of here, I'm going alone if I have to!" Michio plowed toward the door, dragging Takumi and Ishi as they held on to him.

"*Wait!*" Aiko let out a short laugh of disbelief. "Ha! You go, girl!" She turned the face of the phone around.

> I'm ok. Saw kenji. Got our stuff. On my way out. Spooky. Saw a goon i think. Tell ishi not to kill me. Mai

After a collective "Huh?" everyone released a deep sigh of relief. They looked over at the building, imagining the pure-hearted tiny dancer alone in the midst of hell on earth. Michio just stood staring at the front door of the club, struggling with his emotions and slowly clenching and unclenching his fists.

"Okay, she's not out yet. Keep praying and let's disperse. Girls, let's head back around the corner. Michio and the boys, you guys stay and escort our little sister when she comes out. If anything happens, you have my permission to...uh...subdue anyone who tries to hurt her." Michio looked over with a satisfied expression on his face and nodded.

Junko, Ishi, and Aiko calmly walked back down the street and returned to their starting point, out of sight around the corner.

"I think something happened to Mai after the train attack," Ishi reflected with concern.

"I think you're right, Ish. She loves you so much. It had to affect her, watching what they did to you."

"She's not a little girl anymore," Ishi spoke sadly.

"No, but she's all Warrior," Aiko said, looking around the corner toward Mai.

"She's got some balls," Junko said incidentally.

Aiko and Ishi looked at her and let out a laugh.

The door opened and the girl clad in black stepped out carrying a backpack. The head guard noticed her and stopped her. She was answering questions. She turned to go and he stopped her, again grabbing her hand.

Michio had had enough. He walked out the door while Takumi held the others back. "Okay, wait, it won't look right if we all go at once," he cautioned them urgently.

Mai looked up and saw Michio marching across the street toward her with clenched fists. She saw both guards look up at him and put their hands in their pockets. She had to think quickly.

"You idiot! You're always late!" she yelled, surprising everyone. She then walked up and slapped Michio as hard as she could. He stopped in his tracks and stood there speechless, looking down vacantly at Mai. She turned to the guards. "You men are selfish pigs!" She turned back and grabbed Michio's hand. "Let's go. I'm hungry." She stamped her feet like a child.

"Oh...uh...sorry...uh...honey?"

"*Honey?*" She squeezed his hand in frustration. "Don't try to suck up now!" As she led him away, the guards paused for a moment and then started chuckling.

"What a nag."

"Cute nag, though."

"Yeah, cute, but still a nag!" They both sat down and went back to their previous conversation about who was the best dancer in town, not realizing that they had just met her.

Chapter Twenty-three

Hard Knocks

In the bathroom of Coffee Shop, Mai stood staring at the strange dark girl in the mirror. She closed her eyes.

Mai felt strong hands grip her hair and pin one of her arms high against her back. Ishi was screaming and struggling next to her. Suddenly her head snapped forward. Ishi was off the ground kicking and screaming reaching back to release her hair from the train doors. Mai's trembling hands were covered in blood as she touched Ishi's chopped hair.

Mai opened her eyes. *I did it.*

She took a drink and splashed some water on her face, and again looked intently at the face in the mirror. She had penetrated deep into the recesses of evil, and no one had noticed. Somehow, it satisfied the rage that had been burning in her since the attack. Her face hardened and she adjusted her black clothes. The door opened slowly and Ishi walked in.

"Ready for the barrage?" Mai looked up at her friend, nodded, and started for the door.

"Wait." Ishi stopped her. "Why, Mai? Why'd you do it?"

Mai froze. She looked at her like a confused child as tears filled her eyes and rolled down her cheeks. She buried her face in her hands, breathing in short gasps. Finally, she rushed into Ishi's arms, sobbing uncontrollably as Ishi held her close like a protective big sister.

"I…I…had to," she said, trembling. "I'm so terrified, Ish. I'm so afraid of losing you and the others. I'm so scared of what they can do to us, I can't breathe sometimes." Ishi held her as she shook with each sob. Then Mai held her breath and shifted in her arms. She bit down hard, took a deep breath, and focused. In a low, ominous voice she said, "But when I face it, when I challenge it, when I'm the hunter…I…I feel better."

Ishi held her by the shoulders, pushed her back a little, and looked her right in the eyes, to see if Mai was still all there. "Mai-chan, I'm okay. We will not die one second earlier than God Himself wills." She desperately searched her face for confirmation that she understood.

Mai looked from side to side, nodded, and wiped her tears. "Right, but if they touch you again…"

Ishi smiled. "I know, me too! She hugged her close. "I'll tell you what, though, my little dark angel, you rock. Come on, they have questions." Ishi led her to their table in the back room.

Mai endured the group hug that followed and all the scolding that came from her older teammates. At this point, there was more exhilaration over what she had just done than anger for her recklessness.

Aiko gave her a big hug. "Amazing job, little sister." Then Aiko stood back and watched as the group peppered her with excited questions.

"How did you…?"

"What did he say?"

"Who taught you to…?"

"What were you thinking?"

Ishi took control. "Hold it, guys. Give her a chance to breathe." Everyone quieted down.

Koh got in the next word. "Okay, okay, but what we *all* want to know is"–he paused for effect–" Who are you?" Everyone groaned, but also agreed with the question. What that girl had done was awesome and unlike the shy Mai that they all knew.

"Mai, how did you get in?" Takumi asked seriously.

She paused for a moment like the old Mai, but then her eyes hardened a bit as she spoke. "I told him I left my stuff at the party last night at the candy shop and had to get it." She looked up for the next question.

Takumi was rubbing his chin. "Okay, but where did you learn how to…?"

She shrugged. "TV."

Everyone nodded. "Oh, yeah…"

"Then he insulted you," Junko said, moving on.

"Yeah, something about being a sex object and losing track of my stuff because I was so busy with men, but it was more crude," Mai said, wrinkling her nose.

"So you, you gave him the–" Koh flipped the bird hard into the air.

"*Koh,*" five voices corrected at once.

"Come on, you have to admit that was so cool!" he said, chuckling.

"Sure, fast thinking," Aiko said, reaching up and lowering his hand for him.

"Yeah, that's what I mean." Koh plopped down with his arms crossed.

Everyone turned back to Mai.

"I'm just glad I got the finger thing right. I've never had to do that. Sorry, Aik." She broke into an innocent smile. They all laughed.

"Guess you don't have a brother like mine," Kai declared. The brothers glared at each other.

"I swear, I had a heart attack when I saw you walk up to those guys," Michio said, pounding his chest with a fist. They all chimed in.

"Oh yeah."

"Me too!"

"Me too!"

"Who didn't?"

"Really, he's not joking. I think his heart actually stopped, and then went into overdrive," Takumi said pointing at Michio's stretched shirt, where they had hung on to him.

"Dragged all three of us into the pawnshop across the street ready to bash his way in," Kai added.

"Speaking of which, Mai, tell us what you learned?" Aiko asked, seeking to focus the conversation.

Mai paused for a moment, reached into her shirt pocket, and pulled out a small piece of paper. "Thirty-six employees visible on three floors, and more, like, henchmen on the fourth floor, maybe sixteen."

"Henchmen?" Takumi started writing on his own notepad.

"Those would be dealers and armed guards. Ryudan's men," Junko said.

"What about Kenji?" Ishi asked. "When did you see him?" Mai shot a glance over to her friend, remembering her care for Kenji.

"On the fourth floor. He was on a couch just sleeping, or drugged, or something. Men were crowded around him because there's a TV there and it was saying something about Ryudan's trial so they were all distracted. I saw our stuff on the table, walked up, took it, and left."

"Perfect timing," Michio said.

"God's timing," Aiko said. "Mai-chan…demons?" She crossed her arms.

"Yeah, I want to hear this," Koh said and sat up. Everyone leaned in a bit.

Mai stopped, took a deep breath and her eyes glassed over with tears. She bit her lip and shook her head slowly. "I've never seen so many," she whispered in awe. She paused, looking down, and then continued. "I lost count. At least fifty per floor, but I can't be sure, you couldn't see past the room with Truesight on because there were so many." She hesitated. "I think I saw some of your Goons."

"Some! How many?" Aiko asked.

"Just three. One by Kenji, and this other guy I didn't recognize," Mai said, looking down suddenly.

"What about the other?" Takumi asked. Mai slowly turned to Aiko with doubt filling her eyes. She sighed and reached into the front pocket of Aiko's jacket, where she always carried her sword manual, and pulled it out. She opened the first page and extracted the picture that Aiko kept with her all the time.

"The other one was watching *him*." She handed the picture of Makoto to Aiko.

Aiko gasped, and murmured almost to herself, struggling in a controlled voice, "Makoto is there? You saw him?" Mai just nodded.

"He didn't look so good, but, he was…" Mai was also struggling.

"Just say it." Aiko sat down and clasped her hands.

"I think he was helping them; he seemed like one of them." Mai looked at Aiko sadly.

Everyone fell quiet as Aiko sat there thinking intensely and hurting deeply. Then she looked up again and lightly slapped her knees.

"Thank you, girl, you're amazing." Mai just looked down. Aiko walked a few steps away from everyone, deep in thought. She wiped the tears that were gathering in her eyes. The others let her go, knowing that she had been dreading this news. It was confirmation that her brother had turned.

Kai changed the subject. "How did you keep from putting on your armor or pulling your weapons?"

Mai looked up at him. "It was hard." She smiled slightly as she recalled the events. "I almost forgot once." She looked up at Ishi for a moment and then down at the ground. "I wanted to hurt them all," she whispered.

They all took a breath, exchanging glances of concern. Ishi looked at Aiko, who turned toward Mai with a compassionate look on her face.

Michio broke the silence. "Hey, all I know is…" He lifted Mai and gave her a long bear hug. "…you are my hero, girl!" Everyone clapped or cheered or joined the hug. Michio put Mai down and moved on to business. "Okay, we got our target, we know the place, so let's go get them," he said with his arms open wide. Everyone looked at Aiko.

"Okay, I'm not on the math team but we're talking like two hundred-plus bad guys, versus, uh, let's see, *seven*!" Koh raised his eyebrows and held up his fingers.

"Eight," Junko corrected, stepping to Takumi's side. He grinned, pushed up his glasses, and looked down at the paper.

Aiko peered over at Takumi for the count.

"Fifty-two visible employees and say at least eight to ten more guards on the top floor where Mai didn't go. Many of them will be armed and *all* of them will answer to Ryudan or whoever is left in charge," Takumi calculated out loud.

"Keep counting," Koh said pointing at the paper.

"Fifty demons per floor…but why?" He scratched his head. "Why so many?"

"Yeah, and the Goons." Koh tapped the paper. Finally Kai slapped him to make him be quiet.

Takumi looked up as though it was starting to add up. "Something's not right here. What did Akira say about the Goons?" Takumi asked, looking at Aiko and Ishi.

"They gather when something big is about to happen," Ishi replied.

"So, who was the third person they were guarding? Kenji, Makoto, and…who?" Takumi held his palms up.

Then, she heard it. Aiko heard a voice in her heart.

"*Are you ready?*"

She closed her eyes. *I'm ready. Is it time to die, Master?*

"*I will be with you,*" the voice assured her.

Takumi continued. "They're gathering. That can't be normal. They're waiting for something or someone. Aiko, it's going to happen soon; the curse will be passed on."

Aiko stood. "But Ryudan's arrest upset their plans. They can't do anything without him." Ishi looked around the group. "We have to get to Kenji before he returns. Remember, as long as he is alive there's a chance we can change things."

"What about Makoto?" Takumi asked. "We have to turn him back," he suggested, looking at Aiko for confirmation. She shook her head.

"I don't know what the plan is for Makoto, but I'm going after him," Aiko said resolutely, not wanting to hope for too much after so long.

Takumi looked carefully at the paper in his hand again. "Kenji and Makoto will be hard enough to deal with, but then the real battle will happen." He looked up at Aiko.

"We gotta go in!" Michio's voiced filled the room. He stood holding his fist up ready to fight.

" Okay, Takumi, so the final total is?" Koh asked, leaning over his shoulder.

"Oh, uh, sixty-two potentially armed thugs, two hundred various fallen angels who hate us, and three Resistant Ones, otherwise known as Goons, that we can't beat yet, who will be guarding our goals; plus one unknown but obviously important player in all this." Takumi stood, causing everyone else who was sitting to do the same. They all took a step toward Aiko.

"When do we leave?" Ishi asked for everyone except Koh, who was watching in disbelief, shocked that no one was listening to him.

"Can't we just call the police?" Koh whined.

Junko shook her head. "Ryudan owns them."

"Can't we invite them to a meeting and trade them something for Kenji?" Koh was struggling for an easier solution.

"There's nothing we have that they want. We have nothing to bargain with," Takumi replied simply.

"But, this time someone could die." Koh mentioned dismally what they all knew but refused to talk about.

"Hey, you know how it works. If the Master calls, we go out and we trust Him. Right?" Ishi looked over at her leader and friend, but Aiko was looking absently into the far distance of another reality. She knew in her heart that *Mai had shown them the way.*

It had struck her hard. They *did* have something they wanted.

Her, a Called One. And…they wanted her really bad.

"Okay, I know you're not going to like this, but I'm going in alone. It's what they would least expect." Everyone stood expressionless in silent disagreement.

"But Makoto," Takumi objected. "He'll recognize you."

Aiko nodded. "The problem is the humans. If we can just neutralize them…"

"I hope that includes their guns," Koh added.

"…then I can focus on the spiritual side of things," Aiko finished.

"Not alone, I'm sorry. There's no way," Ishi insisted with her hands on her hips.

"I agree. Not alone." Takumi crossed his arms.

Aiko was thinking and praying. She looked over to Mai, who was standing just behind Ishi. "Mai-girl. Wanna party with me tonight?" Mai's eyes hardened and she smiled in agreement.

"Do I get to fight this time?" she asked grimly.

"Yes, Mai-girl, time to hit them back–hard." Mai nodded slowly, and clenched her fists at her sides.

"What about the rest of us?" Ishi asked, with Michio nodding next to her.

"You will clear the escape route, which really is the hard part. I'll just distract them," Aiko stated, still figuring it out. She sat down, grabbed a napkin, and pulled out a pen. "Okay, this is how it will work. Takumi, did you notice…?"

They gathered around the table for an hour, planning. Ishi, Takumi, Michio, and Kai leaned forward as Aiko talked. Junko made comments and filled in gaps with Mai about the inside. She also taught Aiko and Mai how to talk their way into the party upstairs. Koh sat with his hands behind his head with a look of despair on his face, reminding them every step of the way of all the dangers they would face. They decided to go when the club was busiest instead of in the early morning hours, so that it would be easier to cause confusion. They left together at midnight. Aiko was last out of the door and as she watched them all walk ahead of her to the station, she prayed that they would all return safely and unhurt with Kenji.

But, she knew it wasn't to be.

Chapter Twenty-four

Aiko's Folly

THE SAME STREET LOOKED DIFFERENT AT NIGHT. WEALTHY CUSTOMERS ARRIVED IN luxury cars with hired drivers, and a constant stream of taxis were dropping off and picking up. There was a line of party-clad young girls waiting to get in. Some came in groups, others were with half-drunk businessmen, and still others hung on the arm of a rough-looking boyfriend or date. The building was lit up. Neon lights flashed the name "Dragon Palace," "Men's Entertainment Club," and "24 hours." From the street nothing could be seen on the inside, but one could hear the constant *thump*, *thump*, *thump* of a heavy bass dance song. The same two guards were outside, still wearing their sunglasses at night. However, now there were other bouncers standing at the corners of each building and in the front where the cars came in. One of them was talking and laughing and sharing a beer with two beat policemen.

Down the street, a plan was unfolding.

"Okay, how do we look?" Aiko said, with Mai standing next to her. No one said anything. They all looked up at Aiko speechless. They had never seen the young woman standing in front of them. Aiko was wearing a short skirt with dark nylons and high heels with a low-cut blouse pulled off her shoulders. Junko had spent an hour putting on her makeup, styling her short hair, and accessorizing. Mai had refreshed her dark look but Junko added glitter around her eyes and a touch of purple to the ends of her hair.

"I'm losing these as soon as I can," Aiko looked down at her heels. She looked up again. "Well? Will we fool them?" she asked.

The guys were stunned, not wanting to say what all of them were thinking. She was beautiful. They had never seen her dressed like that before.

"Uh..." Takumi shrugged and adjusted his glasses.

"I think you just got your answer, Aiko. You are one hot babe tonight!" Junko beamed and stepped back to admire her work. She looked Aiko up and down and nodded. "You have the most beautiful eyes." Junko looked at Takumi and motioned toward Aiko. He smiled and nodded at her.

Michio cleared his throat. "I'm a little partial to the dark look. Mai is like, wickedly hot." The guys all grunted in agreement and Ishi walked over and put her arm around her protectively. Mai looked up at Michio with a slight smile that grew when their eyes met. Michio put his hands in his pockets and looked away.

"Ah, but she's deadly, and don't you forget that." Ishi shook her finger at the guys.

Aiko surveyed herself one more time and took a deep breath. "Okay, you all know what to do. We work as one."

"Wait, can you say that again, I'm still getting used to *you* being our leader," Koh said, and they all laughed.

She smiled for a moment, then thought, *Good. Thank You for these light moments before battle. Thank You. Good way to finish if*… She didn't complete the thought, but reminded them, "Remember, our priority is getting Kenji out."

"Makoto?" Ishi touched Aiko's arm.

"I don't know, Ish. The Master hasn't given me clarity on his path." She paused. "But if I see him, I'm going after him."

"Tell me again how you are going to beat the unbeatable ones?" Koh had his hands on his hips.

"I can't," Aiko said. "At least, I don't think I can."

Koh waited for his answer, tapping his foot.

She finally answered, "If we move fast enough, we won't have to beat them. Just…outrun them."

"Yeah, but if you don't move fast enough…" Koh began. Kai threw his hand over his brother's mouth. "Time to rock and roll?"

Aiko looked around at each one of them. "Okay, take your positions. Mai and I will wait twenty minutes from right now." They all looked at their watches. "I'll signal you with my cell when we're inside and ready." Everyone gathered around her. She nodded and they declared with one voice, "For His Honor." As they broke, she paused and caused everyone to stop.

"I, um…I love you guys."

They all smiled and moved out. Michio gave her a big hug. "You two be careful." He hugged the little one, lifting her off her black Keds.

Ishi simply gave Aiko a nod and looked directly into Mai's eyes. "Get some for me." Mai's eyes flared slightly and she smiled grimly. They moved out.

♦ ♦ ♦

Michio lifted the manhole cover off, grunting with effort, and laid it aside. "There you go. Okay, see you guys soon. Be careful down there." He trotted off and joined Ishi, who was waiting for him at the entrance to the back alley.

Koh and Takumi looked at each other for a moment and pointed their flashlights down a dark ladder that descended into blackness. "Would you smell that? How did I get sewer duty again?" Koh closed his eyes and held his nose shut.

"Because we needed two down there," Takumi answered, "and everyone else had something else to do. And you've never had sewer duty, this is a first," he finished matter-of-factly.

Koh grunted and climbed down the ladder. "Roboto, we're going to smell for weeks."

♦ ♦ ♦

Kai pulled the van into the alley from the other direction and stopped by a large garbage bin. "I've thrown up in this alley," Junko said, making a face.

"I didn't need to know that." Kai grimaced, peering out into the night. He looked in the rearview mirror, to the front and sides, and then the mirror again.

"Hey, don't worry, no one comes out here. Just keep the lights off and they'll think we're a delivery truck or something."

Kai looked out again. "I hope you're right. Look, there goes Michio and Ishi." He pointed toward the building.

The two Warriors wearing black climbed cautiously up a ladder. They crept up the fire escape to the window outside the fourth floor. No one had armor on…yet.

Junko turned to Kai. "Okay, let's practice again, you only have a few minutes."

Kai took a deep breath and gripped the wheel of the van tightly. "Are you sure about this?"

"Don't worry, we'll turn up the music really loud, and as long as you get close to it, they'll buy it. Remember, the name of the game in their world is, 'save your own . . .' uh." Kai glanced over. "I mean rear end." She smiled. "Oops."

♦ ♦ ♦

"Here goes, you ready, girl?" Aiko asked, looking at her watch one more time.

"Yes." Mai nodded.

"Okay, let's get some help first." Aiko knelt, prompting Mai to kneel with her. "Master, give us Godspeed, blind the eyes of our enemies, foil their evil schemes, and quicken our swords to strike ever so deep into the heart of evil tonight. We're going after Kenji and…and Makoto. Go before us and do battle with us. For His Honor." Aiko pushed her send button and sent out a group text message to her team: "Party time." Both girls stood up and walked around the corner toward the front door.

♦ ♦ ♦

"Okay, this is it." Takumi pointed to a cable in a circuit box.

"You sure I won't…you know…zzzzzt?" Koh jerked both hands and shook violently.

Takumi smiled and looked at his phone. "You can never be sure." He held up his phone. "Party time, let's be ready."

♦ ♦ ♦

"You see anything?" Michio asked as Ishi peered in the window of the fire escape from the darkness.

Ishi looked back. "Demon mosh pit. Pray hard, Mich."

He reached into a pocket and pulled out his phone. "Party time," he whispered.

♦ ♦ ♦

Junko jumped when her phone buzzed. She checked it and looked up excitedly. "Dial, Kai. It's party time."

"Okay, here goes." Kai took out his phone with trembling hands and dialed the number.

"Remember, keep your voice low and angry…you're evil and demanding, and don't hold back on the cussing," Junko reminded him.

♦ ♦ ♦

Mai called out to the head guard. "Hey, I'm back! Can we cut in line? We have an appointment." Mai and Aiko tried to walk right past them, but they were blocked.

The guards looked them over and paid special attention to Aiko before glancing down at Mai. "Hey, Frankie, you know this little girl?" the head guard asked.

The other guard looked her over. "Nah, Louie, I don't think…Ha! Wait! Yeah, remember she nailed her boyfriend across the face today, remember, bad little chick?"

Louie smiled, remembering that funny break in their day. "Oh yeah! So, what's this about an appointment sweet cakes, and who's the babe?" He looked Aiko up and down and smiled. "Hi, gorgeous, you're new." He stepped close to Aiko, who forced a smile in accordance with Junko's instructions and let him step closer, almost inviting him. *A kiss on the cheek will get you far*, Junko had said. But Aiko couldn't do it.

"Hey, guys, I'm Sayaka. I have an appointment upstairs." She spoke confidently, expecting them to recognize her name right away. They just looked at each other, bewildered. Mai and Aiko exchanged nervous glances.

"Uh, I don't know nothing about no appointment, girls. You trying to pull something?" The head guard rubbed his chin and looked at his partner. "Anyone call you?" He shook his head.

Mai looked down for a moment and mouthed, "Kai?"

♦ ♦ ♦

"Shoot, I hit the last number wrong again! My hands are shaking too much!" Kai yelled in frustration.

"Give me the phone." Junko dialed as fast as she could.

♦ ♦ ♦

"Who is this appointment with?" the guard asked.

"Uh, he didn't want me to say." Aiko fixed her hair. "And I never ask questions." She smiled and touched her lips, trying to be convincing.

"Hey, Louie, you think Kentaro ordered some fresh meat? Better not send her away too quick. He won't like it." Louie looked at his partner with a serious expression on his face, and nodded slowly. Then he added, "Wait here," and reached for his phone and started dialing. The girls glanced at each other, holding back the panic.

OhGodOhGodOhGodOhGod, help us, please! Mai kept a forced smile.

Kai!…please…Master? Aiko glanced to see if an escape route was available. Both guards watched them closely.

Just as Louie got to the last digit, his phone rang. He abruptly stopped and stared at the number. "Hey, you recognize this?" he asked Frankie, who looked at his phone.

"No, maybe one of the ones we lifted from those…"

Louie cleared his throat. "Hey."

"I mean, uh, one of the new phones." He nodded to his partner then scratched his head. "I thought we lost those this afternoon?"

"Guess they didn't get everything." Louie shrugged and stared at the number on the phone.

He put the phone to his ear and immediately cringed. Music blared through the receiver and a voice barked orders at the guard.

"Uh, yes, sir…a girl is here now…Sayaka? Yes…uh, no sir, no delay…they just got here." He held the phone away from his ear while a string of profanity poured out of the phone. "Ye-ye-yes, sir, of course, they're coming right up," Louie stammered, and then hung up. He looked at the girls. "I hope you know what you're getting yourself into. Go on up." He let out a short breath and shook his head. Mai and Aiko slipped through the front door. Louie made a quick call, clearing security for the girls.

"We're in" was broadcast to the team, and they all held their breath.

♦ ♦ ♦

Kai fell over the steering wheel and let out a big sigh. "How could dialing a phone be so stinking hard?"

Junko patted him on the shoulder. "Try asking a girl out."

He sat up immediately with a serious look on his face. "Right…ha!" He nodded and let out a nervous laugh. "Okay, maybe that wasn't so bad."

"Hey, they're in…nice cussing."

Kai shrugged. "I guess I'll take that as a compliment, but right now I feel like taking a shower." He smiled and pulled at his collar.

They all watched their phones for the next signal. It was the most crucial one of the night.

♦ ♦ ♦

Inside, the music was blaring. To be sure they didn't slip up, Mai and Aiko had agreed that they would not put on Truesight till it was time to fight. They pushed their way through a crowd of well-dressed businessmen with sexy young girls on their arms. Everyone was drunk or high, or on the way there. The whole place was shrouded in smoke and smelled of alcohol and sweat from the dance floor.

Suddenly, Aiko saw something that caused her to stop in her tracks. In the middle of the dance floor, the focal point of the building, there stood a statue of a god-like figure. It was an obvious symbol of hedonistic pleasure. He was covered by a toga, but obviously naked underneath. He was surrounded by naked women. The one on the right side had grapes that she was feeding him, on the other side a woman offered a cup of wine. At his feet a kneeling woman had her hand on his crotch, and behind him a fourth woman was placing a wreath on his head.

"Men's club, huh?" Aiko frowned.

"Gross, yeah?" Mai looked disgusted.

"They squeeze so many people in here, and they run these all over town?" She shook her head sadly.

The music droned on and the place was pulsating with activity. Four floors reverberated with loud gambling machines, throbbing music, glasses clinking and people laughing, screaming, or barking orders to the waitresses. Amid all of this, young prostitutes were making their moves.

Aiko and Mai turned right, just past the crowded entryway, and walked toward a waiting elevator. The guards had been tipped off, so they waved them both past. Finally, they got to the elevator.

Both girls stared at a sign and then at each other. "Out of order. Sorry for the inconvenience." They saw a guard on a chair next to the door who took notice of them and pointed to the back of the room.

Mai looked up to Aiko for orders. "Stairs it is," Aiko said with a grim smile. They walked toward the back of the room.

"But your escape?"

"He knows, little sister," Aiko whispered, trying to reassure her. Mai looked at her for a moment and then took her hand.

"This way."

Oh Lord, we need a break, Aiko thought, following her guide. Each stairway was disconnected from the others. It was designed so that a patron would have to cross the floor of each room and be tempted to stop and spend a little more money on the way in or out. Each floor had a large circular hole in the center of the room just over the statue so that revelers on any floor could gaze down upon their pleasure god.

At the last banister leading up to the fourth floor, they separated. Mai went ahead to mark where she had seen Kenji. When Aiko got to the top of the staircase, she noticed that this room that had a different layout. These were high rollers and rich drug users. There were diamonds, high heels, and low-cut, high-slit dresses on most of the women. Some men were snorting cocaine from glass tabletops with their dates. Others were lounging around flirting or making out with a paid hostess or stumbling to private rooms off to the side. It was painfully over-crowded.

Good. A crowded room is good. She looked across the room at what seemed to be a more private area that was separated from the rest of the room by transparent curtains. She saw Mai walk over and enter past the curtains, grab a drink off a tray, and sink down on a couch next to three other girls pawing a man. She sat back, blended in, and looked toward the direction where Aiko should go.

Aiko was approached by several men who made lewd suggestions about what they wanted to do with her. "Taken." She smiled sweetly. "Maybe next time." They stumbled on, disappointed. She got ready to march into the curtained area when she saw a young girl come out on the arm of an overly aggressive customer. He pulled her close and kissed her roughly on the mouth and neck. Aiko could see her effort as she tried to stay cheerful and willing. He kept pulling at her clothes while she attempted to drag him in the direction of the private area. Others who were watching from the side appeared either amused by the scene or totally unconcerned.

The world went silent for Aiko as she let the morbid scene unfold. As she watched, the girl's face changed and it was…"Shiho," she whispered. "Is this how you ended your life? Here, like this?" Tears formed in her eyes and her hands turned to fists as she pictured her little sister sinking into the depths of filth and pollution, never to return. She stood there, paralyzed, as the struggle continued.

Mai saw the look on Aiko's face. She tried to make eye contact with her, but she was too focused. She pulled out her phone and got ready. Just then a giggling, screaming girl fell on Mai, spilled her drink, and knocked her phone to the floor where it was abruptly kicked under the couch. She dove after it amid silly screams and laughs and searched for it desperately.

Aiko decided she would change her route to the curtained area. She walked directly toward the drunk, rude man, stopped, and pushed up enticingly against him, almost eye to eye. He smiled wickedly, still holding onto his date. "How about joining us, gorgeous?"

Aiko smiled and put a hand on his shoulder. "Oh, I'm sorry, but…" She kneed him hard in the groin. "I don't think you can handle me." His expression changed instantly to extreme agony as he froze and sank to the ground, unable to speak, with his young prey still standing by his side, unsure what to do. People around them laughed at him unsympathetically; they must be used to this kind of scene. Aiko's eyes met the girl's and held them, speaking volumes while she prayed silently for her.

After a moment, the girl smiled thankfully. "You're not really from here, are you?" Aiko looked at her with misty eyes and smiled warmly. She shook her head then turned and surveyed the room again. Her hands slowly formed into fists and her smile disappeared.

This has to stop right now.

Without a word, she walked into the curtained area. It was designed as a lounge, big enough for forty or fifty people. There was the window that led to the fire escape, a large flat-screen TV, and…*Kenji*!

He was surrounded by a group of gangsters dressed in suits. *Okay, the henchmen…armed.* Aiko looked over to signal Mai…but she wasn't there.

♦ ♦ ♦

"Now?" Koh asked with the wire cutters in position.

"For the seventeenth time, no! Wait for the signal," Takumi said sharply, pacing back and forth, looking at his phone, and glancing up toward Aiko from time to time. "Come on, girl."

♦ ♦ ♦

"I'm going in. We're on their home field and they're all alone in there," Michio said, fiercely. He pushed up from his stomach to his knees.

"No, Mich, we're in their locker room. They're not ready for this," Ishi grabbed his shirt and pulled him back down. "Be patient."

"OK, but let's hope we get to the bat rack before they do." He slumped back down and shook his head.

♦ ♦ ♦

Aiko had just spotted Mai down on the floor when she heard Makoto's voice.

"Aiko? Aiko!"

She turned and saw Makoto looking directly at her barely ten feet away. They stood staring at each other, stunned.

"Gotcha." Mai opened her phone and dialed from her hands and knees.

"What the…?" Another voice cut in as a young hoodlum stepped up to her from the side. "Is this babe really your sister, Makoto?" He looked her up and down and a few other henchmen looked over with interest. He wore a tight gold-colored business suit opened at the chest revealing gaudy gold necklaces. His hair was long and greased back from his face. He had a young girl on his arm and, jutting out his chin and sneering at Makoto, he pushed her away.

Makoto slowly shook his head. "I have no sister, Kentaro."

Kentaro. Aiko looked at him, unflinching.

He shook his head, smiled, and opened his coat. Aiko saw that he had a bloody ponytail attached to his belt. Mai saw it too.

"Aiko, no!" Kenji murmured and reached out to her from the couch where he lay with his eyes half-closed, his arms pulled close to him, trembling.

"So, it ends tonight. We end the legacy that has hounded us for generations," Kentaro sneered again, then laughing, he pulled out his gun. "Nice gift for Ryudan."

"Aiko, you really are an idiot! What did you think you would do here?" Makoto looked at the gun pointed at her and then back at her and threw his hands up in disbelief.

She stood tall and poised as Kentaro raised the gun to her head. She hadn't taken her eyes off Makoto the whole time. *Wait, wait, wait,* she thought for what seemed like an eternity. Kentaro's finger started to squeeze the trigger slowly. She took a deep breath and said, "Makoto, I love you."

Suddenly the world went black.

Kentaro fired into the darkness. Then all at once the entire club gasped and started to panic.

In the dark, two warriors crossed paths. A swift dark dancer sprinted across the room and shoved Kentaro with so much force and surprise that he flew backward, fired his gun again into the air. The weapon tumbled into the darkness as he reached back to break his fall. People started screaming and stampeding for the exits.

In the meantime, Aiko turned on her sight, armored up, and pulled out two swords. A room that was literally filled from wall to wall with a dark demonic presence suddenly shuddered as a bright Warrior appeared in its midst. They all froze. Without the slightest hesitation, she closed the gap between her and Makoto. From her peripheral vision she could see the demons in the room retreating at the sight of her glowing swords. She also saw a Goon hovering near Makoto, turning toward the light she gave off, but she was too quick.

Before Makoto could even raise a hand, she drove her two swords into Makoto to the hilt; one entered his eye and went directly through into his brain. The other sword entered his heart, directly into the pulsing mass of evil.

He screamed, pulling at the handles, but she was too strong. She whispered a prayer that caused the swords to glow first blue then white hot, and Makoto was filled with light. He writhed and screamed louder.

People were ducking, running, and hiding in every corner in a mass of confusion. The demons were regrouping. Makoto's Goon acted first. Behind Aiko, he unsheathed a grotesque sword, took his time, wound up, and swung hard at her.

"Stop!" Makoto screamed, but Aiko held on with a look of fierce love. She heard the sword unsheathe behind her and heard the swish of a blade coming at her, but she wouldn't let go of Makoto. *Trust,* she thought. *Trust.*

Just before the blade hit, a translucent purple shield appeared out of nowhere and blocked the blow in a hail of sparks. The Goon spun around, searching, and screeched, "Warriors! Find them!" Now the demons were in a mass of confusion as well, looking in every direction for another gleaming Warrior, but they saw none. Mai stayed in the shadows, looking like the others, ready to throw her shield again whenever needed.

Makoto sank to the ground gripping his head. Aiko was done.

Kentaro yelled at the top of his lungs, "Get the stupid lights on!" His shoe hit something fleshy that crunched when he stepped on it, and he tripped. "Morons! Don't let anyone out of the club!"

Time to draw a crowd. Aiko turned toward the screaming melee.

She spun around in time to see the Goon in full backswing getting ready for his second blow. Kentaro's Goon was right behind him hurrying to get into position. "Little skank, do you really–"

Aiko kicked him hard in the chest and sent him flying backward into the other Goon.

"No time for speeches." Aiko set her stance and selected her next targets. Both of the Goons were swallowed into the confusion of demons who were now swarming up out of the hole in the middle of the room.

Aiko ran the length of the room. She spun both swords like crisscrossing windmill blades, and heard demons cry out in agony and confusion as they burst into dust before they could pull their weapons. She had banished eighteen by the time she reached the stairway. She paused there, dodged people who were clawing their way out of the club in the pitch black, and faced demons coming at her two and three at a time. She spun, ducked, rolled, and thrust her way through each attack. Nine more burst. There was a short pause as the demons stepped back and started calling out signals to each other.

Eight demons the size of higuma bears circled her and on command all charged simultaneously. Aiko glanced for an escape but they had cut her off completely.

She went to one knee and threw up her shield but knew that her back and sides were exposed. "This is going to hurt," she said to herself. They charged, snarling at her. As their weapons flew, three more shields appeared around her, covering her back and sides. Michio and Ishi had entered the room during the confusion in time to see the attack and joined Mai to block for Aiko.

Sparks flew from the lies hitting truth so hard, and the demons all drew back in surprise. "Find them!" a demon leader screamed above the noise.

When the sparks settled, Aiko was gone. She had raced down to the next floor. The Goons yelled orders and rushed down the hole to find Aiko leading most of the remaining demons down with them. That was the Warriors' signal to move Kenji.

Aiko would be alone now.

♦ ♦ ♦

Kenji sensed people sitting next to him. They stood him up and started leading him in the darkness. He tried to look at the person struggling to hold him up. "It's Mai," a quiet voice said in the darkness. He felt strong hands grab him and throw him like a bag over big shoulders.

"Hurry…this way." It was Ishi's voice.

♦ ♦ ♦

As she ran down the stairs, Aiko tried to stay calm and think logically. *Okay, Aiko, no more stopping. Goons are close behind. Keep the swords always moving like Akira showed you.* She reached the bottom of the stairs and saw a multitude of glowing demon eyes fixed on her, her gleaming armor drawing their attention like a beacon. She could smell an evil stench. "Okay, who's first?"

An Overlord stepped forward, towering over her, while the others screamed hideously for her death. He growled and lunged in an attack. She sidestepped his powerful swing, then leaped upward and ran up his huge arm, decapitating him as she passed his head, and somersaulted off his massive shoulders. *Whooosh!* The demons gasped.

Before they could react, she was chopping them down at a rate of one per second as she worked her way to the stairway. She spun, rolled, jumped, blocked, and stabbed her way, always moving forward.

One demon managed to grab her foot as she ran past. She crashed on her face and heard the whistle of arrows coming her way. She spun faceup and called out a command; her shield appeared instantly as fire and sparks fell all around her. She felt large, powerful claws grip her shoulders, shake her violently, and lift her almost to the ceiling in order to throw her to the floor. The demons cheered. She grunted as she powerfully swung both swords in front of her like scissors and severed the head of yet another demon Overlord, who burst leaving a cloud of dust while Aiko fell to the ground.

Immediately, another Slayer demon leaped through the dust of his fallen comrade and kicked Aiko forcefully across the room, slamming her into the wall. As she slid down, a demonic spear penetrated her armor and pinned her to the wall. Pain spurted through her shoulder and she cried out. The spear protected the demon from the reach of her swords and she was immobilized, pinned hard, and vulnerable.

"Kill her!" she heard from an approaching Goon who had finally caught up. The demon holding Aiko glanced at the approaching Goon to get approval for his catch. When he turned back, Aiko's thrown sword entered the front of his neck and came out the back. The spear went limp and she was freed.

The moment Aiko hit the ground she retrieved her sword and rolled toward the stairway, staying low, slicing the feet of demons who tried to jump away. She descended the stairs in a controlled roll, slashing at them on their way up and banishing them before they knew what was happening. She glanced ahead to the bottom and noticed a Goon waiting there with a terrible-looking spiked mace. "You want me?" she yelled, grabbed a fallen demon ax, and flung it as hard as she could. As the Goon reacted, Aiko flipped over the rail and dropped the remaining eight feet to the second floor. By the time the Goon turned to see where she had gone, there were six clouds of demon dust settling. *Whoosh!*

Aiko finally reached the mass of people trying to escape. Her progress slowed significantly. She turned quickly to her shoulder that was still smoldering with a spiritual wound, issued a healing prayer, and the wound started to close. She inched her way backward with the crowd, praying fervently. *Master, may they be safe, no matter the cost.*

The masses of demons renewed their charge, the Goons in front.

♦ ♦ ♦

"You sure you got him?" Ishi looked down as Michio began his descent.

"Hey, I did this before, remember? I just wish we didn't have to leave Aiko alone," Michio said with regret, carrying Kenji over his shoulder and moving as quick as he could without banging him into anything down the fire escape.

"Mai? Come on, let's go!" Ishi looked into the window at all the confusion. She couldn't see Aiko.

♦ ♦ ♦

Mai stood gazing into the darkness. She could just make out Makoto lying on the floor, dazed and being helped by men dressed in dark suits. In the spiritual world she saw the residue and carnage of Aiko's charge still hanging in the air. She wanted so badly to race in and help Aiko but knew that she could not. She grunted in frustration, shook her fists at her sides, and turned to go. The next moment she heard Kentaro yelling into his phone.

"Idiot! What do we pay you for? Turn on the emergency lights! Send out the order, I want her shot on sight. And be sure you guard Kenji!"

A henchman said, "We've got him. Don't worry, boss, I won't leave him." Mai smiled because she had replaced Kenji with a passed-out druggie who was about the same size, and in the confusion the guy just lay there in the dark where Kenji had been.

♦ ♦ ♦

"Come on, come on, come on, come on!" Kai watched the big baseball player make his way down the alley toward the van with Ishi as rear guard.

"I don't believe it…they got him!" Junko looked up at the club. "I hope Aiko is okay."

"That's what we're all thinking, Junko," Kai said with a worried look on his face. Suddenly, the back door burst open.

"What's happening?" Takumi demanded as he leaped into the back of the van with Koh close behind.

"Oh wow, what happened to you?" Junko's mouth fell open and her eyes fixed on Koh. He was smoking slightly and his hair was a chaotic frizz. He blinked his eyes and put one hand on his forehead. With the other hand he shoved Takumi weakly.

"Uh, I forgot to tell him not to step in the one puddle of water near the line he cut," Takumi tapped his own chest. "My fault."

"That makes me feel a whole lot better," Koh answered sarcastically. He started patting himself all over. "Whoa, I hope nothing got cooked."

"Here they come!" Kai shouted. Ishi ran ahead, opened the side door, and helped Michio carefully unload his cargo. Kenji was gingerly laid down on the floor. Ishi looked out the door, concerned. "Here she comes." Mai came running gracefully down the alley and slid into the van. She acknowledged everyone with a relieved look but sniffed and made a face when she saw Koh.

"Aiko?" Takumi asked, and all eyes went to Mai. Even Kenji, half conscious, looked up at the sound of her name.

"She's ripping the place up," she said with a wicked smile, "but, I want to go back in and help. They're giving orders to shoot. Ish?"

Ishi glanced back to the building with a worried look. "No, we move to the pickup point and trust she knows what she's doing."

"But–"

"No!" she ordered more fiercely.

"We've got to…"

"*Hey!* Aiko's strict orders. We've got Kenji, now we have to keep him from them or all this is wasted," Ishi answered, reminding them of the bigger picture.

"Ishi, I agree with you, but I made a promise." Takumi leaped out of the van.

♦ ♦ ♦

Aiko blocked another Goon attack. She was fighting two of them. They would come in together and send a flurry of sword attacks at her and like lightning she would block them all. When her swords were engaged with one, her shield would deploy to block the other. They couldn't touch her, but she couldn't hurt them either. Her stabs and slashes penetrated but caused no wounds. They just laughed at her. The other demons circled around, forming a demonic arena waiting to see the generational champion taken down.

"Just a matter of time, skank!" one of them hissed.

"You really don't believe that do you?" she shot back. "Once the Master decides, my swords will send you to hell," Aiko said evenly.

The Goon looked at her hard, wondering if she knew something that he didn't. He stepped back with the other Goon and looked at her hatefully. "I despise you, Warrior…and I despise your weak Master too. You can't win this." He looked at the gathered crowd of angry demons and commanded them: "Destroy her!"

The moment she heard the command she dropped to the floor with hands raised, and whispered to the heavens. It took a moment for the demons to hear the Goon's command, lock on their target, and then begin to move. It would take another two seconds to reach her. That's all the time she needed. When the mob had closed to within inches of her, a spiritual wave of power exploded outward from her, leveling the room. Even the Goons were slammed against the far wall.

As Aiko stood, the red emergency lights went on, bathing the room in hellish colors. At the far stairway she saw Kentaro, who locked eyes with her and raised a gun. "Everyone get down! Shoot her!" he yelled.

She heard the sound of guns being pulled and saw confused employees scanning the crowd. She dropped to the floor with everyone else. They were looking at Kentaro, wondering *who* was to be shot.

"There! There! You idiots!" He pointed across the room at fifteen people sprawled panicking on the ground. Aiko was camouflaged by the confused mass of bodies, so in frustration he started working his way toward her.

Aiko knew the demons were regrouping and knew she had to move. But by doing so she would paint a big target on her back.

Move, girl. Move.

She stood and ran toward the opening in the middle of the room.

Kentaro yelled, "There! Kill her!" He raised his gun and fired wildly as he raced to catch up. With the target finally clear, at least three other employees also joined in creating a hail of gunfire.

Aiko sprinted the distance, putting columns and pieces of furniture between her and the bullets. She could hear the angry volleys and the *pop* and *crack* of shattering objects around her as she strained to reach the hole. She dove over a chair, rolled, and slid under a coffee table to the other side as it exploded into splinters. *Keep moving, keep moving, keep moving*, she thought, crawling, rolling, and dodging her way to the middle of the room.

♦ ♦ ♦

"Wow, it sounds like a shooting gallery in there," Michio gasped.

All eyes were riveted on the front entrance where people were still pouring out into the street. Takumi stood just outside, waiting. He looked back at the team.

They didn't like what they saw in his eyes. "No…Tak…no," Ishi whispered.

Takumi ran into the building.

♦ ♦ ♦

Aiko popped up just as she finally reached the banister, but Kentaro had gotten there first. He raised his gun quickly and pressed it against the middle of her forehead. "You and your stupid God…*lose*!" He glared at her with hatred.

"Never," she replied calmly, glaring back with intensity, unafraid. *I'm ready, Master.*

Takumi had reached the statue. He heard Kentaro's voice and looked up. He saw Aiko with a gun against her head. She glanced down to him with a look of resignation. *Why did you come here, Tak? I didn't want anyone to see this, if . . .*

He cried out in a loud, desperate voice, "No!"

"I am *so* going to enjoy this." Kentaro sneered and cocked the hammer.

"Kenji," she said, causing him to catch himself and pause. "You'll never beat him, you're not as good as he is." She glanced upstairs, smiling, knowing it had to be a sore spot for him.

His face contorted in anger. "Hmmph. Kenji!" He growled with clenched teeth. "Forget Ryudan's orders! After I put this bullet through your pretty skull, I'm going to put this gun in his mouth and blow his head off."

"Only God can take my life," Aiko said calmly.

"Then today…I…am…God!" he announced triumphantly and pulled the trigger.

The whole world seemed to stop. A group of loving friends were praying their hearts out down the street. Demons were rushing to converge on Aiko again. People were still screaming and rushing in mass confusion to get out of the club, and Kentaro was shouting at her, but now, everything seemed to be clothed in silence. Aiko thought of the world. *How many battles are being fought right now, Master?*

How many angels are in deadly struggle over a precious child?

How much filth and evil is being poured into the minds of the young?

How many of the weak and lonely are being bullied and tormented?

How many are being deceived into hate and bitterness?

So many, Master…so many . . .

And…so few, so few of us…Am I done now?…Is my battle over?

She heard a voice responding in her heart. It said simply, "*Not yet.*"

The next instant, she heard two beautiful sounds. The first was the click of the gun's hammer on a spent bullet casing followed by Kentaro's incredulity as he stared at his weapon. "What the…"

The second sound was the crash of porcelain breaking as Takumi shattered the statue of a naked woman over Kentaro's head, stunning him.

Kentaro went down.

"Let's go!" Takumi grabbed Aiko's arm and they both jumped over the rail as the gunfire resumed.

They both landed on the shoulders of the statue. "Thank God you're tall," she said to the stone idol and proceeded to climb down and jump to the floor with Takumi. They sprinted through the thinning crowd of people trying to escape the gunfire. They ran toward the exit.

"There!" Ishi yelled as Aiko and Takumi broke out of the crowd.

"They're not going to make it!" Koh yelled.

They could see the club's security trying to control the crowd, but with no orders from Kentaro, they were unsure of how much force to use.

The rest of the team broke out, yelling encouragement to Aiko and Takumi as they sprinted the block and a half to the van. Halfway there, Takumi faltered. Aiko caught him and dragged him beside her, her face filled with concern. They reached the van, jumped in, and slammed the door closed.

"Go, go, go!" Michio yelled. Aiko landed on the van floor on her hands and knees. She was breathing hard, tears were streaming from both eyes, and she was gasping out loud trying to calm down. She was shaking hard, still filled with adrenaline and her eyes were filled with rage and relief at the same time.

Ishi and Mai jumped on Aiko and gave her a big hug. Aiko reached up and returned the hug, starting to realize that she had gotten out alive. *God, how?*

Junko left her seat and ran to the back to check on Takumi, who sat against the side of the van trying to catch his breath.

Koh jumped into the shotgun seat abandoned by Junko and started to torment Kai about the best getaway route.

Michio waited his turn to hug Aiko and finally just threw his big arms around all three girls. They were all covered in sweat and reeked of demon dust.

"Kenji?" Aiko said, breaking free from the group hug to see him lying on a futon near the back of the van.

"Still coming down from whatever they pumped into him," Ishi explained, looking concerned.

"Ai…Aiko?" Kenji struggled to say. "Don't…don't come for me…"

"Yeah, I wish you'd said that earlier," Koh yelled back.

Aiko looked at him and smiled slightly. "Too late."

"Ish?" Kenji said, noticing her hovering over him.

"This is three times, gangster boy. You owe us." Ishi smiled and stroked his brow.

♦ ♦ ♦

"What do you mean he's gone?" Kentaro yelled. "You said you had him!"

"Uh, in the dark we couldn't tell, he might have stumbled out with everyone else.... We could find him," the frightened guard offered.

"No," Kentaro replied coldly. "They've got him," he said thinking. He looked over to Makoto, who sat on the couch with his head in his hands, staring at the ground. Makoto looked up at him briefly and seemed somehow different to Kentaro. "What happened to him?" he asked.

"Not sure, boss, he hasn't said a thing. In shock, I guess, from seeing his sister here or something, I don't know," the guard said, glad the attention was off him.

"His stupid little sister!" Kentaro started to stew again. "She's nothing but a worthless skank who–" He was interrupted by laughter.

Makoto, still looking down shook his head and continued with an ironic kind of laughter. He looked up with tears streaking down his cheeks.

"No, Kentaro, look around you!" He chortled. "Nothing but a worthless skank? No, she's a Warrior, a Called One, and she's better than both of us." Then he shook his head. "You'll never beat her," he said with finality.

Kentaro stepped back and frowned, but before he could respond a guard behind him spoke up.

"Uh, boss, what happened to your hair?" Kentaro reached back and felt a huge gap of missing hair. "What the..."

***

"No way." Ishi said, looking at the ponytail that Mai handed her.

"And..." Mai reached into her pocket and pulled out another lock of hair and showed it to Ishi.

Ishi just laughed. "No way."

"Way," she said, a smile reaching all the way to her dark eyes.

"Ha! Is that...?" Michio looked over curiously.

"Yes, Kentaro's hair," Mai replied, with a satisfied grin.

"This girl is majorly bad! *Yes!*" Michio laughed and high-fived her.

"Will wonders never cease?" Takumi smiled weakly, still trying to catch his breath, with Junko at his side.

"Oh yeah, girl!" Junko exclaimed when she saw the hair.

"Hey, be careful, it's probably diseased," Koh said, looking back. "Keep your eyes on the road!" he yelled, as Kai had to swerve the van.

Aiko came over to Mai. "Now, Mai-chan, you know what we believe about revenge, right?"

Mai looked at her leader. "He had Ish's hair on his belt like a trophy, and he was going to shoot you. I had him on the ground and it was dark."

"Mai?" Aiko put a hand on her shoulder.

"I know, I'm sorry." She looked down.

"No, girl, I met him too. He's a royal jerk and will be wearing a hat in your honor for a while." She paused. "Let's just remember who we are and Who we represent."

Mai nodded. Then Aiko pulled her into a tight hug. "Thank you for saving my life tonight."

"Thank you, too, Tak, but you disobeyed orders."

"Yeah, but I kept a promise," he replied weakly.

Junko looked at him closely. "Tak, wait, lean forward." She reached behind him. "Oh no. Please no." She covered her mouth with one hand and looked at the blood on the other one. "Tak, don't you feel it?"

"There was a pinch..."

"He's been shot," Junko said, tearing up.

"Kai! Hospital now!" Aiko spoke sharply, rushing back to Takumi.

Takumi liked it when she was being strong. She was amazing. He saw Junko looking at him closely. Now that the swelling was down, she had the most beautiful eyes...so pure.

The world faded and went black.

Chapter Twenty-five

CASUALTIES

TAKUMI LOOKED UP AND SAW KENTARO HOLDING THE GUN AGAINST AIKO'S HEAD. SHE *looked down and saw him. She could say so much with her eyes.*

"Why are you here?"

"This is the price we pay, I'll be okay."

"Let me go, Tak..."

An eruption of love and loyalty poured out of his mouth. NO! He rushed up a banister like a salmon working against the current, pushed his way through a screaming crowd and dreaded the sound of a gunshot that would send Aiko out of this world.

Must go faster. Must go faster. Legs felt like lead.

When he reached the top, he grabbed a fallen statue. As he approached, he could see her eyes looking at Kentaro, calm, defiant...she said something. No! The hammer on the gun went down. Please, God, no! Huh? Aiko was still there and Kentaro was looking at his gun. No bullets. He swung the statue down hard on Kentaro's head, shattering it with a crash.

Then there was climbing down...running...ouch! A pinch in the back...running...getting weaker...she's okay...we're going to make it. I counted them...all here...all here.

"We're all here, we're all here," he said out loud. Suddenly, it was quiet except for a gentle electronic beep that kept rhythm with his heart. He opened his eyes and saw a face come into focus.

"Wow, nice eyes," Takumi said weakly and smiled, eyes half closed.

"If you weren't so drugged I'd take that as a compliment," Junko said, smiling over him. "God, we thought we were gonna lose you," she said, and gently hugged him.

"Huh, what did I just say? Um...what did you say?" Takumi raised his head a bit.

Junko laughed lightly. "Well, thanks for making my point. How are you, Takumi, my dear?" she asked cheerfully placing her palm on his forehead.

He opened his eyes wide, trying to shake the drug-induced drowsiness. "I feel so groggy. What happened?" He raised a hand and saw the tubes and probes connected to it.

"You just had an operation to remove a bullet from you," Junko replied. Takumi looked at her for a moment and then glanced around the room for the first time. It was dark. He squinted at the digital clock next to him. It was 3:30 A.M. He tried to sit up, cringed in pain, and then lay back flat.

"Hey, don't move, just take it easy." He stared up at the ceiling, trying to clear his head, and let out a breath.

"Kenji. Did we get him out okay?"

"Oh yeah, and managed to thrash Kentaro thanks to Mai and you," she said with a proud smile on her face. He tried to recall the events of the night again and suddenly it hit him. He blinked his eyes and slowly raised a hand to his forehead.

"Whoa. Okay, I remember now. I was afraid we were going to lose Aiko. I don't think I've ever been so scared. I tried to help her. I think I hit someone pretty hard."

Seeing the worry on his face, she said, "That was Kentaro you hit. Don't worry, you just gave him a mean headache. You didn't kill anyone."

"That's a relief. I'd get kicked off the math team," he sighed. Junko laughed at his joke.

He glanced at the clock again. "Isn't it a little past visiting hours?"

"No, actually, there *are* no visiting hours yet, that is until tomorrow." She smiled a mischievous smile and raised one eyebrow.

"The others were here and wanted to see you but the hospital wouldn't allow it till tomorrow night. Besides, they all needed the rest and had to find Kenji a good place to hide."

"So how did you…?"

She stepped back with her arms out and did a spin. She was wearing a nurse's outfit. "My hat's over there. How do I look?" she said. He stared at her and opened his mouth to speak but nothing came out.

"Oh." She looked at him and shrugged her shoulders. "I thought you should wake up with a friend, you know?" she said and handed him some water. "Small sips. Then you need to rest," she instructed in a soothing tone.

"I don't think I can…rest that is. Now I'm wide awake," Takumi took a small sip of water.

"You're not tired?"

"No."

"You're not in pain?"

"No."

"Feeling weak?"

"Not really." Takumi pushed up to his elbows and looked at her.

"Okay then, Takumi, show me everything; train me."

"Huh?"

"I know I've been changed and I've chosen sides," she said, choosing her words carefully, "but there's this spiritual…thingy…" she said, struggling.

"Spiritual warfare," he said, helping her.

"*Yes!* Spiritual war…whatever you said." She waved her hand in the air.

"I hear you talking and see you all go out there and I don't fully understand, you know?" She looked up toward the sky. "It's sounds horrifying and dangerous, you know? It's the most radically crazy thing I've ever seen. I mean, why get involved? That's stupid." She looked at him sincerely and took his hand. "People like me, people caught in that world, don't have a chance without someone like you willing to be stupid-crazy committed, and now that I've been given a second chance, I want to help."

Takumi's eyes got moist; he let out a short breath and smiled. *After all you've gone through*. He nodded. "I have to introduce you to a friend named Akira…"

"*That* was his name!" Junko blurted out and slapped her forehead. "Akira. He was here tonight after the others had gone. When I was about to sneak in, he showed up. He gave me this." She pulled out a new sword manual from her pocket. "He told me I should ask you to teach me everything. I snuck him in and he put his hand on your head and prayed for you."

"Akira? Really…what else did I miss?"

"Oh, well, you talked a lot in your sleep; even sang me a love song." She chuckled. "It was so cute."

Takumi eyes opened wide and his arms tensed at his sides. Then he caught a hint of a mischievous grin. "Don't even joke like that." He laid back and sighed.

Joke?" She hummed while she fixed his covers and tidied up his bed.

Takumi frowned. "What song?"

"Ha! Gotcha."

He just groaned and shook his head.

Junko looked at Takumi. She giggled and after a moment looked very sincere. "Don't worry, Tak, I know what you're probably thinking. I know the others can see it too. I really like you a lot. I feel safe around you." She pulled up a chair and sat next to him.

Takumi listened, looking up at her. He raised a hand to fix his glasses, but he wasn't wearing them. She clasped her hands in front of her and looked down.

"I don't expect anything from you, but, I mean, you're my freaking knight in shining armor. I trust you. You respect me, you see me like a person, you know? That's why I want to be trained by you. I think the others are great, I do, but I want you. Besides, Akira said it was okay." She finished and glanced up into Takumi's eyes waiting for his answer.

He looked at her intently, then looked upward, took a deep breath, and nodded. "You have a…a pure heart, Junko." Junko's eyes started to tear up. "Okay, give me your hand." Junko slipped her hand into Takumi's. He tried to ignore the electricity that filled him when he felt her warmth and softness. "Close your eyes, and know that you're about to get involved. You may regret this one day, but if you say you want to be crazy-stupid committed, then you qualify." Junko nodded once slowly and closed her eyes. Takumi joined her. "Master, in Your name I impart the gift of sight to her. Anoint and commission her with the full protection and power of a heavenly Warrior." They both opened their eyes and looked at each other.

"Okay, let's get to work. First, focus your heart and say, 'Through His Eyes'…"

♦ ♦ ♦

Terror etched the face of the demon messenger who cowered before the Dark Lord. He had just finished his report and looked steadily at the ground, awaiting the Devil's wrath. His evil Lord had his back turned and the messenger hoped it stayed that way.

"What was the count again?" Satan asked, staring at a map on the wall of his office.

"Five Overlords, eight Slayers, twenty-two Harassers, and forty-three Grunts. All banished."

He tapped the map at one point. "That will lower our activity in that area somewhat. Very disappointing."

The messenger looked up. "Sire, we still have thirty thousand suicides to date in that country. Our murder squads are reporting an increase of multiple murders. And lust is at an all-time high." Satan turned and his eyes flared with anger and bore a hole in the messenger.

"Are you suggesting that I should be happy?" He stepped toward the fool. "That thirty thousand is enough?"

"No, I…" The demon looked down and started to shake in fear.

"Take human form." The demon slowly looked up with panic in his eyes. "Do it!" Satan's voice echoed off the walls. The demon stood and slowly morphed into a male human wearing a business suit. Tears formed in his eyes as he stood resigned to his fate.

Satan moved close to him now. "Extend your hand." The devil smiled and took the trembling hand into his own and then slid his other hand to get a firm grip on the extended arm. "Let me remind you." Satan jerked hard and there was a snap. The businessman cried out.

"They are so fragile." There was another crack. The man's eyes opened wide and his mouth opened to scream; nothing came out but a high-pitched squeal. The devil looked into the eyes filled with horror and pain and beamed at his work. He released him.

"P–Please…my Lord." The businessman fell to his knees, holding his broken arm.

"You see. Just flesh and bones made from dirt." He looked up. "His precious weak creation. Easy prey." He turned and walked back to the wall. "Not thousands dead. Millions. I want millions." He raised his arms across the map.

The messenger stood again and slowly morphed into a fallen angel with pain still filling his eyes. He gasped to recover.

Satan rubbed his chin. "How many Warriors were there? Is our enemy redeploying resources?"

"W–We're not sure, it was very confusing."

"How many *confirmed* Warriors?" the Dark Lord said sharply.

"One, but there could have been more."

Silence.

"A Called One. What was lost?"

"They rescued the anointed heir, and…"

"The Son of Ryudan?"

"Yes. Kenji. They did something to the backslider. He's not cooperating anymore.

"Purged. Then he'll have to die."

"Yes, my lord. Do we delay our plans to anoint a new leader, Lord? Your servant Ryudan won't be out of his cell for two weeks. Our enemy…"

Satan pointed up and down the map. "That city is key to the whole region and that region keeps a lock on their country. It's been ours for centuries." He tapped the map. "The banished ones will need that time to get back to the area anyway."

"Yes, my lord."

"So, in two weeks we'll pass the torch and secure the next generation in that city. Since Ryudan can't seem to do it alone, I'll come to personally oversee the process and send someone to deal with this warrior." He stepped back and surveyed the whole map.

"Very well, my lord."

"Now, tell me about this warrior. What is his name?"

"*Her* name is Aiko. She's a teenager; seventeen years old."

He tilted his head and nodded. "Ah, yes, I know her family. Stubborn people. I was told they were done. Wiped out. Like so many before them." He chuckled wickedly.

"Just one child left to deal with, my Lord."

"*Just* a child? Don't be so foolish." He clasped his hands behind his back. "They're the dangerous ones. Young enough to dream, to hope with no bounds. Add faith to that and..." He shook his head.

"She's become very strong and she doesn't fight alone."

"Well then, you know the rules of engagement."

"Never fight fair."

"Never. We need to plant one of ours close to her. We may have a sleeper nearby already. But first, divert two full legions to the city and send for my Slayer general to keep her from disrupting our plans. She's of no consequence."

"Yes, my lord. Moloch will be contacted."

The Dark Lord tapped on the map again and then held up three fingers with long, twisted nails. "Aiko..." he hissed. "Make that three full legions and be sure the Faceless Ones are with them as well. I want all resistance in that city crushed. We will break their legacy this time for good." He waved his hands across the map. "We have other places we should be concentrating on. This is a bother."

"It will be done, my lord."

♦ ♦ ♦

"Something really big is happening in two weeks," Kenji said. "I tried to listen when I was conscious and my head was clear. I found out that I was supposed to be killed and that Kentaro was to take my place...receive the curse."

"Wow, your father would let them do that?" Ishi asked. Mai sat up next to her in surprise.

Kenji caught the emotion in his throat. "Uh, father? My father was going to kill me with his own hands." Akira stepped up to him and placed a hand on his shoulder.

"He had to find a way to show his total commitment to the Dark Lord. Killing you would accomplish that."

Ishi just shook her head, and looked at Kenji with compassion filling her eyes. Mai leaned into her friend.

"That sucks," Koh said and took a big bite out of an apple.

"I'll say," Kai chimed in.

"Okay, but their plan is toast since Kenji is still alive. So what will they do?" Michio looked around the room.

Akira walked over to the window and stared out. "They haven't seen anything like this for generations. What Aiko and the rest of you did has scared them. You've countered their every move and, against all odds, retrieved Kenji." He thought for a moment. "They will send the best they have against you, probably call in more help. The Dark Lord himself may come."

They all looked up at Akira.

"Uh, define 'more help,' and is the Dark Lord like old and feeble, or how does that work?" Koh put down his apple.

"He is evil incarnate, the source of all that is wrong in the universe. God made him more powerful than the others before pride caused his fall. You can feel his hate when he gazes on you, and he hasn't lost personally to a Warrior in over a thousand years."

"That can't be right." Michio stood up. "Really?"

"Not that I know of. He's a wily creature. He hates losing. He'll let his hordes do the dirty work and fights only when he knows you are ready to fall. It's a terrible setback for the leader of the fallen angels who works in lies to be banished by a human."

"So he cheats?" Koh said, standing next to Michio.

"Oh yes, always. But don't be fooled. He's very good at combat. Thousands of years of experience."

Koh frowned and sank down in a chair.

Ishi shook her head in disbelief. "How many have faced him?"

Akira was silent for a moment. "Thousands."

"Have you fought him?"

"Not personally. With him present, just once. I lost." The whole room became somber. Akira, still looking out the window, seemed distant. "With it we lost our chance to change things, but I think you have a better chance." The room sat in stunned silence.

"We've hurt them." Aiko broke her silence. "We've ignored their lies and taken down their leaders. They're scared." Her eyes were calculating.

"And when you are scared, you make mistakes." Akira gazed at her.

"What mistakes?" Koh looked from face to face.

"They might go defensive," Aiko said. Akira nodded.

"What does that mean?" Koh pleaded.

"Ha! I get it. They're going to play not to lose, instead of playing to win," Michio smiled and slapped his thigh.

Akira crossed his arms. "So, they'll do everything that they can to protect the curse now, and get it to Kentaro."

"That makes sense to me," Kenji said, "because they kept talking about protecting a legacy and destroying yours. You really messed them up, girl." He looked with admiration at Aiko.

"Okay, I think I get it. So you're saying the bad guys will build a fortress and protect it with hordes of demons including the evil champion of all time, the Dark Lord himself. I vote no." Koh sat back and let out a big sigh.

"Don't suppose I can take this one alone?" Aiko asked.

Akira tilted his head slightly and shook it slowly.

"Sorry, girl, we're not letting you out of our sight ever again." Ishi put her arm around Aiko. Mai nodded in agreement.

♦ ♦ ♦

"Junko. It's okay, he's one of ours. Besides, I can't breathe!" Takumi said, with Junko huddling against him. Her first gaze into the spiritual world was terrifying; a seven-foot Watcher hovered at the head of his bed. Her face was buried in Takumi's chest. He grimaced.

"Oh, Tak, I'm sorry, I forgot." She got off him and faced away from the guardian angel that she could now see with Truesight. "Is he still there?"

"Yes he is…and he's called a Watcher…he's a good and very powerful angel. Look at the eyes, that's how you can tell." He pointed and spoke soothingly. Junko slowly turned to face the head of the bed. She looked tentatively at his eyes, tried to smile, and waved awkwardly. She saw a purity and a love that just shone through his eyes.

"Can he talk? Can I talk to him?"

"Yes, you can, but they will usually only speak to us when they are given messages to share. They're God's servants."

She started to relax a bit, her eyes opened wide with wonder. "Wow," she whispered.

"Yeah, they go back and forth between here and heaven; they actually stand in His presence. Amazing, huh?" He smiled.

"He looks really, like, powerful, you know?" she said, looking him over.

"Oh yeah, you should see when they fight."

"So why don't they do all the fighting?" She cautiously sat on the bed next to Takumi.

"They do some, but mostly God uses us. We're actually more dangerous. They were created to be God's servants and some chose to reject that and became demons, but we were created to be image-bearers." He noticed her confusion. "That is, we kind of display some of God's qualities to the earth He created. That's why they hate us so much. They hate God, and they hate his image-bearers," Takumi explained.

"Yeah, they still look a whole lot more dangerous than we do." She turned to Takumi and then back to the angel.

"Ah, but with our power of choice, we can bear truth. You see, the demon's biggest weapon is lying. They hurt us most when they tempt us into trusting in lies, but when we take truth and engage their lies, that's when the sparks start to fly."

"How do you know all this?" she asked.

"It's all right there, what you're holding in your hand." She looked down at the sword manual.

Takumi leaned forward and looked across the room. "Okay, now it's time to look outside the window and see more spiritual beings, especially the other side." He took her hand. "Now remember, we have a Watcher here, so we're totally safe." He waited until she nodded. "Okay then, go ahead and look." Junko slowly walked over to the window and pulled away the curtain with her eyes closed. She put both hands on the windowsill to steady herself and then opened her eyes. On the dark street below she saw a strange, dark creature the size of an ape. It was hunched over with its back turned. After a moment his head jerked up. Only then could Junko see that his claws were wrapped around the skull of a teenager who sat listening to music at a bus stop. It turned toward her and rage filled its glowing yellow eyes. The face twisted into a snarl and opened its jaws revealing filthy jagged fangs. It growled viciously at her.

Takumi watched her with a worried look. The first time was always the hardest. "Well?" The next moment, she let out a short scream and fell to the floor.

"Junko? Junko?"

♦ ♦ ♦

Kentaro put the phone down slowly with an angry, shaken look on his face. He was surrounded by his department heads and bodyguards. "He's not happy. He wants us at the warehouse."

"Uh, all of us?" his head of security asked.

"Yeah, stupid. All of us. He's turning over the security of this place to new management," Kentaro said, very deliberately fixing a hard look on him. The security man's face went ashen. He knew what that meant. All the guards of the Red Dragon were dead men. You failed Ryudan only once.

"Take Makoto to the warehouse, he's still useful, even if he's confused." He looked closely at Makoto, who sat staring out the window. He looked over to meet Kentaro's stare.

"I'm going to put a bullet in your confused little head, in front of your sister." Kentaro shook a fist at him.

Makoto just stared back, unmoved. His face seemed to say, "It's over, you've lost," like a chess champion who sees the win twelve moves ahead but doesn't want to take the time to explain it.

Kentaro, trying to keep his confidence high, continued in a disdainful tone, "You'll both be rotting in the ground in two weeks' time, and I–ha!–I'll be like God!"

"Is that what he promised you?" Makoto shook his head.

"Shut up!" Kentaro shot back.

"He's a liar." Makoto stared steadily at him.

"I said…shut up!" Kentaro turned to his personal bodyguards and henchmen. "Move, idiots! Let's get out of here."

♦ ♦ ♦

"You'll need more help," Akira said, finally coming out of deep thought. "It's clear the Master has brought you and your friends to this moment, Aiko, but there might be others who can help you."

"Yes! It's about time someone saw things my way," Koh exclaimed. "How about, say, five legions of Watchers to start with?" he pleaded. Akira glanced over at him with a wistful look.

"You may be more right than you think, Koh, but you'll need Warriors too. I'm not sure any can get here in time." Akira walked to the door to leave. "Nevertheless, I'll try."

"In the meantime?" Aiko stood and faced him.

Akira stopped in the doorway and looked back thoughtfully at the group.

"Get Takumi on his feet. Junko will be important as well, see to her. Watch each other's back, and pray your hearts out." He paused as though something had hit him. "Yes, prayer…the Old Ones…I must go…God be with you," he said and closed the door. They could hear his hurried footsteps as he left the building.

♦ ♦ ♦

"Uh, Junko?" She was cuddling close to him again in fear, like a child hiding in her parents' arms. Takumi was in pain.

"Junko, I can't breathe!"

"Oh, I'm really sorry. I don't think I can do this." She pulled away a little from Takumi and gave him an apologetic look.

"Did I mention to you that they are more scared of you than you are of them?"

"What?" She looked at him in disbelief.

"It's true. Once you realize who you are and Who you serve, and Who is with you everywhere you go, then nothing can stop you."

"Nothing?"

"Nothing, except believing in lies. That's why we study our manual. That's why we spend time together talking about what we're learning. That's why we fight together in a team. We watch out for each other and protect one another."

"Will you watch out for me, too?"

"Junko, once you learn how to fight, you'll be watching out for me," he said, and smiled.

She sighed and took in a deep breath. "Okay, let's start again."

Over the next week and a half, Takumi showed her everything.

Chapter Twenty-six

The Gathering

THE GUARDS HAD STOPPED SMILING AFTER THE FIRST HALF HOUR. THEY COULD HEAR the slaps of Kentaro's palms against the young girl's skin, and her screams that later turned into retching and pleading. Another hour passed, until all they could hear was the faint sound of whimpering followed by the sound of their boss's voice. "Get out of my sight!" After a moment, the door slowly opened and what was left of a young girl stumbled out of the antechamber. Her blouse had been shredded; she pulled the tattered remains around her bruised and bleeding body. Her short skirt was twisted around her hips, and scrapes and bumps covered her arms and legs from when Kentaro had thrown her around the room. Dark smears of makeup marred her cheeks, and her eyes were sad and empty. She carried her shoes in one hand and a wad of cash in the other. The guards gave way as she passed them and wandered down the hall to the bathroom to clean up before leaving. "She looks real bad, boss must be tense," one guard said to the other, who abruptly put his hand up to shush him.

"Hey!" Kentaro yelled. The head guard opened the door to Kentaro's office.

"Yes sir?" He saw Kentaro wearing a silk robe that hung open to show off the well-formed bulges of his muscular abdomen. He was wiping his face with a towel and drinking a beer.

"Get the car…it's time to pick up Ryudan."

The guard nodded, holding back a shudder. "Yes, sir!"

♦ ♦ ♦

"One week left, huh? So we know *when*. That's good! We just need to know *where*." Takumi turned from the TV that was giving an update on Ryudan's trial status. Aiko nodded and turned to look out of the window of his hospital room.

She continued to update him. "We've been doing our best to figure it out. Kenji knows several major hideouts where they could do this kind of thing, and we've checked them out, but saw nothing unusual at any of them. I even sent Mai to find out more at the club."

"What?" Takumi sat up straight.

"Takumi, you know I wouldn't take a chance with the little one. She insisted her cover hasn't been blown yet and promised to stay outside to chat with the guards. Besides, we know Kentaro isn't there anymore, *and* Michio is trailing behind her. You know he wouldn't let anything happen to her," she said, trying to reassure him.

He stared a moment, sighed, and then sat back. "You're right, of course, it's just so…"

"Dangerous." Aiko looked at him earnestly.

Her expression made him realize he was more fearful than ever for the safety of his friends, but never as much as Aiko would be. He would have to trust her.

"Koh and Kai are working today," she said, "and letting Kenji work in the back of their kitchen out of sight. They're also keeping a watch on the streets, which are unusually clear of demons."

"They're gathering for the transfer of the curse." Takumi spoke with a sense of finality.

"They're avoiding us, that's for sure. Ishi is having trouble finding live fighting to train Junko with," Aiko said.

"Really?" Takumi felt a trace of a concern. "So, how is she doing?" he asked without trying to seem too interested.

Aiko turned to face him. "She's amazing; still a little frilly, but there's an innocence about her that shows up in her faith."

"Yes, I've seen it too. Those who are forgiven much, love much," Takumi said philosophically.

"Yup. Good job, Sensei Takumi." She smiled and bowed slightly. He looked up and blushed. He hadn't seen it like that at all, but everything that Junko knew, *he* had taught her, and somehow he felt fully responsible for her.

♦ ♦ ♦

"Okay, Junko, hurry. I think I see one in that alley." Ishi spoke urgently. The two armor-clad Warriors dashed into the alley with swords out.

"Is hunting always this hard?" Junko asked, slightly out of breath.

"No, this is very unusual. They're pulling back or something. Oh! He sees us...okay good, he's going to fight."

The demon Grunt was lagging behind the others, who were gathering and had stopped to harass an old man. They could hear him spewing out hatred as he drove a jagged blade into the man's heart.

"What is your life worth now? You failed your family. You lost all your friends..." He noticed the Warriors and turned to face them. He twisted his neck grotesquely from side to side, cracking his neck, and moved in to attack them.

"Okay, Junko, he's yours," Ishi said, and stepped back to observe and coach her.

Junko stepped forward and, in barely a whisper, prayed, "Second chance...thank You, God." She walked straight toward the demon, who tried to surprise her by flinging a fiery arrow at her. The point glowed orange and red and the flames left a trail of smoke as it streaked toward her heart. Junko didn't even blink. At the last moment her shield appeared in front of her and the arrow crashed into it, bursting into sparks.

"Good," Ishi said, ready to jump in if needed.

Junko locked eyes with the demon and her sweet voice became firm and commanding. "Leave him alone!"

"You worthless whor–"

"Silence!" she commanded and the demon's voice cut off and became a muffled rage.

Ishi nodded in approval again.

He swung his sword high and charged the new Warrior.

Swords clashed for only a second and then there was a loud *whoooosh*!

"Wow. So fast." Ishi trotted up. "How many is that?"

"Forty-two in six days," she said, still looking at the dust settle–dust that was once a demon. "Is my hair messy?"

"It's fine, princess. You have a good memory," Ishi replied, slapping her on the back. Junko turned to her.

"It's kinda important to me...the count, that is," she said with a tinge of emotion.

◆ ◆ ◆

Michio lowered the magazine he was hiding behind in the convenience store as Mai walked up to the front of the club. There were no guards. She peeked in a window and then read the sign on the door as she pulled out her phone.

Michio's phone rang and he looked at the text that she had sent him.

People cleaning up inside. Strange. Few demons.

When he looked up, she was reaching for the door to go in. It suddenly opened and a large guard almost ran her over. He reacted, throwing up his large hands and knocking her back. "What the–" He reached out and caught her.

"Ah, girl, you scared the tar out of me!" He set her gingerly on her feet.

Mai straightened out her clothes and looked up innocently at Louie, the head guard, and saw in his eyes real fear. *What's going on?* "That's okay. Where's your friend? Frankie?" she asked sheepishly. He froze and his words caught in his throat.

"He's been…uh…transferred." He looked away quickly and took a deep breath.

"Oh." She looked closely at him. "Are you being transferred too, because, I mean, you're my ticket to this club, you know?"

He paused a moment and with a contrite tone responded, "Honey, listen. Go back home and stay in school. You're still young and have so much *life* ahead of you." Mai stifled a gasp when she figured out what was happening. He would never be disloyal to Ryudan by chasing away a customer if he planned to be alive anytime soon. Louie was going to his own death.

"Uh, thanks," she said, and then reached up and put both small hands on his massive shoulders. Across the street Michio tensed up.

"Louie, excuse me for just a second." She bowed her head and took a deep breath. He looked at her as though she were going to sneeze. The moment her sight went on she was face-to-face with a Slayer and his assigned demon guardian. They both growled in rage at her. Her armor flashed on and the dancer unleashed a fierce attack. It took only a few seconds and then she looked up at Louie, who was blinking, wondering what he was feeling. "You don't have to retire with Frankie. Okay? You don't…have…to…retire," she said very deliberately. She kissed him on the cheek, whispered something in his ear, and left him.

Michio was halfway out of the convenience store when she came trotting up. "What happened?"

"They're murdering their own men, the ones in the club."

"Wow, don't they have any rules at all?"

"Be loyal or die, I guess. They've moved everything for now."

"Did he know anything?"

"He's out of the loop now, they wouldn't tell him."

"What did you say when you…uh…kissed him?" He crossed his arms.

She looked up at him. "I told him to…"–she pecked Michio on the cheek–" change sides." He was speechless. She trotted off, and he followed.

♦ ♦ ♦

"Okay, one more and we'll be done for the day. This time let's find a group and fight together again. I'm so proud of you, girl," Ishi told Junko as they walked up the street.

"It's Takumi, he's a good teacher." Junko smiled, keeping up with her fast stride.

"Yeah, Roboto is really cool. He's one of the bravest guys I've ever met." Ishi softened a bit and asked, "So, you never left his side, did you?"

"No…uh…" Junko looked down, glanced up, and looked down again. She let out a breath. "It's not what you think. He's just really special to me…he doesn't look at me the way other men do." Ishi nodded with an understanding look on her face.

"Jun…"

"I didn't do anything with him."

"Jun…"

"I could never…I mean I could…but not like that."

"Junko." Ishi reached out and grabbed her shoulders. "Calm down, sister." Junko stopped talking and looked like a child about to be scolded. Ishi continued, "He's smart and sincere. He's a gentleman, an awesome spiritual warrior, and one of the nicest boys in school. Any girl would be lucky to have him as a friend…or more." Junko looked up at Ishi. "I know you feel connected to him, but just know that we *all* love you and feel like you are part of our family now."

Junko looked down, almost embarrassed, "Thanks, Ish."

The next instant they heard a loud sob. There was weeping coming from the next corner. They looked at each other and hurried around and into a dark alley.

"All right, we asked for it," Ishi said as they looked upon four demons harassing a young girl who was weeping in despair. Her clothes were torn and her body badly bruised. From the looks of her outfit she was apparently a prostitute. Junko reacted at once.

"Oh, Ish, let's help her."

"Why four on this one?" Ishi moved toward them. "You remember what Takumi taught about tandem fighting?"

"Yeah, first we strike the middle, then they'll try to flank, so we go back to back." Junko counted each step with her fingers.

It was a textbook attack. They banished two in the initial flurry and then two more that tried to slide around the sides. It took only thirty seconds. Both Warriors then turned to the weeping girl.

Ishi knelt down to talk to her. In a gentle and loving voice she said, "How can we help you? Let us get you to a clinic..."

Junko stood back. She saw herself in the girl. She was fighting a boiling emotion deep inside. Something was welling up from the depths of her soul. A girl, someone's precious daughter, had been trapped by evil, like she had been, and was considered nothing more than an expendable piece of meat. The emotion continued to build. Now she recognized it. It was rage. But not hate. A pure form of rage against all that is evil, an overwhelming righteous anger.

Ishi's attention was focused on the girl and she was facing Junko, so she didn't see the demon who appeared behind her. Junko didn't hesitate at all. Still filled with rage, she leaped past Ishi and blocked a blow that was meant for Ishi's neck. She immediately noticed that this one looked different. It was robed, more wiry, and had no face, but it was just as hateful as the others.

Ishi turned and followed Junko's charge with her eyes as she heard the *ring* behind her, but horror gripped her when she saw the demon...it was a Goon.

She shouted a warning as fast as she could. "*Wait!*" The Goon kicked Ishi in the chest, with hellish strength, before she could finish and sent her tumbling backward twenty feet, crashing into a Dumpster. "Aah!" She snapped to her feet as fast as she could, shook her head, and looked toward the fight. She could see Junko exchanging blows with the Goon, blocking, ducking, getting slashed, grunting in pain, and then being knocked against a wall hard. "Junko! Don't try..."

Junko, undaunted and naïve, charged back toward the Goon. Ishi broke into a sprint with all the speed she could muster, but she hurried and was too reckless in her attack. The Goon locked swords with Junko and swung his shield with so much force that Ishi slammed against the opposite alley wall and slid to the ground dazed.

"Ju...Junko...no..." she said weakly. "He's a...a..." She could hear Junko grunting with effort with each blow and block. The fight was intensifying.

"Just...just run!" Ishi said, scrambling to her feet and trying to clear her head. "We can't..."

Suddenly, there was a sound like a lightning bolt followed by a horrible high-pitched screech. Her eyes cleared and she saw Junko, with clenched teeth, shove her sword the last few inches to the hilt into the chest of the Goon, whose head was thrown back with his arms spread and trembling at his sides. There was a sound of rushing wind and then a huge *whooosh* as the Goon disappeared. Junko fell to her knees, exhausted.

"That was a hard one." She blew a strand of hair out of her face. "Guess my hair's gone now. Are you okay?"

Ishi stood transfixed by the ex-prostitute. Finally she spoke. "You have no idea what you just did, do you?"

Junko blinked innocently.

♦ ♦ ♦

"They could change the place at the very last minute," Takumi continued to think aloud.

"Tak, I think this might be my last battle," Aiko said, out of the blue, as she continued to gaze at the sky outside the window.

What makes you say that? Please don't talk like that."

"Um...I'm sorry...I'm just tired." She sighed. "Guess I haven't recovered from the other night yet."

"You can tell me about Makoto if you want to," Takumi said gently. Aiko hadn't spoken to anyone about it yet. Everyone just talked around it and waited for her to be ready. Tears started rolling down her cheeks.

"I was only able to glance back on my way out. I saw him drop to the ground, after the...purging." She paused. "I, um..." She wiped tears rolling down her cheeks. "I can still hear his screams." She pressed her lips together to keep from sobbing.

"Did he try to fight you, as you thought?" Takumi asked.

"Oh no," She took and deep breath and composed herself. "I didn't give him a chance. I knew if I hesitated I wouldn't be able to do what I needed to."

"So, did you get it all?"

"I think so, I don't know. That's just it! I've been asking God but He's been silent! Why? Why is He silent?" Now her tears were tears of frustration. "I'm not asking for much, I just want to know that he's okay. Or did he snap back to evil?" She paused, looking up into the sky. "I just wanted to give him one more chance. Why won't God let me know? I *need* to know!" She slammed both fists on the windowsill.

This was rare because Aiko never questioned God. She just trusted. Takumi knew that Aiko's greatest source of pain and only weakness was her great love for her family. Demons were ruthless and immoral and never fought with any sense of fairness or honor. If they couldn't get you, they'd go after those you love.

"Hey, getting to him was a gift, and you did what you had to do. Now it's in His hands," Takumi offered. Aiko looked at him without expression. He started shaking his finger in front of him. "I have to say, in my seventeen long years on this earth I have never, ever seen a display as brave, loving, or amazing as when you fought your way out of that club, and you even looked great doing it." Takumi smiled. "Did you ever lose those heels?" Aiko looked up and finally broke into a light laugh.

"Yeah, on the first stairway down. I'll never wear those again." She shook her head and smiled at him. Takumi was relieved that she had pulled out of her dive.

"Now *they* are so afraid, they're not attacking anymore." He pointed to some unknown battlefield. Now they're just waiting, probably afraid that we'll show up and ruin their little ceremony, which we will."

"Tak, can you get out of bed?" Aiko said, suddenly cutting him off, her eyes transfixed on the sky. He slid off the bed and gingerly walked over in his hospital robe, followed her gaze into the sky, and turned on Truesight.

"Oh my…I guess we know where they're heading now." His eyes opened wide in fear and wonder.

"Start counting," Aiko ordered.

♦ ♦ ♦

The tray of dishes crashed on the ground as Koh froze in fear while staring at the sky over the alley behind Coffee Shop.

"What?" Kai yelled, coming out with Kenji right behind. They both looked up.

"We're dead."

"Okay, this is new." Kai placed a hand on his forehead to shade his eyes.

"Oh wow, they want this really, really bad," Kenji gasped, almost out of breath.

♦ ♦ ♦

Two blocks from the hospital, Mai's eyes hardened as she watched hundreds of demons flying high overhead. Michio looked defiantly into the sky, clenching his hands into fists. "Wow, looks like they called in the reserves." Mai was silent. They both sighed and sank onto a nearby bench, continuing to watch and feeling very, very tired.

♦ ♦ ♦

In the soundproofed basement, Ryudan pulled the trigger again. He shot the last of the kneeling security guards, who fell forward with a head shot from behind. He sidestepped over and put the gun to Makoto's head. "And now the traitor," he began. Makoto looked straight ahead with no fear and closed his eyes. Ryudan stopped smiling and huffed. He pulled the gun away and thought a moment. "No, he's not afraid anymore, it will be much better to shoot him in front of his sister. Take him away!" A henchman roughly pulled Makoto to his feet and marched him off.

Ryudan took a cloth, wiped the gun clean, and removed the white gloves he was wearing. "Is that all of them?" he demanded. Kentaro stepped forward. "We lost track of just one, but we can find him." Ryudan looked over at his heir. "No, he'll live in fear for the rest of his life. Don't waste anymore time on him or Kenji."

"But Father…"

Ryudan looked at him and growled. "Listen, you idiot, you had your chance, and you messed it up! But don't worry, soon you won't have to choose anymore. You'll be serving the Dark Lord and will be his slave to command." Ryudan spoke with an evil intensity that choked the air.

He paused and stood for a moment as if he were in another world. His eyes glazed over and he turned his head from side to side. He wore a strange smile and trembled slightly. "Ah, Moloch is here, Aiko's executioner, and he has brought some friends. Good. Almost time to spoil our enemies' maggot-filled little *world again!*" He let out an evil laugh that echoed throughout the basement of death.

♦ ♦ ♦

"I'd say two legions of mixed demon types, mostly Grunts." Takumi held a clipboard and was scribbling while he surveyed the flying formations.

"Did you see the Goons?"

Takumi nodded slowly. "Yeah, not a lot, but enough to keep us at a disadvantage." He shook his head in defeat and sighed. They both sat down and looked at each other.

Aiko looked upward. "*Oh God, we need a break.*"

◆ ◆ ◆

Wherever they were, they were sitting silently, feeling helpless and overwhelmed. A sudden weariness and heaviness fell on all of them. So many enemies; so many filled with hate and evil; so many against them. Just before they went under and were completely enveloped in despair and discouragement, their phones rang with a text message sent to each of them.

"Huh?"

"Ohhh, yeah!"

"I don't believe it."

"Tak, look at this." He read the text and his mouth dropped open and his eyes blinked in disbelief.

It read simply: "**Junko banished a goon!**"

Chapter Twenty-seven

Last Minute Moves

A week later the door to Coffee Shop burst open and the Warriors returned from another night of training.

"I could go for a Coke."

"Me too."

"Me three."

"I'll take iced coffee."

"I'm hungry, training always makes me hungry."

"Everything makes you hungry."

"Lemonade for me, please."

"All right, all right! Hold on and let me get in the door first," Kai pleaded as they all filed into their room in the back and plopped down. He went straight to the kitchen to help his parents, who were expecting them. They had faithfully shown up every day after school. It was the same routine. They would put down their books and then train together for three or four hours. Next, they would come in hungry and thirsty, do homework together for two more hours, and then head home around ten o'clock. Tonight was special for two reasons. They were expecting word from Akira, who promised to come; and according to what Kenji had overheard while held captive at Ryudan's, it was the night before the transfer of the curse. They would fight for their generation tomorrow.

"Food!" Koh called out, and walked in with a tray of hamburgers.

Kai followed with a tray of drinks. He placed it on the long low table opposite the couch. They all gathered and took their orders.

"Whose turn to pray?" Michio looked at the food and rubbed his hands together.

"I'll pray." Aiko bowed her head. They all paused and closed their eyes. "Thank You for this food and for this fellowship. We belong to You. Strengthen us and go before us. In His Name." They all said, "Amen!" and dove into their meals.

Aiko stood back and watched everyone.

Kenji and Ishi walked to a corner and were having a spirited talk about battle strategy. As soon as they put their food down and took a bite, Kenji motioned with his hands and described some move. Ishi shook her head and made a face. She looked really good in short hair, but Aiko missed her ponytail.

Junko and Takumi sat down and pulled out a chessboard. He had been teaching her the game since his stay in the hospital and she had picked it up very fast. Now he was teaching her how to think in battle. After setting out the pieces, Takumi adjusted his glasses, which prompted something in Junko. She said something, with a big smile on her face, and Takumi looked up and fixed his glasses again, shaking his head. She leaned over, took off his glasses, and sat back to take a look while he squinted. She tilted her head from side to side and then started nodding. Takumi pointed to the board and reached for his glasses. She pulled back and giggled, and then gave them to him. Aiko could see that Takumi enjoyed Junko's less-than-serious approach to life.

Aiko laughed to herself. *What a pair.* She looked over at Mai, who sat alone, surrounded by papers and an open math book. She ate slowly and kept her head down, working, looking from the book to her paper, back at the book, and then writing. From time to time, she jumped up and trotted over to Takumi, who would pause, scan the paper and nod, or point out something to her. Then, she would run back and plop down to work again. Aiko shook her head slowly. *Oh, girl, you are so dangerous…my little dark angel. What will you become?*

Michio yelled, "Boom!" as he simulated a homerun swing and put his hand to his forehead as though he were watching the ball go into orbit. Koh and Kai were shaking their heads. Koh also got up and simulated a strikeout, swinging hard, and then looking back at the catcher who had caught the third strike. "No!" Michio shouted and they all laughed. They were bickering with him about his big game on Sunday. All three were putting hamburgers away at an alarming rate, but still managing to argue about whether Michio would be able to hit the famous pitcher, Tanaka, from the team up north. Michio would make an exaggerated, incredulous face as if the outcome were obvious. No question at all about who he thought would win.

Win. Aiko sighed.

Win.

All week long they had talked about Michio's game on Sunday, homework and assignments due before the end of the school year, summer plans, and other upcoming life issues. No one had mentioned Akira's disastrous battle and the fact that Saturday night could be anyone's last night on earth. *Confidence is okay when you add concentrated preparation*, she thought. That's how she had kept them focused. With Junko's miracle came the hope that God had given them everything that they needed to win. Well, almost everything. They still didn't have a plan.

♦ ♦ ♦

Makoto was handcuffed to a chair in Ryudan's office. It had been a while since he tried anything spiritual, but he decided to risk it. He closed his eyes and in his heart whispered to the Master.

Through His eyes.

When he opened his eyes, he had to fight the sudden fear of being in a place with the complete absence of good. Six of the Resistant Ones, Goons, stood equally dispersed around the perimeter of the room. Ryudan was at his desk, yelling at someone on the phone. "What do you mean insurance doesn't cover gunfire? We run a reputable business and you treat us like filth?" Makoto had to keep from reacting when he looked over at him. Sometimes, he could see the convoluted image of five evil faces overlaid on Ryudan's human face, all growling or snarling in deep guttural tones. Sometimes, one or more of them would turn another way and lean out of his body creating an eerie Hydra-like image, and then return back inside his body. One of the demons looked over and glared at Makoto.

A deep, evil voice emerged, and declared with alarm, "He sees!" Ryudan immediately looked over and hung up the phone.

"What are you looking at?" Ryudan sneered at him. Makoto could see the overlaid demon faces leering, mocking him.

"A slave," Makoto said with no emotion.

"Well, I'm looking at a dead man," Ryudan replied with contempt, then added with a piercing glare, "Oh, or should I say, dead family?"

Makoto thought for a moment and figured that he had nothing to lose. "Are you so sure? You can see what Aiko did to your club. One Warrior. Believe me, she's coming for you next, and she won't be alone." He shook his head and grinned.

Ryudan turned his eyes upward impatiently and scowled. "Well, that's what you get when you leave it to a two-faced traitor, an ambitious underpowered heir, and an army of leaderless, disorganized fallen slaves. That won't happen again, because next time she'll have to deal with *me*!" he thundered and drove his finger into his chest.

Makoto's eyes opened wide with fear as the five demons all fanned out from Ryudan's waist and drew their weapons. The swung them with deadly coordination creating a horrific shredder effect. Then they combined their voices in a thunderous *roar*. He shuddered, thinking what they might do to Aiko.

♦ ♦ ♦

"Hey! I saved this for you." Kenji handed Aiko a plate with a hamburger. "I noticed you hadn't eaten yet, and the boys won't stop till the food is gone." He gave a lighthearted chuckle. Ishi had gone over to sit and talk with Mai, who was putting her books away.

Aiko took the plate and looked at him. "Thank you."

"No, no…thank *you*, Aiko. I know I've been saying it, but let me say it one more time: Thanks for coming after me, again. What you did in that club…"

"…shows what teams can do that work together." She nodded toward the activity in the room.

"But, you were alone."

Aiko smiled slightly and looked him in the eye. "Kenji, I was *never* alone," she said firmly.

"All right, all right! I give up, but I still think you're amazing." Kenji raised his hands in surrender.

There was a pause as they looked at the ongoing fellowship around the room.

"So, what do you think? Your life's changed a bit in the last month," Aiko said reflectively.

"Tell me about it. Oh man, I'll never look down a dark alley the same way again," he said, with a grim smile and raised eyebrows, "but, you know, I think I kind of always knew there was something going on behind the scenes; something deep, like a struggle between good and evil. I felt like a pawn, with no control over what happened, but now…" He glanced at the room of Warriors. He paused and rubbed both hands on his thighs for a moment and then continued. "Sooo, do we have a plan yet?"

Aiko knew that everyone was waiting patiently for her to sit them down and talk it through step by step, as she always did. She just looked at him.

"This one's different, Kenji. I'm still waiting on God." She paused, took a deep breath, and shook her head slightly. "Maybe Akira will help tonight. I'm…I'm afraid my love for Makoto will take me away from the right focus. There's also Ryudan to deal with *and* Kentaro, who seems evil enough without the curse." She blew out a breath. "Thank God for Junko. At least we can now handle the Resistant Ones." She looked over at the chess game. "Sweet girl…pure faith…"

"Nooo…" Junko bounced in her chair and waved her arms. She slapped the table and screamed theatrically. "You keep blocking what I'm trying to do!"

"Junko, there's no screaming in chess." Takumi smiled and moved a piece on the board.

"Watch him, Junko, Roboto will trick you," Koh called out and pointed his hamburger at Takumi.

"Yup, smokes me all the time." Michio squinted trying to see the board from across the room.

"Uh, we're playing a game here." Takumi raised his voice above the din and held both hands up. The others waved a dismissive hand at him and returned to whatever they were doing.

"I'm going to kill your king." Junko focused again on the board, her forehead wrinkled.

Aiko and Kenji just laughed. "Goon-Killer is what the guys are calling her," Kenji said, still watching the chess match.

Aiko stopped smiling and looked troubled. "I don't feel right about all this. I just can't get clarity on it. Something's wrong, but I can't put my finger on it. How do we stop this curse? How does one turn the tide?" she said, searching for answers.

"Well, remember, *you* are just as much a target for *them* as Ryudan is for us. They're trying to erase you too. Maybe you're sensing a trap? Or, maybe the Dark Lord will show up again after what you did to their stronghold," he added with concern, shaking his head again at what she had pulled off.

There was a flicker in her heart, then a faint whisper, "*He's coming.*" She looked at Kenji. *There's something there. Think, Aiko…God, come on.*

They heard Junko raise her voice and they looked over.

"Okay, I don't mind that you let me win. But let me jump your King…I want to clear off *all* the pieces. Why do you just quit?" Junko complained in fun.

"The King is never really jumped." Takumi held up the chess piece. "When you know you're going to lose you just retire him; he never really gets jumped. Okay, clear the board."

Junko frowned. "Huh? I don't like that rule, leaves you feeling frustrated even if you win." She reached down and helped set up the board again.

Something gripped Aiko, and the world went quiet. Her look hardened as she watched the pieces swept off the board and then replaced pawn by pawn, piece by piece, back in place. Suddenly, it hit her.

"I know what we have to do." She spoke out loud and looked at Kenji, who didn't know what she was talking about. The whole room went quiet as everyone looked up at her and a plan instantly crystallized in her mind.

"I know what we have to do," she repeated, still looking at the chessboard, "but you're not going to like it," she said with a frown and beckoned to everyone. "Okay, gather around!"

♦ ♦ ♦

"Unfortunately, I don't get the fun of destroying your sister alone." Ryudan pulled a box from his desk and opened it. "You see, first we'll destroy her faith. That's very important, we can't have her die as some holy martyr; we've learned that lesson. No, first we make her hate and curse her God." He gagged on the word. He pulled out a needle and filled it with dark green liquid from an unlabelled vial. "By the way, I called in the demon general, an assassin, to do just that! He's what you might call our ace in the hole." He spit and plunged the needle into Makoto's arm. Ryudan held it there and watched Makoto grimace and press his lips together hard. "He happens to be the one who destroyed your sister's faith." He chuckled and then abruptly stopped smiling. "Although, she tried to turn back again too. Stupid family."

Makoto's ears perked up. "Wha..."

"Yeah, the skank tried to crawl back to her God in her last moments...we had to assist her." He nodded with a mocking smile.

"You *murdered* my sister?" Makoto pushed against his restraints and raised his head.

"It was...uh..." Ryudan searched for the right word. "Fun!" He laughed and yanked the needle out of Makoto's arm.

Makoto looked down as the realization slowly dawned upon him. "My sister was killed, she didn't commit suicide." He closed his eyes and thanked God as he felt a burning sensation enter his veins. *In her moment of despair, she trusted Him.*

Ryudan returned the box to its drawer and stood. "The Dark Lord himself, who gave the order to kill your parents, will see that the job is done right." The next moment, Ryudan heard something that made him stop smiling. Makoto sighed deeply, slowly shook his head, and laughed weakly.

"You..." Makoto blinked and wavered. He formed each word with great effort. "You...

"Just...

"Lost...

"Your...

"Ace..."

He fell into what was meant to be a bad dream. But it wasn't. For the first time in many years Makoto felt peace.

"You and your family are worm food!" Ryudan pointed hard at him. "I have my ace!" He stared a moment, wondering if he was missing something.

♦ ♦ ♦

The room was so quiet you could almost hear people's thoughts. Everyone's eyes fixed on the chessboard that Aiko had used to outline her plan.

"All right, I'll talk first." Koh stood up. Kai pushed him back down.

Takumi looked up from the board with his glasses in one hand. "It makes sense. There are always more pawns; even when the board is cleared, he'll just keep setting it up again. We need to get him to leave the table."

"So, how do we do that again?" Michio rubbed his chin.

"We challenge him, beat him in front of everyone else, and claim this city." Aiko pounded a fist on the table.

"Are we sure he'll be there?" Ishi tapped the chessboard.

"Odds are pretty good." Takumi wiped his glasses. "Look at the past month. Finding Kenji, meeting Ryudan, Kenji's conversion, the generational clash. It was all..."

"God's plan," Aiko finished. "From the beginning, He's opened one door after the other to get us face-to-face with the one moving the pieces. The Dark Lord."

"Hello? Hasn't lost in a thousand years...that makes him...hmmm, let's see...five million wins and no losses!" Koh motioned over the board and then held out five fingers in one hand and a closed fist with the other. Everyone ignored him and looked at Aiko.

"What do we know about him?" Aiko looked from face to face.

"He was made more powerful than the other angels." Koh buried his face in his arms on the table, shaking his head.

"He's a liar, the Father of lies."

"He's a strategist and always hits your weak spot." There was a brief pause.

"He's proud." Ishi picked up the queen and held it in front of her. "*That* was his downfall–his pride." She looked at Aiko.

"Pride." Aiko tapped the chessboard. "He uses our weaknesses. We'll use his."

♦ ♦ ♦

Ryudan had his feet up on his desk. He held a cigar in one hand and the phone in the other. "No, I just need the usual protection, nothing big. I want to get there by eleven thirty P.M. The…uh…ceremony will take place at midnight. Don't be late!" Ryudan gruffly slammed down the phone and sat up. He took a puff and looked at Kentaro who sat watching Makoto jerk about in his fitful sleep.

"Let me slit his throat now!" Kentaro spit out with contempt and hatred. "Two-faced traitor!" He looked up at Ryudan. "Then I want Kenji."

Ryudan bared his teeth. "A man after my own heart." Then a moment later his smile faded as he contemplated further. "Not yet. He'll be useful to stop her."

"What? She's just a weak has-been." Kentaro huffed.

Ryudan stormed across the room and grabbed a surprised Kentaro by the shirt.

"Shut your ignorant mouth! She'd slice you to ribbons up in two seconds." He pushed Kentaro away from him in disgust and fixed his hair. "If you're going to lead, you better know how to read an enemy. She's a *Called One*…she's put in this world to stop *you*. Until you are infested, you can't touch her." Ryudan paused. He looked up briefly. "Besides, Moloch is here. My killer angel," he whispered.

Kentaro yanked his shirt back into place. "Just give me the pleasure of wasting this one," he demanded and glared again at a semiconscious Makoto.

"Done." Ryudan waved his hand. Makoto groaned as if he had heard the exchange.

As he drifted on the edge of lucidness, Makoto made a choice.

Chapter Twenty-eight

GENERATIONS

THE BOARD WAS SET ON BOTH SIDES.

The Warriors planned thoroughly and trained hard. Calls were made, and quick trips home to pick up essentials after which the team came back to Coffee Shop for their last night together. The girls got the back room and boys got the front area where the television was. Koh tried to get a game of cards going, but no one was in the mood. Everyone was settling down for the night. Michio retired early because he had an early Saturday morning practice with his baseball team that he couldn't miss.

Ishi and Kenji sat at a table at the front window of the shop and looked out into the night.

"Do you think she's okay?" Kenji asked, referring to Aiko, who had left an hour earlier and not returned.

"Oh yeah, the spiritual streets are deserted. Everyone is gathering." Ishi gazed out the window. "Besides, I think the name *Aiko* strikes fear in them right now." She smiled and held up a fist.

"Yeah, she's pretty amazing. You *all* are."

"Don't you mean *we*?" Ishi looked at him sideways and nudged his shoulder.

Kenji shook his head regretfully. "My first battle alone, I walked right into an ambush. There's a part of my old self that just reacts. When Kentaro showed me your hair, I thought…well, I was afraid…I just lost it." Ishi listened intently.

"I was totally out of control and just snapped," Kenji huffed and looked at Ishi.

"Because you thought he hurt me?" She met his gaze.

"Oh yeah. I don't know what I would do if that happened." Kenji leaned against her shoulder and nodded.

Ishi looked away and sat up so that they weren't touching. "Yeah, we're all kind of attached to each other." She glanced back and then away again.

Kenji looked at her directly. "Ish?" He waited a moment until she looked up at him.

"Ishi, I'm talking about you. I care for everyone on the team, but there's something really special about you."

Ishi blinked. Her cheeks turned a deep red. Kenji kept a steady gaze into her eyes.

♦ ♦ ♦

Eerie mists rose from the cemetery, shrouding the rows of lampposts and the new gravestones laid out in order on the perfectly trimmed lawn.

However, the ancient part of the graveyard had only snatches of light that blinked between the moving branches of the trees. Stubborn weeds clung to moss-covered gravestones; and in the far corner, almost hidden from sight, was a small section for crosses. Only a beam or two of light penetrated this far, but there was enough light for Aiko to find what she was looking for.

The weary Warrior sat on the ground with tears streaming down her face as she pondered two ancient crosses that, along with about a dozen others, were desecrated. Sometime, long ago, someone had taken a sharp instrument to hack at them in a show of utter contempt, but here lay her ancestors. She reached out and ran her hands along one cross, letting her fingers trace each nick and cut. *We're so hated.* With glassy eyes she looked up at the starry night and started to pray.

"I can't do this." She stared at the sky . "Master, I'm tired, tired of being strong." Her eyes looked down to her hands that she held open in front of her. They were trembling. "Can I ask You again why You chose my family? Why?" Her voice got sharp. She sat back as though in conversation with some unseen friend and talked aloud. "I…I just want to be normal: to walk down the street and only see people; to love my friends; to find someone to share my life with…to…" She released a deep sigh of frustration. "Why again do I need to care? Can You tell me why?"

She took out her sword manual and placed it in front of her. "Can I resign?" She looked up pleadingly. "It's just…my friends have been dashed against walls, and mugged and bullied, and forcibly drugged, and…and…shot. What's next? Huh? Rape? Disfigurement? Murder?" She picked up the manual and threw it on the ground. "They're so, so evil, Master, and we're just…kids. Why don't You just take my life now and save them the trouble?"

♦ ♦ ♦

Kentaro held the straw to his nose and snorted up the white powder spread on the coffee table in front of him, breathed deeply, and leaned back on the couch. He smiled and then looked up suddenly. He remembered something he had to do.

"Hey…" He shouted to a guard standing in the shadows, "Hey, *stupid*! *Get over here when I call!*" The guard came up to him. Kentaro tried to focus but couldn't, he just blinked his eyes and shook his head to get a clear thought. "Okay…listen. Give our special guest one more dose, a double dose in fact. That will keep him quiet till I blow his brains out." He laughed.

"Yes, sir," the guard answered obediently. Satisfied, Kentaro lay back again.

The guard watched for a moment to be sure he was fully spaced out on his drugs. Kentaro could not see the look of disdain on the guard's face or the slight grin as he walked over to Makoto and gave him a different kind of injection.

♦ ♦ ♦

Ishi took a deep breath and her eyes darted from side to side, and Kenji continued. "I don't expect anything from you. I don't even think I deserve you as a friend. You are so…beautiful and loyal and courageous…I'm not even worthy…" He looked down and shook his head.

"Stop. Don't say that." Ishi placed her hand on his. "Kenji, we all start broken." He looked up from the floor, glanced at her hand on his, and met her gaze. Their hearts were pulling hard at each other and their lips were getting closer. Then a mischievous grin formed on Ishi's mouth. She put her hand back in her lap. "Of course, you were mo-o-ore broken…like smashed!" She pounded a fist into her open hand.

Kenji's mouth dropped open, then he caught the tease and shoved her.

"Hey…what about the 'we *all* start broken' part?" She shrugged and crossed her arms.

In his heart he thanked Ishi for lightening the atmosphere. "By the way, the new hair rocks."

"You better say that. Mai and I call this the Kenji-cut. You hang out with him and…" She pointed to her hair with both hands and then her eyes flashed playfully at him.

Kenji rocked back. "Ohhh, ouch…stop, girl. I'm sorry and promise to shave the rest of Kentaro's head for you."

"Hey." She reached into her pocket and pulled out the lock of Kentaro's hair. "I want the full set. I'm making a wig for my dog." They both threw back their heads and laughed hard together.

"Yo! People trying to sleep here, you know, epic battle and all." Across the room Koh peeked from under his sleeping bag.

"Sorry, sorry," Kenji and Ishi replied in unison, containing their mirth for a few seconds and then bursting into laughter again, wiping tears from their faces.

♦ ♦ ♦

Aiko was on all fours before God in the graveyard, deep sobs wrenching her. "It's...uh...really simple, You see. Just use someone else. I've done my part, right? I've done my fair share...so now it's somebody else's chance to share the burden. That's not asking too much, is it?" She looked up with frustration in her tear-filled eyes. "*Is it? Say something!*" she yelled into the night. She sat back on her haunches and with clenched fists cried out to the heavens. "How much blood do You want? You've taken my father and mother and sister...and soon my brother! How much more? My friends too?" She fell face down in the grass, weeping uncontrollably.

A few moments had passed when she heard a faint sound from across the cemetery that sounded like a car door closing. She ignored it at first, till she heard voices. It was a woman's voice, and a child's. No, it was more than one child. Aiko composed herself, sat up slowly, and looked in the direction of the sound. She could see the lights of a taxi parked in the newer section of the cemetery. The little family, a mother with two children who must be ten and twelve or so, walked amongst the gravestones, searching.

At this hour? Aiko watched the scene unfold. The mother's uniform told her that she must have been an off-duty nurse. The clear night allowed the voices to carry well.

"Here it is, Mommy! Shinji Matsuoka," a little girl exclaimed. The younger brother came running over, and the mother walked over too, opening her bag.

"Please, be quiet, children." The mom spoke gently. She looked around and pulled out flowers from her bag and knelt before the grave. The kids watched curiously and knelt down too.

"Mommy, what happens when you die? Where is Shinji now?" The little girl ran her hand over the smooth gravestone.

"He's just sleeping. He's at peace now." Her mom placed flowers on the fresh grave.

"Why are we sneaking, Mommy?" the boy asked. His hands were in his pockets and he looked over his shoulder at the empty cemetery.

"Because we don't want Daddy to know. He misses Shinji very, very much and doesn't want to talk about it. Please promise you won't tell him."

"We promise." they chorused.

"Why did Shinji kill himself...was he mad at us?" The boy looked at his mother. Aiko gasped and started to tear up again.

"No, honey, he was just very, very sad."

"Will we see him again?" the little girl asked. The mother hesitated, searching for the right words.

"I hope so, honey." She bowed her head and started to gently weep. Both children hugged their mommy.

Aiko watched with emotion pouring into her soul. Her fists clenched hard as her heart exploded with compassion. "Dark Lord, you like this.... You enjoy their pain.... You're even laughing right now, aren't you? In the end God will damn you to hell where you belong." She watched the little family as they concluded their secret memorial service and made their way back to the waiting taxi. "You laughed when my sister died...and you'll laugh when my brother dies." She sat up straight and took a deep breath and wiped her tears.

She looked up and resumed her prayer, but the tone had changed. "It's for them, isn't it?" She turned to the taxi that was driving away. "The next generation of children who will walk right into his hands if he's not stopped?"

She closed her eyes and started to drift. She could see children everywhere. She saw them in the malls, lining up in uniform for their schools, asleep on their parents' shoulders in the trains, and playing in the parks. She heard the voice of her mother,

"Makoto, slow down! Wait for Aiko...she's helping your little sister." She felt little Shiho holding on to her hand tightly as they tried to catch up with their brother. "Stay together," her mom said caringly.

A tiny voice pleaded. "Don't leave me."

Aiko looked down and squeezed the little hand. "I'll never leave you behind, Shiho-chan. I promise."

She considered a whole generation of children who were filled with hope, innocence, and potential; and she could see a vicious and evil Dark Lord waiting to devour them.

Someone's got to stop you...someone . . .

She opened her eyes again and sighed. "I'll stop you."

She put her hands together. "I give You my allegiance and worship, O Lord my Rock, who trains my hands for war and my fingers for battle. I am already dead. My life is in Your hands and hidden away with You in the heavens. The battle is Yours alone, and Master, I claim the victory that You have already won over the Dark Lord. Give me wisdom and quicken my sword to strike deep and push back the darkness."

♦ ♦ ♦

A beam of light peeked in the room and fell across Makoto's face causing him to squint. He had a splitting headache and squeezed his eyes shut again, trying to clear his head. Everything was blurry. He was so thirsty. He opened his mouth to lick his lips and his tongue felt dry. He felt a movement nearby and a glass of water appeared in front of him. His hands shook, so a pair of strong hands held the cup for him while he drank. He heard a reassuring voice:

"Sleep as much as you can, they can't know you are clean or they'll dope you up again. I'll get you some food later. You can't just treat men like dogs, you know?"

♦ ♦ ♦

The door to Coffee Shop opened and the morning light poured into the room. Ishi and Kenji raised their heads from the tables where they had fallen asleep waiting for her. The others were roused by the light as well and stirred. They all sat up, rubbed their eyes, and looked toward the open doorway.

There stood the tall figure of Aiko. The bright sunlight bathed her, creating a regal silhouette. She stood silently for a few moments, looking at the friends whom she loved so much. Finally she spoke.

"Everyone, it's a big day for us. Today, we show the world that there is always, *always* hope that evil can be defeated by good. It's time to take our city back from the darkness and free Kenji's family from the curse."

"Today, He has called us to make a difference; to force the Dark Lord and his slaves out of our city and stop him from taking so many innocent lives." She looked around the room. "So together, in His strength and for His honor we're going to do just that. No matter the cost."

She squared her shoulders as she spoke her last sentence. *I'm ready, Master.*

"What if some of us don't come back?" Koh asked grimly and sat up.

Aiko paused looking at each of them in turn. "If even one of you doesn't come back, I promise I will be standing next to you when you meet the Master today."

"Well, sister, that means I'll be there too." Ishi stood with her hands on her hips. Mai walked up and stood next to Ishi and nodded her head once.

Michio threw his covers off and stood. "Nobody's meeting the Master without me!

Kai stood and pulled Koh to his feet. "Or us!"

Koh sheepishly scratched his head. "They have food in heaven, right?" He looked at his brother and nodded. They bumped fists.

Takumi put on his glasses and walked over to Junko. He extended a hand, she took it, and he stood her up. Then he turned to Aiko. "He calls and we go out together. That's just how it works. We all come back or we meet in glory tonight. Sorry, Aik. You have no choice in this."

Aiko stared hard at each of them and her eyes misted up. She smiled and nodded. "Okay then." She extended her hand in front of her, and Takumi came over and placed his hand over it. Then the others stepped up and huddled around stacking their hands. "For the Master, for each other, and for our generation. Let's send them to hell."

They worked until evening with single-minded purpose. Honing spiritual weapons, kneeling in prayer, encouraging each other before the coming battle. As the sun descended over the city skyline, they grimly armored up. No more talk. It was time to fight.

Chapter Twenty-nine

BATTLE FOR A GENERATION

"I THINK I'M GOING TO THROW UP." KOH HELD HIS STOMACH AND TURNED AWAY FROM the crest of the hill overlooking the demon gathering.

"Uh, could be the *whole* pizza you ate before we left!" Kai pointed his brother's full stomach.

"Or not!" Koh rubbed his belly gingerly and looked back at the horrible sight.

The Warriors were all lined up looking at the greatest mass of evil they had ever seen. It wasn't a jumbled mass. There were ranks upon ranks of demon Grunts led by captains, Overlords, and Goons. An abandoned industrial park gave them the expanse they needed to layer their defenses all around, and make it near impossible to penetrate all the way to the central core, the main warehouse, where the ceremony would take place.

Junko breathed out. "Why so many?"

Takumi shook his head slowly. "This happens only once in a generation. They have to guard it, because it guarantees they stay in power another thirty to forty years."

"Do you get the feeling that this is somehow bigger than a battle for a city?" Ishi stretched her hands over her head and then touched her toes. Their runner needed to be limber.

"I think you're right." Aiko stared at the countless mass of enemies. A voice suddenly spoke from behind them.

"Yes, it's a regional strongpoint for the entire country *and* they've had this country locked up for a long time…too long."

It was Akira. They all let out a burst of relief and gathered around him.

"It's really good to see you!" Aiko reached out and clasped his hand.

"Weren't you going to bring some help?" Koh looked past Akira and craned his neck to see.

"It's good to see you all, and yes, I brought some help." Out of the darkness walked a group of ten people.

"There's more, right?" Michio blinked into the darkness.

"This was all that could get here on time; they are spread pretty thinly over the world. Besides, God knows just what you need." Akira stepped back to let the groups meet.

A tall young foreigner strode up. He had long blond hair, blue eyes, and a strong, athletic build. "You're Aiko, right?" He extended his hand. "I'm Daniel. My friends and I are here to help you. We've been preparing for this for a long time."

Aiko looked at him curiously, as did the other Warriors, and took his hand.

"Go ahead and take a look." Akira grinned and pointed a finger to his eyes. The Warriors spoke a silent command in their hearts and their vision changed.

Before them, there stood seven Warriors glowing with armor of light. They all had blond or brown hair and were slightly taller than Aiko's group. There were four guys and three girls.

"Oh yeah! Our chances just doubled!" Michio slapped his hands together.

Mai grinned and nodded her head.

Koh looked past them again. "I…uh…don't suppose you have one or two thousand friends close behind?"

"No, just us." Daniel smiled. "We'll do what we're called to do, nothing more and nothing less." Aiko stepped back and they exchanged nods.

"We are so glad to see you. Okay, this is Ishi, Kenji, Takumi, Junko, Mai, Michio, Kai, and Koh." She pointed to each of them in turn. As she said their names, they nodded or waved. Daniel responded and turned to his group to introduce them.

"Okay, this is Skeeter, Sanchez, and Ricky-boy. They have real names but never use them." He chuckled lightly. "The girls are Kitty, Suzie, and Sarah."

They all hesitated, looking each other over. It was the first time either group had actually met another team of Warriors. The girl called Kitty stepped forward with tears in her eyes. "I don't know about you guys, but it feels so good not be alone." She walked over and hugged Ishi. That started a spontaneous group greeting with handshakes, pats on the shoulder, and hugs. Aiko quickly filled Daniel in on the plan while the others talked. Akira stood back and smiled. After a moment, he broke up the chattering.

"I also want you to meet these very special people…Agamata-san, Nishimura-san, and Komatsu-san." One elderly gentleman and two women, all in their eighties, stepped forward and bowed. Akira continued, "They have fought for three generations. Their prayers are unbelievably powerful." Both groups of Warriors paused and returned their bow, showing respect for those who had lasted in the battle so long.

"Akira?" Aiko beckoned him to the hill's crest, where she pointed toward the battlefield. "We don't have much time."

♦ ♦ ♦

"Well, your time has come, my son," Ryudan said to Kentaro as they looked into the night sky. Twenty armed men surrounded them. They wore business suits, sunglasses, and carried automatic weapons. Makoto was on his knees behind them with his hands tied, looking dazed and weak.

Ryudan turned to his chosen heir and beamed with pride. "When he arrives, you will kneel and he will ask you to pledge your whole existence to him and worship him. While you are bowed down, he will touch you and give you more power than you can imagine!"

Kentaro smiled and clenched both fists at his sides. He thought of the moment he would touch the Lord of the underworld and felt fear rising in him. He swallowed hard and took a deep breath. He glanced at the sky again. "Are you sure twenty men are enough protection?" He looked at the men encircling them.

"Don't worry, we're expecting her. That's why her brother is alive...live bait!" Ryudan looked back at Makoto, who remained listless. "Besides, you wouldn't believe what we have here guarding us on this special occasion. Nothing can penetrate the forces surrounding us." Ryudan touched his shoulder; a dark power surged through Kentaro's body and his Truesight was enabled. His eyes opened wide and he shrank back at first, but then he recognized the horrible-looking creatures as allies and relaxed.

He could see now that the large abandoned warehouse was filled with fallen angels. Ryudan and his men were ringed by nine Goons, each commanding a group of twelve elite demon warriors, creating an amphitheater-like effect. Through the partially caved-in roof he could see an array of demons flying in groups above. "Hundreds of them," he murmured breathlessly.

"Thousands!" Ryudan opened his arms toward his legions. Kentaro noticed a taller demon standing nearer the middle than the others. He looked much more powerful than the others. His armor was uniquely colored with a deep, sinister red and black hue. His face was expressionless.

"That's Moloch. If our little white witch shows up, he'll deal with her personally."

Ryudan put his cigar to his lips, took a long drag, raised his head, and blew out a stream of pungent smoke.

"She *will* try." Kentaro glanced at Makoto.

"Oh I know, and she may even get to us. I won't underestimate her again."

Kentaro looked around again at the daunting layers of spiritual power. "But how..."

"If she manages to get here, we have a special treat for her. There's nothing quite as entertaining as killing a family member in front of another. Then all of hell will collapse on her and her little friends. She'll be dead, and we'll end the legacy of resistance in this area and claim it for the Dark Lord once and for all."

♦ ♦ ♦

"What do you mean you're not going to fight with us!" Koh pulled at Akira's sleeve.

"It's not my battle. God has forbidden me from fighting. My call was only to train you, and then pray." Akira squeezed Koh's shoulder to reassure him.

"But, but, but..." the Warriors stammered.

"That's how God wants it." Aiko stepped up and everyone quieted down.

"Yeah, we're here for a purpose too." Daniel scratched his head. "It's been a real puzzle for us. What we know for sure is that we have to help you get in, and then handle a demon named Moloch. He's major bad news, a Slayer general. That's why we were close. We hunted him down and followed him here."

"You can hunt them?" Mai took a step forward.

"Yeah, cool, huh?" Daniel winked at her.

Mai blinked, looked down at her closed fists, and toward the battlefield.

"Once there, we'll watch your back and take him out, but there's something here only *you* can do...that's what we get from the Master, anyway."

"Okay, this is weird." Koh pointed at the sky. They all looked toward the battlefield and saw that dark clouds were forming quickly over the city. It seemed as if they were bubbling with evil life. There was rolling thunder and flashes of lightning, giving the whole night an eerie strobe light effect.

"Look at the army." Aiko motioned toward the forces on the ground.

As they all gazed down the slope, what they saw filled them with foreboding. The entire demon army was falling to its knees, one rank after the other. Thousands of them with heads bowed, all faced the same direction. A deep, dark song in a language that they couldn't understand, like a relentless and monotonous chant, pierced the air in a pulsating, drum-like rhythm.

"He's here, and thanks to his army, we know which direction to go." Aiko looked down to her side and her sword materialized. She drew it and held it in front of her. She took a deep breath and turned to the others. Their eyes were fixed on the telltale sign that the Dark Lord himself had arrived. Some were breathing hard and others clung to the one next to them.

"Hey." They all looked at her. "We'll never leave each other's side in this one. At all costs, stick with the plan and we'll be fine." There was a collective sigh.

"Final check!" Aiko ordered, going into battle mode.

"Gear up!" Daniel said to his group. Both groups of Warriors did a quick check of armor and weaponry.

Aiko walked up to Akira. "Thanks, Sensei…for everything."

Akira looked at her lovingly like a father. "You know everything you need to know. He's brought you here, He will be with you. " He hugged her. She took one last look at him. "Right…His power, not my own."

Aiko then turned to the Old Ones. "Do you take requests?"

♦ ♦ ♦

"My lord…my god…my everything." Ryudan lay flat on his face before a beautiful angel clothed in white, with elegant silvery wings, and gold flowing hair; the creature descended to a soft landing in the middle of the expansive abandoned warehouse which became a house of worship. His marble countenance had the look of nobility. He had a mocking grin, and his eyes smoldered with hatred as indescribable evil radiated from him.

Standing before them was the creature who chose to wage a war against the Holy Creator, and was cast to earth. He chose to call evil good, and good evil, to take all things beautiful and to defile them with any device at his disposal.

Full of malice and without a hint of mercy, he waged war on all that God loved and those who loved Him. He was the undefeated prince of the world until the Master had defeated him in the desert. Now, generations later, the Master's Warriors continued to wage war for the future of the human race.

After surveying the room, he lifted his powerful arms toward the rolling sky and received the worship that was being given him. His smile betrayed a mouth filled with blacked evil fangs turning him from beautiful to horrific.

The entire room was laying flat on its face. Even the humans had been ordered by Ryudan to lay prostrate, and though they couldn't see anything, he knew that they could feel a presence enter the room that scared them to the very depths of their souls.

"Ah, Moloch, rise my friend," the Dark Lord said with a silky voice. "Always good to observe you work. I take it you will deal with the *Called One*?"

"Yesss, my lord…one called Aiko, the last of her family." Moloch continued to look down.

"Be warned, your friend from America is here looking for you."

Moloch looked up. "Ha! Then you will see my true skill, my lord, and I will give you double the pleasure."

"Just do me one favor." The Dark Lord closed his eyes and grinned. "Make it last!" He turned to the rest of the room. "Rise, everyone, rise."

♦ ♦ ♦

Aiko's eyes darted from formation to formation as they stood and returned to their alert status. She waited, for what she didn't know…except that she *would* know. All the Warriors were next to her. They watched eagerly for her signal. They exchanged nods and steadied each other with a quick nudge or slap on the shoulder. Daniel and his team stood immediately behind them, also waiting for Aiko's signal.

Akira stood with one foot on a rock looking over the scene. He glanced back at the Old Ones and nodded. They slid to their knees in a tight triangle and began to pray with hands raised to the heavens.

♦ ♦ ♦

"Ryudan, my servant. You have done well. Are you ready to pass your legacy to your son?" Ryudan stood, head bowed and eyes fixed on the ground, with Kentaro at his side.

"It has been my pleasure to serve you, and my son is ready." He stepped back and Kentaro stepped forward. The Dark Lord looked him over and then went eye to eye with him, looking deep in his soul.

Kentaro could smell his sulfurous ancient breath and trembled in fear. He looked down for a moment and then caught sight of Makoto on the ground. His faced twisted in hate and he stood tall before Satan and held his chin high.

"Yes….you *are* ready. But…" He turned to Ryudan. "What of Kenji?"

"They got to him before we could finish him, my lord."

"Three times he escaped you, if I'm not mistaken." The Dark Lord shook his head.

Ryudan's eyes darted back and forth and he spoke quickly. "Yes, my lord, it's been very unusual."

"Not unusual, when you've fought Him for thousands of years." He paused and looked around the room and a grotesque smile formed on his lips. Then he thundered, "Is there no one to fight for this generation? Is there no one left to resist us anymore?" Demons grinned with satisfaction across the battlefield.

Ryudan hesitated and Kentaro saw his chance. "My lord, there are only a few stupid kids. They caused some trouble, but we've set a trap for them. We have her brother here...the skank will see him die. That feeble excuse of a brother, Kenji, is with them and will come for me, but he will die as well. All will be dealt with right here, for your pleasure, my lord. We have summoned legions of demons who will crush her friends on your command."

The Dark Lord looked hard a Kentaro and then produced a smoldering smile.

♦ ♦ ♦

Aiko could see the Warriors exchanging glances and starting to wonder. She stood patiently waiting, trusting. No one wanted to see or face the Dark Lord, but with him now present, the ceremony would certainly take place. Aiko checked her watch. It was almost midnight.

"By the way, what was your prayer request for the Old Ones?" Michio broke the silence. All eyes moved to Aiko as she turned to answer the question. She had the hint of a grin.

"Something even Koh would love." She looked at him.

"Yeah...right," Koh said, rubbing both hands and fidgeting.

"*Look!*" Takumi yelled and pointed to the sky above the battlefield. A bright mass of light pierced the clouds and grew brighter by the moment. It was moving quickly toward them.

"I can't make it out." Kai held a hand to his forehead.

"Me either." Koh stared with his mouth open. They all squinted together and waited as the glowing mass got closer and then began to divide into ranks.

"Hey! They're angels...Watchers!" Michio pumped his fist into the air.

They all turned to Aiko again.

"I asked for twelve legions, to be exact." She looked at them all. "It's time. Let's go." She ran over the crest of the hill in a full sprint toward the waiting demon formations. The Warriors obeyed and despite their fear, ran straight toward the largest mass of evil any of them had ever seen.

The demons now stared at the sky in utter surprise at the sudden appearance of their ancient enemies. However, the approach of glowing armor caught the attention of a demon officer near the front who immediately ordered his twenty-five to attack. From behind, the Warriors saw a volley of flaming arrows streaking toward Aiko. Just before they hit she dropped to one knee and braced herself behind her shield. There was an explosion of fire, sparks, and smoke. Everyone gasped, but when the smoke cleared, Aiko was still on one knee whispering to the heavens. Then she yelled, "In His Name!" A sudden *boom* rocked the battlefield and a wave of power erupted from Aiko's position, cutting a swath into the demon line. They had a moment to organize, so she turned and called out, "Form up! Battlefield formation!"

The Warriors moved quickly, staring with dread at the thousands of enemies in front of them, and set up as planned. Michio and Takumi watched the right. Ishi and Mai watched the left. Koh and Kai watched the rear. Junko stood directly behind Aiko so that she could run to whatever side encountered a Goon. Kenji stood with Aiko at point.

"Good, and remember, don't break formation! Stay next to your partner and if a Goon attacks, go defensive and call Junko. Fight while always moving forward. Don't forget, keep moving forward."

"Why do we have to keep moving forward again?" Koh scratched his head. At that moment a single flaming arrow appeared on the left.

"You see that, Ishi, Mai?" Aiko pointed.

Ishi moved instantly. "Got it." The arrow crashed against her shield. Before the Warriors could turn back to hear Aiko answer Koh, a hundred flaming arrows appeared from all around them. The demons had recovered from Aiko's blast. They all took a step back. "Circle up!" Aiko ordered. The Warriors formed a tight circle, knelt down, and locked their shields together. There was a series of loud crashes. They could feel the heat of the arrows as their shields shook with each hit and smoke filled the air with a hellish odor. The arrows that missed created a ring of fire around the Warriors, making them stand out on the battlefield.

"That answer your question?" Kai yelled at Koh.

"It was just a question!" Koh peeked from behind his shield.

"Harder to hit a moving target, okay?" Aiko looked around getting her bearings.

Koh nodded. "I get it."

The barrage was over and the Warriors stood. Only now did they see Daniel's squad behind them, standing up from a defensive circle as well.

"Is it always this much fun over here?" Daniel called out with a grin on his face. His Warriors were clearly shaken at the sight. They looked over to see Aiko's group, who still seemed a little tentative. Suddenly, there was a loud rolling crash like thunder across the sky, as if worlds were colliding. They looked up and saw heaven and hell in a deadly struggle; the Watchers had attacked. The Warriors felt like ants in the middle of a barroom brawl.

"Let's do this!" Aiko shouted, jolting them away from the mesmerizing scene of thousands of angels in battle. They started their run across the battlefield. "Stay focused!" Aiko pointed her sword forward and charged.

♦ ♦ ♦

The Dark Lord gazed at the struggle in the sky above him and all over the battlefield. He shook his head. "Too late. Too late, my old enemy."

"My lord, they have no chance of getting through," Ryudan assured him.

"They have Ancient Ones with them. Dispatch a squad to attack them while they pray," the Dark Lord commanded a powerful demon at his side.

"Yes, my lord." The demon flew away immediately.

"By the way, Ryudan, forgive me while I change your plans."

"Of course, my lord."

"Moloch, go and kill the Called One now, then they have no chance of stopping this. Make sure her friends see you do it." He turned to Kentaro and pointed to Makoto. "Before I endow you with power, show me your allegiance by ending this failed Warrior's life, now."

Kentaro smiled, filled with sudden pleasure. "As you wish, my lord." He pulled a switchblade from his pocket, flicked it open, and walked to where Makoto lay.

Ryudan watched the battle around them and wiped his brow. "My lord, and if any of them should reach this room?"

"Have your men gun them down." Satan chuckled at Ryudan. "Don't forget, my friend: *Never fight fair.*"

♦ ♦ ♦

"Here they come," Ishi called out, pointing her sword.

Despite the angelic attack, there were still hundreds of unengaged demons on the field. They converged on the two groups of spiritual warriors as they made their way across the field toward the main building.

"Swords," Aiko ordered. Everyone started talking to each other with excited high-pitched voices.

"Aiko, demon officer dead ahead." Kenji gripped his sword and his shield.

"Okay, watch my right flank for a second," Aiko answered quickly.

"Fast and efficient," Takumi called out.

"I got this first one, Roboto!" Michio exclaimed.

"Stay close, Mai-chan." Ishi looked at her young friend. Mai's eyes were grim and determined, her dual swords out and ready.

"Goon coming up behind...I knew it...why me?" Koh looked back shaking his head.

"Uh, Junko, we'll need you here in about two seconds," Kai said without turning.

"Oh, okay, that's me! Okay, I'm here...God, I can't believe I'm here," Junko exclaimed and moved to the back to meet her first Goon of the day.

All at once, each one of them was in combat and the air was filled with the ring of swords, the clash of shields, and the whooshing sound of demons being banished.

Aiko drove a demon captain back. "Keep moving!"

In addition to the opponents in front of them, each Warrior had to block flaming projectiles that came from all directions. It took all of their speed and clear communication for them to last even one minute, but they did.

They heard a ripping sound like a lightning bolt and a loud, popping *whoosh*. They glanced back and saw Junko standing in a greenish cloud of dust with Koh and Kai.

"Oh wow, now that's awesome!" Koh yelled, having seen his first Goon banished by Junko. "And oh yuck." Koh held his nose.

Before she could say anything, Takumi called her. "I need you here!" Junko ran over for her next Goon.

The second wave hit the Warriors, and they fought it off, then a third and a fourth and a fifth. All the while, they called to each other and Junko ran from side to side, facing Goons. A wave of Watchers suddenly swooped into their part of the battlefield, disorienting the demon attack. The Warriors had a few moments.

"Everyone okay?" Aiko called out, looking back for the first time and checking their forward progress.

"Still here and the right side is solid," Michio called back and high-fived Takumi.

"I don't know how, but..." Koh shook his head.

"We're here." Kai clapped a hand on his brother's mouth.

"Mai-chan?" Aiko asked. Mai looked at her and just nodded that she was okay.

"Junko?" Takumi looked at her with concern.

"Uh...there's this thing sticking out of me, it's like a dart or something and it hurts really bad. And, that last Goon hit my shoulder." She cringed in pain.

"Who's wounded?" Everyone's hand went up. Ishi cried out and rushed over to Junko.

"Okay, heal up quickly," Aiko ordered. Ishi pulled the dart from Junko, who flinched and let out a short squeal. She then prayed and the wound closed almost instantly.

"Uh, Mich, let me get that for you." Takumi pulled a black twisted dagger from the back of his partner's shoulder and prayed. Michio looked back surprised. "Oh. Hey, thanks. Didn't know that was there."

They all quickly examined each other and their healed wounds; burning gashes mostly on the arms and legs. A few errant arrows had crossed over a Warrior only to hit or graze another in the back or shoulder.

They suddenly heard a cry coming from their left. "Aiko? What is this? We can't kill it!" It was Daniel. A Goon had penetrated their formation and was now fighting him. Three Warriors lay wounded on the ground.

"Everyone, let's move. Get over there quick. Support Junko's attack," Aiko ordered.

♦ ♦ ♦

Kentaro stood eye to eye with Makoto, who listed from side to side, dazed. "So how does your God feel about double traitors? First you turn your back on Him and then you betray us? I'll tell you what, you can find out right now, you worthless maggot!" Kentaro propped him up and put one arm around Makoto's neck to pull him hard against the knife in his other hand. He looked back to the Dark Lord, who nodded his approval.

When Kentaro looked back he wasn't staring into the eyes of a wasted addict. Instead, they were clear and full of righteous fury. Makoto grabbed Kentaro's knife hand and twisted it until the knife dropped, and threw him to the floor. He hit hard, snapped his head into the ground, and sprawled out dazed. Everyone remained in stunned silence for a few seconds while Kentaro struggled to get to his feet, then fell down again.

Makoto dropped to one knee and closed his eyes.

"Crush him," Ryudan roared to his waiting demon guards, who immediately began to move toward Makoto. As they converged on him, there was a sudden burst of light and when Makoto stood, he was fully armored and brandishing a gleaming sword.

♦ ♦ ♦

Junko was fighting her twenty-seventh Goon since the fight began. The demons had renewed their attack with added fury; the Warriors found themselves only twenty meters from their goal, yet they couldn't move on until this Goon was banished. He was in the middle of their formation. Aiko, Michio, Koh, and Kai filled the holes in the line while Ishi, Mai, and Takumi went to heal up the wounded Warriors. Sanchez, Kitty, and Ricky-boy were down, holding their injuries. Kitty was crying from the pain. All the other Warriors were engaged in combat.

Sanchez looked up at Takumi as he knelt to help him. "Dude, what's with the skinny demon? I hit him. I know I did. Then he raked my thigh."

"They showed up in town recently; they're called Resistant Ones. We just call them Goons. Our girl can handle them."

"But how…" Sanchez strained to see the fight.

"I'll explain later, okay?" Takumi examined the spiritual wound.

Sanchez leaned back while Takumi extended his hand over the wound and prayed. It took longer than usual to heal a Goon wound; they festered and spread. He had to pray hard to catch up with it.

A loud whoosh filled the air.

Another Goon was gone. Junko sighed and ran over to Takumi. "How's it going, babe?"

Takumi's eyes opened wide with surprise.

"Uh…oh, they'll be fine…gonna hurt for a while though. Good work, girl." Junko gave him a quick hug and ran back over to her position behind Aiko while fixing her hair. Takumi and Sanchez watched her as she trotted away.

"Hooo, dude, she's yours? Wicked. I want one of those." Sanchez gave Takumi a thumbs-up and nodded in approval.

Takumi smiled. "We're…uh, chess buddies."

Sanchez looked at him with raised eyebrows. "Right, bro…whatever. Hey, thanks."

"Hurry, guys, we have to move. We're attracting a crowd," Aiko yelled back.

Daniel's three Warriors got on their feet again. The hurried back to the line and awaited orders.

"Okay everyone, form a wedge and drive for that set of double doors over there." Aiko pointed toward their objective. The two groups became one and marched forward. Their swords flashed, shields repelled fiery arrows, as they slashed their way to the door.

♦ ♦ ♦

"You're an arrogant boy. Do you honestly think you have a chance of leaving this room alive?" The Dark Lord raised a hand to stop Ryudan, who had pulled a gun and now held it to the back of Makoto's head.

"That's not my goal, fallen one." Makoto stood tall and answered evenly.

"Well my goal is to rob you of your faith again and then take your soul to hell with me," the Dark Lord hissed. He motioned the demon guard to attack. Ryudan put the gun away and stood back to watch.

Makoto moved with the same incredible agility as his sister. As the first three demons approached him, he quickly closed the distance between them, bashed one on the left with his shield, and stabbed one into the barrens. *Whoosh!* He then spun quickly and took out the other two. *Whooosh! Whooosh!* Suddenly, a Slayer decloaked in front of him and launched him backward. He smashed against the wall and slid to the ground, blinking his eyes.

"Tch, tch, tch, out of practice, are we?" the Dark Lord mocked, arms folded.

♦ ♦ ♦

As they approached the entrance to the door, the rear attack became intense. Kai and Koh were fighting as well as they ever had as a team, but this time it wasn't good enough. Daniel's rear guard was going down too.

"Kai's down!" Koh cried, looking back for help.

"Kitty and Suzie too!" Skeeter called out. He ran over when he saw them fall and now tried in vain to heal them. There just wasn't enough time to heal some wounds now.

"Our rear is collapsing," Daniel yelled to Aiko, who was engaged with an Overlord that guarded the door they needed to go through. Junko responded and ran back with Ricky-boy. They helped drag the wounded Warriors away from the line while Mai stepped in to hold the rear alone.

"Mai, be careful." Ishi glanced back with a worried look while still fighting. Michio turned from banishing a demon and ran back to help her. They were immediately engaged by a rush of demons attempting to collapse the rear guard altogether. Aiko went down on one knee and after a moment the ground shook and power rolled outward, leveling all attackers for twenty-five meters. The Warriors sighed in gratitude for the reprieve.

"Quick, into the door!" Aiko surged forward. They all turned to follow, but as Aiko neared the opening a blast of power burst the door open toward them and hurled the Warriors to the ground. The door caught Aiko in the head, throwing her back and cutting a gash just above her hairline. As she sat up and shook her head to clear it, blood trickled down her face.

A dark figure emerged from the doorway.

Moloch.

♦ ♦ ♦

The squad of twelve demons drifted slowly from the trees, their eyes burning with hatred toward the three elderly people kneeling in prayer.

"Attack their minds with every murderous and lustful thought you can conjure. Listen for their names, so we can go after their children and grandchildren too! Go...Now!" the demon captain ordered.

There was a sudden movement from the shadows and a bright light appeared in the clearing where the prayer vigil was being held. "I can't let you do that," a voice said grimly. A Warrior stepped out in full armor with two swords.

"This isn't your fight! You already lost your battle, Akira!" The captain circled him.

"This place of prayer *is* my fight! And my battle is never truly over. Consider my involvement trans-generational."

"There's no such word," the demon argued.

"Sure there is; it's fueled by something you hate and something you'll never understand...*love*."

The demon's face twisted into a scowl and he spit foul yellow phlegm on the ground. Then he drew his sword to join the attack on the older Warrior.

"Love makes you weak, Akira."

"Well then, let's find out how weak I am." He readied his weapons.

The demons rushed him. Akira glided through each attack without wasting one inch of movement. He was calm and confident as he banished the entire squad until only the captain was left.

"Face it, you're a loser, Akira! Those three ancient bags of dirt can't–"

"*Silence!*"

The demon's mouth fused shut instantly.

The demon turned to flee into the trees. After fifteen meters, he laughed and looked back over his shoulder. The twirling sound of a thrown sword made him gasp. A second later it penetrated the middle of his back and stuck out the front…and *whooosh*, he was gone.

"Thank you, Akira," one of the Ancient Ones whispered, and kept on praying. Akira smiled and then looked toward the battlefield.

"Aiko…" he whispered.

♦ ♦ ♦

"Aiko, you're bleeding!" Kenji wiped the blood from Aiko's face with his sleeve. The next instant a loud voice boomed.

"Where is the one called Aiko?" Moloch demanded as the Warriors got to their feet. The Warriors' eyes flared with terror and their mouths hung open. "Where is she?" His voice thundered again and he stamped his clawed foot down and shook the earth.

The Warriors exchanged glances and then Mai, Ishi, Junko, and Koh stepped forward and spoke simultaneously. "I am!"

Moloch frowned at Koh. The girls all gave him sideways looks.

"Uh, after my…uh…grandmother." Koh's voice cracked as he spoke.

Moloch looked past him.

"I'm Aiko." She pushed through the human shield her friends had made around her.

From the look on her face, he knew she was telling the truth. There was a resolve in her voice and a grace in the way she moved. Her armor was nicked and cut from many battles, her sword was sharp, and she inspired unbounded loyalty in those she led. She was a Called One.

"I'm Moloch. I specialize in ending spiritual legacies." He leaned forward as he said those words and smiled. "Today, I will finish what I started when I helped the Dark Lord kill your parents."

Everyone braced for Aiko's response. She walked up and stopped in front of him. She looked up at the nine-foot demon general with a straight face, observed his mocking smile, and shook her head. She wiped a trickle of blood from her temple and straightened her armor. "Listen, Moloch, so you understand once and for all. When my parents took the field against you, they had already surrendered their lives and considered themselves dead–as do I. They are in heaven, a place you will never see. So your threats mean nothing to me. As for killing me, I won't waste my time fighting with one of such a low stature."

Moloch got angrier with each word. She wasn't afraid, and that bothered him. Nor was she offended by the evil he had done to her family; that bothered him more. She gave him no respect or concern at all, which pushed him over the edge. His eyes were bulging and he trembled with rage. Before he could act, another voice cut in.

"But *I* have plenty of time for you, old friend!" Daniel stepped up, sword drawn, with his remaining Warriors at his back.

Moloch looked at him with disdain and huffed. "Well, well, well, it's the little Slayer hunters. Aren't you too far from your mommy's grave, little boy?"

"Just so you know, we cleaned out the Slayer base you had in town and decided to find you to let you know, you're *not* coming back. Ever."

"Are you up to the challenge, little white trash?"

"Born for it, slave general," Daniel said evenly and then turned to Aiko. "We'll fight him here and then hold this door and watch out for anything that will come at you from behind. You be careful! We'll see you after the fight. You'll know when to move." He winked at her and turned toward Moloch. His Warriors filled in behind him.

Moloch drew his huge mace and began to swing it over his head. The deadly spikes whistled louder with each revolution.

Aiko stepped back and joined her group. "Ready to move." She whispered a command and they all nodded. The demons in the area stepped back to allow Moloch his fun. With a general on the field they would await orders. In the meantime, the Watchers had deployed themselves in a zone defense over the building. Nothing else was getting in until it was over.

Daniel walked toward his fierce enemy with his sword at the ready. Moloch timed a vicious swing to meet the young Warrior as he got within sword range. But just as the mace started its downward arc, Daniel dashed toward him and rolled past the blow, swinging back, cutting Moloch's leg, and darting into the room behind him. Moloch roared, turned, and charged in to find him. That was Aiko's signal.

"Let's go!" The Warriors all ran in with Michio and Koh helping Kai, who was still badly wounded. Takumi was limping and Junko was holding her shoulder. Daniel's Warriors had rushed in and manned the door, which they shut as soon as Aiko's group was in. They sensed the squad of powerful Watchers that positioned themselves outside the door.

Aiko paused a moment, looking after Daniel. She wanted to help, but it was his battle. His was a different call. He was a Slayer hunter. She had a different opponent waiting.

♦ ♦ ♦

Whooosh! Another demon burst into a cloud of stinking sulfurous dust. Makoto panted hard from the exertion. They just kept coming, until the Dark Lord held up his hand.

"Still fighting? Coming back to you, is it? Now that you're warmed up, let's make it more interesting. Meet the captain of my bodyguard, Cerberus."

A three-headed demon Overlord decloaked in front of Makoto, brandishing a jagged sword. A crimson pentagram pulsated on his black shield.

Makoto sighed and raised his sword toward his new opponent.

The Dark Lord nodded and Cerberus attacked with a surprising quickness, swinging his huge sword. Makoto raised his shield in time to block the blow but its force knocked him off balance. He tumbled backward and into the wall. He looked up and saw the demon with a wicked smile, waiting for him to get up. He wiped the blood off his mouth and picked up his sword.

Kentaro had recovered and stood next to Ryudan. His eyes were filled with loathing as he watched Makoto getting beaten down.

Makoto checked his armor, gripped his sword tightly, took a deep breath, and charged the Overlord. Their swords met and sparks filled the air and both combatants pushed hard for control. Makoto could hear a rush of wind as the demon swung his shield toward him with bone-shattering force. Makoto dropped to the ground on his face and the shield rushed over him, missing completely, leaving the demon vulnerable for a moment.

He shot upright and drove his sword into the demon's foot, speaking a quick prayer that filled his sword with light.

Cerberus kicked hard and caught Makoto in the chest. Flying through the air, Makoto registered the *crack* of broken bones–not his own. He crashed into the ground in front of Ryudan, Kentaro, and the Dark Lord.

The demon's heads twisted in agony and roared. The toes of the foot he'd smashed into Makoto's breastplate flopped uselessly as he turned in rage toward Makoto. Makoto spit the grit out of his mouth, wiped the blood and dirt from his face, and stood, deliberately keeping his back to his enemy. He could hear the irregular footsteps pounding as the demon made a final charge. He could see the anticipation in their eyes as they prepared to see him executed. *Wait. Wait.* As the footsteps got louder Makoto instantly turned and let his sword fly.

Pain, rage, and desire for revenge had so filled Cerberus that he wasn't ready for the sword that spun past his shield and buried itself in his heart. Makoto sprinted and jumped up on the demon's chest and pushed the sword in to the hilt, praying intensely. Cerberus growled in angry dissonance and shuddered uncontrollably and then *whooosh*!

Makoto fell to the ground on his knees, exhausted and relieved.

He didn't hear the dark arrow that streaked toward his back, trailing green flame and black smoke.

He cried out in pain and reached down to grab the shaft of an arrow that was sticking out of his shoulder.

The Dark Lord lowered a horrible-looking black bow, smiled, and said to Kentaro, "He's all yours..."

♦ ♦ ♦

"That was Makoto!" Aiko looked ahead toward the yell she had heard. "Hurry!" They ran the length of the dark hallway that ended in a huge empty warehouse. It was lit only by torches spread evenly along the walls, which framed the room with an eerie flickering light and curling black smoke. The room itself was the size of a football field. Assorted broken shelves and rusted machinery were scattered about randomly. Another set of torches created a smaller ceremonial area about the size of a basketball court. It was surrounded by men in business suits.

The moment they stepped in and took in the sight, their knees turned weak with fear. There, standing at the end of the room, was the ancient enemy of God, the father of lies...and the greatest hater of man. In front of him stood Ryudan and Kentaro.

"Father..." Kenji said grimly to Ryudan.

"And Brother." Ishi nodded toward Kentaro.

They all saw a movement from the left side of the ceremonial area. Someone was moving slowly, in *glowing armor.* Aiko and her team turned to one another to see if anyone was missing.

"Huh?" Aiko looked closely.

"Hey, who is that? Did we lose someone?" Michio asked.

Takumi stepped up and squinted. "Everyone's accounted for. No one could have gotten ahead of us."

"Whoever it is, he's hurt." Ishi adjusted her armor and prepared to move.

From the distance the Warriors could see him jerk something from his shoulder.

Aiko gasped. "It's my..." Her eyes teared up. She took a quick breath to keep from crying. "It's Makoto," she whispered. "It's my brother."

They all stared in amazement as they saw Makoto shakily raising a sword of truth. At the same time, Kentaro slowly raised a gun toward him.

"No!" Aiko yelled in desperation, and started to sprint the long distance. Her team rushed behind her. Makoto glanced at her, gasping at the sizzling pain of his wound.

"Ha! It just doesn't get better than this." Kentaro casually crossed his arms, smirking as Aiko tried in vain to get to her brother in time and Makoto sent a longing, regretful look at his sister.

Ryudan chuckled. "Ha! This generation goes to the Dark Lord! After all you've done, you are the loser, just like your parents!"

The Dark Lord smiled, Ryudan laughed, and Kentaro pulled the trigger. The gunshot thundered.

"No, Makoto!" Aiko screamed. She stopped suddenly at the sound of the gun and extended her hands toward Makoto. She took a last look at her brother.

Three shots rang out.

Makoto instinctively dodged. The first bullet grazed the top of his shoulder and tore a piece of his shirt off with flesh and blood. The second bullet followed his movement and slammed into his shoulder, sending him to the ground.

The third bullet was soft-tipped and designed to enter the body and then expand, leaving a softball-size hole in a man.

It ripped through Kentaro's right forearm and sent the gun clattering to the ground, with his severed right hand still clutching the stock.

The third shot had come from another gun.

Everyone in the room froze. Kentaro dropped to his knees, clawing at the blood spurting from his arm. Ryudan and his men searched the room for the gunman. The Dark Lord looked disturbed. Makoto rolled to his side holding his shoulder, looked at Aiko, and smiled painfully.

"*Huh? Okay, what just happened?*" Aiko was breathing hard, looking both confused and relieved. The next moment, they saw a movement from behind a rusted machine. A dark figure walked toward Ryudan and started firing rounds.

"There! Take him down, and the other intruders too," Ryudan shouted as bullets pelted the ground at his feet. Twenty semiautomatic pistols lit up the room like strobe lights.

"Aiko, the guns!" Takumi yelled as bullets whizzed overhead. They could hear the sound of the mystery gunman taking hits and falling to the ground.

"*Aiko!*" Takumi yelled.

Aiko tore her eyes away from Makoto and looked back at Takumi, regained her composure, and dropped on one knee with her hands raised. It only took a moment before a heavenly Watcher ripped through the barrier between the spiritual and real worlds and blasted the room with holy light. The men in the room all collapsed in a fearful stupor, dropping their guns, and then the angel disappeared. The Warriors looked around and quickly helped each other up.

Only the Warriors and demon-empowered humans remained conscious. Ryudan stood defiantly, wiped dirt from his clothes, and straightened his tie. Kentaro was writhing on the ground. He stilled and, trembling, wrapped his arm with a coat. The Dark Lord stood calmly watching the Warriors approach him. He frowned. His claws formed fists and his breathing became labored.

"So, this…is Aiko," The Dark Lord flexed his muscular back, moved his head from side to side, cracking his neck, and looked directly at her.

Aiko looked over to make sure Makoto was still alive and then broke into a walk that brought her face-to-face with Satan.

"My dear, why are you here?" he said in a sickly sweet voice. The ancient, beautiful angel began to morph. His skin was still marble white, and his face was the same, but he was now in human form. He was dressed in black pants, a crimson shirt, and a long coat that fell past his knees. He wore black knee-high bucket boots.

Ishi and Mai ran over to Makoto and started trying to heal him from the spiritual wounds and stop the bleeding from the gunshot wound. Michio and Takumi flanked Aiko as she faced the Dark Lord. Michio exchanged a glance with Takumi and swallowed hard.

"I'm here to break the curse," Aiko stated simply, though there was far more to it that she'd divulged only to her team.

Satan looked closely at her eyes and then grinned. "I don't suppose I should try to change your mind?"

"No," she said without hesitation.

"If I offer you the freedom to walk out of here with your brother, would you put down your sword?"

Aiko glanced over to Makoto and their eyes met. He shook his head.

"Not a chance."

"Well then, you'll have to fight for your generation." He looked past Aiko and her team. "Ah, he's here." Satan looked to the back of the room from where they had come. "It's your turn, my dear…"

The Warriors all looked back and gasped together, their eyes opened wide in horror.

"Oh no…no…"

"It can't be…"

Moloch stood there flexing his powerful arms with an evil air of triumph. The Warriors exchanged looks with each other.

Koh grabbed Aiko's arm. "It's happening again like before. Akira went in with seven and came out…"

"Alone." Aiko looked deeply into his eyes for a moment and gave him an almost imperceptible wink. "Kai needs you." Koh moped over to his brother.

"Are you ready for this?" Aiko looked at them hard. They all swallowed and nodded grimly at her. She turned to face Moloch.

Satan placed his hands behind his back. "Oh, but that's just the beginning of the fun. Ryudan, you've been very patient, why don't you show them what my generational champion can really do." Ryudan smiled and lifted his hands from his sides, and five demons fanned out from his waist and roared.

"Ishi. Kenji. You take him," Aiko ordered, and the two Warriors started walking toward Ryudan. The Dark Lord looked pleased and motioned eloquently into the air with one hand. "Ah, a father and son reunited…nice touch. And, I'm sure you know that I don't travel alone. I have a…modest bodyguard." He waved his hand to the side.

A rushing sound filled the air as thirteen powerful demons decloaked all around the Warriors. They stumbled into a loose circle.

"Whatever you do, never leave your partner!" Aiko called out. The other Warriors nodded at their partners.

Makoto walked over and stood next to Aiko, sword drawn, while the demons closed in.

"Can I be your partner, little sister?" Makoto said, looking at her warmly.

"I've been saving your place for a long time." Aiko's voice trembled and tears rolled down her cheeks. She gave him a brief hug and then took her fighting stance.

Takumi and Junko stood next to each other, picking targets. "This is it. Stay close." He moved till their shoulders were touching.

"Don't you worry about me. I'm *not* going anywhere you're not." She looked from side to side, pointing her sword from demon to demon.

Michio hefted his heavy sword over his head while Mai's swords moved in a slow windmill motion in preparation for the attack.

"Come on! Let's finish this," he yelled. Mai looked up at her older friend, blinked at the scene in front of her, and then hardened a little.

Kenji and Ishi talked while they approached Ryudan.

"Can you do this? Face your dad?" She glanced at him.

"Honestly? I don't know. I wouldn't exactly call him a dad. I'll need your help." Kenji sighed and gripped his sword tightly.

Ishi nodded. "Let's just stay alive." She braced to meet Ryudan's first attack.

There was an infinitesimal pause. Each Warrior took a deep breath. Partners glanced at each other. This was going to be their most difficult battle.

The next moment, all of hell's demons broke loose.

Moloch fought with a double mace on a long pole. He was incredibly fast with it. Aiko and Makoto attacked together. There was a series of fast rings and as their swords sought their targets and Moloch blocked each blow, always one step ahead.

They stepped back, a current of uneasiness spreading through their ranks. None of their attacks had penetrated.

Moloch smiled coldly and launched into an attack on Makoto.

Aiko leaned in to support him and got hit with a full-force backswing of the mace. It struck her shield and launched her ten meters into a pile of broken shelving. Makoto lunged forward and smashed his shield into Moloch' face, driving him back. He turned to see if Aiko was okay.

It was what Moloch was waiting for. His long mace jabbed hard at Makoto's chest, spun and smashed hard on his shoulder, and sent him stumbling backward cradling a limp arm.

Both Warriors were down.

♦ ♦ ♦

The others weren't faring much better. In his first exchange, Michio staggered back with a deep cut on his sword hand. His opponent had slipped his attack and slashed at his grip. The demon facing Mai locked up her swords with his and leaned his full weight into her, then spun quickly and swept her off her feet...the dancer was down. Michio attempted a spinning attack, but the demon jumped and slashed a gash across his back as he spun. Michio fell forward. Mai tried to recover, but her demon opponent had the initiative and kicked her head like a soccer ball. He caught her chin, and although her unseen helmet absorbed much of the attack, the impact sent the little one flying into Michio. They sprawled on the ground, too winded to brace for the next attack.

♦ ♦ ♦

"Aah! There are too many." Ishi screamed in frustration as they tried to cut through the five synchronized demons. "Opposite sides! I'll take two or three." Kenji yelled, sidestepping to the demons right side.

"If you only knew what you're going to miss, you pathetic little loser," Ryudan hissed.

Kenji held out a hand toward Ryudan. "*Silence!*"

"Ha! That only works on demons. You pitiful excuse for a son." Ryudan's demons separated. One went totally defensive with Ishi to keep her occupied, while four swung to attack on Kenji's side. He was now facing eight weapons that came at him like a high-speed shredding machine. Ishi looked in horror as Kenji blocked the first four or five attacks and then fell back with two, four, six, slashes on his shoulders and chest.

"Kenji! No!" She tried to disengage from her opponent, who now hammered her with an aggressive attack.

Ishi parried and slashed into the shoulder of her attacker, wounding it. It howled, but in the blink of an eye, she was facing five demons. Kenji cried out and fell backward, grabbing at his wounds. Smoke poured from deep gashes criss-crossing his body. They hissed as they seared into his spirit.

"Aaah! God, it hurts!" He reached out toward Ishi with pain etched on his face.

Ishi held on a little longer, parrying and blocking with increasing intensity, but as the demons coordinated their attack, there was a slash across her cheek, another on her arm, and a sword point penetrated the armor near the shoulder, forcing her to cry out in agony.

Ryudan took a moment to gloat while he twisted the sword deeper. "So much for our little Warriors!"

Ishi fell back and crawled over to where Kenji lay moaning. Acrid smoke rose from their wounds, and the gashes deepened and spread.

♦ ♦ ♦

"I...I can't do this. This is too hard!" Junko blocked the powerful swing of a demon sword.

"I'll help you," Takumi yelled, keeping his demon at bay with good defense. "Stay close!" This time the demon faked a strike with his sword and pounded Junko with his shield. She wasn't ready–her knees buckled and her sword clattered to the ground. She slowly sank to the ground stunned. She was totally open to a killer blow. Takumi immediately stepped in front of her. "If you want her, you have to get through me!"

"Tak...no...no..." she pleaded, grabbing at his shirt. With only one target now, the demons went after Takumi. Junko slowly rose to a sitting position. She saw her hero from behind as he fought...for her. He managed to sever a demon arm and stab a foot, but it only made them angrier. She saw his head snap back from a punch, and she gasped as he jerked, one, two, three times as swords found their mark. He slowly collapsed into her arms.

◆ ◆ ◆

A chorus of raucous laughter pealed over Aiko as the horde from hell cheered on the Warriors' defeat. She was on her hands and knees, covered with dirt, splinters embedded in her flesh. Her head felt so very heavy. Blood and sweat streaked her face and blurred her vision. She could just make out the dark, gloating figure of the devil. She could hear the sounds of her friends crying out in pain. She felt every blow, every gash, and every stab in her own spirit as her team crumbled.

Her heart was filled with sadness and despair. She pushed back into a sitting position and saw that Makoto had stood up and was trying to protect her. Moloch pounded on Makoto's shield and drove him down to the ground blow by blow.

She could see Takumi lying over Junko with both their shields being pounded by two demons. Junko was screaming and Takumi cringed with each blow.

Mai and Michio had regained their feet. They wavered back-to-back, with four demons circling them like hungry wolves. "Come on! Come on!" Michio cried, sheltering his wounded hand.

Ishi lay in Kenji's arms with Ryudan crouched over them. Kenji pulled a sword from Ishi's shoulder and she screamed. Ryudan moved in for the kill.

"Wait," Aiko whispered. "Wait!" She pushed to her feet and stumbled toward the Dark Lord.

He looked with interest at her. He knew a look of desperation in a human and he relished it. He held up his hand and all the attacks stopped.

Aiko limped closer and crumpled to the ground before the Dark Lord. "You can have me, but please let my friends go. I'm the one you want…please…" Tears of defeat rolled down her cheeks.

Satan grinned in satisfaction and felt pleasure in the pain he had inflicted and saw in her face. He loved the fact that a Called One lay at his feet. It was after all *his* world. *He* should be worshipped.

"What do you offer?" He crossed his arms and tapped his lips with one finger.

"Myself…my life…for theirs…" She waved weakly at her friends.

The Dark Lord looked around the room at the pathetic scene. The Warriors were beaten to a pulp and suffering from their wounds. Now their leader was asking to die in front of them so they could leave. He pondered it for a moment. They would live in utter torment from the day they saw their leader die, and of course his angels would whisper nightmares into their lives till the day they joined her. He thought a moment more, rubbing his chin, and then he decided.

"I accept, on one condition. It will cost you the life of one of your beloved." He motioned quickly with his hand and before Aiko could answer, there was a loud *bang*.

Kentaro fired the shot from the darkness, where he had waited, trembling, full of rage and vengeance.

Aiko spun to see where he had pointed the deadly weapon. All of the Warriors followed the path of the bullet.

Makoto sank to his knees, clutching his chest, and looked down at the blood spurting from between his fingers.

The low, vicious voice of Kentaro spit out, "Die, you traitor!"

"No! Oh please God, no!" Aiko screamed. She found new strength and ran to her brother's side. She cradled him in her arms and pressed her hand over the hole in his chest to help stop the bleeding. The other Warriors looked at each other with a sense of helplessness, tears forming in their eyes.

"Makoto, can you hear me?" Aiko held back her tears as best she could.

"Aiko?" he said weakly and reached up and took her hand. "I'm so…proud of you…"

"I can't lose you again! Please…please, God…" Aiko pleaded through her tears.

"No, you're not…not losing me…" A fit of coughing seized him. Blood trickled from his mouth.

"Makoto…" Aiko realized he was about to die.

"Y…you need to know…" He coughed again and then willed himself to speak. "Shiho died…fighting." He spit up more blood.

Aiko's eyes flared. "What?" A glint of hope swelled deep in her soul as she sought confirmation in Makoto's eyes.

"They told me she went back…back to God." He let out a painful laugh. "They had to kill her…she didn't take…her own life. Stubborn w…women in our family." He laughed again, wincing.

"Makoto! Really?" Makoto nodded. She took a deep breath and looked away and then up. Years of despair started draining from her soul.

"M…me too. F…forgive me." Makoto blinked his eyes and started to go limp.

"Don't say that. You know I love you." She wiped his face gently.

"I was…angry…"

"It's okay. You came back. We fought side by side." Tears rolled down her cheeks and she pulled her brother close. Makoto smiled weakly.

His eyes started to close, then he opened them suddenly.

"Aiko?"

"I'm here."

"D…don't be sad. I was dead before I…took…"

"I know, I know, Makoto don't go." His eyes closed and his breathing grew shallow. He spoke in a whisper.

"We'll…be…waiting . *All* of us." He labored to take a breath.

"I know you will."

"You're…the…last. You know…what to do." He opened his eyes. "For His…"

"Honor." Aiko held her brother as he breathed out his last breath on earth and closed his eyes. She hugged him, kissed his cheek, and closed her eyes, shaking her head.

The Dark Lord clapped his hands and laughed at her pain. "Now that payment has been received, it's time for Moloch to add another notch to his belt. We've stopped yet another generational call and will pass on our generational curse. A good day for hell, I'd say. So, failed Warrior, any final requests?"

Aiko gently laid her brother's body down.

Satan motioned Moloch, and the large demon raised his awful-looking weapon.

While Aiko was still looking down she spoke. "Yes. I want *you*."

It was so absurd that all those present were sure that they had heard her wrong. All, that is, except her team.

"What did you say, human trash?" Moloch leaned forward. "You want to play with Ryudan before I kill you?" Aiko, still looking down, shook her head and then spoke as she looked up and pointed at Satan.

"I want...*you*." She stood and locked eyes with the Dark Lord with a look of righteous determination. Tendrils of smoke were rising from spiritual wounds all over her body, blood trickled from her forehead down the length of her face and down her neck, her arms hung limply at her sides, and her clothes were torn and covered with grime from being thrown to the ground.

He examined her up and down with a look of mild irritation.

"You can't possibly know what you are asking." The Dark Lord waved a dismissive hand.

"Oh, but I do." Aiko limped toward him. "I challenge *you* and *you* alone...not your meaningless pawns, or your mindless hordes...*you!*"

Satan dropped his hands to his sides and stood speechless at her boldness. Moloch and his bodyguard gasped at Aiko's challenge and looked at their Master and then back at her. They surrounded her, raising their weapons to strike.

She stood in front of the Dark Lord and squared her shoulders.

"You are Lord of nothing, fallen and pathetic, desperate and ugly...the beauty given to you has turned to hideous deformity, and the kingdom that awaits you is nothing more than a place of utter regret and humiliating punishment.

"I'm a servant of the Master, Who is Lord of heaven and earth and the One Who will judge you. I want *you* to leave this place and this city!" Aiko raised her sword in challenge to the Dark Lord.

The room stilled in shock. All of the demons were waiting for his order to obliterate her. No one could believe that a teenage girl could speak to him that way, especially one who had been beaten so badly. He looked around the room at the horde of fallen angels watching the Warrior insult him. Then he looked down at Aiko. His eyes narrowed, his lips were pressed together hard, and his mouth was twitching. A glowing red sword appeared in his hand. "Well then, little girl...I accept."

He didn't notice Mai pressing the send button on her phone.

♦ ♦ ♦

Akira stood, worried and straining to see anything on the battlefield that told him that the moment had come. Suddenly, his phone rang. He snatched it up. It said simply: "Heal now." He turned to the Ancient Ones. "Healing prayer...*now!* The most powerful prayer you can ask for...Quickly!" The three prayer warriors extended their hands toward the warehouse where the generational battle was taking place.

♦ ♦ ♦

"It will only be us…right?" Aiko wiped the blood from her face with her sleeve and looked around the room.

"I can crush you myself, but can I help it if my men have a terrible loyalty for their lord?" Satan looked at his bodyguard. They moved to surround Aiko. He laughed.

"Yeah, I thought you'd say that." Aiko raised both hands to the heavens, closed her eyes, took a deep breath, and waited.

It started from the crown of each Warrior's head and then flowed downward like a wave till it reached their toes. It didn't help the bumps, bruises, or cuts, but every spiritual wound was instantly healed and the Warriors stood up and hurried into a new formation behind Aiko.

The Dark Lord looked past Aiko at what was happening. Ryudan and his bodyguard jerked their weapons up and took a step back.

"I think your men will be too busy to interfere with you while you play with a child." Aiko materialized her shield and raised her sword.

A voice called from the back of the room and a group of Warriors rushed into the room. "Moloch!"

It was Daniel. "Ready for round two?" Daniel's Warriors spread throughout the room. One of them made sure all the guns in the room were secured from Ryudan's men who still quailed in their fearful stupor.

Koh and Kai came running up. "What'd we miss?" They rejoined their team behind Aiko.

The Dark Lord's eyes darted from Aiko to the new situation developing behind her. Something was terribly wrong. His pinioned wings started to twitch. His smile was gone.

"Oh, you can back down if you want to," Aiko said in a loud voice, "but I still want you to leave this city."

All the demons in the room turned away from the Warriors and fixed their eyes on their ruler. He knew every eye was on him. His face hardened as he glared at Aiko and tried to regain the upper hand. He spit his words out at her with hatred.

"Once you strike there is no turning back. Understand this, I will torture you and your friends and their families to a horrible death!" He looked past her at her friends. Aiko knew he would do exactly that if she failed. She turned to look at each of them. *Could I really do this?*

She closed her eyes and her world went silent. All of heaven and hell held its breath waiting to see what she would do. She saw a series of images flashing one after the other in her head . . .

"Our family isn't like other families..."

"Makoto, Aiko, Shiho, I have bad news..."

"Mommy, why did he kill himself?"

"Will we ever see him again?"

"You're already dead..."

"To end it, make him leave the table..."

"You're the last one..."

"You know what to do..."

"For the children..."

*"We'll be waiting...*all *of us."*

"I will be with you."

"Afraid now, are we?" Satan mocked. Aiko opened her eyes and looked at him closely, and decided.

"Fallen slave, you can go to hell." Aiko, the last in her family, a Called One, for the first time in centuries, attacked the lord of hell.

She pressed hard and attacked with amazing speed but the Dark Lord blocked every thrust. Their swords sent sparks flying as they collided again and again. After a quick feint, he slashed her shoulder.

She staggered back and cried out in pain, but her wound closed immediately as Kai prayed from her left flank where he and Koh guarded her from any interference. The Dark Lord frowned and Aiko renewed her attack.

He dodged and backhanded Aiko hard then drove his sword into her shoulder. He forced her to the ground, twisting his blade, and then he wrenched it out. Aiko gasped from the pain, but again the wound closed rapidly as Takumi prayed from her right flank where he and Junko guarded Aiko's other side.

The Dark Lord stood up and glanced at the Warriors behind her. "So, this is how it's going to be? Are you ready to suffer, then, *because I have a lot more to show you, little girl!*"

Aiko stood up and whispered a prayer. "I can't do this, but You can." She reset her stance and charged again with her team following.

♦ ♦ ♦

Daniel's team had their hands full with Moloch and the demons surrounding him. Their battle moved toward the back of the warehouse. "This time I'll make sure you or your friends don't get up!" Moloch spit.

"Uh, this time, we'll actually fight back," Daniel replied resolutely while he walked around the demon with his sword drawn. "You really don't think it was so easy to beat the Slayer hunters, do you? There are a whole lot of your friends who will be in for a big surprise in a few moments. Moloch, the general of all Slayers, who sits in the presence of the dark one himself, will–poof–appear in the barrens after getting an old-fashioned whupping." He glanced at his team, who were all smiles. "And you know what? That little girl over there, Aiko? She's gonna send your lord flying there flat on his face."

Moloch huffed and shook with rage. He stamped his clawed feet and roared and charged Daniel.

♦ ♦ ♦

As Aiko's fight passed Ryudan he moved in to attack her but was blocked by Kenji and Ishi.

"What? Haven't had enough yet?" he growled. "Well then, Son, *come to Daddy*." The demons filling Ryudan's soul roared in hatred. Kenji approached his father, looking him in the eyes.

"It ends with you. From now on, our descendants will serve the Master. No more evil, no more broken lives, no more filth, and no more death." Kenji pulled out his sword manual. "I belong to Him now."

The demons writhed and shrieked in unrestrained fury.

"Come, and I'll shred you to pieces!" Ryudan turned to attack him. He didn't notice the blur from his blind side that came at him like a missile. From a full sprint, Ishi launched a powerful kick to Ryudan's head, snapping it forward and launching him onto his face on the ground in front of Kenji.

"There's a little thing in battle called 'mobility' that really helps when you are fighting," Ishi landed and stood with both hands on her hips.

The demons' host lay unconscious on his face, rendering them unable to attack.

"You guys wanna come out and play?" Kenji stood just out of their reach with Ishi at his side.

With a series of wet slithering noises, the demons extracted themselves from Ryudan and sprang up toward the two waiting Warriors.

♦ ♦ ♦

Kentaro, still breathing hatred through his near-blinding pain, pushed the gun down on his lap and heard the *click* as a fresh magazine snapped into the grip of the gun that had killed Makoto. He looked for a new target and saw Kenji fighting in front of their downed father. He took a deep breath, summoned his strength, and raised the gun.

"Good-bye, Brother!" As Kenji came into focus at the end of the gun he felt a sudden movement from his left. A metal pole smashed into his wrist, shattering it, sending the gun flying. He wailed in pain.

"I was hoping you would do that." Mai tossed the pole to the ground.

Kentaro felt strong hands grab him and haul him to his feet. He was dragged toward an industrial window and was evacuated as the powerful arms shoved him through the air with such speed that for an instant he was flying. The ground rushed toward him. There was a sickening crunch.

Kentaro had left the room and the battle.

Michio and Mai looked at each other with satisfaction and then ran back to Aiko.

♦ ♦ ♦

"Come now, you can't beat me! I've won for *ten thousand years!*" the Dark Lord bragged as he stepped backward, parrying Aiko's relentless attack. She grunted with every swing and block. He anticipated her every move. She was Akira's best-trained Warrior, and she couldn't touch him. She grunted in frustration and continued to seek an opening.

"Stupid, stupid little girl. I'll enjoy killing your friends, like I did your family."

Aiko's eyes flared with anger and she cried out. "No!" She stepped back and dropped her sword arm.

The Dark Lord saw the opportunity, leapt in, and swung downward to strike Aiko's sword-side shoulder.

She spun lightning fast, blocked the sword with her shield, which concealed a powerful spinning kick too fast to block. She hit him square in the chest with full force sent him flying backward, and the Dark Lord–for the first time in a thousand years–crashed to the ground.

He looked up in a cloud of dust, his mouth hanging open, and he glanced around to see who was watching. The whole room gasped. Ryudan's demons, and even Moloch, paused to gape at their leader sprawled out on the ground.

Aiko was breathing hard and dripping with sweat. The Dark Lord directed his gaze at his minions and flicked it over to Aiko in a wordless command. Every demon in the room surged toward her.

Michio and Mai came running up and switched with Kai and Koh, who took the rear again. Aiko was now surrounded by six Warriors who would die for her. A cloud of fiery arrows rained on Aiko. She stood unflinching, totally focused on her opponent. Just before the arrows hit, six shields covered her with an umbrella of protection. The arrows burst in sparks and flame.

As the smoke lifted, Aiko was still standing, waiting.

The Dark Lord frowned.

She raised her sword. "Just you and me."

He leaped to his feet and Aiko charged.

♦ ♦ ♦

Whooosh! "That's one," Ishi called out, then blocked and parried.

Whooosh! "That's two!" Kenji yelled, then ducked and blocked another sword.

"Watch it! He's switching to you!"

Kenji saw the demon coming up from the side and spun and slashed its leading leg, rolled closer, and drove his sword into its heart. *Whoooosh!* "Three!"

Ishi was parrying from side to side, one sword and then another. She sidestepped toward one opponent's shield, bashed him, and then from behind drove her sword through his chest where it glowed brightly…*Whoooosh!* "Four!"

The last of Ruydan's demons stepped back with a look of fear. Kenji and Ishi stood side by side walking toward him. "Your day here is done…you've lost…no more destroying lives." Kenji burned with the intensity of his hope.

The demon spit, and as Ishi moved in for the kill, he turned and ran for the window.

"I'll be back, you'll see." He turned and fled. Kenji saw Ishi toss her sword in the air and catch in the throwing position. He watched her quick powerful movement that buried the glowing sword in the back of the demon's head…*Whooosh!*

"Five," she declared triumphantly, and braced her hands on her knees to catch her breath. Kenji looked at her with admiration. They heard the sound of the last battle going on somewhere behind them and ran together to join it.

In the distance, the two master swordsman fenced without pause. Attacking, blocking, counterattacking, ducking, pushing, swinging shields, punching, feet stepping in an intricate dance of death around the warehouse. The mass of demons hovered over them liked buzzards over a carcass, rushing in to attack at every opportunity, but their attacks were stopped either by the sudden appearance of a glowing shield or a Warrior that blocked their way. Now, eight surrounded Aiko as she relentlessly advanced on the Dark Lord. Takumi and Junko took the right flank. Kenji and Michio guarded the left. Koh and Kai watched the rear. And Ishi and Mai, armed with bows, watched the skies.

"Watch left!" Ishi pointed to an Overlord who charged the line to get to Aiko.

"Got it!" Michio stepped up and blocked his attack.

"Junko, Junko, Junko–to the rear fast!" Ishi ordered. Junko sprinted to help Koh with yet another Goon.

Koh was forced to back up. "Shoot…is it my cologne? Why do the Goons always attack me?" It raised its weapon. So did Koh. "Okay, you want some of this? I have someone I want you to meet." Koh blocked the initial attack and then let Junko step in to help him.

Aiko cried out in pain as her leg was slashed. She fell to one knee.

"I got the heal!" Takumi called and prayed quickly so Aiko could keep fighting. She stood again and continued.

"Mai, with me! *Right!*" Ishi ran over with Mai just in time to stop a charge of five demons formed in a wedge trying to reach Aiko. There was a *crash* as Takumi, Ishi, and Mai met the charge and held. Junko came back from the rear and the four dismantled the attack in a series of *whooshes*. They quickly ran back to their positions, glancing back at the Called One who continued to fight fiercely.

"Get him, Aiko!" Michio yelled. Everyone joined in.

"We got your back!"

"Do it, girl!"

"For Makoto!'

"Come on…you can do it!"

Ishi noticed that the demon lords were calling out orders. "Whoa…they're coordinating. Everyone get ready!"

There was a sudden rush from all sides and above. Mai and Ishi sent a series of arrows heavenward while the circle met the charge. The Warriors held and kept following Aiko as she pressed hard.

All of her exposed skin now glistened with sweat. Blood trickled down her face from her earlier wounds mixed with dirt and sweat, but Aiko didn't slow her pace for a second. Her eyes burned with a virtuous intensity and fierceness, and her body moved instinctively with a holy purpose that continued driving the Dark Lord back.

He grunted and finally gave way, disengaged, and jumped back ten meters to break Aiko's attack. Undaunted she walked briskly toward him to continue the fight.

Just before she got to him, Shiho stood before her. "Aiko? What are you doing here? You came for me. I knew you would come." Shiho extended her arms and tears rolled down her cheeks. Aiko froze.

"Is it…Shiho?" Aiko looked closely, suddenly disorientated. Shiho just smiled and walked straight to Aiko with a thankful smile on her face.

"Shiho?"

Shiho wrapped her arms around Aiko in an affectionate hug.

The instant they touched, Shiho grabbed her by the hair and landed a series of punishing blows to her stomach.

Aiko bent over, unable to move, unable to breathe. Her sister kneed her hard in the face and flung her onto her back. She blinked and shook her head to clear it.

The Warriors glanced back, but had their hands full. Takumi instantly saw what was happening. "He's a liar! It's not Shiho," Takumi yelled. "Don't trust anything you see!"

Aiko heard him just as "Shiho" came leaping at her with a sword aimed at her neck. She couldn't react fast enough. The blow crashed into a purple translucent shield just above Aiko. A dissonant *crack* disoriented "Shiho." Aiko drove her sword upward and it penetrated the liar's abdomen. The girl crumpled on the ground next to her, screaming.

Aiko heard Junko speak a command that dematerialized the shield that had saved her.

By the time Aiko pushed herself to her feet, her opponent had changed again. An old friend pushed himself up from the ground holding his wound. "Aiko, it's me. You've won. He's gone." "Akira" smiled at her.

Aiko hesitated. Then, her face hardened. "You *liar*!" She bashed "Akira" with her shield and sent him flying back. He stood up and now changed to the form of "Makoto," wearing armor and holding his sword.

"You saved me, Aiko. Thank you. Now we can fight side by side."

"You aren't worthy of the image of my brother!"

The Dark Lord laughed and attacked Aiko with ferocity, backing her up. Each time she tried to attack he blocked her before she could even begin her swing. They locked swords and stared inches from each other.

"Now, now, Sister. You were never as good as me with the sword!" "Makoto" pushed hard and she stumbled backward. He raised his sword.

At that moment, Aiko heard Akira's voice in her head. "*You must learn to beat a warrior of light...he's had ten thousand years to learn every style.*" She took a deep breath, looked at "Makoto's" stance, and waited for his attack.

The Dark Lord smiled. He knew he had her now. He had stalled her attack. She knew how to fight demons, that was for sure, but *not* her own. She was disoriented and would hesitate before she drove her sword into the image of her own brother. *Perfect.* "On this attack she dies," he hissed.

He'd made one mistake.

A short distance behind the Dark Lord lay the body of Makoto, in full view of his loving and loyal sister. Her eyes darted from him to the Dark Lord and back. The image drew Makoto's last words into her thoughts.

"*For His Honor...*"

Aiko set her chin, strengthened the grip on her sword, and faced the charging "Makoto."

He came at her swinging hard, knowing she would parry, and spun quickly intending to bash her with his shield and drive the sword through her heart.

Aiko knew the move well. Instead of parrying, with great agility she ducked the slashing sword and stepped into the attack while he spun, so that when he faced her again she was up against him with her sword buried in his stomach.

The Dark Lord changed back to his fallen angel form and the hideous monster roared and gripped her sword with both taloned hands. Aiko started to pray and the sword started to glow.

The Dark Lord drove his powerful arms into Aiko and sent her with her sword flying backward into Ishi's and Mai's waiting arms.

"Noooo! No *child* will banish me!" He screamed and his black shield and red glowing sword appeared again in his hands.

"Go get him, girl!" Ishi pushed her forward. Aiko wiped the sweat and blood from her brow, stood up again, and walked toward the evil one.

"We finish this!" Aiko yelled, and then attacked again. As she charged, the other Warriors watched in awe as she began to glow with holy light. At first it was a dull blue, but as she attacked it became a brilliant, white-hot light.

Aiko spun and jumped. She ducked and rolled and parried and slashed. She sidestepped stabbing attacks and locked up with Satan eye to eye, good facing down evil, and pushed him back.

Then the tide turned.

Aiko switched tactics quickly and stabbed at his claws. The shield flew one way. Aiko spun and cut down hard and the Dark Lord's claw, sword in hand, flew the other way. She kicked him hard in the chest and he flew backward and crashed into the ground. Aiko leapt after him.

"For all the death you've caused!" she shouted and slashed a deep wound across his chest. He roared in agony, holding his clawless arms in front of him.

"For all the lives you've ruined!" She cut swiftly in the other direction. Again his roar echoed across the battlefield.

The Dark Lord glared at her like a desperate animal. "I swear to you, you stupid little whor–"

"*Silence*!"

Satan's jaws locked instantly as he growled through his teeth in absolute rage. The whole room went silent, all fighting ceased, and all eyes went to Aiko. She slammed her foot down on the Dark Lord's neck and pinned him to the ground.

"I've heard enough of your lies." She paused and gathered the last of her strength. "Now…You can *go to hell.*" Aiko drove her sword into the devil's heart and prayed out loud. As she did, the light from her sword started to explode into the Dark Lord's form. It penetrated and filled him till it was pouring out of his eyes and open wounds. He shook violently and gripped her sword and roared.

Truth and lies cannot coexist.

There was an ear-piercing *crack*, like the sky was being ripped open, followed by a deafening *crash* of thunder and a loud, extended *whooooooosh*!

In an instant, the Dark Lord was gone. There was a collective gasp and all fighting ceased.

After a silent pause there was a rush of movement all around. Like a wild stampede, every demon in the place bolted from the warehouse, leaving the Warriors free to look back. Aiko stood in a swirling cloud of dust, holding her sword. She was breathing hard and tears rolled down her cheeks.

♦ ♦ ♦

Akira and the Ancient Ones on the crest of the hill overlooking the battlefield saw the lightning strike and heard the great boom. The ranks broke up in near panic and sped away into the sky in every direction. Akira's eyes filled with tears. "Oh my, my Aiko…Oh, Aiko…you did it." He laughed and raised his hands to the sky with the Ancient Ones, who were cheering and hugging each other.

♦ ♦ ♦

Aiko walked over and knelt by her brother, looking at his peaceful face. She pulled him close. The Warriors gathered around her.

"I'm so sorry." Ishi knelt too and put her arm around Aiko.

"I can see where you got your groove, girl...he was awesome," Koh said sincerely.

"Side by side...that was incredible!" Takumi knelt on her other side.

"Yeah, side by side." Aiko gazed at her brother with a tearful smile.

Mai came running up. "He's gone...Kentaro, and Ryudan's men too!"

"Do we chase him down?" Michio stood up and started checking his armor. Everyone looked at Aiko for orders.

She thought a moment and shook her head. "No, we did what we were called to do."

"What about Ryudan?" Ishi looked at Kenji. They all turned to where he had been knocked out and were surprised to see a large man who lifted Ryudan's limp form and threw him over his shoulder.

"Hey?" Mai trotted over while the others watched. "Whatcha doing?" She looked up at her new friend.

Louie grinned at her. "Choosing sides, sweetie. I'm going to the police station, to turn us both in."

She noticed that he was covered with bullet holes, but no blood. "Are...are you okay?"

He looked at himself and nodded. "Oh yeah...Kevlar." He chuckled. "Hey, little one, I don't know everything, and I'm not sure I understand all this..." He searched for words and then gave up. "Well, come visit me in prison sometime, huh?" He patted her head and walked away toward the parking lot with his human cargo.

The sky opened up and a steady rain fell. Everyone breathed in the fresh air. Aiko let the rain wash the blood and dirt from both her and Makoto.

"Weird. The sun is shining, but it's raining." Koh pointed to the morning sunbeams that were bathing the battlefield in light, turning the rain into a cleansing mist. Everyone looked up to see the phenomenon.

"Satan's crying." Takumi took off his glasses and wiped them. "That's what my grandmother told me once. Guess it's true." Everyone looked around in wonder and just nodded their heads.

Daniel's group came running up pumping fists into the air and cheering. "You guys are amazing. We held our little corner and sent Moloch packing, but *you* guys with your teamwork...and Aiko...seriously, girl–can we take you home with us?"

They all exchanged hugs and handshakes and started telling their battle stories.

Aiko called the ambulance and police to collect her brother's body. Louie's confession had already sent ripples through the police department. Processing would be quick. Mai seemed to sense her pain and wordlessly walked up and hugged her leader and stayed in her arms while she made the call and waited.

"Okay, who's wounded?" Ishi called out. Everyone's hand went up but Koh's. They all looked at him.

"Whaaat? I didn't get hit. So sue me." he challenged defensively.

"I took your hits." Kai pointed to various wounds. Koh waved him off. "Pussssshawww!"

"What's this about your name being Aiko?" Ishi planted a hand on her hip.

Koh looked around and shrugged. "Hey…heat of battle…you know, moment of crisis." Everyone laughed.

"Thanks for the thought, Koh." Aiko smiled at him.

"But, uh, next time maybe do something that will actually have an impact on the battle." Kai slapped the back of his head. Koh hit him in the shoulder.

"Right, everybody heal up," Ishi ordered.

Kenji walked over, pulled out a handkerchief, folded it, and placed it on Aiko's bleeding head, holding it there. "I uh, I don't know how I can ever thank you, Aiko."

Aiko reached up and held the cloth herself. "Just do what He says and you'll be fine…Remember, He'll speak to you."

The other Warriors also drifted to Aiko. It was starting to hit them all. They had won. They had won big. What it would all mean, they couldn't be sure, but it was a new day.

"Well, we got the Dark Lord to leave the table." Takumi hugged her. "I'm so honored to fight with you. I'll never forget this night."

"Me too, Tak," she replied to her faithful friend.

"Thanks for believing in me." Junko stepped up behind him.

"No, thank *you* for saving me back there." Aiko smiled, extended a hand, and pulled her into a hug. "You are a very special girl. You learned faster than anyone I've ever seen." Junko blushed and wriggled out of the hug to hide behind Takumi.

Ishi stepped up, wrapped her arms around Aiko, and just held her. When she pulled back, tears were streaming down her face, so Aiko started crying again. "You did it. Sister, you did it."

"No, Ish…*we* did it." They smiled and hugged again.

"All right, all right, stand back!" Michio gently moved everyone to the side.

"I've got some hugging to do with this girl." Ishi stepped back and Michio picked up Aiko in a bear hug and spun her around while everyone cheered. When he finally put her down, Kai and Koh were waiting.

"We're hungry." Everyone groaned.

"You're always hungry." Ishi waved a hand in the air.

"Hey, fighting the hordes of hell works up a healthy appetite." Koh put both hands on his hips and struck a hero pose.

"I could go for a Coke."

"I need coffee."

"No, I'm thinking thick, juicy pizza."

"Just give me miso ramen and I'm happy."

"Hey, you think my game will be rained out?" Michio asked, remembering the championship scheduled for that day.

"Uh, sure looks like it." Takumi looked at the burgeoning clouds.

The cleansing rain fell all over the city. The ambulance pulled up with the police, who had already started processing Ryudan and Louie. By lunchtime, the team was at Coffee Shop enjoying their bittersweet victory. Akira and the Ancient Ones had disappeared, but the team was used to Akira's mysterious ways, and let it go. They all went home after eating together and slept till the next day…a peaceful sleep.

Chapter Thirty

A Whole New Game

Two weeks later, Aiko placed flowers on Makoto's grave and also on Shiho's, then finally on her parents'. They were all next to each other in the small area of the cemetery where the crosses had been desecrated. She sat down and prayed for a moment. "Thank You, God…so much!" She stood with a peaceful smile. "I'll see you all…soon, when He's done with me." She glanced over toward the grave of Shinji Matsuoka and sighed. "There's still much to do." She turned and walked to the waiting cab and jumped in with all the girls. "To the school!"

♦ ♦ ♦

"Okay, somebody explain this game to me!" Junko made her way to her seat. She wore the school T-shirt, but had tied it in a knot at the waist and had cut off the sleeves to go with her tight cutoff jeans. She had a ponytail gathered at the top of her head, ribboned with school colors. Only Junko could turn a baseball game into a fashion statement. She plopped down by Takumi, who was keeping score pitch by pitch. He wore his math team shirt because it had school colors and a baseball cap that Michio had found for him.

"Well, it really is a game of numbers." He looked up at her and lost his train of thought. "Uh, wow…you look, um, really good, Junko." She beamed at him.

"Hey, I brought these!" She pulled out pom-poms and handed him a pair.

"Uh, I need to keep score." He pushed them away.

"Oh come on, come on, come on, come on, you have to let go sometimes!" She bounced in her seat and shook them. He sighed, pushed back his glasses, and took his pom-poms.

"Okay, here's how it works: The goal is to score..." He went on to carefully explain the rules.

"*There!* You see him, cute huh?" Ishi pointed at the sophomore batboy and leaned into Mai. She looked over sheepishly and wrinkled her nose. Her new black look had taken and she looked really good in it. Ishi was wearing her soccer sweats because she had practice later.

"What's not to like?" Ishi opened her arms palms up. Mai let her eyes drift over to the batter's circle where Michio swung his bat. Ishi saw it, as all girls do, and smiled.

"Ahem, girlie? Do you like older men now?" Mai smiled and pushed Ishi hard.

"We're just friends." A mischievous look crept over her face. "Kenji!"

Kenji turned around from his seat right in front of them.

"Ishi said she li–hmmmph."

Ishi clamped her hands over Mai's mouth with a horrified look on her face.

"Don't you tell any lies, girl!"

Mai pulled at her hand. "She thinks–hmmph–you're *hot!*"

Ishi grabbed Mai in a playful headlock.

Kenji laughed. "No, that's fine." He leaned as though he were going to tell Mai a secret. "I think she's *hot* too. I'm going to ask her out after the game." Mai's eyes opened wide and Ishi turned red, then they all laughed. Ishi smiled and Kenji smiled back.

"Hey, did I miss anything?" Koh arrived with a big tray of food. He had a school cap on backward and a baseball shirt from his favorite pro team, which happened to share the school colors for the *other* side.

Kai started to pass out the food. "No, Michio's up to bat second this inning. What took you so long?"

"Yeah, sorry, had to use the can...and oh man, it smells like someone ate nuclear waste for breakfast! Ew!

"You *did* wash your hands, right?" Kai looked closely at his hamburger.

"Hey, guys, we're gonna eat. Can you stop with the bathroom talk?" Ishi shook her head.

They waved her off and dove into their food. Kenji leaned over to speak to Aiko as the first batter got up. She was looking at the crowd with glassy eyes.

"So, how are you doing?" he asked genuinely. She smiled and thought a moment.

"I'm just thankful...and," she said, "looking ahead a little."

"Yeah? Well, what's next?" Kenji waited patiently for her answer. Ishi and Mai leaned in, and Takumi and Junko stopped to listen too. Koh and Kai were busy eating.

"It's just impressions. You sure you want to know?" They all nodded.

She leaned back against the bleachers and sighed. "Well, the tide has turned here, but he'll be back. The Dark Lord won't give up that easily. I think we all know that. But how and when? We'll have to wait on God for that. I think he'll lick his wounds for a while. For now it's time to push." Aiko took a deep breath like she was catching her second wind. "Then there are unanswered questions. Like your mom, Kenji. Do you want to find her?"

"Yeah, I've been thinking about that." He nodded.

"And what about Kentaro? Is he still alive? If he is, we'd better find him too." She shook her head and looked off in the distance. "But, for now, we wait for orders. The Master knows what he's doing. Still, I have a feeling that our days as a team may eventually come to an end. I think our destinies lie in different places." They all looked at each other sadly, and Aiko caught it. "But not today!" She smiled. "Not today."

"Hey, Michio's coming up!" Kai yelled with a mouth full of hot dog. Michio walked up to the plate, swinging his bat hard. He tapped his shoes and then glanced up at the stands. The whole team of Warriors stood and cheered.

"*Michio, Michio, Michio, Michio!*" Koh and Kai chanted.

"Hit that ball hard...somewhere!" Junko yelled.

"Come on, Mich, you can do it!" Mai yelled.

"Kill it, Mich!" Ishi yelled with cupped hands and stuck two fingers in her mouth and let out a shrill whistle.

"Hey, buddy! You let them know who you are!" Kenji pumped his fist into the air.

"Hey, we're already proud of you! Knock it to forever!" Aiko clapped her hands.

Takumi stood up. "Well, I'm sorry, Michio, but there is a seventy-five percent chance that you will strike out. I'm sorry, but hey, do your best!" Michio stepped out of the batter's box and glared at Takumi. His eyes narrowed, he pointed his bat to centerfield, and then he looked back at Takumi, who laughed. "He's so predictable."

The pitcher wound up and fired his signature fastball. Michio pulled the trigger and whipped his bat with a mighty force. *Crack.* The ball leaped off his bat into orbit, heading toward the next county.

All at once the entire crowd was on their feet. They followed the trajectory of the ball with their eyes, held their breath, and waited to explode in celebration.

For just a moment, people on earth would experience what had happened in heaven the moment Aiko and her friends laid down their lives to make a difference and turned the tide.

The End